Brothers by Honor

by

Janet Yeager

This is a work of fiction. Names, characters, places, and incidents are either the product of the author's imagination or are used fictitiously, and any resemblance to actual persons living or dead, business establishments, events, or locales, is entirely coincidental.

Brothers by Honor

Cover Art by *Lisa Dawn MacDonald*

The Wild Rose Press, Inc.
PO Box 708
Adams Basin, NY 14410-0708
Visit us at www.thewildrosepress.com

Publishing History
First Edition, 2023
Trade Paperback ISBN 978-1-5092-4958-9
Digital ISBN 978-1-5092-4959-6

Published in the United States of America

I look at my four friends. Rolf, now calm, appears to have a channel for the anger at being categorized by beauty. Stein's nefarious skills have been given a platform, at last. Through his words, Paul defies conventions and expresses his resentment toward going along. And Jan, who demands excellence from everyone, holds himself to a higher standard.

Stepping out into the cold, clear night air, a stack of newspapers in my hands, I'm overwhelmed by the sensation of love. My heart beats faster. The trees and flower boxes are etched in high relief, and I'm giddy. And terrified. And filled with longing. Longing to do this again—the printing, the information gathering. The camaraderie of my friends was… no… is a brotherhood. I'm trusting these people with my life, and they trust me with theirs.

I look over my shoulder at my newfound brothers. Like an unposed photograph, all are in mid-position—just about to—leaping into—oneness.

Paul is the last to leave the hut. As he turns off the light, the yard is distantly illuminated by a passing ship's red, white, and blue lights that paint an abstract of the Norwegian flag in the seawater.

I don't hear my friends leave, but I stand alone on the Carhart's lawn. My thoughts follow my gaze out to sea. I'm venturing into the unknown with my brothers.

Dedication

Heroes surround me.

To my loving husband Greg and my children Eric, Janet, Scott, and Kathleen, and grandchildren Chloe and Ginger, I owe a debt of gratitude and patience on this journey. I love you all.

To my friends and family, thank you for your listening ears, your wise counsel, and your unending good humor as I navigated what must have been uncharted waters to bring this story to life.

To my editors, Julie Kimmel-Harbaugh and Ally Robertson, thank you for your guidance in helping me shape the words and craft them into a story.

To Pastor, Elinor, Katie, and Eric, thank you for the sage advice. And a "kiss on the hand" to Heather C.

And to my father Kaare Hitland, his friends Paal Kahrs, Stein Ottersen, Ivar Kristoffersen, Rolf Wik, Inger Johanne Refsdal, and Jan Amundson, you are my compass—my Brothers by Honor.

Heroes all.

Chapter One

"I called to the other men that the sky was clearing, and then a moment later I realized that what I had seen was not a rift in the clouds but the white crest of an enormous wave."
Ernest Shackleton

The Solsvik-Bridge game's protocol failed me, and now my brothers and I are going to die.

My right eye stares at a clump of sphagnum moss embedded with a tiny, pink porcelain doll's finger. Dead level with the top churchyard step, my left eyelash bats away granules of snow flying by.

The guards' conversation raining from the parapet lands on me like shrapnel. I know just enough German to understand they're talking of the litter floating through the air and what pigs my countrymen are.

Litter?

The fingers of my right hand baby-crawl across the leather satchel I carry, brushing against the rough interior that should be latched shut.

Forgetting subtlety, I shove my hand inside and imagine, for a split second, that when I tripped on the staircase, I hit with such force that I tore out the bottom of the pouch.

In answer, one newsletter leaps from my satchel onto the breeze of freedom. Then a second and a third

1

slide out like mousy girls asked to dance by the popular boys in school.

Rolling over, I stanch the flow of information. Copies of *The Whole Truth* flutter like confetti over Cathrineskirken's graveyard.

Circling the church's lamppost, a copy settles upon a snow-covered gravestone like a nesting goose. In plain sight is the headline, *Chum.* Another copy, opened to the article about mines, soars toward the belfry in one of the twin Gothic spires. A third takes a long, lazy flight toward the armed guards, an hour early for changeover.

When the Nazis read what we wrote and then find me—and, following my footprints in the fresh snow, they *will* find me—I…and soon after, my friends and family…will be executed.

Two hours ago—at my insistence—using our largest fonts, we, my brothers in fighting the Nazis and I, used every last drop of ink to get one hundred issues of *The Whole Truth* printed.

When delivering previous editions, and while the soldiers practiced their idiotic changing of the guard, Jan, my partner in crime, and I sauntered through the church's graveyard. Taking the flagstone steps two at a time, we waited for our target, the news wagon of Bergen Norway's daily newspaper, the *Tidende.*

Jan and I followed from a safe distance as the wagon trundled up the steep hills rising above the city's two wharves. Surreptitiously, we inserted our *real* news among the propaganda printed at the Nazi's behest. Then, my best friend and I walked home with our transit passes, our plausibility checked, stamped, and approved.

Per Solsvik-Bridge game protocol, the Queen and Two of Hearts I received in my parents' mailbox meant meeting at Cathrineskirken—Cathrine's Church—at two o'clock. Only my fellow brothers know this meaning, and no one knows who places the cards in the mailboxes. Thus far, those protocols for our newspapers and smuggling operations have worked like a charm.

This time, someone didn't—to use one of Gramps' Brooklyn-America expressions—*wise up.*

Me.

Worse, these are no ordinary editions of *The Whole Truth* that my brothers and I have created. Oh, no.

No, this time, we wrote of our chums—our friends and family—correction, *my* friends and *my* family, who, in trying to obtain liberty for themselves and our country, paid the ultimate price.

One short hour ago, after leaving Paul, the printing press owner, I, with my twenty-five copies to distribute, climbed up Ny Klosterveien, the main thoroughfare in Bergen's oldest district. The English's bombing of the neighborhood the previous summer has offered us timbered and bricked cover from the German's prying eyes.

Now, as the bells in the church's twin towers toll the hour, this should have been a regular following of protocol. But the guards changed their changeover time.

The parapet, part of an old monastery, is now used as a vantage point to watch the activity in Bergen's harbors. If the guard above me looks down—straight down—instead of out toward the Rosenkrantz Hotel's lights and Haakon Hall's slate roof, he'll see a teenaged, red-headed hobbling idiot clutching anti-Nazi literature.

The branches jiggle, but I hold up my hand to the lanky young man who crouches ten meters from me. Bits of gray-brown moss fall on the snow as I pluck out the porcelain doll's finger and turn back to look where Jan crouches.

The Spartan is gone.

"Help! Help!" calls a voice not unfamiliar to me. It comes from thirty meters away and is closing in fast. A lanky shadow dances across the graveyard's snow. Jan runs toward the soldiers, waving his arms, his voice strained. "Help! Have you seen the wagon? I must stop them! This will cost me my job."

The German guards stop talking, and I hear the click of a rifle.

Carefully, I raise my head so that both of my eyes are above the churchyard's stairs. As I do, a clump of moss lands on my cheekbone.

"Oh, no, please don't shoot me!" says Jan, whose long legs rest against the gate leading down into the cemetery. "I've been delivering papers in this neighborhood for only a few weeks." He waves our latest edition at the guards. "Look what some traitors put into the newspapers. I saw this propaganda sticking out at my last stop, and"—Jan sobs—"I must find the wagon. I must find who is behind this. Chums and mines! Those bastards! My father is at sea, and my mother, with the new baby."

He's laying it on a bit thick, but then again, that *is* our opinion of our occupiers.

"Who are you?" demands one of the guards in broken Norwegian.

Is Jan's identity that of Stefan Nelson? Or am I Stefan Nelson? I pat my pocket and feel the small piece of paper used to forge our identities.

Thank you, Crimshaw Brothers and Solsvik Bridge.

"I'm Hans Josephson. I'm sixteen, and I live on

Ovregaten," Jan says. "You can see my boss at the *Tidende,* but I wish I knew where the wagon is so that I can…" He pauses as if turning over an idea in his mind. "Can you help me look? I think the wagon passes"—he points down the hill—"Do you mind?"

He puts his right hand behind himself on the gate. His fingers mimic stroking his cat's back. He doesn't as much run his fingers over the handle as expands and retracts them, probing first with his ring finger, and then with his middle, the tip of which finds the tiny lock. Rubbing the latch, he finds the sweet spot, then turns it with his thumb and index finger. He might not have the speed or flair of our lockpicker friend Stein, but Jan has mastered the subtle art of diversion.

The wind has stopped.

Jan tilts his head. "Do you hear that? Is it coming from that way?"

On a better day, when he isn't trying to cover my ass, I would half expect him—and me—to bay like hounds on a scent.

"Those bastards! It would be great to catch them in the act," he says, patting his satchel.

One of the soldiers lets out an exasperated sigh.

I hold my breath and count, and since I'm in a churchyard, I pray to whatever god might be listening to me.

"Can you help me find who is inserting this trash so that I can keep my job?" Jan moves away from the gate. "The wagon passes at the bottom of this hill, I think."

Straining every peripheral muscle in my eyes, I look where three shadows lie on the snow-covered ground. Two of them have the unmistakable shapes of guns slung over their shoulders. The third, resting his hand on the arm of one of the shadows, points.

"I'm Hans, and you are?" The Spartan's shadow leans to one of them. His voice is cordial and warm. A guttural voice, akin to the start of an old machine, is replaced by a higher-pitched, younger whine. "Josef?" Jan claps one shoulder. "And you are Klaus. Thank you." The points of the guns lower as the guards turn to walk with him. "I appreciate this."

His voice fades as the three figures stroll down the hill. Jan continues to pepper the guards with questions about their lives and their family.

Picking myself up from the stairs and brushing the moss from my cheek, I shimmy sideways through the iron bars of the gate. Drawing in a deep breath, I glance down the hill where Jan appears to be regaling the guards with a story.

I crouch. As I push off, my shoe finds ice and twists. The sharp pain jolts up my ankle and to my brain, reminding me of the ten meters of exposure and my idiocy.

This edition of *The Whole Truth* is, after all, my brainchild. Putting my hands on my knees, I again curse my weakness. As I smooth my coat, the doll's porcelain finger rolls under my fingertips. I pull it out. Still creamy and smooth, the pink polish on the fingernail reflects in the dim light. It's not much smaller than my brother Ray's.

When the English bombed Bergen, it was a warm summer evening, and many people were out near Kloster Park, mere steps from where I am standing. Thirty people were killed, among them, ten children who had been at a summer church camp.

A certainty settles on my shoulders. This doll's

finger, its edge dulled and blackened with unexpected violence, and its owner, who is undoubtedly dead, is why my friends and I use codes and ink to get the message out.

So maybe, just maybe, the gods are listening after all.

Now blanketed with innocent snow, charred beams and toppled bricks strewn in the narrowed passage threaten to trip me. Putting the fingertip back into my pocket, I work my way past the vacant houses to reach my destination. As before, the quiet street, lit in its slumber by gaslight, is empty.

Framed in the shadows of the alley, I glance up and down the street. From this distance, muffled hooves clop on the pavement like rhythmic, slow drips of water. Cresting the hill, a yellowish beam rocks to the horse's hooves.

Right on time. I exhale, my breath curling into the night air, and then gag on the smell of rotted fish.

As the blindered horse passes by, I swear it turns its head to where I hide but trudges ahead as if willing to keep my secret. The wagon stops, and several packages drop with a thud on the street.

I have exactly three minutes to untie the bundles, insert *The Whole Truth* two pages in, retie the piles, making sure they are where I found them, and then slip away. My record is one hundred forty-seven seconds.

The newspaper uses a new knot on the bundles as an extra precaution against tampering—our tampering.

My friend Stein, who worships Harry Houdini, took this predicament as a challenge. Over the past month, using a stopwatch he had lifted—from where he would not say—he taught us how to untie and retie the knot within ten seconds. We rehearsed sliding the newsletter from our satchels, stuffing the papers inside Paul's folded letterhead, carefully straightening it to escape detection, and then retying the bundles.

As I work, I recall that Jan, Paul, and Stein's records were fifteen seconds faster than mine. I don't think I can beat them.

By one hundred thirty-eight, I retie the last bundle. If the newsboy is on schedule—and he usually is—I have forty-two seconds left to escape back to the alley twenty meters away that smells of spoiled cod. The bundles lie precisely how I found them. I admire my handiwork and smile in satisfaction.

Not ten meters from me, a flicker in an upstairs window and faint thuds of the half-asleep newsboy's feet descending the house's stairs alert me that I can't dawdle any longer. I have twenty seconds before he pulls on his boots, hat, coat, and gloves. Pinpricks of fear course over me as I take one last look before rounding the corner into the alley. Have I missed anything?

A door slams. The newspaper carrier is there, right on schedule.

I listen intently, knowing that the boy will start his rounds away from where I stand. Raising my right foot to brush off the snow, I look down the alley in horror at what I missed. A single set of treasonous footprints puddles and crystalizes below me. My footprints. He'll see my footprints.

I am *so* dead. My friends and I are *so* dead.

As I lean against the soot-covered wall, inhaling rotted cod, a calm, like what I think a shroud must feel like, settles over me. In the face of knowing how I am going to die—in an alley, alone, with my best friend living by his wits and unable to rescue me—I draw a long, resigned breath.

I'm ready for the firing squad. I am.

"You!" A voice booms down the alley.

They're here. I look up, ready to face them.

A lanky, curly-haired boy points his finger at me. Then snapping a crisp salute, he says, "Spart."

Through tears, I snap back a salute. "Spart."

"They turned back, something about a dereliction of duties." He eyes me, his face holding the most welcome grin I've ever seen.

We're ready to soldier on.

Chapter Two

Kory–1938

Our family carries a legend how my great-grandfather Joseph won Solsvik and two large outlying islands using a particularly nasty Solsvik Bridge card game variation.

Gramps, peering over his wire-rimmed spectacles, sets down his coffee cup harder than usual when my friends and I venture questions about Solsvik.

"They will skin you alive. I hope you know that." Gramps is laying on his Brooklyn-America accent on a little thicker than usual. His years in New York with my step-great-grandparents mean many American words creep into his conversations, like his insistence on being called Gramps instead of the Norwegian *Bestefar.*

My friends and I are learning English in school. Terms like *hot dog* and *skinned alive* confuse us and are—another American phrase—*funnier than hell* to my wily grandfather.

"Do you own any property? You married?" he asks.

I size up Jan, Stein, Rolf, and myself, with our voices cracking from baby to youth, spotty faces, and ever-shortening trouser hems. We'll never pass Gramps' muster.

"No grandson of mine will not know the rules of Solsvik Bridge. You need to keep your wits about you.

Always look sharp. I guess you are old enough, but my reputation is at stake here. I can't have it ruined because you men are foolish!" Gramps' laugh comes out in a gushing, snorting torrent.

Stein and Jan's laughter is hyena-like.

Rolf remains silent. Gramps knows a challenge when he sees it.

An overpowering cologne wafts in as the door behind us shuts. "Mind if I sit in?" My older brother Jules' shirt has ruby cufflinks. His right-hand index fingertip is faintly yellow. "The more, the merrier, right?"

"Jules, go get a chair. Rolf, you're first." Pointing to me and using yet another Americanism, Gramps cajoles, "*Lickety-split!* Sonny, the rest of you, take some chairs and learn."

"Solsvik Bridge's rules aren't in any bridge tutorials." Gramps harrumphs as Jules raises a quizzical eyebrow. "Jules, your Great-Grandfather Joseph made deals, passing secrets and property on this game's outcomes. No one wrote down the rules. Sure, you must give an overview. Beyond that? If your opponents don't know what signals to watch? That's their problem."

Gramps' eyes hold a mischievous twinkle. "Some say if you leave a card in certain places around the island, packages show up at your door. No money changes hands. It's more like a barter system."

Twenty chair legs scrape and jockey for position around Gramps.

Gramps flourishes the Two of Clubs before us. "This? In certain circles, this card says you have valuables worth more than half of what you possess that you need to get"— he leans in, whispering conspiratorially— "or get rid of."

Jules twirls his cufflink adorning one of his shirt cuffs.

Gramps pushes at his hand. "Jules? That's a tell. They will eat you alive."

My three friends and I exchange glances, and I blanch at the vision of us in a bubbling pot of stew.

Jules' olive complexion flushes while his hazel-green eyes darken to the color of brine in a brackish pond.

Rummaging through the deck, Gramps pulls out the Seven of Clubs. "The-start-of-negotiations card. The I-want-to-know-if-you-are-interested card. You appear confused. Let's start with the basics. And some history."

Jules undoes his cufflinks, places them on the table, and expertly rolls up his sleeves as his eyes move from Gramps' spit-shine crewcut to his Popeye forearms.

Gramps continues. "Kory, your Great-Grandfather Joseph perfected this version, which quickly became known as Solsvik Bridge. Sailors passed the time with it on whaling ships off Africa and in ports up and down Norway's coast. According to the boasters in my family, Solsvik Bridge was used to win a gaucho ranch in South America."

Jan and Stein elbow in, knocking a ruby cufflink to the floor.

Gramps turns his attention to Jules. "You better pick that cufflink up. It might get crushed. I hope you didn't pay too much for it."

Jules grabs the cufflink and pushes it into his pocket. "It's real enough," he says sourly.

"Great-Grandfather Joseph took a backwater port and, with his in-law's connections, turned Solsvik into a place to obtain things not legal in Bergen."

Gramps smacks his lips and pauses. "Ah, those were the days. Solsvik became famous for its whiskey. Your aunt moved to Scotland. When she returned to Solsvik, widowed but not bereaved, her secrets included how her husband had actually died and the recipe for a whiskey rivaling anything produced on Scottish soil." He sighs.

Snapping back to the matter at hand, he surveys us sternly. "And you want to step into that hornet's nest?"

Side-eyeing each other, we, in turn, nod solemnly.

Lecture completed, Gramps clasps his hands and cracks his knuckles. "Let's get crackin'."

Another Brooklyn-America expression to figure out.

So, in the year before the world war broke out in Europe, after countless hours clustered and arguing around our battered kitchen table, my friends and I consider ourselves well versed in Solsvik Bridge.

****

We're to have different covers on our playing cards. Mine features a lighthouse. Jan chooses Bergen's wharf. Stein selects a frightful lion. Rolf's botanical garden choice makes us snicker, and Jules asks a sailor to pick up playing cards from Poland. To meet, we'll leave a card in our parents' mailboxes. We decide our meeting places will have a playing card, too. Jan's cabin is the Ace of Spades.

Playing Solsvik Bridge and leaving messages in our mailboxes, we test the system, looking for failures. The system never fails.

Time for the next step. No persuasion is necessary for Rolf, Stein, and Jan to want to spend a weekend in Solsvik and prove our mettle.

Gramp's weekly Solsvik Bridge game means he leaves every Wednesday and returns early on Thursday morning.

After rehearsing his speech with me for what seems like weeks, Jan screws up his bravery one Thursday afternoon in May. "Herr Molder, are there things out in Solsvik you can't get here?"

Gramps leans back in his chair and shakes his head. "Jan, you are a nice young man. Why do you want to get yourself shanghaied…or worse?"

Jan's face goes from beet-red to white in seconds.

Gramps squints at us. "So, you all think you are ready for Solsvik?"

Time to make tracks. Another "Brooklyn-America."

Chapter Three

Everyone has one friend who's always overprepared.

In third grade, Jan Anderson became my best friend when we set a heaping bag of dogshit on fire by Principal *Hoot Owl*'s front door. Jan makes lists and checks everything. I suspect he'd already tried to set bags on fire at least twice before doing it for real.

I count a knapsack, a small satchel, and two glossy palomino suitcases by his ankles as he waits for me at the bus station.

Waving, Jan shoves the book on the Spartans—his favorite subject—back into the satchel.

"Spart." I salute, my eyes crinkling at him, caught out as a history nut.

"Spart," he answers, snapping a crisp salute.

Routine complete. We're ready to be soldiering on.

"Nice trim," I say, eyeing the brown suede trim and hammered brass nails adorning the suitcases.

"Parents." His sigh confirms another shopping trip to Kloverhuset, the premier department store in Bergen.

Stein Oscarson rounds the corner, a knapsack slung on his back. My experience skiing and camping with him tell me his bag contains one change of clothes, pajama bottoms, a lock-picking set, and pliers. And chocolate. Stein loves chocolate.

Rolf Wik's suitcase and satchel bounce off his

chiseled frame as he runs to us. In the clothes he's wearing, he could give Jules *a run for his money*—another Brooklyn-America phrase, courtesy of Gramps. Crossing Rolf's chest is his most cherished possession, an expensive German camera.

As we bounce along in the decrepit bus from Bergen to Solsvik, my three friends beg me, once again, to tell them the stories about the bootlegging, the money and goods laundering, and the whiskey stills dotting the Sotra Island's jagged landscape.

"I gotta tell you important stuff about Harold," I say.

Jan, Stein, and Rolf's eyes open wide.

I grin. "Nah, nothing bad. Harold is nothing to fear." The bus's muffler blats enormous smoky puffs.

I motion them closer to me to continue. I don't want my long-lost relatives blabbing to Gramps that I gossiped. "People would pick on Harold if he lived in town. He has an ugly scar around his neck, has bad acne, and he limps. To cover his pockmarks, he grew a beard, and a white stripe that looks like the letter *I* grew in on his cheek."

Rolf starts to snicker, but Jan, raising his eyebrows in warning, jabs him in the ribs.

"A scar on his neck resembles a rope burn. I asked Gramps about it once, and Gran hit my arm and shushed me."

Stein takes his finger to his neck in a bad imitation of a burn.

Now, Rolf and Jan jab him, giving him contemptuous looks.

Maybe this was not a great idea.

Hoping they will grow up, I continue my story. "Harold's mother took a long time to have him. She nearly died several times."

Three gasps from my friends address this statement.

I continue. "The cord was around his neck, pressing tight in one spot when Harold was born. The midwife unwrapped the cord, breathing life into Harold because he was a *blue baby.* He should have died, but the midwife saved him. No amount of rubbing can make that scar go away."

In the far distance, I see the lighthouse. We have another ten minutes on the bus.

"Gramps says, 'Harold can read the sea.' He knows where the fish are and can read storms. He's special that way. That's why my uncle lets him have the boat. He's good at getting on and off the sea without trouble."

I gaze out the window. The lighthouse is as tall as my thumb. The bus driver drops down a gear and a massive exhaust blast unfurls through the open window above my head.

Directions for the approach to the harbor come to me as the bus lumbers on. Straight for the green warehouse with the white shutters. Veer sharply left. Slam on the brakes. Although it has been a while since I've been to Solsvik, instinctively, I brace right, clutching the seat in front of me.

My three friends slam into each other, colliding with the seat's metal edges.

Coughing from the last exhaust blast, we clamor off the bus, anxious to see the tawdry town.

In the harbor's center, a man wearing a yellow slicker and work boots packs up the day's catch at a small fish stand. To my right, an empty bakery advertises coffee and sandwiches. Next to the bakery is a bank and the bus stop. Standing near the bus stop are a tall young man and a man who could pass for my mother's twin.

"That's Harold, and that's my Uncle Bertin," I whisper.

Jan glances around surreptitiously.

Rolf and Stein clutch their suitcases in white-knuckled terror.

"Welcome to Solsvik," I say.

****

Uncle Bertin's hug is, apart from the whiskers on his face, identical to his sister's—my mother's. "Kory! It's been years!" Taking my hand, he shakes it three times. Pulling me toward him, he inspects me. "Harold, come meet the boys," he calls over his shoulder to a tall young man dressed in the yellow oilskin worn by every fisherman on the coast. "Don't mind Harold." Bertin gives my shoulder an extra squeeze. "He's shy but nice. And a talented sailor and fisherman."

Releasing me, Bertin turns to Jan, Stein, and Rolf, extending his hand and chattering the whole time. "Hello!" My uncle bows, shaking my friends' hands in turn. "There's not much to do in Solsvik, but we can take you around on the boat and do some fishing."

Stein's stomach lets out a growl.

Clasping Stein's shoulder, Bertin walks toward the bakery. "Hungry? We have the best bakery in Western Norway. Old, too! Kory's Great-Grandfather Joseph and his wife, Janice, ran it. People came from all over to get their baked goods and even traded things for them. Neptun Konditori in Bergen, jealous of this little bakery's reputation and its reluctance to sell its recipes, created trouble in olden times."

Placing his hand on my back, Uncle Bertin opens the door to the Solsvik Konditori. The scents of cardamom, yeast, and butter—lots and lots of butter—waft out.

"Mmm…" is all I hear from my friends as we walk in and settle ourselves at a table

Glancing around, as if asking for permission, Harold sits down on a chair next to ours.

His picture had shown him with an *I* shape in his beard. Being clean-shaven exposes his deeply pockmarked cheeks. A dark red mark, like a fingerprint, juts above his shirt collar. His blue eyes twinkle as he breaks into a grin displaying the whitest teeth I've ever seen.

"Not a leading man, but a good fisherman. That's me!" says Harold. "I hear your grandfather, Andreas, is teaching you to play bridge."

"Harold, do you know how to play Solsvik Bridge?" I venture.

Uncle Bertin sets a tray loaded with glasses of milk and mounds of sweet rolls in front of us.

Harold laughs. "Papa, Andreas filled these boys in on Solsvik Bridge. We should take them out tonight, and we can all play."

Uncle Bertin claps his hands. "A great plan! We'll have dinner at the house, and we can play bridge tonight. I must warn you, though, people in Solsvik take no prisoners. Are you boys up for that? Or fishing? It's a nice night for that, too."

Stein, Rolf, Jan, and I glance at each other. Once again, I win … or lose…the vote.

"Uncle Bertin," I say, "let's go on a boat ride tonight and hear the stories about the islands. Can we do that?"

My thought is to buy us time before walking into what could be a hornet's nest. Solsvik Bridge can wait until we have better information on what cutthroat pirates might be lurking around here. As everything appears normal in Solsvik, this could be difficult. The houses are identical to other island houses, right down to their white clapboard exteriors, red shutters, gardens, and drying racks for cod in every backyard.

"This is nice." Bertin hoists Jan's palomino suitcase into his hand.

I shoulder Jan. "Nice."

He shoulders me back and blushes.

Rolf and Stein snort.

Behind the main street are buildings with long roof lines. These are the fish shops and canneries, which are identical to the canneries in Bergen.

A suitcase swings into my calves. Looking over my shoulder, I see Rolf.

"Trap," Rolf mouths. His eyes dart everywhere.

Raising my eyebrows, I shrug.

Stein and Jan's expressions are the same.

Bertin's house dominates the neighboring houses. Leaded glass windows, a rounded front door, and a slate roof declare this house the grandest in Solsvik. To the right, a large garden, a pen, and several outbuildings suggest the owner holds property. A dock has a trawler, a sailboat, and a rowboat tied to it.

Opening the rounded door, we see a grand piano and shelves filled with books and artwork.

"Constanse is visiting her mother." Bertin investigates the kitchen. "I think we have things for dinner, though. Afterward, Harold can take you on that boat ride." Uncle Bertin points to two nearly identical bedrooms.

"Here are the bedrooms. I will start on dinner, and you boys can unpack."

Within a few minutes, Stein and Rolf come into the bedroom that Jan and I share.

Jan breaks the ice. "Look, this is a wonderful place, but I think your grandfather is telling stories. This place is like where my family stays on the coast."

Stein and Rolf murmur agreement.

I don't know what to say. Fortunately, Harold's timing couldn't be better.

Large carrot tops peek out of his overall's pockets. Wiping dirt off his hands, he says, "I can show you around the place while Papa is getting dinner together. Our family's a big part of Solsvik's tumultuous history."

I nod, smiling smugly to my friends as if to say, "See! There are villains everywhere. We simply haven't been introduced."

Harold leads us to a shed that houses a copper barrel with tubes going in all directions. "This shed is famous around these parts. Janice—you know about her?—well, her aunt lived in Scotland and learned to make whiskey, bringing the recipe back to this island."

My friends are having trouble keeping their mouths closed.

Closing the gate, Harold scampers up the rocky path behind the shed. "Come with me."

We follow, eager to hear and see where the villains might still be. Massive gray-green boulders, stacked and squared off, are half as large as cars. Lichen and juniper protrude from the crags just below the summit, a forlorn looking bluff.

Harold points to them. "Another landmark around here. Joseph got the land through a card game people hadn't seen before—Solsvik Bridge."

We nod.

At last!

We jostle for a spot next to Harold. Who among us will be the first to hear the truth about Solsvik Bridge and about how people lost their land and women?

Bleating sheep scatter as we trek up the bluff.

Breathless, Harold stops at the top, and we gather around. The lighthouse is as big as my hand. Two large green islands lie a short distance west of the harbor, with an isthmus holding the remnants of what looks to be a wrecked boat. A narrow channel of lighter water slithers between the islands. I notice how oddly the waves crash against their shores.

"There," I point. "What's that narrow channel of water?"

Harold claps his hands as if we have discovered a good secret. "That? That's a part of the Gulf Stream. The current flowing there does funny things when the tide goes out. Do you see how the water hitting that sheer wall spins?"

Eagerly, we squint.

The water, instead of crashing directly against the wall, coils like a snake as it spins and ebbs.

"The current's power is underneath the surface," Harold says. "When the tide goes out, you will see that this shearing causes pockets to develop under the rock. It's an ideal place to hide things. Your great-grandfather rowed out there at low tide and discovered a large dome about two meters high." Harold wags his eyebrows and winks.

Slapping Jan and Rolf's backs, Harold chortles. "It will be low tide early tomorrow morning. Do you want to go? We've found pottery, whiskey bottles, and one time—" Harold stops.

Seconds later, we hear a chime's faint tinkling. Far below, a figure is hitting a triangle. "Supper's ready!" Harold says. He raises his hand, and Bertin raises his hand back.

As my friends call out, "Woo-Hoo!" I think they're as excited about the food as they are about all that Solsvik offers.

Jan leads the call as we tramp down the hill. "Spartans!"

Bertin's broad smile greets us.

Breathless, I gasp, "Uncle Bertin! What a wonderful place! Can we go on the boat ride tonight? We want to go out to the island and see the hiding place. I thought Gramps was teasing us. He wasn't!"

Uncle Bertin nods his head. "I can put your dinner onto tin plates, and you boys can go out in the boat now if you like." Eight pleading eyes stare at Harold.

I hardly notice what is on the plate Bertin hands to me. It doesn't matter. Gramps' stories are true!

Running to the sailboat, we climb aboard. After casting off, we get around the long tongue of land, heading past the harbor toward the outer island.

Sailing due west, we pass the closer island, dotted with summer homes, before heading south toward the second, more impressive island. The sun lies low on the horizon with a few clouds. Content, I cock my head back, the sea spray hitting my hands and arms as Harold talks to us about the island's history.

I look back toward Solsvik and am surprised that its buildings are now mere dots on the horizon. The Gulf Stream's current, appearing as a gray band, is broader here.

Harold leans over, his index finger carving a figure

eight into the water, and he peers westward.

"Boys"—his voice edges up as if he wants to make sure he has our full attention—"we'll have to save the other island for another time. I don't think we'll be able to go out tomorrow morning. There's a storm coming."

Changing tacks, Harold turns the boat toward Solsvik. I notice the lighthouse keeper turning on the light across the bay, but it is daylight. The sun is shining. The storm is upon us in minutes. A wall cloud, reminding me of the children's Ghost game in which someone covers himself in a sheet and lurches toward you, first sent cooler temperatures. We shiver, as a drizzle of salty spray sprinkles our heads. As Harold expertly navigates the choppy waters, rain starts to pour, and lightning flashes in the distance. Loud cracks of thunder roll overhead. We crouch but soon see lights and buoys, telling us that we have arrived in Solsvik's harbor.

Harold circles back, and flooring the boat's motor, he drenches us. The waves are slapping high, unfurling a blasting spray upon us. The rain lashes our backs as Stein jumps from Harold's boat to tie up.

I know the walk from the dock to the door with the yellow lantern is one hundred meters, but we can't get to the door fast enough to suit me.

No one should be on the rain-slicked streets. Instead, men in yellow slickers hurry to a building up the hill from the bakery, where a yellow, blue, and white light blinks.

Looking to dry off inside the house, we discover that Bertin has other ideas as he greets us holding yellow rain slickers and matching bucket hats.

"Put these on and run. Storms bring out the card players, so the card game will start earlier tonight."

Bertin waves us out and hands a roll of money to Harold. "Take care of them," he says in a low voice. "I'll be up in a few minutes. I have chores to finish."

Our heads down, we sprint up the short path to the main street, where we see feet and shadowy footprints grow brighter, casting a blue-red glow in the puddles.

The building is a low-slung mushroom-brown wooden building set with narrow glass panes.

Ducking into the alcove, I'm reminded of mustard flavored sardines. Twenty or thirty men, all clad in yellow oilskins, jockey for the wooden pegs on the wall. With strategically placed elbows and rolls of their shoulders, the men pull off their slickers and then hang their mackinaws so that the rainwater drips into a long metal slat in the floor. Whiffs of diesel, cigarette smoke, and—curiously—the pungent scent of mustard permeates the alcove as the men file through the narrow doorway.

Chairs scrape as an announcement is made that the game will be starting in five minutes. Above the scraping and chatter, the director announces, "Bets exceeding ten thousand kroner require cash up front and proof of deeds or other property you might have."

I swivel my head to see my friends' faces. Gramps wasn't kidding!

We shake off the water like golden retrievers, quickly discarding our rain gear. Shoulder to shoulder with Rolf and Jan—Stein, thinking there might be a chocolate bar in his pocket, retrieves a fishing lure—we survey our surroundings. There is not a woman in sight. The low-ceilinged hall, holding probably fifteen card tables, is filled with cigarette smoke. Men sit at the tables wearing expressions identical to those seen in a doctor's office waiting room. Two men carry out coffee urns. Then they return to the back. The taller man, whom I recognize as one of my distant cousins, brings an amber bottle to his lips. Laughing, he shakes his head in what to anyone else would be shock or disbelief, but I recognize the gesture. It's the same reaction we had when drinking alcohol at Jan's cabin.

Gramps' voice fills my head. *They distrust outsiders. There have been too many skirmishes and robberies. Remain polite and let them look you over.*

Bertin, who is now standing behind us, quietly comes forward. "They're my guests, Klement, and I will settle with you."

Klement's ruddy complexion contrasts with his silky white and black sideburns. He motions for us to sit at an empty card table.

Bertin and Harold sit directly behind us, and over his shoulder, Harold tells us what will happen next.

"It's like how Andreas plays," Harold counsels. "You'll catch on after the round."

Stein mutters, "We'll be the judge of that. Look at these people."

Harold hands us each one hundred kroner. He shakes his head when Jan and Stein immediately attempt to return the money. "Remember to ask for change."

Long wooden boards are handed out. Each board has four slats with a notation showing a compass direction and a number. Sitting on top is a deck of playing cards.

Gramps taught us well. Stein takes the cards and shuffles, taking the playing cards, dropping them from one hand to the other to a count of three. Distributing the playing cards to each receive thirteen of them, we place them into the slats. Stein passes the board and a twenty-kroner note over his shoulder to the person sitting directly behind him as part of the ritual.

Jan and I stand up and walk to the card table behind us, shimmying past two men smelling of cod.

Performing in near-synchronicity, people clasp shoulders, pass money, and change positions with the people at the next table.

Jan and I glance at each other and at the cod-smelling men sitting across from us. Gramps' crusty instructions are in my head. *Politely say hello and ask their names. Keep your knees close, and your cards, once taken out of the holder, should be placed as far down on your lap as you can and still see them. Breast your cards. And no smiling or frowning! Play in tempo, and don't snap the cards. Those are tells, and you will lose your money. No verbalizing. Use the bridge box.*

"We haven't seen you before." The man speaking bears a scar on his hand and is missing a finger below the knuckle. Somehow, balanced between his shortened knuckle and his other fingers, he holds a pencil, a pad of paper, a ten-kroner note, and a saucer with a cup of what I'm sure is not only coffee.

My knees scrape the table, sloshing the coffee cup's contents. "Kory." I nod to the Spartan. "And this is Jan. We're from Bergen."

This introduction is met with a slight smile by both men.

The chatter dies away, and we study our cards. Knuckles' partner bids and Jan tells me through his bid what he has. I respond, and we settle the bidding with me playing the hand.

It's textbook. Knuckles writes down our score. Then he clasps his hand to his shoulder. A board appears from behind him. Knuckles passes the board containing the cards we played to Rolf. Rolf smoothly moves the cards they played to Knuckles.

Knuckles and his partner win that bid, and we play. Jan signals he holds hearts by playing a high diamond. I follow, and we end up beating Knuckles and his partner.

Gramps' instructions must be in Rolf, Stein, and Jan's heads as I hear them say, "Thank you for the game."

Rolf and Stein return to our table, and Knuckles' partner clasps Rolf on the shoulder.

Rolf grimaces. There must have been fish oil or slime on his hand.

We inspect our scores. We're looking for mistakes. One extra trick for our side—one signal that worked well—counted, and it worked.

Stein rose. I could almost see Stein preparing Gramps' speech. "Do you agree? Thank you. I will take that."

Stein returns, twenty kroner richer, and adds the money to the twenty kroner on the table. "Gramps knows what he's doing. One of those men doesn't have all his fingers," he says.

I interrupt. "Did Knuckles cause you trouble?"

Stein grins, shaking his head. He leans forward, motioning us in. "I think we need to hide the money we're getting or pass among ourselves. Knuckles' partner could rip our heads off. It's good we're with Bertin and Harold."

After three hours, I'm exhausted. But we had taken Bertin's one-hundred kroner stake in us, and each had added three hundred kroner for the evening.

Bertin and Harold come over, their faces expectant.

Stein flourishes the money in front of us.

Bertin's expression darkens. "Not here! Robberies have happened, and the people get on the boat and go to a different village. That man you played against on the first round—the one missing a knuckle—do you know how he lost that knuckle? He tried to rob someone, so they say. In the process, a knife fight broke out, and he lost a portion of his finger. We'll settle up when we're back at the house." He smiles, realizing we are now scared to walk the one hundred meters to his house.

It could be my imagination, but it appears that Knuckles lit a cigarette in the entryway and is waiting for us.

The red, yellow, and white lights flicker off as we step outside, leaving only two streetlamps. A man is leaning against one, smoking a cigarette. His head turned toward the door.

Bertin walks to him and calls out, "Hansen! Did you have a good night? Boys, come and meet the bridge game's organizer."

The man's head is still down, but as we approach, he looks up, revealing, not Knuckles, but the man who was drinking the amber liquid earlier that evening.

Harold smiles at Hansen. "I'm taking the boys out in the morning to see the hiding place."

Hansen grins at us. "It should be good weather. I hope you find treasure."

After trying to give Uncle Bertin the one-hundred kroner stake, we walk to the house and tuck the money into our bags.

#

"Spart, you awake?" Jan asks. He stretches, his fingers falling short of the bedroom's ceiling. Pushing a curl from his eye, he reaches into the top suitcase and pulls on shorts, and wrests a white shirt over his head.

"One of these days," I say, "your mother is going to button every button, and you are going to look like an idiot when you do that."

He grins. "Mother stopped after I careened into everything in the laundry room."

We turn as light footfalls, the squeak of the icebox door, and clattering utensils come from the kitchen.

Jan opens the door. "Good morning!" he calls, turning to me as Harold mentions we could go out to see the islands and the Smugglers' Rock. "I'll go wake the others."

There is a flurry of activity across the hall, and Stein and Rolf walk toward the kitchen.

I dress, padding out to where Harold has laid out four cups and plates, rolls from yesterday, three kinds of cheese, smoked salmon, and bread.

Turning down the stove, he pours warm milk over small chocolate bars placed in the cups. "The storm has cleared out. If we leave in an hour, we'll be safe to go to Smugglers' Rock and maybe walk around. We might find buried treasure!"

We make short work of breakfast, and the five of us go down to the skiff. The now calm water, a faint blue-gray, changes to navy and green as we leave Solsvik's harbor.

"I'm sorry we weren't able to go all around the islands yesterday, but we ended up with a good evening, am I right?" Harold teases. "Watch for the gray band of water and the swirling motion. I'll take the sail down, and we can row carefully to the sea stack."

The gray band is quickly spotted, and within a

minute, Harold and Rolf take down the sail. The boat is not moving of its own accord.

Stein points as the grayish green band swirls and lazily spins out. "That looks different from last night. That's because the tide is going out. Right, Harold?"

Harold answers by taking the oars and pointing them downward in a poling motion. A large rock appears a meter below the surface.

Rolf, Stein, and I put our heads over the boat's edge, calling directions to Harold, who poles through the water like a gondolier.

Dropping anchor in the shallow water, Harold jumps down onto a small sandbar.

Rolf follows and then Stein. I turn to look at Jan, who appears perplexed. "C'mon, let's go check it out," I say, walking the bow.

Jan rises slowly and, as carefully as a tightrope walker, edges along the bow toward me. His eyes never leaving mine, he holds out his hand.

Harold pulls on the rope, bringing the bow closer to the water. "Jump!"

The distance is only a meter. Jan swings his long legs over the side and eases himself down into the water. Once again, his eyes never leave mine. Pursing his lips and furrowing his brow, he continues to stare out over the horizon.

"There it is! I see the indentation." Stein calls. "It resembles—"

I interrupt. "A troll. That's what it looks like."

The sea stack resembles a water troll's head in the cartoon "The Water Spirit" by the Norwegian artist Theodor Severin Kittleson. As the water ebbs, two misshapen eye sockets appear, with one of the sockets deeply hollowed. Strings of kelp hang over the sockets like mats of dirty hair. Rocks, barely visible below the surface, strongly resemble The Water Spirit's nasty, warty nose.

Harold wades through the water, leaning against the nose and gripping the warts. All the while, he inspects for algae, wiping his foot on each stone. Then he pulls a piece of paper from his pocket. "This is how you know you'll be able to stand inside without going deeper than your waist. Watch this." He ducks his head under the troll's nose and disappears.

The four of us follow. I take up the rear in case Jan needs help. Since he's splashing through the water to the ever-widening gap in the rock, his earlier fear must have passed.

A wave slows and curls around the opening. As it unwinds, Harold calls from inside. "I think we can all fit in here!"

Mimicking his movements exactly, we join Harold in the rounded alcove.

Harold brings a small flare out of his pocket. In his other hand, as promised, the piece of paper is completely dry. "The water, over time, collapsed a portion of this rock, and the area up there"—he points to a sharp shelf projecting upwards—"is where we discovered artifacts—bowls from the East, ancient trinkets, and a runestone. This opening probably took millions of years to create."

The flare sputters, and the oily smoke causes us to cough.

"Let's see if we can catch fish for lunch." Harold turns to retrace his steps.

Later, recalling the perfection of Harold's boat and

the bridge game, I realized that this was the day my childhood ended.

Chapter Four

Walking up the Goat Trail reminds me of my life's narrowing choices. The path—rock-strewn and brambly—leads to Jan's family cabin and is the one we have used since he and I became friends in grade school.

"BST? That's a private school! What's wrong with Granvin?" my mother asked me over this morning's breakfast.

I had no clear answers to her questions. Other than Jan nagging me at every turn to join him at the school he would be attending in a few months. And he and I were always getting the best grades in our classes. And I wanted to. Wasn't that enough?

A rock about the size of my foot tumbles in front of me on the trail. Kicking it like a football, I gleefully watch the serrated stone sail over the trail's edge and, like a butcher knife, peel the bark from a downed tree. Taking my walking stick, I stab where the rock was as if killing the memory and its daring to be in my way.

Three days ago, Jan's tone was one used when explaining the basics to a child. With an exasperated air, he said, "BST—Bergen Science and Technological School—is the best school in Bergen for science and mathematics and a near-automatic approval to go to the university in Trondheim, which is the best in the country." Jan pulled a sheaf of papers from his desk, shoving them into my hand. "Fill them out. You belong there."

Blue Man and *Little Red Riding Hood*—Floien Mountain's beloved funicular cars grinding out a greeting to each other on the mountain's mid-point jolt me back to the present. I pause, and by leaning my head back, I make out the white railing surrounding the viewing platform. The views are spectacular, and on a clear day, all seven of the mountains surrounding Bergen are easily visible.

When we were kids, Jan and I nicknamed this trail "the Goat Trail." We'd met on a playground. I'd lost the fight—about what, I've forgotten—but gained a best friend.

We shared a love of the boy-detective series The Crimshaw Brothers. We dubbed Jan's parent's cabin "Fort Spartan" for two reasons: a shared love of the tale where Ned and Tom Crimshaw saved a platoon by camouflaging a hut with leftover paint and Jan's obsession with the Spartans of Ancient Greece.

The cabin lies in a bunker of trees and rocks within spitting distance of the main path connecting the funicular and other mountains. Painted, as it is, in a mix of olive drab, dark green, and brown, the cabin is reminiscent of a military installation. Without a doubt, the place uses leftovers from some unknown country's failed defense project.

But this location has unique geological features. A sheer slate wall makes it easy to hear the funicular cars clank in their slow climb to the restaurant and overlook of Bergen's harbor. Better yet, all sounds coming from the cabin are undetectable.

Soon after making friends with Jan, we tested this phenomenon by yodeling and singing at the top of our lungs. Our friends Rolf, Stein, and Jules, who had come up the mountain on *Little Red Riding Hood*, and who walked toward the cabin, had all sworn they never heard a thing.

The Crimshaw Brothers Detective Series authors would have a *field day* with it. Another Brooklyn-America expression from Gramps.

Happier times. Today, all I want is to scream my lungs out without anyone hearing me.

I want to go to BST. A tear wells up in my eye as I duck into the copse of trees leading to the cabin.

Damn, another plan has been thwarted.

Jan is outside, gathering firewood.

As I come into the cabin, Stein is wiggling the liquor cabinet handle, pushing it this way and that.

I explode. "What do you think you're doing? We can't break into that cabinet! We're going to get in trouble! This isn't our place."

"Baby," he mutters as he rummages in his knapsack.

"What did you call me?" I like coming up here and the Andersons. I don't want my welcome to end because of this jerk. And if Herr Anderson says I'm rotten to the people at BST, I can kiss that chance goodbye…all because of someone who must always tinker with things that don't belong to him.

"Relax! You're afraid all the time. You never want to get in trouble. Jan knows. He asked me to bring my tools." Stein inserts a long tool into the lock.

Bewildered, I ask, "What's that?"

"Shh!" Stein cautions. Slowly, he twists the tool and places his ear against the cabinet—like in the movies.

Jan walks in with Rolf, talking and laughing.

I quiet them, pointing toward Stein.

There is a click as Stein pulls open the door, but I, unlike the others, don't cheer. Bowing to all of us, he takes an extra low dip when he turns to me.

"This is not okay." I scowl, going outside. I expect Jan to come and find me or Stein to come out and apologize for screwing up my chances to go to BST.

Loud laughter and whistles come from the cabin.

Assholes.

I go through the copse of birch trees out to the main path, turning to face the restaurant and funicular lying no more than thirty meters away.

A group of women, chattering about the scary climb, exit the funicular and walk toward me. I want them to shut up so I can hear if any of my so-called friends miss me. The women stop to admire the harbor view, and I crane my neck in the cabin's direction.

Complete silence.

What a bunch of assholes.

Walking toward the funicular, I turn because what I want to do is—

"Are you lost?"

It isn't who I want there, but he will have to do.

Rolf holds a kindling bag out to me, his other hand protecting his camera. "We need more firewood. I took your picture when you were standing there. I wish you could have seen the expression you gave those women."

"Have you thought about school?"

Rolf thinks about my question and holds up his camera.

"Is this about BST?"

I start to shake my head, but the guilt of maybe laying open my argument with my mother, our lack of money, the easy lives others seem to have has shut down any truth I might expose. I gaze up at him and nod.

"Not all of us have our lives mapped out, and some don't worry when they should." Rolf rolls his head toward the cabin. "That new job of his father's, the move to Eidsvag—I don't think he's going to have as easy a time of it as he thinks."

"He's moving? Who's moving?"

"Shit!" Rolf clasps his camera strap. "I thought you knew. I thought that's why we came up here. To celebrate his going to a new school and the fancy, new house. He says he'll stay in contact."

Asshole.

"Ingrid. Ingrid told me."

I'm barely listening.

Rolf's voice rises in pitch. "Jan didn't tell me, Kory. Ingrid did. She was at the post office getting change-of-address cards, and I asked. I thought you knew." Rolf's voice drops to a whisper. "I forgot Jan and Stein can hear us. Let's gather firewood and head back."

Mechanically, I fill the kindling bag, but I'm thinking about Rolf and his camera. Over the summer, he brought it everywhere. I know from firsthand experience that he's sensitive about being in front of a camera.

To explain, my mother calls Rolf *fine-boned*.

****

When we were younger, none of us knew what that meant, so I decided to ask Rolf about it one warm summer day as we splashed around the lake behind Fort Spartan, scrutinizing rocks. Big mistake.

Rolf half-charged, half-swam over, pushing me in the chest.

I tripped backward. As he jumped on top of me,

Rolf's hand yanked my hair and face. I tried to roll to the side, but he seized my nose and ear with his hand and kept pushing. My hand reached down and grasped a rock.

When he saw me swinging the rock, he let go.

Muffled giggles were replaced by a shout of terror, as, through the splashing and waves, Jan yanked Rolf off me.

Pushing off a rock, I sprang to my feet. Coughing and spitting, I was mad as hell and stunned by what just happened. "What the hell?" I lunged toward Rolf, but Stein and Jan blocked me, their arms extended, mean expressions on their faces.

So, there we stood—me with a welt rising above my ear, Rolf looking like a coiled cobra, Stein and Jan looking like Centurion guards—all glaring and snarling at one another.

"I was simply asking," I said. "A phrase my mother said, that's all. God almighty, what's wrong with you?"

Rolf glowered at me. "You don't think I'm as tough or as strong as you. I'm merely a tagalong. That's what you think."

Now, all three of us gaped at him.

"Rolf! It was only a question!" Stein shouted.

Jan glanced sideways at me and shook his head. "You know how old women are."

I lunged forward again.

This time, Jan stood directly in front of me. Rolf stood behind him. There was no remorse in Rolf's face.

I tried to bob up over Jan and past him. No dice. Jan's reflexes were faster than mine, and once again, his arms extended. "No. No discussion."

"Look, it was dumb to say, and I'm sorry I said it to

you." I wiped the water from my eyes, trying to get a read on Rolf's face. "I didn't know what it meant, and I wondered. That's it. Nothing more." Rolf's anger shocked me.

Rolf didn't give in so easily. "Listen, I get that from my mother and her friends. It's constant, and I hate it." Rolf struck a fake modeling pose straight out of a magazine. His voice took on a mocking, cooing quality. " 'Oh, Kristi, you should get him into a modeling agency, with those blue eyes and blond hair. Ooh, Kristi, what a nice smile. Ooh, Kristi, he can wear just about anything.' "

Rolf shook in anger. "I hate it, and I wish they'd leave me alone! My mother brings it up at least once per week, usually after her bridge parties. I go in the opposite direction. I like coming here—drinking and swimming, being away from people I despise."

"I'm sorry, I—" I was incredulous.

"I know. Forget it, all right? And, for the record, it means I resemble a doll. Like I'm made of china." Rolf glared at the three of us.

The way Rolf acted still made me uneasy. He was angry at me, and all I'd done was ask him a question. As we walked back to the cabin, we collected kindling wood. Rolf was a few yards away from me. He leaned, flexing his muscles, foot upon a branch. Then he stamped it down, breaking the limb in half.

His hair genuinely did reflect a glint of gold, and though it was momentary, he did appear like someone you'd see in a magazine.

Catching my stare, he scowled at me. His shoulders lowered, and his head dropped, ready to charge like a bull.

He wasn't over my remark.

I made a half-hearted wave, indicating that my stumbling upon him was accidental. I didn't glance back as I walked to the cabin. I couldn't look back. His anger had been real, and the fierceness of it scared me.

Now, years later, back at the cabin, Rolf is either beating me to the punch or giving me time to simmer down. "Jan, tell us about your move."

Jan pours a clear liquid into two cups, handing them to Rolf and me. The contents are acrid, even from fifteen centimeters away.

"Well, wham-o!" Jan drains the remnants in his cup and pours more clear fluid into his cup. "Papa called Ingrid and me into his study three days ago."

Taking a sip, Jan winces as the pungency and memory water his eyes. "Papa's promotion covers all of Western Norway. He must entertain clients, and that, more than anything, is why we're moving to Eidsvag. The former salesman is moving to Eastern Norway, and my parents are buying his house. I'm applying to BST." He lowers his head but tilts his eyes up toward me in warning. "Ingrid will go to the Eidsvag school."

Jan sets the cup down to let us know he didn't like the alcohol he was drinking or the situation. "Papa says it is a great opportunity. And it's not far away. We'll still come here."

Right. Wham-o.

Chapter Five

"What's on your mind?" Among Gramps's many talents is the ability to read sullenness at fifty meters.

I'm sitting cross-legged on the brown suede couch in our living room, a sheaf of papers spread out around me.

Gramps walks over, a newspaper in his hand.

Hastily, I gather up the documents.

"I'll ask again. What's on your mind?" Gramps' tone is one of discussion.

"Jan. Jan wants me to interview with BST. He's moving. Did I tell you that?" I hope to avoid the topic and don't want to rat out Mother. Pissed by her automatic dismissal of my going to BST, I don't know what other options I have.

"It's a good school. Did I tell you about how I met your grandmother?"

I knew they were childhood sweethearts. I'm puzzled by the trajectory of this conversation. "You were childhood sweethearts. Your parents went to America. And you went back to marry Gran."

Gramps nods. "That's the gist. Mali and I grew up together in Solsvik. Her parents had that grand house her grandfather built, and my father worked for her father at the cannery. Like her sisters, Mali was to get married when she turned eighteen, have children every two years, and be supportive. I was one of nine, and there was no way for us to live on the farm. My father worked in the cannery and supplied fish to restaurants so he could support the family."

"In 1880, he slipped, and a cannery machine sliced his right hand from his wrist to his elbow. They thought he would die, and he realized he couldn't work at the cannery or on his boat after getting stitched up. When my brothers and sisters turned eleven or twelve, they were sent to Bergen to work as maids or on ships. My oldest brother Hans went with his father-in-law to New York— Brooklyn, America—and got work as a tugboat operator. One of my nephews was very smart, learned English quickly, worked as a teacher—at first, to help the Norwegians learning the language off the boat, and then, in a local grade school."

Sliding off the couch, I walk to Gramps' desk, bending to study a sepia picture of a young man holding a large paper. I have passed by that photograph many times. Looking now, I see that the young man is not holding the certificate in an ordinary way.

He holds the certificate out from his body, and I recognize pride, like that of an athlete who has won a great victory.

"Right," Gramps says, his tone the same as when he talks of the Brann, his beloved football team. "That's his diploma from the university. New York University. He became a university professor of English. Ten years before, he spoke only one language, and there he was, ten years later, teaching men who were not much younger than him."

"Do you think I should go to America?" I turn this thought over in my head. "Maybe go live with your nephew?" I'm still not getting the point of this conversation.

"I think you work hard, and I think you are smarter than Jan."

I don't believe I'll get answers, though Gramps' tone holds pride.

"BST is a private school. You can't be the first boy to have more brains than cash. I think you should make an appointment and see what they say."

That evening, after finishing my letter of introduction to the Selection Committee, I bring it to the living room, where my parents and grandparents sit. I hand the message and the completed application to Gramps.

Dear Herr Bye:

I'm writing to apply for admittance to the Bergen Science and Technology School's Fall 1940 term. I have requested that Granvin Gymnas send my transcripts for you to consider… .

He silently reads it and passes it to my mother, who quickly raises her head to scowl at her stepfather and me.

"You spoke of it to Papa?" My mother's voice is of the wounded. I have exposed a gap in her mothering skills to her parents.

My father takes the papers from my mother. Then he considers me.

Tipping my head back, I swallow hard, fighting back the tears of anger and frustration. Gramps turns to look at his nephew's portrait. Then he turns, and, with the slightest dip of his head, nods to me.

At that moment, I change my tone to one of conciliation. As if I had planned for every objection, I say, "I will interview with them now, but with the term starting shortly, maybe there will be an opening or a way to afford this. I'm willing to work and help pay for the tuition so I can go next year." I need all of their approvals, but I know who holds sway in my house.

****

My mother looks at the faint stripes on my pant legs where she's let out the hems. Taking money from the cookie jar in our kitchen, she carefully counts out my bus fare and hands it to me. "We'll have to buy you another suit soon. I can't let those pants out any farther." The crease in her brow says, "Another expense. With the money we don't have."

The bus ascends the narrow streets and then grinds to a halt with an expectant *whoosh* from the opening doors. In the bright outdoor light, the white stripe in my pants might as well scream, "I'm poor!"

Walking with impending dread up the last half block, I enter the Bergen Science and Technology Institute—BST. It appears to be a castle.

The school sits on a large outcropping overlooking the harbor. I think it's meant to intimidate. And it does. The walls have imprints of *B's* engraved into them. With nary a stem out of place, the garden's hedges appear pruned with embroidery scissors, and turrets jut upwards like spears. Everything is fresh, as if dirt or litter anywhere would be an insult.

I walk up the dozen stone steps and open a large, ancient door. Jan didn't tell me about the overwhelming smell of wax. The stone floors gleam, and the banisters reflect the light from chandeliers that have—only recently, I'll bet—converted to electricity. To my left is an alcove where a man sits reading papers. He looks up as I close the heavy door and walk toward him.

"I'm Kory Mowat. I'm here to see Herr Mueller?" I

venture. I practiced meeting the professors and what I'd say, but I didn't know about a gatekeeper.

His finger traces the lines in a ledger. Then he picks up a telephone. He speaks quietly, so quietly that all I hear is, "Very good. Shall I guide him? I will let him know."

His eyes scan my cowlick, sprinkle of freckles, and my tie, whose knot must not be in style. He purses his lips. "Please have a seat. They will be here, momentarily." He waves to a gigantic pew.

Sitting down, I slip back—faster than I intend—the waxy finish making me slide like a well-oiled toboggan. I imagine this was a castle at some point. Too high for a moat. Doors open above me, and I hear the rhythmic clattering of a typewriter, abruptly cut short by a door's slam. As I pull on the crease of my blue gabardine pants, I see two pairs of polished black shoes. Two shadows appear on the floor. One shadow is of someone wide; the other, of someone leaning over.

"Mister Mowat? Kory Mowat? I'm Herr Mueller," says the man who is old and stooped.

I didn't see the cane in the reflection of his shoes. "This is Herr Simonsen. Please come with us."

I follow them past pictures of men in formal robes. All look old and solemn. Probably dead. At the hallway's end is a large bay window overlooking Bergen's Nordnes District—the steepest, most crooked, scariest part of town. I can make out the monastery atop the hill where—if the campfire stories are true—evil people will spontaneously immolate if they walk by and don't repent.

"They burned witches there. Can you believe it?" Herr Simonsen follows my gaze as he opens the door to a classroom full of beakers.

Chemistry laboratories smell the same. What makes this different from Granvin is the fact there is no way anyone shares anything. Beakers, burners, test tubes—all are neatly lined up in the hutches holding them. Through a door, I spy walls of chemicals.

"What do you think of Pluto?"

"Pluto?" I answer questioningly. "Our newest planet?"

Herr Mueller leans forward as if prodding me to speak more.

"Um, I wonder how long it will take to go around the sun?"

Herr Simonsen takes a file from the desktop and opens it.

Swallowing, I recognize my letter.

"You have good marks. Your teachers at Granvin say you are curious. What would you like to get out of your time at BST?" Herr Simonsen pulls at an imaginary thread on his lapel. "Well?" he repeats.

The interview is not going as I want. "I do well in math and science, and I like to build things," I blurt out. "I...want to...I...start...save up money." I'm getting lightheaded.

"You want to start in the Fall 1940 term? Why not now? With your friend, Jan?" Herr Simonsen pulls out another sheet of paper.

The oil company letterhead from Jan's father. Oh, no. That's why this isn't going well. Why did I bother? *Out with it.* "I want to help pay for my tuition, and by starting next year, I can do that." I realize my mistake almost immediately.

"Are you working now?" Herr Mueller asks.

I shake my head. "I want to do this. Be an engineer." The monastery at Nordnes appears through the trees and then evaporates. I'm going to pass out.

"We'll contact you."

A voice, or voices—I am not sure—seem to come through panes of glass. They move toward the door, and before I know it, I am moving past the bay window, down the stairs—the banister's more slippery than before, or maybe it's my damp hands—and I'm out looking at the turrets.

The interview, if that's what you can call it, lasted all of ten minutes. I look at the manicured gardens and the gate of what I'm now convinced—more than ever—had to have been a castle.

This is one moat I will never cross.

Chapter Six

The wet maple leaves smell rank. Pushing and pulling on the rake in the clockwise manner beaten into me, two metal tines nudge a striped body. I lean over, gently pressing against the furry ball and gasp.

So that's where Tuffy went. We searched everywhere.

Scooping up a rhododendron leaf, I suck in my breath and reach down to pick up the dead kitten. As I tuck the leaf under the body, the kitten's head lolls. How did it break its neck? A dog didn't do that. There aren't any marks. Tuffy looks perfect. Asleep. With a broken neck. Tuffy's fur along his spine dries, and I run my index finger across his spine. No marks?

"What happened to Tuffy?"

I don't hear Jules come up behind me. Wearing navy slacks, a cream-colored knit sweater, and a knotted scarf, Jules looks to be every inch the *dandy* that Gramps has begun calling him.

Months earlier, Jules' friend, Petter, mentioned a sales job at Gold Dust Pawn, suggesting that Jules would be a *natural*. Over dinner, Petter talked of marketing certain items. "If you listen carefully, people will often supply clues to what they want but cannot afford. An easy sale!" Petter oozed confidence. "Suggest they might want to trade up and that having the right things is the mark of the right man. They owe it to themselves."

Jules, capitalizing on this advice, was promptly hired. Our grandmother, Mali, calls Jules' way of dressing *as having a knack with clothes.* But Gramps, ever the realist, says "all flash and no cash."

Jules' finger points to Tuffy. "That smells awful. You need to bury him. Dead things attract rats and mice, and we don't want that." The tip of his two-toned shoe nudges at the raking pattern I started. "Glad to see you're following my advice. It's easier if you go along with learning things properly. Finish up soon; I'm sure dinner is almost ready." His fingers curl under, the better to dig his nails under my clavicle as his hand slides across my shoulder.

I flinch at the remembered—and his favorite—way to inflict pain on weaker prey. In the process, I drop Tuffy on the ground.

"Is that any way to show respect for the dead?" I reach down and pick up Tuffy, cradling the balled figure a little tighter.

Jules' fingers, still curled under, leave my shoulder. His smile is that of a viper sighting its prey.

I jerk away, putting my fingers across the recalled space centimeters below my clavicle and the unanswered pleas for mercy.

"I'll tell Mother Tuffy is dead, and you are burying it." In the dimming light, Jules saunters across the yard and into our house.

Moments later, in our kitchen, as I wash the garden dirt from my hands, a phrase from my catechism pops into my head. "Whoever is righteous has regard for the life of its beasts."

Shoving a heaping mound of potatoes into his mouth while wiping the melted butter dribbling down his chin onto his napkin, Jules eagerly fills us in on an exciting day at the Gold Dust. "Two Polish sailors came in. Their Norwegian was horrible, but luckily, Petter could understand a few phrases." Jules wipes his mouth and takes a slurping chug from his water glass, his eyes lighting up at the memory.

"Anyway," he continues, "two Polish sailors were talking about the September Campaign. They were upset. Their neighbors disappeared—rumored, taken to camps. The Germans showed up—" Jules shoves another bite into his mouth. It doesn't seem to matter that my mother and grandmother are giving him the evil eye. He wipes his mouth. "So, the Germans planned the September Campaign, and the next thing you know, people don't show up for work. Orders aren't delivered. It's weird."

Jules divides the salmon on his plate into two palm-sized bites, ferally gulping and swallowing them.

My mother's fork clatters onto her plate.

"Standing a meter away were two regulars of ours, both from Hamburg. One broke out of the line, grabs a Polish guy by the collar, calls him a liar, and tells him to shut up." Jules slathers thick, creamy butter on a roll.

Gran stands up and takes her plate to the kitchen.

Oblivious, Jules chomps on the roll. "Petter stepped in and escorted the Polish guys to the door. Clapping his hands around the Germans' shoulders, he offered to cut them in on a special deal. One German sailor shook his head and said, 'It's not a campaign. It's called *Case White*, and we're transferring people to better jobs. It's simple."

Jules' butter-drenched fingers reach for the cake but receive a hard slap from my mother's hand.

Buttery oil seeps into my shirt as his fingers slither across my shoulder, once again finding my clavicle. "And Kory disposed of Tuffy this afternoon."

Chapter Seven

Herr Henricksen, the man interviewing me at Marine Techworks Center, resembles a clarinet. His long, thin nose, black shirt, brown vest with piano-key-like black buttons, and his honking, barking voice only add to my mental image. And to my distraction.

"We need help filing invoices, cleaning the shop, and putting away the workmen's tools," his voice—like a musician wetting a new reed—cuts over the buzzing, stamping, and grinding of machines. "Let me show you around."

The workshop is a chaotic hive. Staring at the machines, I linger, gawking at the machinists' creations and marveling at the sparks flying off the grinders. One machinist, holding up his product, evaluates the crafted engine part like a diamond, reminding me of Jules examining a pawn-shop trinket through a jeweler's eyepiece.

Herr Henricksen continues to honk ahead of me, pointing to the janitor's closet and the office.

There's a tap on my shoulder as I stand near a metal lathe. Sheepishly, I blush at Herr Henricksen. Waving my hand apologetically, I motion toward the janitor's closet.

He crooks his finger at me, and I follow him to an empty station holding a metal lathe. "You have stared long enough," he says. "I will teach you how to use the lathe. Watch me now!"

Over the next few minutes, Herr Henricks transforms from being a comic figure to a magician. He hands me goggles, picks up a chunk of metal from the floor, and sets it at an angle on the lathe.

Like a sorcerer, he's in complete command, and the machine appears to leap to do his bidding. His nose, mere centimeters from the spinning device, seems to be in constant danger of being lopped off. With blinding speed, the machine hums and whines, turning the metal and spewing burred, curled metal around like carnival lights or confetti. Herr Henricksen conjures calipers from his pocket to measure the thickness, and—in another sleight of hand—a vial of oil appears as if grasped from thin air. He expertly adds a small drop of oil to the white-hot lathe. A holder soon appears through the smoke. It's dull, its edges burred. Then Herr Henricksen moves to another machine. The chunk of metal, with quick precision, is transformed into a shiny part, worthy of inclusion in any device.

I regard him with unabashed awe.

Grinning, he says, "I understand you like math, and you can draw. We can help you create the designs that come in. That is, if this is what you would like to do."

Shaking his hand, I'm too enthusiastic, but I can't help myself. "When can I start?"

"Tomorrow? Or maybe sooner?" Herr Henricksen says. "Would you like this?"

Dancing the still hot part between my fingers, I continue to shake my new boss' hand and singe both our palms in the process.

I flush with embarrassment, but Herr Henricksen laughs. "Tomorrow, then."

The part has now cooled to the touch, but my enthusiasm for what was created has not. I need to share this with the Spartan. Clamoring off the bus, I race down the tony lane to where he lives. Jan is silhouetted in his bedroom window. I hoot our secret greeting to each other. He looks up and waves to me.

"Look at this!" I thrust the holder into Jan's face.

His blue eyes narrow, and he takes a step backward. He sniffs.

Taken aback, I raise my voice. "This takes skill!"

"An engineer will tell the machinist how many to create. Do you want to think it up, or do you want to do the manual labor? You are smarter than that. No one disputes you are good with your hands. But if you come to school with me, you can design these and have someone else make them for you."

Jan's logical answer pleases him, but it infuriates me. "Jan," I say through gritted teeth, "I dreamt up this design, which many machinists in the shop do. An engineer comes in with a design, but sometimes he doesn't have the hands-on skill to know if it will work. Often, the machinists have to rework the plans because the engineer has missed an important detail."

"Some machinist overriding a design?" Jan eyes me up and down as if the next thing I say will be that the moon is made of green cheese.

Heat creeps into my face. "The people who work there are not dumb, and not all engineers are smart." I draw in a long breath.

I can't believe we're fighting about this.

Jan waves his hands in mock defeat. His tone is apologetic as he speaks. "Spart! It's a rare thing to have the ability to do both. You can create these things in your head *and*"—he raises his finger in the air to signal a point— "you can show people on the machines a better design. That's rare, and it's why you will be a good engineer."

Chapter Eight

April 9, 1940

On the morning of April 9, 1940, I awoke to hear my mother use combinations of words and violence against inanimate objects.

Our household's rituals carry a rhythm and hum. My mother turns on the radio for Papa to listen to as he shaves, chattering about our doings, and in lower tones, commenting about Gramps, my siblings, and Gran. I can hear the clattering and bustling through the ceiling of the basement bedroom I share with Jules, who either left early or has not come home, which is something that's been happening increasingly.

The radio—always tuned to *Radio Andorra* programs in the morning—is set on full volume.

"German paratroopers? In Stavanger?" Mother asks.

The radio responds with a squeal, static, and then silence.

"You goddamn piece of shit! Bootlicking bag of..." my mother blusters.

I'm shocked, not only by her choice of language— "scum-sucking bag of monkey shit" will be added to my new list of words to shock my elders—but the fear and anger coming from the person vocalizing it—my mother.

"What the hell is wrong with the radio?" Mother demands.

Whatever is happening upstairs is out of sync. Haphazardly, I find my school uniform, run a razor across my reddish stubble, and do a quick swipe of my teeth.

Leaving the bathroom and passing by the rakes and canned goods arranged along the walls, I enter the bustling kitchen.

I know what will be waiting on the dining room table—creamy white cheese, salami, dollops of canned jams, and my mother's yeasty home-baked bread. Breakfast will be followed by a stolen gulp of Gramps' or her coffee, an admonishment it will stunt my growth, and a kiss on my mother's cheek. Then, I'll head off to my last year of school at Granvin.

Today, however, the topic is that the radio is silent and that there are paratroopers in Stavanger. German paratroopers.

Gramps' solution to the problem with the radio is simple. Like many things in his life, he believes that a direct approach is the best way to handle situations.

Banging on the radio's top, he puts a chip on the instrument's glass face, which accomplishes two things: a high squeal of surrender and a higher squeal from a ticked-off woman who tells Gramps how much her social hour programs uplift her.

But I don't care about my mother's radio programs. Radio Andorra has reported shocking news. Paratroopers. German paratroopers. German paratroopers in Stavanger.

Papa has come into the kitchen to lend his expertise. His solution is even more direct than his father-in-law's. He unplugs the radio and plugs it back in. The dial begins to glow, going from a faint honey color to a soft orange.

Absently, I drink from Gramps' and my mother's cups of coffee, shoving in pieces of bread and white cheese.

Everyone leans in to hear the radio announcer. Everyone questions. Everyone is hopeful.

Papa points to the clock in the shape of a coffee pot on the wall and then to me.

Scampering out the door, I skid to a complete stop at the sight of a familiar figure.

Jan is waiting for me.

Angling my head toward him, I call out, "Spart."

"Spart," he returns, and we salute identically, ready to soldier on.

Except he's here. "What are you doing here?" I'm becoming more direct by the day.

Jan scowls at me. As I come toward him, he pivots on his heels and walks for a moment without saying anything. I wait.

"Well?" he says, in a tone demanding an answer. "Well? What do you think?"

I shrug as I fall in with his long stride. "I dunno. What? The paratroopers in Stavanger?"

"Germans. Here," he says, like a Norwegian One radio station announcer.

My news has had a chance to settle in with the Spartan. Jan cocks an eyebrow at me. "Paratroopers?" he asks.

Jan's low voice fades in and out, making me hunker in closer as one of Bergen's famous *mists* starts. "The Germans came to Bergen early this morning and are meeting with people from our government," the Spartan says, wiping drizzle from his coat and chin, "but from what Papa heard—He even got a phone call! He never

59

gets that!—they're now in our harbor and in Oslo to take over our country! The King and his cabinet have fled to the woods."

Stein is waiting on the corner as he does each morning and, like Jan, demands to know what I think.

Of course, since Jan has brought me up to speed, I have an opinion.

The three of us chatter on our way to our schools, but as we walk, we are joined by the other citizens of Bergen and—probably—of Norway that day. All the people I see heading to their schools or jobs share the same grim expression, all huddled in their raincoats, shivering as they lean into their fellow countrymen to make sense of it all.

The snippets of conversation, tossed around like a bad game of dodgeball, center around a central question. "Why would the Germans come and for what?"

As my friends and I near Granvin, I overhear a girl's conversation with her friends. Like Jan, her father received a phone call notifying him that the Germans were here and that our government was cooperating. Her next words make me shiver: "Norway is now a part of the German government."

What a liar!

Stein asks us if we think our German is good enough to be German soldiers.

"I don't think that's an option for us, Stein." The Spartan's tone of voice could have cut ice.

Jan claps Stein and me on the shoulder as we near Granvin Gymnas. "I'm going to be late for school at BST. Fortunately"—he pats his coat and grins—"I forged my mother's signature on a doctor's appointment note. Meet me after school at the *Latinskole*."

My favorite teacher, Herr Tveit, looks like he's playing dress-up in adult clothes. Standing outside Granvin Gymnas on the decidedly unmanicured lawn, my English teacher's brown Harris Tweed overcoat hangs to his ankles. A creased bowler hat covers the tops of his ears. He waves a gray and white knitted glove in a swooping motion to direct us up the brick stairs.

In the gentlest of voices, Herr Tveit says, "Good morning, Laird Mowat," in what I now know is a Scottish burr, before addressing the girl behind me as "Lady Johnson."

My clan's tartan is not on the wall of Herr Tveit's classroom and never will be. A map with a red lion holding a banner proclaiming England is on one wall. A larger map with men in colorful kilts is nearly half the chalkboard's size. *Stewart Clan* is written in medieval script on the map, and I recognize the shires of Scotland, the Shetland Islands, and the Orkney Islands.

Herr Tveit calls me Laird Mowat in jest. Papa discovered the Mowat's clan was not big enough to have a Lord—a Laird—unlike Herr Tveit's. He proudly claims to be a Sinclair.

"Lairds and Ladies! Good morning?" Herr Tveit asked us a question instead of stating a fact.

Yesterday, or any of the other days before, our response would have been a resounding "Good morning!"

Herr Tveit pulls his bowler hat from his head, and he rubs his ears and hair. Removing his overcoat, he folds it on the detention chair next to the door. He smooths his jumper, straightens his tie, and perches on the corner of his desk.

"Good morning?" he says again, walking over to his

desk and taking a long draught of his cinnamon tea. He looks at us, in turn. "Much has happened since yesterday. We know the Germans are here. Our King and his family are safe, and so is our government. That's important." He stands as if at attention, his voice rising with every word. "The Germans say they're here to protect us from England, who they say is trying to invade us. The warships in the harbor are here to protect us. From England."

He clenches his jaw. Then—as if he were able to—he throttles his thoughts, stuffing them into a drawer. He gives a small shake of his head. "Let's start on our English assignment for today. Lady Johnson, can you read the first paragraph, please?"

Pedra Johnson rises from her chair. Blushing, she finds the paragraph and stammers, "Deh, um, *beklaget*—" Pedra apologizes. It is a strict rule that we speak English in Herr Tveit's class. "Sorry. Deh—the girls val—walk to deh—the beach."

As if on cue, two greenish-gray airplanes appear over the harbor. The German crosses on their fuselages are unmistakable.

Herr Tveit stops in mid-sentence as thirty of us abandon our desks, upending pencil boxes and pushing aside chairs.

The girls wipe the glass and press their faces to the panes.

I crane my neck in time to see a third plane join the two as they head south. Then, in exact formation—*exact formation!*—they tip the noses of their aircraft up, roll over, and head back over our school, shaking the desks and rattling the windows.

Squealing with fear, we reach for one another's

shoulders for comfort.

The planes return, doing another rollover maneuver. All around me are whistles and whispers of awe.

In my mind, I picture Jan looking at the planes with other plans. The Spartan talked about becoming a pilot. Once, his reading focused only on Greek history, but now he prefers the Red Baron's exploits and Charles Lindbergh and Wiley Post. After Post died in Alaska, Jan bought every book he could find and listened intently to the newsreels about Post's death and that of his friend Will Rogers.

Over the course of the day, our teachers refuse to dismiss us. Instead, talking to us about the King and the Parliament, they tell us to listen carefully and think for ourselves.

One girl talks about how her family's maid is Polish. Late last fall, posters claiming that Poles invaded Germany appeared, declaring Germany was only defending itself.

Herr Tveit moves to comfort her, but she waves him away.

"My maid's sister disappeared." Wiping a tear from her eye, she shakes her head.

At long last, the bell rings, dismissing us for the day.

Running past the large lake near the train station, I careen through a narrow side street near the Domkirken, on my way toward the row of ancient wooden buildings lining the harbor's east side. My foot hits a gray mound. Looking down, I see the shiny black brim of a hat and a tripod. The tripod has the most massive gun I have ever seen.

The gray mound rises, sweeping mud off his raincoat, and reaches down to pick up his hat. He's middle-aged, clean-shaven, and he hates me. His mouth forming the perfect sneer, he unleashes a torrent of German as he points toward the gun, his hat, and the harbor. From my German language classes, I understand that I'm an idiot boy who ruined the man's coat. I've also set him back in his demonstration, as he now must check everything on the gun again.

He repeats that I'm an idiot and that I should leave. "Schnell!" The one word I understand entirely, and I take off running.

The bell on the Domkirken bell tower tolls the half hour.

Rivulets of people are coursing down the Sandviken's streets, immediately above the wharf known as *Bryggen*. The rivulets join and jostle, becoming a tributary, and finally, a jeering river of chattering citizens curious to see what lies in the harbor and in their future.

The Spartan appears nearly flattened against the goldenrod-painted wall of Bergen's oldest school. Seeing me, he salutes, ready to soldier on.

"What a day!" I say, gasping for breath.

At the wharf, another gray mound is setting up a tripod.

Jan and I walk down the half block to the Hanseatic Museum, and I shake with fear.

Near Rosenkrantz Tower, a seaplane takes off, occupying the entire space, dwarfing the little boats.

The Spartan shakes my elbow. "We're being blockaded. At least six ships are in the harbor and a submarine. It's a hike, but I think we should go see them."

"How do you know? Did you hear from your papa?"

How could Jan have advance information on everything?

Jan rolls his eyes in pity at how clueless I am. "BST. They flew over BST today. We watched the planes swoop and fly in formation. I want to be a pilot, but not for them!"

The harbor is full of people who, like us, are braving the crowds to see what we cannot believe. Like Poland, we have been invaded. We didn't ask for it, and we can't understand why. Other than land mass, what do the Germans want?

In front of us, a little girl astride her mother's shoulders and bouncing in time to faint march music, blocks our view of what's happening. Wearing her hair in pigtails tied with red, black, and white satin ribbons, the child clutches a German flag in her chubby hand. She's not much younger than my brother Ray.

I think the German's have a three-tiered pecking order for the work they display. The lowest level belongs to the pudgy and soft Germans handing out flags who act like salespeople on commission. They go so far as to stoop down to the children's eye level and thrust a flag into their unsuspecting hands with a smile and a gentle nudge of their shoulder.

Slightly above them in the pecking order are the adults that pander their flags to the Norwegian adults, who—I'm amused to see—rebuff their advances.

The highest tier belongs to the Military Police trickling through the crowds. They remind me of guard dogs, right down to their olive-brown fitted coats with black trim and their alertness. It's as if they're continually smelling the air for trouble.

But I'm gravely mistaken. With a sharp crack that sounds like a rifle shot ricocheting off the windows, the highest level of the pecking order arrives.

Our Spartan training fails us as Jan and I clutch each other's coats, taking cover by pulling each other down.

The little girl in pigtails screams as her mother swiftly sweeps her from her shoulders, carrying her away. One of the child's legs kicks furiously as Jan and I catch a sharp jab in our arms. The girl's German flag falls to the ground, and she wails, her hand outstretched, all the while kicking her mother's back.

Jan and I push our way down to the trolley tracks running along Bryggen. A sharp drum cadence and trumpets remind me of our citywide competitive bugle corps. Is it our bugle corps? Spirited military marches boom down the street, and I start tapping my toe to the music, turning to see where the music is coming from.

A half-curtain of gray, framed by Haakon's Hall and Rosenkrantz Tower, flows toward me. Soldiers march in formation, backs erect, rifles straight up. As they hold their legs out straight in front of themselves, their swaying gray coats flash behind them.

A soldier glances in our direction. His jawline and cheek have an outbreak of pimples.

He's no more than a boy! I wonder how old he is. I nudge Jan and point, but the soldier is now too far away.

Jan holds up his hands questioningly.

I look at the soldier and shake my head. "Kids, Jan. Just like us."

A man near us whistles. "I can't believe my eyes," he says. "It's like the newsreels, except the men are here. Those bastards are goose-stepping!"

The din—shouted whistles and commands, murmured chatter, boat horns blaring in the harbor—frightens me. Anguished cries erupt at the sight of the soldiers, but, as the soldiers pass, we're stunned into silence. We appear to submit to them being here. The precise movements, meant as a display of dominance, signal that they could kill those in their way.

I'm not a soldier. I'm a boy playing at being a soldier with Jan and my friends. "How could I, or any of us, stop people like that?"

While I'm impressed by the precision, the meaning terrifies me. These soldiers are boys our age, and yet, they're being entrusted to do what men do.

"I want to see the warships, don't you?" Jan says. "How long before this display is over, do you think? I get it—the German's might—but how much longer before this parade is over?"

A man standing next to us glares at Jan, putting a finger to his lips and then to his ears as a warning. The man's eyes are wide with fright.

Jan nods an apology and then looks at me. "When this dies down, let's walk to the other harbor to see the warships."

One hundred meters away, a large ship occupies the harbor's center. Men walk down the long gangplank, carrying boxes and shouting orders above and below them with synchronized precision.

Jan points at the gray hulk in the harbor. "That submarine looks like a sardine," he says sarcastically.

I glance around. "Keep your voice down!" Jan is right, though. The submarine looks like a gigantic sardine. It's gray with a narrow snout and gills that—according to local experts—help the submarine dive.

We stare. On silent cue, the submarine lumbers to life. Five muffled metallic taps follow a loud *shish!* The surrounding boats, tightly clustered—as if recognizing a common enemy—pitch and heave. One of the taller boats rises higher than the others. The mast catches a neighboring boat's flagpole and shears the Norwegian flag from its mounting pole.

"I'm getting hungry," I say irritably. My heart races. A trickle of sweat runs down the back of my neck. "And the most direct route to walk home takes me through the worst part of town."

Jan smirks, then looks at his watch, a gift from his grandparents for getting into BST. "You're right. It's getting late." As he makes his way through the crowd, I see him snap a salute.

Snapping one in return, I quickly bring it down, realizing that I'm in a sea of gray uniforms and attitudes.

I want my familiar.

Fresh flowers grace the newly painted planter boxes and doorways. The worst part of town has put on a bit of an effort for the Germans.

A young girl leans against a trimmed-out entry. She looks at me intently and then, on second glance, at nothing in particular. "Gotta light?" she calls.

I do, but with my schoolbag, I don't think I'm what she wants.

"Spreken zie Deutsch?" The voice is older, and I suspect, far more experienced.

The girl laughs and opens the door as I pass.

Inside the dimly lit interior, an olive-skinned hand carries a box in a most peculiar fashion. Accentuating the crisp shirt sleeve above the hand is a ruby cufflink, and I do a double take as I recognize its owner.

Jules breaking his wrist was an accident. That's the family story. His trying to teach me to go down the stairs when I was six months old was his being incorrigible—

also part of the family story. His tripping on the outside step, fracturing the ulna, the silence as to who—exactly—was chasing him, and why, all are shrouded in the telling of the story.

But this much is true. Jules favors one arm over the other and hates carrying anything heavy, so the incentives to work at the West Indian must be compelling. The door shuts, and so does any naivete that I might have had about my brother.

I skip as the familiar comes into view. And as I open the door, climb the stairs, drop my bag, and gaze into the eyes of the familiar, I cry—cry for the day, cry for the unknown, cry because a part of me knows that the familiar will be slipping away.

Static. A voice is coming over the newly repaired radio. "Hello, this is Vidkun Quisling. The King and his parliament have fled. A new government is being formed for which I will be the leader. We're working with the Germans in forming a new government and will work on a peaceful transition. We look forward to working with our new allies."

I'm not a soldier. I'm a boy playing at being a man with Jan and my friends.

"How could I—or any of us—stop people like that?"

Chapter Nine

The playing card in my family's mailbox is the *W* of
diamonds.

I know who sent it. I don't understand why he can't
come inside and ask the question about my going to
Solsvik with him.

I hold out the card to Jules, who is in our kitchen,
having a smoke. I lean over, and he takes the Polish
playing card, passing the expertly rolled cigarette to me.
Inhaling—my habit of smoking now six months old—I
lift the cigarette in the general direction of Solsvik.

Jules shoves the card in the pocket of his pinstriped
jacket. Taking the cigarette back, he relights it with an
engraved lighter. "I heard strange things this past week."
He looks at the lighter, a small smile crossing his lips. "I
have a new job. I'm still working at Gold Dust, but now
I'm helping a friend with her deliveries." The lighter
disappears into his expensive-looking pants.

"You are starting at BST this fall with your friend,"
Jules says, tamping out the cigarette. "And did you hear
about the Germans going to Shetland after the southern
part of Norway came under German rule?"

I shake my head, continually amazed at how much
information Jules gets on a daily basis.

"Some dumb sailors took them over for free, and
some—who know the value of money—charged them."
Jules pulls another smoke from a silver cigarette case

engraved in the same way as the lighter. "I'd like for us to go out to Solsvik and have fun. We can celebrate your getting into BST. See Harold. Drink hooch." He pulls the *W* of Diamonds playing card out of his pocket and waves it at me. "What do you say?"

****

Two weeks later, Gramps clutches his valise with red knuckles as he and I wait for Jules at Bergen's central bus station.

Gramps' valise is black with a tartan inset of the MacDonald clan, and it's one of his most valued possessions. When he talks of his time in Brooklyn, America, he always references Lapskaus Boulevard, a Norwegian restaurant and marketplace. Gramps worked as a *busboy*—another Brooklyn-America expression— before coming back to Solsvik to marry Gran. I can hear him saying, "When I left the restaurant, the customers chipped in with the owners and bought me this valise." The smile on his face is thinner, and his eyes are always a little brighter when he tells this story.

If Jan is an overpacker and planner, Gramps' habit is to get to places early and wait. "I don't mind," he says. The rest of our family does, but since I was a little boy, Gramps and I have played a game while waiting called *Invent*, in which we invent stories and destinations for the people around us.

Today, after seeing an old couple squabbling about leaving a cake at home, we decide their story is about star-crossed lovers in their nineties who are reunited after seventy-five years of separation. We also agree that the woman hurrying by us, holding a child and a bag of live lobsters, is going back to the nightclub where she works to demand payment in cash, not lobsters.

There's a serious side to our game. A soldier by the platform entrance eyes the people buying tickets inside and those departing the various buses that have come in. We wait long enough to see the soldier's routine. When a bus arrives, the soldier goes to the bus' doorway, climbs aboard, takes a headcount, talks to the driver, and watches the people get off. He selects a passenger and asks to see the purse or satchel's contents.

We continue to stand. Gramps refuses to take a seat since that is a privilege for old people, and he isn't one. At least not in his mind.

With a push on my arm, Gramps silences me. "Eh?" Gramps calls, cupping his hand to his ear and leaning into me. "Eh?" he repeats.

Gramps can be described in many ways—irascible, a true force of nature, and a cagey bridge player—but definitely not as deaf. Now, he's playing to an audience of one—the guard.

He turns his body away from the soldier. "Wait until the soldier boards the bus. We must warn *the dandy* about being checked."

Right on time, Jules' head bobs among the other passengers in the waiting room. Spying Gramps and me, he waves his ticket in the air and comes outside.

Gramps gathers Jules in a firm embrace, his back to the soldier, and whispers into Jules' ear. Jules' nose comes to Gramps' shoulder.

Jules' eyes widen, widen further, squint, and then close. Message received.

Since July, we haven't been able to get real newspapers. The papers, still printed in Norwegian, are filled with many stories of what an excellent job the Germans are doing.

Earlier this summer, orders were sent for our radios to be confiscated and destroyed. All is silent. No music, no news, and we discovered our letters—no matter how innocent—are being intercepted by the Germans.

The bus door opens, and we board.

The driver smiles at Gramps. "Andreas! Another card game? Are these your grandsons that I hear about?"

Gramps nods. "Karl, are you going to be playing tonight?" The driver, shaking his head, looks past us. "Solsvik?"

We take our seats while other passengers climb aboard. Wedged between the seats is a newspaper. Pulling it out, I see it's from Oslo. I point to the paper, but Gramps frowns, glancing at the bus driver.

The bus leaves the station, passing the lake, Grieg's statue, and Hotel Norge, and winding around the narrow roads leading west to the island. I glance down at the newspaper.

"Raid on Shetlands!" reads the top headline, followed by "In Flames!"

Gramps' bony knee gouges my thigh. His knee then gouges me a second time, and I push him away. Gramps stands up. Pulling his valise from the overhead rack, he sits back down and opens his bag, rummaging around until he finds an apple, which he hands to Jules. Pushing the bag onto my lap, he says, "Look inside. You should find two oranges."

As I peer inside and push a shirt and pants aside, he leans over to me, takes the newspaper from my knees, and presses it against my chest. "Take a long look out the window to see if anyone is looking at you. Put the newspaper in the side pocket of my bag. Make sure there is no paper sticking out."

Gazing into the bus window, my breath shortening, I use the reflection to see who's sitting around us. A couple sits several seats back, and two others are seated near the front. The bus driver looks at the road before glancing back at the passengers.

Continuing to rummage, I find the two oranges, handing them both to Gramps. The newspaper slides into the valise's interior pocket. I push the paper down with my thumbs, pulling Gramps' shirt and pants back into place, and zip up the suitcase. Gramps hands the oranges to me and, standing up, puts the valise back on the shelf above us.

We brace for the descent into Solsvik as Jules hands me his apple core. My hands sweat, sticky from the juice from the oranges and what's left of the apple.

Jules and Gramps exit the bus and walk to where a young man in a gray uniform stands next to Harold.

Getting up, I see that Gramps has left his valise and is now outside talking to Harold. My fingers stick to the leather handle as I descend from the bus and walk to Harold, Gramps, and Jules. I'm bracing for when Gramps grouses that my sticky hands marred his bag.

"I'm going to wash my hands from those oranges," I say, walking past the soldier and depositing the rinds and core into the trash can. I wipe the handle with my sleeve. Is the soldier going to come in to inspect the valise? Gramps wanted me to hide the newspaper.

I slip inside the restroom, which—surprisingly— smells of lemons tinged with cinnamon from the bakery next door. I rest the satchel on the edge of the sink. The newspaper wouldn't be visible if the valise were inspected, right? I turn to wash my hands, starting as the door creaks open and a fellow passenger walks past me to the toilet stall.

Drying my hands on my pants, I go outside to find Harold, Jules, and Gramps chatting. The soldier talks to a woman who rode the bus with us. Her purse is open, and the soldier is feeling the bag's exterior.

Setting off for Bertin's house, Gramps and I fall in behind Harold and Jules, whose walking together reminds me of *Mutt and Jeff.* Harold's loping walk, his hands thrust into his overall's pockets, contrasts with Jules' sharply pressed trousers and sprightly gait.

Turning to laugh and punch Harold's arm, Jules has his charm turned on full throttle. "So, it's a plan, Harold?" I hear him ask. "We'll play tonight and fish tomorrow?" Jules' laugh is like a child receiving a long-awaited toy at Christmas.

Harold shoos sheep out of our way as we climb the hill behind Bertin's house toward the still. "Bringing your friends out now would be viewed suspiciously by the townspeople," Harold says. "I will have to mention to Hansen that you are my cousins. I don't want someone seizing my boat." Pausing by the boulders to catch his breath, Jules pulls out the cigarette case and lighter from his pocket, offering Harold and me a cigarette.

Taking the lighter from Jules, I can now inspect the inscription. *J ——Always, Bella*, it reads.

Jules flushes and stammers, "Gramps didn't say anything. I didn't realize it was so bad. I'm sorry. So are you, Kory. Right?"

We're not welcome here. Why didn't Gramps tell us? How awkward. I'm half listening, drowning in embarrassment as Harold continues, his voice in a measured monotone.

"One of our bridge players coming from Movik had

his boat seized by the Nazis. There have been sightings of German boats, and planes make regular sweeps along the shore to make sure no English troops or anyone else can invade." He motions toward the house. "Dinner will be ready soon."

Jules, Gramps, and I help set the dinner plates. Bertin's wife Constanse is making a favorite dinner of cod and carrots. We step back to admire our handiwork,

Gramps clears his throat and wipes at his crewcut. "Boys, I'm not playing with you tonight. A friend of mine is sick, and I want to see him. So, you'll be all right without me." He straightens a dinner knife to line up just so with the napkin and dessert fork.

I thought Gramps loved Solsvik Bridge almost as much as life itself.

After dinner, Jules and I clear the plates over Constanse's protests. Then we walk up the hill to the bridge club with Bertin, who gives Jules and me a slight, reassuring shake of our shoulders before turning to leave.

The card game that night has five tables—twenty people. Hansen goes to the trouble of introducing us as Bertin's nephews. Though the conversation is polite, and Jules wins, I feel like an imposition as we walk back to Bertin's house.

Late that evening, a storm pummels the windows. Jules' bed is empty. Tiptoeing through the kitchen, I see a lit cigarette under the back porch's eaves.

Jules and I watch the rain and wind. Reaching over, I take the cigarette. Inhaling deeply, I gather the smoke in my lungs. The scents of motor fuel and salt drift over us, along with the incongruous combination of roses and compost wafting from the nearby garden.

Jules smells of cologne, smoke, and caramel. The

lighthouse beacon swings around in a sharp light the size of a kroner coin. "Good game tonight," I say. "We should come out here, after this war is over, and play together."

Jules nods. "After this passes. But, apparently, not now. I wish Gramps had told us."

Over the next morning's breakfast, Harold's announcement that he has boat repairs to work on takes no one by surprise.

As we stand in the bus station waiting for the bus to come, Harold apologizes.

"Let's hope for better weather and better times." He raises an imaginary glass in the air.

Jules and I raise imaginary glasses in return as the bus lumbers down the hill toward the station.

Climbing onto the bus with Jules, I turn to wave at Harold. He's rounding the corner past the bakery. As the bus climbs the hill, I see Harold walking down the pier with Gramps in the bus window's reflection.

They—despite the rain—turn to gaze at the bus.

"To better times," I say on a breath of air.

Chapter Ten

At Techworks, Herr Henricksen rules the work floor, but Fru Martin is our problem solver and mystery woman. Her age, while impossible to guess—and I have tried—is not ancient. She wears white gloves and a Chesterfield coat with a Burberry scarf wrapped neatly around her neck to work every day. Her hair, tinged with gray, is curled under, making her look like Deana Durbin, my mother's favorite actress.

Rolf whistled when we spied her one Saturday morning, buying fish at the fish market. "That coat cost money!" Rolf said.

He squatted, reaching for a lens, and snapped a picture.

I was perplexed. "How do you know?" I asked.

"I've been taking photography classes," Rolf answered. "A model came in with a coat and scarf similar to Fru Martin's. Annika went to London before the war broke out and bought them. She likes to tell people how much clothes cost, and Fru Martin's coat and scarf are nearly a thousand kroner."

Fru Martin always carries a white, monogrammed handkerchief. She's waving her handkerchief at me now.

Herr Henrickesen walks over, tapping my shoulder, nodding toward Fru Martin.

Turning off the drill press—an action that fails to reduce the racket—I walk toward Fru Martin. A small smudge of whipped cream is on the corner of her mouth.

"Kory, you have a visitor." She smiles coyly like a schoolgirl being asked—at last—to dance.

Is she blushing?

She motions for me to come with her, and I walk through the double doors, leaving the loud machine clatter behind.

The Spartan jumps up from a chair in the reception area.

Jan smiles at Fru Martin. "Dear *Hilda*, you are so wonderful."

Hilda!

"Enjoy that cake I brought you." Taking her hand, Jan bows slightly, clicking his heels together.

Is he going to kiss her hand? Unbelievable!

She curtsies, waving him off with a lopsided smile and a slight shake of her head.

"Until next time, Hilda."

Thus, the mystery: How is it that Jan can call Fru Martin, Hilda? Neither one is confessing.

"Kory, walk with me," he exhorts. Once outside of the reception area, the Spartan not so much pushes the outside door as muscles past it.

Jan slows to give a friendly wave to Hilda through the window. Then, like being shot from a cannon, he barrels toward the crosswalk.

Although we're the same height, his legs are longer than mine, and I break into a jog. "I can't be gone long," I say. "Where are we going?"

His walk—my jog—takes us west toward one of our three secret entrances to the Goat Trail. "I don't have time," I say. Jan needs to tell me what the hell is going on. "Stop! I mean it!" I half turn back, pleased that the thuds on the trail stop.

A stone squeaks in the mud as he walks back to me. "Look! Unbelievable!" Anger tinges Jan's voice.

Squinting in the direction that the Spartan was walking, I see the spit-and-polished boots and black woolen pants of our enemy. The teenaged German officer stands next to a makeshift sawhorse that blocks the trail. He is holding a clipboard and yawns.

"What's the rush?" I call, following Jan as he stalks east, beating back a branch daring to cover his intended path.

Jan remains silent as he walks past the steepled lepers' hospital. His pace slows as he takes a faint trail leading up the brambled hill. At a small outcrop of rocks, Jan halts.

I follow suit.

His words spew out like machine gunfire. "I don't know who or what to be most pissed off about. Our families go along to get along. We're no longer able to walk anywhere we want. We're supposed to relinquish our radios. We have a fake government lying to us. Everyone is to watch everyone." Jan balls his fists as he speaks. "I wanted to go up to the cabin, and I could not because I didn't have the proper documents. Why am I not allowed to go to a place my family owns? Jesus!"

My breath increases as I survey the area, looking for a place to sit. On edge for any hint of movement, I spy a small hollow with a downed tree twenty meters away. I point to the tree.

Jan nods and follows me. He sits opposite me on the downed pine, his shoulder touching mine. "Get this— Papa's having foreign visitors come to the house."

I raise an eyebrow. "Like…Germans?" I recall

reading of Herr Anderson's promotion in the newspaper's business section. It made me choke: "From his humble beginnings." Edvard Anderson has many facets. *Humble* is not one of them.

Jan is talking. "Two men. Herr Mitchell came to Bergen from Copenhagen, but he's British. Ingrid and I were introduced to Herr Mitchell like little children late for bed. He doesn't work for the oil company with Papa. From what I overheard—the air vents are like those tin cups you use to play telephone—Herr Mitchell is concerned about oil shipments Norway promised to Britain. Shipments are to be properly tracked, so he wanted to make a firm connection with us. Papa asked him how he would be getting back to Britain, and Herr Mitchell said, "On a boat.""

Jan rolls his eyes. "How is a British man getting through a German blockade? There are patrol ships." The Spartan drops his head closer to mine. "He used a phrase that made me wonder. Herr Mitchell said, "Britain is not your enemy. We would like your support and diligence in this matter.""

"The other man is a guy my father works with—what an asshole! He talked about how right we were to allow Quisling to take over, how the King should have stayed, and how the Germans help our economy. 'The Germans will bring jobs! Prosperity for Bergen and Norway.' " Jan's impression of a stuffy bureaucrat is dead-on. "I wanted to punch him. I did this instead." Jan points to a paper clip pinned to his chest. His shoulder is moving.

I peek over my shoulder to see what he's doing.

His fingers press against his thumb—a habit he has when he's working out a problem. "Herr Mitchell said a curious thing, and I'm glad Papa asked him to repeat it." Jan's shoulder stops. "Herr Mitchell said the Germans already destroyed a small resistance group, and he asked Papa if he knew of any new groups."

I gasp. "What did your father say? Resistance Groups? Who is Herr Mitchell, again?"

Since we're sorting out all the world's problems, I decide to add my story to the list. "Rolf's father is angry because the Germans are setting up a training camp next to their cabin."

Jan expels a long air column, picking at a sarvisberry leaf and twirling it in his hand.

I continue. "A few weeks ago, Rolf's father found two German soldiers stealing belongings from a neighbor's boathouse. One German soldier apologized for not knowing, but the other one was smirking. Rolf's father wanted to report it but didn't want to cause a problem. He was mad, though. I can tell you that."

Not wanting to let questions go unanswered, I ask the Spartan again, "Does Herr Mitchell work for your father? And what did your father say about the resistance groups? Are there any?"

"Couldn't hear." Jan's tongue works at the remnants of Hilda's cake that are stuck in his teeth. "There's more." He turns to me, his mouth puckering as if he's taking a dose of cod-liver oil. His tongue stabs successfully at the morsel, dislodging it. "Herr Simonsen and Herr Mueller are no longer at BST. My mother joined the school's parent-teacher organization and invited the ladies and the teachers over yesterday for a fancy lunch. Mother introduced me—God, I hate it when I'm trotted out like a prize farm animal to be inspected and examined!—a teacher spoke of BST having to promote two young teachers to take over Herrs Mueller and Simonsen's classes! The biddy sitting next to her said, "We have new, young powers in the government. If those two were unwilling to teach the new ways, they should be sent North."

All the air gets sucked out between us. Putting my fingers in a praying position, I rub my nose up and down, hoping for answers. I'm too old to cry. I am. I wipe a tear from my eye, inhaling my snot.

"They…they were sent away? Where? Why?" My head is reeling. "Are *you* going to school at BST this fall? Become a cog in the German machine?" I swing my legs over the log so he and I face the same direction. Before us lies the circular lake, the fountain in the middle, the art museum, and the train station's golden dome. "Are you?"

Jan's shoulder starts twitching again.

I reach over, slapping that annoying tic. "Answer me! Are you going?"

Pine bark is on Jan's raincoat as he stands up. He extends his hand to me, pulling me up. "We need to get these bastards out of Bergen and out of Norway."

"How are we going to do that?" I inquire. "We're kids!" My eyebrows shoot up.

Jan glares, shaking his head. "I don't know. I know I needed to talk to you. The Spartans may need to start training again." He smiles ruefully.

Over the treetops below us, I see Festival Park. People are marching, making columns, and walking with military precision. Jan and I stare, and in the distance, I hear drums.

"Shit!" Jan says. "That's where we have our Independence Day celebrations. Nazis are desecrating our Festival Park!" He wipes drool from his mouth. "I will come by in a few days. Do you think you can get a day or two off? I'd like you to go for a hike in the mountains with me before it gets colder."

Jan waves, making his way down the slope. Twenty meters down, he stops. Turning toward Festival Park, he raises his hand, extending his middle finger.

That gesture sums up my life.

Chapter Eleven

For the first time in nearly a decade, I'm trying to avoid Jan.

The Spartan rests against the stamped *B* wall. Having saluted and begun to soldier on, he launches into the day's topic—prepping me for the upcoming term. "Have you received the post about the books we're to buy before the term starts? I thought we could go to the bookstore and go for coffee afterward."

A cement path winds below the promontory where BST sits. With its filigreed *B's* set in every other fencepost, the iron fence is ostentatious. Jan's chatter is background noise to the conversation I am having in my head.

The Spartan has asked me a question. Based on the eye roll and the thin-lipped line his mouth gets when he's pissed, he has apparently asked me several times.

I can't fake this. I stall by staring at a moss-covered spring that nearly hides a drinking fountain. Even the fountain's handle has a curlicued *B*. *Out with it, Kory,* I tell myself.

"I can't go to BST, Jan."

"It's the money, right?"

I'm about to break family codes that state you don't talk about money. Or what you genuinely think about other people's families, especially their parents. Or how easy you think people have it. Or how you don't want your best friend to turn into his father. The collaborator. Which he will. It's about Germans arbitrarily— randomly—taking teachers, dismissing them, or moving them like so many pawns on a chessboard. It's about inking in the hem on my pants to fit in with my friends. And the look on my mother's face that says that I think I'm better than the rest of the family.

"I can't. I'm sorry." I state, praying that my best friend will not press for answers I can't give.

It might have been hot that day. The sun might have been shining. I might have gone through a couple of checkpoints, told the officers I was returning home, and "No, I wasn't lost." Or maybe I was.

My blue gabardine pants are on top of a pile by the bedroom door. The hemline is visible, with my mother's meticulous stitches faintly showing. The white line I wanted to ink in all those months ago is now a line of demarcation between all that is and all that will never be.

Can't be.

I go downstairs to my basement bedroom, past the rakes and the canned goods. Lying on my bed is a suit.

"It's a surprise," Mother says, with a smile reserved for the completion of difficult tasks. She steps from the laundry room door next to my bedroom, rubbing lotion on her chapped knuckles. "For your first day of term." Her thumb pauses as she peers up into my face. "But maybe you can find another use for them."

I reach up and dab away the tear trickling down my cheek.

Chapter Twelve

My life in the fall of 1940 is about filling two uniforms. The uniform of my present is new suit pants and the shirts, vests, and ties of Granvin. The uniform of what will most likely be my future is what I change into every day after school before going to Marine Techworks.

To be fair, Herr Henricksen has begun leaving diagrams of parts for which he wants my input. So, after sweeping up and throwing out the trash, I find myself spending time, pencil in hand, diagramming, constructing, and experimenting with the tools at my disposal.

Behind the Center lies what I call *the boneyard*, a cavernous storage shed filled with remnant parts from scrapped projects in every size and shape imaginable. About twenty meters high, the shed is made of whitewashed brick, with large doors and windows. Facing the back of the Techwork office building is a large bay door, which has never been closed since I've worked here. The parts, piled into large mounds of varying heights, are covered in grease, rust, salt, and dirt—or as I have come to look at them—possibilities.

I have permission to rummage through the mounds, creating categories. Within those categories, I get to judge what has redemption and what has expired its possibilities.

To use one of Gramps' Brooklyn-America phrases, I'm in *hog heaven.*

Thumbprints bearing grease or rust always mark my homework. I should care, but I'm finding justification for staying away from Jan and the life BST offers.

It took two people to design the box for the part I'm to take to the post office on a bright fall afternoon in early September. Reinforced with extra sheets of thin steel and heavily riveted, the contraption is part of a new cannery operation. Usually, I get to see the latest designs being invented or improved upon, but this part was boxed up in the back and brought to Fru Martin's office. I had no idea that it was under construction.

"It's too large to carry and too small for the cart," Herr Henricksen says. "Do you need help?"

My thought that Herr Henricksen honks when he talks has not gone away. I flex my muscles and laugh. "I can handle it!"

"Oh, to be young like you, Kory!" Herr Henricksen turns and waves.

Five minutes later, as I grapple with the box, I realize that Herr Henricksen's comment has several meanings. Determined to succeed—and prove my boss wrong—I find carrying it above my head, setting it down, resting, and then taking it in my arms is the best approach.

Trudging by Neptun Konditori, my favorite bakery, I hear tapping on the window and a muffled "Hoot!"—a call from my childhood—followed by more tapping and a familiar laugh.

Through the panes of glass, I see Jan motion for the other boys to make room at a table, already laden with cups of coffee and *skillingsboller,* the cinnamon rolls that are a *Bergense* favorite.

Like an iceman carrying bags of ice—complete with the gray twill overalls—I lug the heavy parcel over my head to Jan's table, where several boys sit.

One boy covers his head with his arms.

A blond, curly-headed boy nearest me jumps up, throwing his hands in the air. "Here, let me help you."

Shoved under the table are school packs and a battered suitcase. A chair, pulled from an adjoining dining area, is ratcheted under me.

Jan signals for the waiter. "Coffee with extra milk. We have a youngster in our midst!"

Flexing my already aching muscles, I give Jan a good-natured punch in the arm, grateful to sit down and be back with the Spartan.

Jan introduces Klaus, who's heading back to the university.

Klaus scans my hands, declining my handshake, continuing his story of a girl in Oslo whom he's trying to win over. Standing up abruptly, he grips his suitcase, jostling the package I'm to take to the post office.

The box lands on my foot, and I pull back in pain.

Klaus doesn't notice.

The blond boy does notice. He leans down, righting the package. "That will smart, I think. He's like that—gets in a rush and forgets his manners. I'm Paul. I've heard about you from Jan. *The brilliant engineer*—that's what he calls you."

Sipping the pale brown coffee, I grimace. "Baby formula. Disgusting!"

Paul slides his coffee over. "Here's the real stuff. I'm having a party at my house on Friday. Would you like to put those engineering skills to use?"

Chapter Thirteen

My mother holds up three playing cards with the Two of Clubs on them. "Do you have big plans?

I peck her cheek, stealing a sugar cookie she made with our rationed sugar. Sugar, coffee, and flour are becoming scarce commodities.

"I'm turning sixteen on Saturday. And I didn't know you paid attention to the rules of Solsvik Bridge, Mother!" So, while I know who sent the cards, I have no idea what big plans might be in store for me. I continue to carry a pack of cards with me, but months have passed since I left anything in anyone's mailbox.

The following day, three Jacks of Hearts are in our family's mailbox.

The next day, three Aces of Diamonds appear in the mailbox.

The day after that, three Twos of Hearts and three Nines of Hearts appear.

At Granvin, I corner Rolf and Stein. "I've deciphered most of the puzzle. It's big, Involves me. At Rolf's cabin. On my birthday? What time do we get on the train?"

My answer came upon finding three Three of Spades lying in our mailbox—3:00 p.m.

On the morning of September twenty-ninth, my sixteenth birthday, I awaken to the best cacophony in the world—my family standing in my bedroom doorway, singing a happy birthday song. Gramps follows up with a recitation of a Brooklyn-America shanty involving a stair and a woman from Eau Claire, making me blush.

After breakfast, the gifts wrapped in tissue reveal books, a pair of skates, and pens to be used in my diagramming and designing.

At two thirty that afternoon, climbing aboard the trolley taking me to the train station, I see Rolf has already boarded. Rolf is quiet. A smudge of makeup is on his cheek.

"Hey, some girl left her mark on you," I tease, pointing at a spot on my face, and he quickly rubs away the smudge.

"I thought I got everything."

"Was a girl involved?"

"Shut up! I don't want you thinking I'm *fine-boned*," Rolf snaps.

"Aw, not that shit again. My mother, remember? Not me." I see the trolley driver raise his head in a questioning way, and I shake my head.

Rolf kneads his jawline, leaving deep red marks.

As we approach the train station, he jumps up quickly, heaving his bag over his shoulder. As I follow him off the trolley, it seems that Rolf is making every effort to stomp on the trolley's stairs and the pavement leading into the station.

Rolf's blond head bobs through the crowd to where Stein and Jan stand near the platform.

Jan holds a bunch of purple daisies in his hand. "Mother made you a special treat." Jan pats his backpack. "In honor of St. Michael. And your birthday."

I'm pleased he has not brought the palomino bags with him again. I'm staring at the flowers. "What in the world are you doing with those? Visiting your old gran?"

"The Spartans." He snorts with glee. "For later. I've been reading—"

"C'mon, the Spartans did not have daisies. What are you doing?" I like hearing Jan's history stories, but I'm sure those daisies have nothing to do with the Spartans. What prank is he going to pull now?

Looking pleased with himself, Jan clutches the flowers and smiles enigmatically. "You'll see."

I wish Jan's prank were the only thing to be nervous about today.

The train is carrying more than mail and passengers today. Pallets of supplies, stamped with an official-looking black eagle, are being loaded into the boxcars. Soldiers gesture to the conductor and engineer, pointing to them and the pallets with warnings of dire consequences.

We board the train, and Rolf and I sit next to each other. Rolf clutches his ticket. Two soldiers climb aboard with the conductor, taking seats in front of us. I want to move but don't want to draw attention to us. There goes any chance of asking Rolf what's going on with the makeup and the buffed nails.

I count fifteen stops between Bergen and Vika, the whistle-stop near the Wiks' cabin. If Bergen is the equivalent of Alpha Centauri, then the train ride reminds me of riding on the tail of a fading constellation, one that can be seen only by the strongest of telescopes.

At last, the conductor announces the hamlet of Vika as the next stop. Rolf has not spoken more than five words in an hour.

In Solsvik, the walls surrounding the hardscrabble, rocky outcroppings called *farms* are haphazard. Vika is pastoral. Its rock walls are straight and tidy.

Descending Vika's train-platform stairs to the main road, I catch a whiff of apples. The town's expansive orchards are pruned to maximize production. Small barns and huts used for storage or to press the apples into cider have sodded roofs.

Strolling toward the cabin, Rolf stops and cups his ear. Pausing behind a small grove, we listen as a buzz of German commands—like bees in a hive—wafts across the cove.

Rolf's eyes widen. Then he motions us to him, whispering, "I didn't want to believe my parents. The Gundersons have allowed the Nazis to use their land and build a camp. Nothing is safe around here anymore."

Including that cabin of yours, I say to myself.

The Wik-family cabin abandoned hope years ago. Its squatty first floor tilts at an angle, ready to leap off the rounded hill with the slightest provocation. A walkway—*balcony* is too strong a description—has boards reaching out from under the first floor like skeletal fingers. I know from firsthand experience that the boards are uneven, broken, and soft.

Clawed out of a hillside, a misshapen barn door covers what my family privately calls *the manger*. Since my last visit three years ago, twin birch saplings have leaned together to best the upturned wheelbarrow, stacked axels, and boat motors tossed in front of the door—a close contest, but one in which the saplings have the upper hand.

The exterior is Rolf's father's responsibility, and he's failing miserably.

Rolf lifts a broken flowerpot, dusting off a key, and inserts it into the lock. Shouldering the door, we open it onto Rolf's mother's domain.

A small dining table sits in front of two medium-sized windows overlooking a fjord. Two chairs with pillows angled jauntily rest in one corner, while a sofa hugs the space in front of the fireplace. I recognize Rolf's photos along the wall, enlarged and framed. Behind a curtain is a bed, and behind us, a ladder leads to a loft where a white duvet peeks out.

On this day in late September, the sun creates a golden trail to the west in the blue-gray depths of the fjord. The water, which is always choppy, is not ideal for swimming. It works hard to push against the shore, as if to say, "I'm warning you! You will be swept back to your land. Do not come out unless you think you are stronger than me. But I will win."

Jan walks and drops his clothes at the same time, never skipping a beat. Kicking off his shoes, pulling off his shirt, and dropping his pants, he's in the water, diving under the current and reappearing ten meters out. The elapsed time is under thirty seconds.

Not to be shown up, Stein is next. His head disappears, and then, like Jan's, reappears ten meters out.

My turn. What a stupid idea! I do battle with the current, which yanks me toward sharp rocks, and with numbing-cold water. I float for a few seconds. This turns out to be a horrible mistake, as the stones now loom over my head. Dirt clods rain down on me as I push away from the rocks.

Rolf, his camera swinging wildly, is above me. He points to a calmer section five meters down the shore. "Go out there. You can avoid the strong current."

He's right, and I swim a hundred meters into the fjord to get a better look at the camp the Germans are setting up. The Gunderson's pasture teems with activity. The scene reminds me of an illustration in one of my long-ago Crimshaw Brothers novels in which Tom and Ned go to a Native American village. Teepees. The tents matching the uniforms appear to make heads float and hands hammer tirelessly. Makeshift shelters emerge from random stacks of boards laid out in the mini-city.

The sun is low in the sky when, rested from my brief swim, I go into the cabin and pull out the sleeping mats.

My friends have other ideas.

Strutting into the cabin, Jan brandishes two fancy wine glasses, followed by Rolf and Stein. They raise their glasses together.

Where did they get those? Did they bring them?

"A quiet speech! A quiet speech!" Rolf whispers, using his hands as megaphones. He jerks his head back toward the Gunderson's farm.

"Ahem!" In mock seriousness, Jan says his voice is going raspy and also uses his hands as megaphones. "Stein, Rolf, and I had a *look-see* for alcohol at my parent's cabin. We have special surprises for you, Kory. Stein, would you care to do the honors?"

Stein digs into his backpack, pulling out chocolate and pliers. Kneeling over a table made from a piece of driftwood, he exposes the pajamas he has plans to wear tonight. Rummaging deeply into the bag reveals more chocolate bars, and finally, the lock pick. Tapping the table with the lock pick, he waves his hand over the counter and holds up his hand. "Silence!"

He pulls back the table and rug to reveal a trap door. Then he inserts the lock pick and raises the door. Silently it rises, and Rolf scrambles into the hole in the floor and out of sight.

Within seconds, his hand shoots triumphantly from the opening, holding a wine bottle. "Ta-da!"

I whistle and stamp my feet.

Stein holds the bottle in triumph and reads the label. "Cham-pag-nuh."

So much for Fru Wik's décor.

We throw pillows at him, chanting, "Champagne! Champagne! Oh, yes, champagne!"

A sharp *ping!* hits the window.

We duck as frothy liquid spews from the bottle. Eagerly passing the bottle around, we taste the warm champagne. The bubbles tickle my nose.

Jan pulls out four bundles smelling of sugared crust from his pack. "For all of you, but especially for the birthday boy."

The small pies are slightly squashed and broken, but I don't care. As I bite into mine, delectable blackberries and juice drip down my chin. Fru Anderson is great at making pies. This is the best birthday I have ever had.

Jan taps his finger against the bottle. His face is serious. "I was reading about Michaelmas—"

Rolf belches.

Jan glares at the interruption.

Then, according to the Spartan code, we must—and do—sing the national anthem.

"Shh!" Jan points toward the Gunderson place." I was reading about Michaelmas—after St. Michael— who fell in a blackberry bush."

Stein lets out a fake snore.

Rolf chucks a piece of pie crust at Stein and points at Jan with an air of deference.

Jan rolls his eyes and continues. "As I was saying, Michaelmas is, historically, about the settling of accounts for the year and making plans. For deciding what to do next."

Silence.

"I thought so," says Jan. "We have decisions to make… to settle accounts. I brought the flowers—the daisies… the Michaelmas daisies… so we can decide who wants to settle accounts and make plans. If you want to, signify by drinking champagne and putting a daisy behind your ear."

I'm not going to embarrass myself. "Oh, come on, Spart! I'm sixteen. I'm not going to do that. I'm too old to dance around with a flower behind my ear."

Rolf grunts. "Count me in. I'm not afraid."

Stein reaches for a daisy. "I'm proud to be a daisy."

One by one, we take a daisy, solemnly tucking the stem behind our ear, taking a swig from the bottle.

"To the daisies of September!" I call out.

"Daisies!" comes the refrain in unison.

****

"I fell asleep holding playing cards last night," I say.

The curly-headed boy and the boy whose hair really does glint in the early morning sun nod to me as I peek around the cabin's corner.

Rolf says, "Cups are inside on the shelf."

Shouldering the door, I step inside. Christ, what a mess!

An empty champagne bottle—one of the four we confiscated from the manger—lies sideways on the kitchen table. Around two in the morning, we decided that spinning the bottle would determine who the dealer was since we were too drunk to remember any other way. At three, Rolf said his parents got those bottles on their honeymoon in France to open on their twentieth anniversary. Cracking open the fourth bottle, Rolf said, "No chance of that anniversary happening."

Muddy, dark footprints track up a duvet hanging over the loft ladder. We were going to recreate Fort Spartan. What happened to that plan? Fru Wik's pillows are stacked like a Battle of Verdun reenactment. Stein is missing. He was going to create another bunker in the bedroom.

A church bell is pealing as I open the cabin door. *From whence he shall come to judge the quick and the dead.* Shaking my head at remembering any lectured Confirmation catechisms, my bare feet crunch down the path where a thin wisp of campfire smoke and the smell of coffee offers redemption for my sins.

Rolf and Jan sit staring out across the fjord, drinking coffee. They turn to look over at the neighboring yard as commands and hammering interrupt the quiet.

Rolf nods toward the Gundersons' house. "I don't know if I should drink this coffee. If I do, am I helping their cause? Being a collaborator? Or am I being a polite neighbor?"

I pour a cup for myself and drink deep, pausing as Rolf's questions sink in. The coffee burns my inner lip and tongue as I swallow. *Polite neighbor.*

Rolf rolls his cup between his palms, welcoming the warmth, but maybe not accepting the entire gift as he continues. "Last spring, right after the Germans came, Herr Gunderson had a tree limb fall near his house. My papa and I helped cut the wood into logs and stack them into piles. At first, papa refused payment of any kind, but he eventually relented, and we accepted chocolate and coffee from Herr Gunderson's store."

Rolf's finger rubs at an imaginary spot on his cup.

"The Gunderson's took the easy way and allowed the Germans to come in and set up. No fight, no resistance. Only what's good for business. My Papa is disgusted, but I'm not supposed to say anything because I could get into trouble. And, of course, my parents... the fights they're having. All because of my... you know." Rolf lifts his chin, and his hair and profile truly do glint in the sunlight.

I tense, and Jan places his hands on his thighs, as if he might need to get up fast. My fingers prepare themselves to toss the cup aside in case Rolf is going to be angry again.

Instead, Rolf braces his cup on his knee and stares at the eastern horizon's dark blue demarcation. "My photography instructor came to the house, telling my mother he'd suggested I become part of an advertising campaign since I look "the part." Rolf contorts his face into a sneer.

Jan and I interrupt.

"What?"

"Are you a model? For what?"

"You're going to see my photographs eventually." Rolf scowls at the thought.

He's preparing us for unpleasant news.

"The Germans are recruiting male models to be *the face* for camps that they'll be offering to elite Norwegian youth," Rolf continues. "Mother was excited—told me that this was my big break and that Hollywood could be next. She said she signed the modeling contract and insisted I try out, and I got the part. I had to pose in their uniform. Afterward, the photographers and the German guards asked if I wanted to keep the uniform. As if I'd ever wear it! Again, my mother insisted I keep it. The campaign is part of a big push by the Germans to get everyone over eighteen to enlist to fight the English. There will be an elite guard of people who get to supervise the lower ranks, and I'm supposed to be the face of that guard. They want me to be a recruiting tool."

Rolf brushes away the campfire's smoke and sighs. "Yeah, my parents—I think they're going to split up. Papa—he's out here all the time now. Mother likes to tell everyone about my so-called modeling career. *The Face of Norway* is how she refers to me now."

He grimaces. "Mother called me The Face of Norway in front of Papa. He threw his drink in the fire and then threw a book at her. The book missed her head, but not by much. Papa started in about the Gundersons, and Mother commented on how I was more handsome than any German boys. I want to say no, but if I don't do it, what then? I'll put everyone in danger. Shit, I see what you guys are doing, and I feel like I'm betraying you. And, of course, I can't say anything to anyone."

Seeing an opening to be candid, I nod. "I'm glad Jan brought up the daisies last night— that we're going to start settling accounts. Am I to roll over like a dog obeying a command and never once put up a fight? And be left with people who want to tell us what to do? Be guided like puppets through the war? I'm not a marionette."

Jan pokes a stick at the fire. "I don't agree with your reasons for not going to BST, Kory." When I tense, he holds up his hand. "You never told me the truth as to why. Not all of us are going to be collaborators if we stay, if that's what you're thinking." Jan's voice could filet a fish. "That's why I wanted each of us to take a daisy. I'm with you, Stein, and Rolf. And Paul, too."

Rolf looks puzzled at the mention of Paul.

I break in. "Paul's a classmate of Jan's at BST. I went out to his house with Jan a few weeks ago. His life is—"

"Paul has it made." Jan finishes my sentence and my thought. "Parents and family who love him and don't ignore him. Connections everywhere. And he gets along with everybody." He pokes the sputtering orange ember and breathes a flame back into it. "Paul hates BST. He thinks the school is full of Nazi recruits and spies. He wears a red hat, pretends not to speak German."

Rolf is quiet for a moment. "I don't think we're alone." He looks at us, in turn. "Jan? Stein? And your friend Paul? We can't be. Jan's right about the daisies. But who to talk to and who to trust? I don't know, and I am scared." Rolf blushes. "Sorry, I shouldn't say I'm scared. I sound weak."

Jan and I jump in at the same time. "No, no! I feel the same way."

I sigh. "Everywhere I turn, I have just a few people I can trust...beyond our parents and friend's older siblings, that is. Although I'm reasonably sure all of us feel the same way about having the Nazis here, I'm not totally sure. Not entirely."

Rolf raises his hand and lowers it.

Telling the truth feels good. My voice rises in frustration. "So, I stand silently, listening, watching. And I can see how my life is unfolding." In a mocking voice, I continue, "I go to work and eat dinner with my family and do the same thing each day. Each weekend. Each month."

The rising sun illuminates remnants of snow capping the mountains. Next door, the camp has quieted.

Rolf pats me on the back. "Time for us to go back to what we know."

But is the world I know listening?

Chapter Fourteen

On a chilly November afternoon, the uniforms of my life intersect in the basement of a police station.

Fru Martin, wearing a Burberry scarf tucked into her Chesterfield coat, stands on a chair, holding a clipboard. Her white gloves peek from her coat pocket like lace. Behind her, a police officer writes the names of the people in line on a giant chalkboard. Four lights in the hallway create spotlights that the next victims step into as they move up in line. Fru Martin calls out a name. A man answers and steps into a pool of light.

Every man holds the identical pose: hands defending their crotches. They step forward from the pool of light to size up the room and their odds. Then, once inside, they nod to the unseen and turn.

The first brilliant flashes of light blind me. I look down at the greenish stones beneath my feet, count to five, watch the corona explode on the floor's reflection, and then glance upward. As the men pass me to leave, blinking into the dimness, their shared odor of grease and sour sweat lingers, melting into the smell of cornered prey.

They are terrified.

I had taken off my school shoes when Herr Henricksen came into Techwork's locker room.

"A German officer told us we're to report at four this afternoon to the police station to have our pictures taken," he said, drumming his fingers on his vest. "We're to always carry our documents with us. The papers are no different from a passport—a method to identify who you are and ensure you're where you should be. Get dressed and come with us."

I pulled on my work boots and went with the other employees following Herr Henricksen.

A policeman held open a wide wooden door that had barred windows. Once inside the building, telephones ring, sharp-suited men—who must have been lawyers—climbed the stairs, talking in code to one another, and the photographed faces of wanted men grimaced from behind a glass display case.

Fru Martin's voice summons us down the stairs and into a dark, low hallway, where we form a line. My co-workers and I won't be talking to lawyers or having a chance to look at the wanted men.

I take my suit jacket's hem and curl the scratchy wool over my knuckles, rubbing the rough fabric until my joints are red. The suit pants, bagging at the knees, puddle around my work boots. "You're a disgrace!" Jules would say. Jules would never allow me to walk around looking like this. Not that I've seen him lately.

The hallway offered no shelter from the wind. Every time the doors open, cold blasts sail down the stairs, scurry up my back, and find comfort between my shoulder blades. Long shadows pool around Fredric, a designer who started at Techworks a few weeks before me. The effect resembles the lights at the Forum Kino Theater, where Stein recently introduced me to my first taste of espionage.

Stein came to Techworks the Tuesday after we celebrated my birthday. "Can you come to the movies with me on Friday?" he asked. His eyes lit up. While I walked to the locker to get my coat, he exclaimed, "This is where you work? Look at those machines!"

I called over my shoulder to Herr Henricksen. "Can I show my friend the boneyard?"

Herr Henricksen honked a *yes,* and Stein and I walked toward my favorite place.

Stein's fingers caressed the piles I had set out as I explained why I sorted them that way.

We walked past my bench on which my diagrams lay, and Stein paused.

"This is a dream job! They let you do this? Design?" Stein's tone was one of awe and wonder. "Can you go to The Forum Kino Theater with me? I want to show you the latest movie."

Stein didn't say *go.* He asked to *show* me a movie. He's one to stay at a friend's house, listen to the record player, or maybe have girls sing and dance with us.

Although I agreed, I was uneasy.

That Saturday night, I met Stein at the movie theater. Situated on a bluff in Nordnes, the theater was—before the war—highly visible. Now, due to the blackout restrictions, The Forum Kino's windscreen Art Deco lights, usually a neon greenish blue, were dark. Smaller lights, designed to look like headlights on a stylish car, which would have served as mini spotlights at other events, were also dark. Dim lights bounced off the interior's black-and-white checkerboard floor.

We sat down as the movie started with a newsreel about the war, accompanied by rousing march music on a piano played by a young man wearing thick eyeglasses. The dais he sat on was positioned to the side of the theater, and a small lamp arced over the keyboard. He seamlessly transitioned into a jazz version of a popular song and turned another one into a ballad. An eruption of cheers came from Germans clustered in the theater's best seats. During intermission, the pianist played nonstop for twenty minutes from requests called out by the Germans. Not a wrong note. Not a misstep.

"He deserves this position," I told Stein. "He's much better than Jules."

After the curtains closed and the lights came up, Stein called to him. "Mathias! When the show clears out, let's talk."

At hearing his name, Mathias waved an arm to Stein, beckoning us. Mathias's gap-toothed grin diminished at the sight of me. Pushing the thick and smeared lenses up the bridge of his nose, he glanced from me to Stein.

"Good playing tonight." Stein's tone was overly cheerful. "You are good. And so many songs, too!"

"Yeah, you are terrific!" I said. "You're a better player than Jules. You are!" I hoped Mathias knew I meant it. "You won this spot fair and square. I don't care what my brother said or threatened. He gets that way sometimes."

Mathias, flustered by my flattery, bent to pick up his sheet music. His hands slipped, scattering the pages around the bench.

The cold wind snaps me out of my reverie, and I step forward, grateful that the gusts are now hitting only the back of my head. My shadow has lengthened, creeping up a wall covered with photographs stamped "Captured!"

Lost in thought, I miss that two people have moved forward. I stride to the open position as if my lapse were intentional.

What happened next at the Forum Kino was, indeed, intentional and seen only in movies.

Mathias abruptly left us kneeling on the floor, picking up sheet music.

Rude, I thought as I grabbed a march's third and fourth pages.

Stein's fingers ran below the bottom of the piano bench. Pulling a piece of paper out, Stein read it. Then, he swallowed the paper.

I was—and remain—dumbfounded.

I've replayed that event and what followed over and over in my head. I never draw a different conclusion. Stein's actions were straight out of a spy novel.

The theater ushers opened the doors, carrying brooms and dustbins. Behind them, the chatter and laughter in German combined with the slamming of the Forum's front doors.

Stein tugged at my arm and held out a sheet of music. "Kory, would you mind returning this to Mathias?"

Standing up, I shrugged, playing it off as a normal consequence of any Saturday night at the Forum Kino.

The theater's red curtains were heavy, and I had difficulty finding the opening. Frustrated and shocked, I walked to the side of the stage, where Mathias awaited me.

I handed the music to Mathias. "I do think you deserve this position. You're much better than Jules ever could be."

Mathias flushed, pushing his glasses up his nose, smearing them. His voice barely audible, he said, "Thanks."

Stein came through the curtains, nodding to

Mathias, cocking his head at me for us to leave.

After walking outside the theater, into the cigarette-and-popcorn-scented night air, I had a million questions about what I had witnessed.

Stein stared hard into my face, and with the slightest shake of his head, confirmed that I was to know about this and be a part of it but could not ask questions.

The next morning, I woke to the sound of twenty birds hitting the window of our front door. Scampering upstairs to investigate, I saw the heel of a person's hand striking the glass.

"You're going to break the goddamn glass, and you will pay for it!" I yelled. Flinging open the door, I found not a menacing troll, but our next-door neighbor.

Fru Eklund, a thin, young, and ordinarily quiet red-headed woman, nearly hit me as I ducked back inside.

My mother bustled down the stairs, standing behind me to see what the ruckus was.

Fru Eklund raised her hand again. Eyeing us as if we were roadkill, she shook a fist in my face. "How dare you!"

She turned her eyes from me to my mother. "I'm not surprised. That tomcat son of yours! What kind of mother allows her son to live where he wants?" Fru Eklund was at full boil, her words needling. "How can Jules live in two places? Have two sets of ration cards? People are starving, and your son thinks nothing of taking advantage of bad situations!" At last, she drew a breath.

My mother's voice was like honey on warm toast. "Tilda, I'm as shocked as you are." My mother smiled gently and turned to me. Her voice was smooth as a chocolate bar melting in a deep cup of warmed milk,

"Kory, please check the desk in the living room for Jules' cards." Syrup flowed from her mouth as she explained that Jules, *her headstrong boy, always wanting to go his way,* had recently moved.

I retrieved my brother's ration cards, watching as my mother, a virtual vat of caramel, explained Jules' recent move closer to his workplace.

Fru Eklund nodded. "No doubt a clerical error. Nothing more than that."

My mother patted Fru Eklund's shoulder. "I'm so glad you came to tell me. I wouldn't want us to be unable to continue our long friendship over a misunderstanding." Mother took a handkerchief from her dress pocket as Fru Eklund mopped at her eyes.

Then Mother turned to me. "Kory, can you get a tray of cookies for Fru Eklund? Friendships are important."

Fru Eklund bit into a cookie, pronouncing it to be delicious, and walked away.

Mother closed the door. When she's angry, she gets quiet. I inherited that trait from her. Then comes the storm.

She marched upstairs, closed her bedroom door, and I heard her fling several books at the wall, followed by a sharp cry of frustration. Years of seeing this habit had left the family with clear instructions on what *not* to do. She'd come out when she was ready. We were not to ask. We were not to try to comfort her. What was in her soul remained there, never to be captured.

Several meters from where I stand under a bare lightbulb, its cord frayed, a shadow—sharply etched—fades to a point under the photographer capturing the soul of the man in front of me. My shadow disappears as more flop-sweat-smelling men walk past me. Shifting my weight, I realize I'm not creating a shadow, or notice for that matter, in my war resistance efforts.

That evening, as the sun cast long, dappled shadows over my house, Stein and Jan hooted outside my door. They were both sweating and panting.

"Spart," Jan began, clasping his hands on his knees to catch his breath.

Stein panted, "It's Jules. That two-ration-card situation is causing problems."

I had news of my own. "Yeah, I know—old news. A neighbor came over and called Jules a tomcat! I'm glad people are finding out what kind of guy Jules is. I felt bad for Mother. I mean, she gave back her ration cards for him and apologized for the oversight. She was embarrassed, but he's such a jerk. Only Jules would pull this crap."

Jan's fingers were rapidly drumming on his arms. Uh-oh. I was in trouble. From the speed of his fingers, I could tell that he was not pleased with me yammering on. I blushed and stammered. Jan wanted me to get back to the subject.

"What about the cards?" I asked.

Stein piped up. "Jules is in trouble for claiming them. He agreed to be a monitor and to start watching people, your family included. He's supposed to watch who is here and who is not, reporting information to the neighborhood committee and the German guards. That's becoming important."

I thought Jan was glaring at me and down at Stein. I had messed up.

Stein was fidgeting and hard to understand. He motioned to us. "Let's walk. I have to tell you exciting news."

I looked at him, but he was clipping along, and I turned to get a clue from Jan.

Jan blurted out, "Spart, this is big!"

His voice held a hopefulness I had not heard before. The Spartan was plotting.

He whispered, "Spart, what do you have going?"

Stein stopped in front of a fountain commemorating an ancient person no longer remembered.

The water splashed cold drops on my arms as I faced Jan and Stein.

Both fidgeted and glanced at each other.

Jan nodded at Stein as if he had decided to let Stein tell me the big secret. Instead, Jan blurted out, "Stein's brother, Bill, is on a boat, trying to reach England."

I studied Stein. With his shoulders slumped, his eyes downcast, he looked crestfallen.

Stein opened his mouth to speak, but Jan, oblivious to Stein, kept talking.

In a staccato cadence allowing no interruptions, Stein broke in. He glared at Jan, launching into his news. "Yeah, the boats leave from several places along the coast, and they put you to work when you get to England or the Shetland Islands."

At this, Jan jumped in again. "I think we should plan to go."

I now understood why we were next to a fountain. No one could hear us unless they were standing next to us.

"But Jules—what about him?" I asked. "How would my going to England affect my family? Jules is double-dealing, and a sharp-eyed ninny from the neighborhood caught on." I raised my eyebrows. "They caught him, and he's not at my parents' house much, so people will notice if I disappear. I can't do that to my parents. My mother—that old ninny was yelling at her—it mortified her. I don't know how I would get away with it."

I pondered the possibilities before looking at my friends, in turn. "How do you know about Jules being on the ration-card committee? Even considering Jules is incredible. How low is the recruitment bar?"

Both shook their heads.

"It's true," Stein said. "The committee suggested my mother's cousin, but she doesn't like the chairwoman, *a dirty rat bitch*—that's what she calls her—*that snoopy old biddy*. It would mean my mother's cousin would have to keep track of her friends and family. She just couldn't."

Stein ran his fingers through his hair and continued, "I have never heard my mother's cousin talk like that. She swore! And the woman—that old biddy! Patriotic, *my foot!*—That I should be proud of how I was doing my part!" Mother's cousin turned them down and had to lie, but others—like your brother—are eager, especially since they think they can get perks."

Stein's words came rapidly. "We're going to have to take action, maybe like my brother. I don't know the arrangement. My mother is so agitated. Between my mother's cousin and Bill's leaving, my mother picked a fight with my father, and now they aren't talking to each other."

"So now your mother must lie," I said, "and people are going to ask or gossip about where Bill is. And that leads to questions, and that leads to—" I cut myself off. A woman was walking her dog, and as she walked past, I changed the subject to which soccer team might win the Regional Cup.

Jan waited until the woman was clearly out of earshot and motioned for all of us to huddle closer.

We heard the catcalls and the truck backfiring several blocks before it appeared. As it rounded the corner and menaced toward us, soldiers positioned on the truck brandished their rifles.

One gripped a bullhorn. "Hey, you! Get back to your homes!"

Startled by the bullhorn, I raised my hands in defense.

A voice cackled, "Ohh, look at the big strong Norway boys—scared of everything!"

The soldier with the bullhorn bellowed, "All of you boys, stop gossiping like old women, or we'll run you in!"

I turned to go, my hands raised in submission.

Stein started walking away in another direction.

It wasn't until I was about thirty meters away that I realized Jan wasn't beside me. I whirled around.

He sneered, a look of contempt on his face, at the group of soldiers, not much older than us, on a ride around town with their unchecked belligerence.

When he opened his mouth, I ran to block him from speaking. "You idiot! Not a word! They will kill us. No! *Nooo!*"

Jan drew himself up. A deep huff rolled from his chest. His eyes were not on the truck any longer; he was staring at other possibilities. He continued to stare down the street, past the catcalling soldiers preying on another set of victims several blocks away.

The Spartan—in full battle mode—suddenly noticed me. "Kory! Let's go!"

"You were going to…." I began.

Jan was not keeping pace with me. He was just waiting—no—hoping for the truck to come back. He walked purposefully, taking time to look at the flowers closing their petals for the day. He was taking it all in. Breathing it in. Taunting, cajoling the truck into returning.

"I'll see you later," I said.

He stood again, for a minute or so, like a statue, his head leaning toward the left.

"Hey, you, all right? Those soldiers, you think they would have…"

Before turning to leave, Jan considered me, saluted, and then smiled. He had calculated his odds. They were in his favor.

Here in the dank, sour-smelling basement, the casting of my lots shows that there are no favorites or exceptions written on the police photographer's chalkboard. And the odds of my co-workers—my fellow countrymen—being taken from the gloom of this war, thrust into the spotlight of scrutiny, discarded to end up terrified or dead are good.

I stand under the light, casting no shadow.

The man taking my picture has a burgundy smudge on his tie. It reminds me of the daisy of commitment bearing the blackberry juices from a more optimistic day that I'd pressed between napkins in a Crimshaw Brothers novel from my childhood.

I stand, my hands by my side, looking straight ahead. I do not smell of grease or sweat.

The image captured by the police photographer is, at first glance, that of an unproven boy, with my wide yellow-and-green striped tie and shock of hair pushed haphazardly out of my eyes.

I know better.

The shadow I will cast is long.

Chapter Fifteen

In the Gold Dust Pawn Shop's twinkling holiday lights, Jules' ruby cufflinks and gold pinky ring flash while the first white candle of Advent flickers in the window. His suspenders, in a cheery red, match his cufflinks. He demonstrates a camera to a customer, laughing uproariously at a joke the man had made in what sounds like Dutch.

Another man calls to him. Jules' lips create a perfect *O,* and his pronunciation of what has to be French takes over. Ever the consummate salesman, he greets the second sales prospect as one would a spiritual comrade, drawing him deeper into the fold of brotherhood.

Then, he continues to describe the camera's features to the first man, mentioning that it's a Leica Mountain Elmar. Soon, through Jules' suppleness with words, both men are admiring the camera. Jules brings out another camera from the cabinet but points out that this camera, while good, is not an Elmar. The whole time, Jules seamlessly slips from Dutch to French and back again.

Benny, whom Jules has said is the owner's son, comes to me and asks if I need anything.

"Only looking," I answer. I should correct myself and say I am *seeing* because I am transfixed by what's happening before me.

Pantomime goes on between the original buyer and the new person. From what I can see, now, both men want the Elmar.

Jules pauses, as if sorry for the turn of events. He puts the second camera back into the cabinet, then pauses in a deep squat and even deeper thought. "I thought we sold this!" he exclaims. "And what's this?" Jules shakes his head in disbelief as another Leica Mountain Elmar emerges from the recesses of the cabinet. He shyly puts the camera on the counter, apologizing in three languages for not remembering.

He bends into the cabinet again, pretending to root around some more, and making a joke about Saint Nicholas and his knapsack of gifts. As he comes back out of another deep squat, he sees me.

I watch as Jules, still slipping from one language to another, makes the two sales and walks the men to the door where he wishes them a Merry Christmas and safe travels.

A few weeks earlier, Jules had moved out after announcing that he'd finished with school for good. 'I'm fixing radios and record players," he said. "The shop near the pier does a good business with the sailors that will need money. I have picked up enough German and Dutch on the job to understand what the soldiers and others are saying about the war. The same Dutch and German men put their watches on the table and take a loan. On the next trip to the shop, their bills are paid, and on the subsequent visit to the shop, their watches are hocked again." Jules' finger twirled in the air. "There has been a steady increase in Germans over the last few months. Business is good. Brisk and good indeed!'

At the time, the family was incredulous of Jules's audacity.

Gramps was at odds with my mother and Gran.

"There are limits to freedom!" he groused. "Jules is still a boy. Yes, he is independent, but I think he's hanging out with the wrong kind. Where is your head?"

My wonder must be apparent. I disagree with my family. Jules is doing fine.

The ruse I am to use is to remind Jules about our Christmas Eve dinner. Now, after seeing the ease with which he conjures the possible, the thought of bringing him back to an ordinary life makes me feel grimy.

"Did the parents send you to check up on me?" Jules says and slaps me on the back. "Sales are good. Tell them I will see them for Christmas, and I am doing fine. I have to get back to work."

You are a natural at sales and in getting information. I say to myself. *You don't need schooling for those things.*

Lighting the second Advent candle, I tell the family the truth about what I saw—Jules' audacious talent for making sales and his ability for languages. "He is good at what he does," I say, more defensive of him than I realized I would be. "So, he moved out. So what?"

The subject isn't brought up again in my presence.

Each successive Sunday, a white candle is lit, and an empty place held at the dinner table until, at last, the blue candle of Advent marks the end of my family's traditional Christmas gatherings.

Jules is singing a Christmas carol as he opens the door to our house with boxes tucked under each arm. An oblong box with a big tag that said *Ray* is for my younger brother. A skinny present sports a card with my name.

Jules sets the gifts down. "Open them!" he commands.

Ray opens his present to reveal a magnificent gold

trumpet. The instrument's filigree stamp winds around the bell with an '*R*' rising like smoke from a fire. Ray had been borrowing a friend's instrument. Like many things in his life, from his clothes to his books and music, his instrument had been secondhand.

Jules continues as if he's talking about the weather. "I have begun buying jewelry for myself and better clothes than before. I must look the part, after all! A Swiss watch was my first purchase. Next, came a gold ring containing my birthstone. And remember, Mother, for your birthday, I brought you roses and a bottle of French wine." Jules strokes his fedora's crease and smooths the lapel of his pinstriped suit jacket. "I work hard for those things, and it pleases me to be able to give you nice things, Mother."

Gramps gets up and leaves the room. As he passes Jules, he mutters, "You're a pimp. No better than those whores. My grandson is a pimp. I never thought you would stoop so low."

Jules pulls out a French cigarette, his hands trembling as he puffs. Then, turning to watch Gramps leave, he waves his cigarette around, making sure his gold ring catches the light.

He tells my parents he has a place in the basement near where he works.

Gramps comes in from the other room. "Close to the West Indian?"

Jules flushes, his eyes widen, and as if by an unseen hand, a calm comes over him. "I don't know that place. Is the West Indian a restaurant?" He smirks at Gramps.

Gramps stares long and hard at Jules while he talks and turns to look at my mother.

The Advent candles and any chance of reconciliation were snuffed out.

Chapter Sixteen

The Ace of Diamonds lying in my parents' mailbox in early January is not of a lion, of Bergen, or even Polish. Running my thumbnail along the edge, I check for crispness or the faint acrid odor of newness. Neither are present, but there is a third test for the not quite familiar.

Clustered between Rolf, Stein, and Jan—Paul—the not quite familiar, stands on the icy platform. Given my friends' slouched positions and animated laughter, he has easily aced the third test—that of being one of us.

Paul is the first to board after we present our bags and new identification cards to the bored German agents for inspection. Still, he waits for the four of us, helping us hoist our packs, helping a young mother with a stroller—waiting—always waiting.

Paul sits in the corner, his eyes taking in everything.

I glance at Jan, who has turned to look at me.

Jan's blue eyes move toward Paul and back to me, looking for an affirmation.

I nod, giving him raised eyebrows and a quick grin. What will Paul think of the Wiks' cabin? It's a far drop from his accustomed style.

A light dusting of snow and sleet are falling when we get off the train at Vika. The trees, groaning with fruit only short months ago, are now bare and brown in the dimming light. A halo of grayish-white light appears like a low-hanging cloud over the Gunderson farm's stone wall. I smell stew and a sweet dessert—apple pie.

Fru Wik has obviously not been to the cabin, as the interior appears to have given up hope. The tablecloth hangs unevenly. The pillows lie beside the chairs, and the duvet holds gray spots where we once climbed on them. The kitchen cabinets reveal cans of peas and carrots, while the coffee tin contains enough beans to tide us over for one meal. Fortunately, there is firewood and kerosene, and we soon heat the peas and carrots, mashing them to make a stew.

Digging in the back of the cupboard, Rolf pulls out two tins of kippers, waving them around for takers.

I purse my lips, taking a long swallow of the beer we managed to smuggle into the cabin.

A hand appears on my knee, and I reel back. "Hey!"

Paul pulls back his hand apologetically. "You look lost in thought, Kory. I hear you're good with machines and can fix things. A machine I have needs your help. I was hoping you could come over to look at it after we get back."

I take another long sip, glancing at Jan, who has pulled out a pack of cards and is shuffling them in Gramps' riffling one-two-three *waltz* style.

"Let's play bridge," says the Spartan. "I told Paul about you and how you're good with machines. Paul has a press, and he and I want to know if you could come and help us get information out."

****

Uniforms are not a consideration to the boy silhouetted in Techwork's main office.

I wipe the burrs off my overalls and switch off the lathe.

Paul's pants don't puddle. His shoes shine, and after a long day at BST, his shirt is crisp, and his vest is without pills. Fru Martin—no calling her *Hilda*—works at her typewriter, looking up with an expression between intrusion and curiosity as Paul and I talk for a few minutes. I agree to meet him at the leper hospital.

Paul is enshrouded by a leggy rhododendron drooping over the hospital's stone wall. Like a willowy Medusa, the bush appears to rise out of his head, and I can't help but snicker. In greeting, his head brushes against a large plume with yellow buds, and dew runs down the front of his face. Spitting out a bud, Paul says with a grin, "I didn't mind waiting. This is a good place to meet. How far are we from the Goat Trail?" Wiping the last of the dew off his chin, he continues, "It's a hike, to be sure, and you might need to convince the Germans, but I'm going to be having a party this weekend at my house, and I was hoping you could come. Here's an invitation in case anyone asks."

He shoves a card reading "Paul's birthday party, Saturday, 3:00 p.m." into my hand, slaps me on the shoulder, and walks away.

I'll need to bring a gift. Maybe music, and I know just the person to sell me a good album.

Django Reinhardt's "Daphne" is playing in the background as Jules sets up records in the stalls of the Bibop.

"Hey!" He looks up. He isn't quite so flashy today—just a pair of brown pants, work shoes, and a blue shirt.

"I need a record for a birthday party I'm going to. Is that Reinhardt?"

Jules pulls out his silver case, offering me a cigarette. After I take one, he lights it and mine with the

Always-Bella lighter. " 'Quintette du Hot Club de France,' " he says. " Paris jazz. Reinhardt's a genius. Listen to this!" He pulls an album from a sleeve, setting the stylus down on the spinning record. "Si, j'aime Suzy," he waves his cigarette in time to the bouncy rhythm, and by the second section, we're shaking our shoulders together to the beat. "The piano is infectious, don't you think?" he says as we both break into a little shuffle.

Jules seems to want to be on neutral ground.

He leads me to a rack of jazz albums. "Paris jazz is *verboten*—strictly black market—by the German higher-ups, but try telling that to the people who come in here. The soldiers buy everything we have. I can let you have it for a little off the price, but I'll have to check with the boss to see how low I can go."

"Oh, fine. I'll just take it." I reply evenly. So far, our remaining in neutral corners seems to be working.

"A party, huh? For a new girl?" Jules' voice is teasing, but I'm not sure I should bite.

A song—very downtempo—comes on, and so does the mood.

"Nah," I say, "no one special right now. Mother's birthday is in a few weeks. Can you come by?" The second the words leave my mouth, I see my mistake.

Jules smiles thinly. "I don't know if I'm welcome there anymore. A *pimp,* you know. I'm more comfortable being with people who like me for what I'm doing and respect me for the information I can give them."

He waves his hand at the things he is clearly the master of—the instruments, the record stalls, and the ability to persuade. "And you, with your country club friends. Such big plans! No BST or university, I hear. What *will* you do?" Jules' tone is solicitous and sarcastic. He never blinks while he speaks, his eyes boring into mine, a small sneer playing on his lips.

I flush at the hostility. The gloves are off. Everything has changed within seconds. Me and my big mouth.

"Jules, I'm sorry I said that. The family was worried, but I told them about you at the pawn shop and how good you are. Leave my friends out of it. They like me for me, just like your friends like you for you. They don't care where my family comes from. I think we have that in common. As for school, I'll continue to work and hope I can get into the university when the time comes."

He laughs. "Yeah, you do that. The big engineer wannabe. Lots of talk—pretty talk. Do you want the record? I wouldn't want your big friends to think less of you."

My shoulders and neck feel as though I've boxed fifteen rounds. Why did I bring up the family? I'm an idiot!

That night, record album under my arm, I approach the checkpoint.

"Who is the artist?" the guard asks, staring at the wrapped present.

I'd seen the name of a German jazz player in a record stall—Peder Krueder—and blurt out his name. I breathe a silent sigh of relief when the German waves me through.

****

I hum "J'aime Suzy" as I walk to the Carharts. Even though the window boxes, trellises, and flowerpots are bare, Paul's house exudes a glow, as if cuddled in a soft blanket.

Paul, dressed in woolen pants and a knitted ski sweater, comes to the door, motioning for me to follow him, thanking me, with a laugh, for the gift.

Walking past the Carhart's softly lit, art-lined library—books shoved into shelves all akimbo, Chopin playing on the phonograph—I hear hellos from his parents, and they greet me like an old friend.

Herr Carhart, sitting behind a large book, looks perplexed, as if he's compounding chemicals. He waves me in, asking my opinion. Like Paul, Herr Carhart is dressed in a ski sweater and woolen pants, but his shoulders give away his powerful past. Months ago, Jan told me that Herr Carhart won a medal in the 1924 Olympics in Chamonix, France.

As I come closer, I see that he's looking at the gigantic cookbook by Fru Henriette Schonberg Erken, which is always sent as a wedding present. I draw my hands up in defeat, saying I have no idea about cooking.

Fru Carhart sits with one leg tucked under the other on a floral davenport, rummaging through an old tin chocolate box and squabbling with her husband, laughing over her shoulder at how preposterous the preparations for an upcoming dinner party are.

As Paul and I reach the kitchen, where sandwiches are set out for us, Herr and Fru Carhart reach a consensus that their ration cards can get them the needed supplies, but fish would be the best main dish, as cod is free and plentiful outside their door.

Paul and I descend a narrow flight of stairs leading to a large room. The exterior doors, with massive window inserts, accentuate the twinkling lights across the bay.

"Our company's prototype." Paul points to a wall of woodworking planers and files. "The doors are popular south of here."

Opening the sliding doors, we're out on the lawn. Paul's house has a carriage house—now, a guest house—and a garage. Tucked behind the garage is a small stone building, about two by four meters large, that I didn't see when I was here last fall.

"The shed was behind a tree we had here," Paul says. "The tree was starting to die, and Papa had it taken down. He wanted to tear the shed down, but I talked him into keeping it. Tool sheds. Everyone needs one, right?"

I look down. Mixed into the cement and grass are wood chips.

Paul continues, "Anyway, down in the basement of our office was a—" He nods to a workbench. "Look!"

A wheel resembling the sewing machine my mother uses is propped against a workbench holding hammers and screwdrivers. On a wooden stand, a slanted chute rests atop old catalogs. Jumbled small blocks, with letters and numbers embedded on metal strips, sit in a box. A stack of paper embossed with the logo of Carhart Lumber is in an open folder. Something that looks like a bicycle pump's tube has a skinny, pointed tip with a cap. A blackish-blue splotch has soaked into the workbench.

"A printing press?" I ask, furrowing my brows. Then with a laugh, I say, "I can't help myself," as I press my fingers around the tube. I'm pleased as a large viscous drop falls onto the bench. I dip the block into the oil, pushing the raised letter onto the folder. I look up at Paul, who is wearing the biggest smile I've ever seen.

Paul continues. "We must cut off the bottom of the page so we don't involve Papa's business. Some pages have a watermark…like stationery". He picks up a piece of paper and holds it to the light. A saw, a *C,* and a tree—the Carhart Company's logo—appear. "We can't use full sheets of paper for our newsletter, but we can use the paper for practice to see if the settings are right."

There's a slight tap on the door. Jan's voice says, "I'm here." Breezing in, Jan, also dressed in wool pants and a ski sweater, *cuts to the chase*—another Brooklyn-America. "Can you make the press work?"

I'm intrigued. "What's the problem?"

Paul grips my shoulder and smiles. "That's why I wanted you to look. A part is missing, and I don't know what to do. We need a person who can design a replacement."

Lifting the top, I push the mechanism up and down, and the typeset rattles slightly. "Hmm, let me open the top."

"Careful!" Jan says.

Too late. A small vat of oil spills out, spreading to the pages and lapping at the edge of the workstation.

Jan pulls the vat back before I can react.

Squatting, I pull on the back of the press. "I need a flat-head screwdriver."

Jan squeezes through the space between me and the wall. Seconds later, he hands me the tool.

Unscrewing the back of the press to see the inner mechanism, I tap on a key and watch how the levers press against a plate. Like a piano tuner, I place my ear against the housing, listening, putting my hand on the machine, waiting for a misstep or hiccup. I find I'm holding my breath, as if breathing would not allow the device to tell me what's wrong.

I hear the faint click, like an arrhythmia, and my

fingers confirm where the lever was pressing against the key that didn't connect. Like a heart surgeon, I listen and feel for the other malfunctions while making mental notations.

I see why Paul wants me here. The boneyard at Techworks has small tubes. All I need is to come up with a design. Lifting another piece of the press, I slide a cylinder off the mechanism. "I'll need a few tubes from the shop, but I can fix the printing press. Anything else?"

What I'm feeling as I leave the shed has the same components as being in love.

I think.

Not that I would know, but the giddiness, the excitement, and the "I can't wait to do this!" feeling must use the same hormones.

Walking back through the checkpoints and boarding the bus, I daydream about how I can obtain the cylinders and manipulate them to get the press working. Aching to sketch my ideas and play with whatever abandoned parts might be in the salvage yard at Techworks, I covet the pencil and paper a fellow passenger is using.

It is Saturday night. Techworks is closed, and I have school on Monday. It will be over forty hours before I can start working on this project. *Forty hours!*

Jules's moving out means I have the basement bedroom to myself.

When I get home, I rush to my desk. Shoving the English and math assignments aside, I pull out my mechanical pencil and draw the cylinder, but realize that I need measurements. *Measurements!*

Taking the stairs two at a time, I rummage through my mother's sewing box for her cloth measuring tape.

I bound down the stairs and measure out the

specifications like a grown-up engineer.

****

Monday afternoon is cold and bright. I tell Herr Henricksen I'm having a late lunch outside in the boneyard.

Picking a sunny spot, I open my backpack, all the while sneaking looks at suitable parts candidates. The candidates fall immediately into two piles: too big or too far gone. At Paul's, I said, "Is that it?" as if finding the perfect tubes would be the simplest thing in the world. Now, I am going to have to eat my words.

Wait!

I spy a box filled with old keys—the kind used to wind up antique clocks. Perfect!

A shadow crosses my face.

Herr Henricksen sits beside me, pressing the buttons on his brown vest. Craning his neck back, he looks up at the sun, absorbing its warmth. "You came up with a good idea, I think. It's nice out here."

I want those keys.

Finishing my late lunch, I look at the box. It's now or never. I need those keys. I promised.

"Is that a set of keys for wind-up clocks over there?" I ask. "I haven't seen those before. Are they new?" I point, trying to act nonchalant. "My grandparents have a clock like that, but they lost the key. Can I take the set home to them and see which one might work best? You can take it out of my salary if you like, but I think they could use one of those."

Herr Henricksen waves his hands in the best answer of all. As he goes back into Techworks, he calls over his shoulder, "Take what you need."

Upon closer inspection, I don't think I'm going to

be able to keep my promise to Jan and Paul. The keys are too thick; the brass cylinders, brittle. Of the dozen keys I pick up, half are too small. Seeds of doubt creep into my head that I'm not cut out to be an engineer.

Throwing away the keys is out of the question. Bringing them home will lead to problems because I can't use them. Now my heart is racing. I'm an idiot.

Herr Henricksen has left, and I have Techworks to myself.

I try to shove it into my backpack, but the box is too large. I dump the keys out of the box and slam the box on the ground. A key flies out and rolls under a curtain in the back.

I walk over, parting the curtain, and pick up the key—not the right size—and see precisely what I seek.

My heart stops. I was told I didn't need to clean behind the curtain, so I've never been back here.

Gun cartridges. Hundreds of them. In every shape and size, but every one of them is a tube. I can make adjustments. They'll be perfect. Herr Henricksen will never know.

A flashlight shines through the window, and I come out, waving apologetically. "Closing up!" I call out. "Heading home!"

I told Paul and Jan that I could fix this. Not without breaking the rules.

****

The cylinders are perfect. My stomach hurts at what I'm contemplating.

The bus ride to my neighborhood is quiet after leaving Techworks with my keys and my curiosity about the cylinders. So, when my little brother Ray slams into me, hitting my gut, my swat pushes him into the house steps and knocks me onto the wet grass.

"What's the matter with you?" I shout, rolling onto my knees.

Ray comes up to my waist. He's eight. He's bent over. He's sobbing.

I don't remember the last time I cried this hard. I crawl across the grass and cement, pulling Ray toward me.

His fist, the size of a large plum, pushes against me.

I pull his chin up, and the terror in his dark blue eyes is palpable.

He doesn't trust me. He's scared of me.

"I'm so sorry, Ray." My fingers press against his head as I kiss his forehead and hair, my tears coming in streams. I pull my hand back, praying there's no blood, and wipe along the back of his head, feeling for bumps. "Sorry. Jesus! I'm so sorry."

His fists push against me. "The trumpet is gone! Jules is going to be so mad at me! I've looked everywhere, and I cannot find it." His words come at me in puffs of air.

"Have you told Mother and Papa?"

Ray's head shakes his head no. His fingers tug at my coat. "What's lying on the ground?"

"What?" I straighten up, looking at my backpack. A half-dozen keys surround it. "Nothing."

Five minutes ago, I was scared about gun cylinders. Now, Ray is scared out of his mind.

"Ray," I say, "we have to tell Jules what happened. Sometimes people will try to sell things they've stolen, and it might show up at Jules' shop or one of the other pawn shops. Let's go there tomorrow after school, and maybe we can get it back for you if it is turned in. But let's not tell Mother and Papa just yet. We don't want to worry them."

His fingers, a third the size of mine, curl around my index finger.

I kneel. "We can't look like this. People are going to know we had an accident. And that's what this was—an accident, right?"

His fingers squeeze mine.

****

This Tuesday afternoon, the pawn shop is doing a brisk trade. Jules looks like a magician in a circus. Speaking German and what sounds like Dutch, sailors stand before Jules, his hands conjuring sleight-of-hand deals in all directions.

I lean down to Ray, protecting him against any unruliness. "Look at your big brother Jules. He's a great salesman. He's going to get those people to bid against each other. Just watch."

Jules performing his sales magic is mesmerizing.

Ray tugs on my coat. "Does he know *everyone?*" His eyes, wide with wonder, dart between the sailors and the cases of shiny instruments, watches, and jewelry along the wall in front of us.

I whisper in Ray's ear, "He does know everyone. I'll bet Jules can help us."

Benny, the owner's son, weaves his way from the back with an oblong case. With a flourish, he presents it to Jules. Jules takes the case. He opens it and snaps it shut, teasing the sailors. Then, he opens the lid slowly, provocatively, until the instrument is laid bare in all its glory.

A sailor, turning to his friend, makes a bugling noise. "Louis Armstrong!" His hands fly up in the air, his fingers waggling as if playing a song. Reaching for the oblong case, he pulls out the instrument for his friend to see.

In the light is the filigreed bell of a trumpet. On the top, an *R* rises like smoke.

"*R* for Ricardo!" says the sailor.

He thrusts the trumpet in the air, bugling notes with his mouth. After a handshake with Benny and Jules, the sailor and his friend exit the store.

Ray's knuckles are white. He wipes his nose on my coat.

"Jules, that was Ray's—" My mouth falls open. I reach down to squeeze my baby brother's shoulder. "What have you done? Why?"

I want to beat the holy living shit out of my conniving excuse for a big brother.

Jules stands still for a second. The only sign he's bothered is that he swallows and coughs. He smiles broadly. Looking at Ray, he shrugs his shoulders, twirling his ruby cufflinks. "You misunderstood. It's not like it was a gift. It's too nice for someone your age. I got a good price for that. It was just for you to see what a nice trumpet looks like."

I know what Jules' tell is. He twirls his cufflinks. That's how I know he has given a person the shaft.

Jules smiles and turns to his customers. "So, who is next?"

Chapter Seventeen

"How'd the keys work?"

I look up from the lathe and to the heavy curtain. I heard Herr Henricksen's question perfectly. Raising my fingers in a wait-and-I'll-answer fashion, I turn off the lathe, praying that the high-pitched buzz will take a minute to wind down fully.

Less than five seconds later, Herr Henricksen repeats the question.

Those gun cylinders would be perfect.

"The keys turned out fine," I say. "Fine."

Herr Henricksen's smile tightens, his eyes squinting.

Or his anger could be my imagination. Out with it.

"Herr Henricksen, I spilled the keys when I tried to put them in my pack—the box was too big—and a key fell underneath." I point at the curtain and rush my next words. "You told me I was not to go past that curtain, and I opened it to get the key." I wipe my hand over my face. "I'm sorry."

Herr Henricksen's lower lip is topping his upper lip. He's blinking. I think he's been blinking for a minute or longer. All noise has vanished.

"I see," he says.

I had promised, with blind confidence, that I could deliver the goods as if it were nothing. The screwdrivers, the chute, the letters, the wheel, and my friends—I have the task covered. Anything else?

What was I thinking?

Herr Henricksen turns toward the curtains and holds one back. "Come with me."

"The key dropped right here." I point at the floor—at the *exact* spot—"I didn't mean to look. I'm sorry." My words aren't enough. I'm sure of that.

"Kory, we have kept the curtain closed from the machine shop work area for many reasons. Many years ago, I built a gun for a friend. I liked the challenge, and my friend was happy with the results. Word got out, and I took on more designs—most are hunting rifles—so I keep the cartridge supplies back here. The guns are not part of Techworks. We don't sell them through the Company, but since I own the building, and the machines are here, keeping the parts in the back makes sense. Since the Germans came, I have not sold any guns, and every part matches what's on the inventory. When the Germans came in, I had to provide an inventory, and each month, a soldier comes by to make sure no parts are missing." His lip has dropped back to normal. He claps me on the back. "Your honesty and hard work are going to take you far, Kory. I believe that."

I want to cry. I can't do this. I'll have to figure out another way.

****

Exiting Herr Tveit's English class with Rolf and Stein, we are burring—Scottish style— our English phrases.

"Char-less Dee-keens," Rolf says.

From inside the classroom, Herr Tveit corrects him. "Dick-ins!"

As we move to our math class, Rolf and Stein pull

Aces of Clubs from their pockets. "Do you know about the invitation to Paul's house on Saturday?" Rolf asks.

I, too, got an invitation and an Ace of Clubs in the mail. The invitation, printed on paper from Herr Carhart's company, is typed so the letters that would make sense are missing.

I should be relieved. I am. But I have sweated, blubbered like a baby, and contemplated theft to honor my promise to Jan and Paul. My friends found another way and didn't tell me. A telltale ache makes a home for itself in my upper back. Rolling my head toward my shoulders to ward off the pain, I ask Stein and Rolf to meet me at my house.

We walk through the checkpoint closest to Paul's house. The guard looks at Stein and my passes with disinterest.

Then the guard's eyes widen as he turns to Rolf. "The Face. "You're *The Face*!"

Like a nutcracker soldier, Rolf stands ramrod straight, his feet welded together, his hands—fingers outstretched—by his side. His mouth is in a grimace, and his eyes stare out at the harbor. Only his clenching jaw gives away his anger.

The Germans continue examining The Face. Like hunting dogs, they circle their prey, sniffing for an opening, any weakness at all. While the Germans are not touching him, they are mentally strip searching him, noting every muscle tic and flinch, ridiculing him in the height of German politeness.

The lead soldier goes so far as to sniff the air—looking for another candidate. Finding none worthy, he bows like a waiter, extending his hand out to wave us on.

The three of us walk toward Paul's house with what

I'll bet is the identical question.

What constitutes earshot?

****

Paul is waiting for us as we trek to the shed. We crowd inside the hut, which has undergone changes in the past week. The assembling of the machine is complete.

I turn the wheel, and the chute lifts to feed paper.

"Papa found an identical machine to the one we looked at last week in another warehouse," Paul says.

Rolf's parents aren't speaking. Stein's parents live in fear of being discovered and sent to prison for ration cards they keep for his brother Bill. Jan's father might be a German collaborator. My family thinks my brother is a pimp. And Paul's papa finds another machine. Am I the only one who believes Paul has a charmed—

Jan, always straight to the point, interrupts my thought. "Do you have parts we can use?"

Paul pats the machine.

Jan removes a vial of toner from inside his shirt. He holds it as if the contents are radioactive.

As I watch Paul instruct the others on working the printing press, I notice that the shelving wrapping the hut's interior is a series of planers, files, and joiners butted against one other, sandwiched between sanded and varnished wood. Wood runs in Paul's veins.

After imperfectly crimping and adjusting the paper, we set type, preparing what will be our first newsletter. Paul's abilities as a writer are apparent. I can provide commentary, and Jan has flair, but Paul has created news we can pass along.

We're calling the newspaper *The Whole Truth.* Our article entitled "*You* Are Protecting Us?" details the

German soldiers' catcalls and a warning to the Norwegian girls not to listen. We wrote about how ration cards worked. We threw in a quick story about the labor camps and the importance of not believing German propaganda.

Rolf holds each sheet of paper to the light, looking for watermarks as if he's in a photography darkroom. Then he cuts the paper, and again, makes sure no watermark is showing.

Stein takes over the typesetting, his fingers rapidly assembling the type and ingeniously combining letters like an *l* and a *c* to make a *d*.

"Kory? Are you going to crank the press and watch the paper come to life?" asks Jan.

I decline the honor, deferring to Paul.

We unanimously decide for Paul to print the first edition, cheering as the first edition exits the chute.

Rolf and Stein tag-team the process, and an hour later, we have five stacks of newspapers on the workbench.

I look at my four friends. Rolf, now calm, appears to have a channel for the anger at being categorized by beauty. Stein's nefarious skills have been given a platform, at last. Through his words, Paul defies conventions and expresses his resentment toward going along. And Jan, who demands excellence from everyone, holds himself to a higher standard.

Stepping out into the cold, clear night air, a stack of newspapers in my hands, I'm overwhelmed by the sensation of love. My heart beats faster. The trees and flower boxes are etched in high relief, and I'm giddy. And terrified. And filled with longing. Longing to do this again—the printing, the information gathering. The camaraderie of my friends was…no…is a brotherhood. I'm trusting these people with my life, and they trust me with theirs.

I look over my shoulder at my newfound brothers. Like an unposed photograph, all are in mid-position— just about to—leaping into—*oneness.*

Paul is the last to leave the hut. As he turns off the light, the yard is distantly illuminated by a passing ship's red, white, and blue lights that paint an abstract of the Norwegian flag in the seawater.

I don't hear my friends leave, but I stand alone on the Carharts' lawn. My thoughts follow my gaze out to sea. I'm venturing into the unknown with my brothers.

Chapter Eighteen

Three playing cards are used in the months after the first edition of *The Whole Truth* came out. The Seven of Clubs—the start-of-negotiations card—is our notice that we should be listening for stories before we publish another edition. The Two of Clubs—the I-have-valuable-items card—means a significant story will be going into the paper. The last clubs card varies, and none of us gets the same one. That card will tell us when we can go to the Carhart's for our printing session.

Rolf, Stein, and I live within blocks of one another. Jan and Paul check when the guards take their breaks and find that the security follows a two- to three-hour cycle because of where they live and the guards' habits. As Jan says one afternoon in February, "After two strong cups of coffee, a bathroom break becomes a necessity."

I shake my head as I come through the door to the work area. Jan is kissing Fru Martin's hand.

Oh, those two!

In turn, they bow and curtsy, turning their heads to me with fiendish grins, winking at each other. Worse, Jan bows again and says, "Hilda, as always, a pleasure." He glances at me, then nods toward the door.

I now know better than to ask for an explanation. My jaw set in fake exasperation, I walk with Jan outside into the uncharacteristically cold air. Frost fog mingles with an uncommon sunset, giving the buildings and people walking home from work the appearance of shapes etched with charcoal.

Jan is walking faster than the cold air dictates, and I know I should not ask for an explanation of this either. After slipping on ice, Jan stops behind the leper hospital.

As I reach down to haul him up, his camel coat opens, revealing a London tailor's name. Seriously? Maybe I made the right decision in not going to BST.

"I'm going to need you to meet me at the Goat Trail. Bring your knapsack and tell your parents we're spending the night at the cabin." The Spartan's rat-a-tat commands leave no opening for argument.

"I have a date with a girl Stein is setting me up with." The girl Stein has suggested is someone, I suspect, he himself has passed over.

"Break it! I need you to do this. I have a mission—" He broke off and looked at me out of the corner of his eye. "I need your help. You are not to mention this to your parents, our friends, or that girl. Sheesh! You've been hanging your tongue out over her, and you haven't even met her yet. Knapsack and a weekend at the cabin. Got it?"

"New coat?" I ask.

The Spartan does not care about clothes, but his parents do. Still, this looks like a new coat—from London yet. I can't get him to confess his relationship with Fru Martin, but I might have better luck with his clothing choices.

He nods in a confessional kind of way. "Do you remember Papa talking to Herr Mitchell, the man from Copenhagen who is British?"

"The eavesdropped conversation with your father?"

Jan flips over the bottom of his coat, looking at the

label. "He came to see Papa two weeks ago. Papa had several officers over—Germans—and a representative from the Amsterdam office. Herr Mitchell's name came up. And"— he picks at the tiny stitches holding the label with *Bond Street* on it—"Papa's voice stayed the same in tone, but I've heard him talk like that only once before. When he lied—when he told Ingrid and me about how our dog had gone away on holiday, when the truth was the dog died after being hit by a car. He lied. He lied with a straight face."

Jan pulls at a rhododendron branch, taking pleasure in the ability to warm the ice into water. "Later, after the Germans left, I heard him make a phone call to a colleague in Amsterdam. And here is what's weird. He waited a long time, and he switched from Norwegian to English. He slipped at one point and said "Mitchell"—I heard that distinctly—and then he immediately apologized. Papa said the shipments could begin."

Curfew is looming. I shudder, as much from Jan's instructions as from the sharp, cold harbor wind that causes me to pull my jacket a little tighter around me.

"Shipments are coming in," Jan whispered. "And we're going to help. If you hear or see odd things, go with it."

The Domkirken bell struck six times. "The coat?" I asked. "A gift?"

"The coat came in with a shipment. Papa took it home and had me try it on. Look here." Jan points to the label.

The stitches on the label are newer.

"Inside the lining was a piece of paper saying, "A perfect fit.""

Chapter Nineteen

Above the leper hospital and behind a high wall shielding us and the neighborhood from prying eyes, Jan and I scurry through an alleyway lined with garages and sheds.

He stops, swinging his backpack onto the ground and stretching his shoulders. As he rolls his head, the cords of his neck tighten and release. The pack shifts as if holding large tomcats.

"What's in the pack? And why?" I ask.

I peer inside. Cylinders, looking like the pipes for a small sink, have small bags tied around them. Opening one, I pour the contents into my hand. Gaskets, washers, and screws spill out. Jan has also included two pipe wrenches and banding for the joints. Two small clips in another bag need to be separated. "We're transporting sinks. Again, why?"

"My story is I'm going to my uncle's cabin to work on a leaking sink," Jan says. "You're to follow me twenty minutes later, and you are working on a job at a restaurant near the funicular. Say that you forgot parts for the snack shop, and you'll catch it if your boss finds out. You must look like you are in a rush, and that it's important that they let you through. Show them the pipe and the pipe wrench."

"You are out of your mind. The guards are stupid, but there is no way they'll buy this."

The Domkirken bell rings five times.

Back before our newspaper—now going out every week—before Herr Mitchell began sending supplies—if it was him—back before I'd stood in a police station willing myself to be a different, braver person, there was human nature. Anatomy is what sets our newest mission in motion.

I follow Jan for one hundred meters and rest against the wall, smoking a cigarette and pretending to look at my watch as if exasperated at someone's tardiness. Leaning forward, as if scanning for people walking along the tree-lined street, I see a pair of shiny boots shifting their weight at the checkpoint, but not who's wearing them.

The boots stride toward me. Coming into view are gray pants and a tight-fitting coat with a fur hat. The guard glances at me.

I give a stern glance at the clock and, then, at my watch.

He rounds the corner, heading toward the church.

A long-legged person carrying a hiking pack walks through the checkpoint. He veers to the left and disappears.

How long will it take? I walk toward the checkpoint and look behind me. I might be imagining it, but I see Domkirken's back door open and close and a black hat bouncing along the top of the wall.

I run, counting off the seconds it takes for me to barrel through the checkpoint and run to the Goat Trail. Fifteen seconds. Or an eternity.

My lungs burn as I scamper up the trail. I'm dead sure I'll be identified through the leafless trees.

I reach the fork in the Goat Trail. We always go to

the left, where the path zigzags gently up the slope to the restaurant. The right fork, as I remember, is steep and strewn with rocks. The forks come back together at an overlook—the same overlook where Jan saw the Germans marching last year.

Diving into the woods, I jump over a little stream, my foot sliding on the mud-covered rocks.

There!

Tucked behind downed logs, slippery with thawing moss, are upended shale sheets. Though lower than I remember, the tombstone-like stones are narrow enough to trip the unwary. Too late, I realize they have another flaw—untrampled clumps of snow.

Stupid! If they check here, they can follow my tracks. Idiot!

I'm panting and not thinking clearly. If the guard saw me, he would have given chase or yelled, right?

Pushing off the log, I stand, listening for a footfall or the twittering or flight of birds, which will let me know I'm not alone.

I hear footfalls. I hear a c*lunk,* and I know who is above me, taking a short rest.

Scrambling through the brush, I hear the pack being picked up and rapid footfalls.

The long legs pump like pistons, and the pack sways like a pendulum.

A few minutes later, as the sun sets, I walk through the newly bare copse of trees near the Andersons' cabin. A dull-red birdhouse swings in the faint breeze.

Jan walks to it and pulls out a piece of paper.

Is he going to eat it like the paper Stein ate that was underneath the bench at the Forum Kino?

He reads it and, like Stein, pops it into his mouth.

Unlike the Wiks' cabin, the interior of the Andersons' cabin retained a woman's touch. Although faintly musty, the pillows lining the banquette are upright. A vase stands ready for wildflowers, and old books and magazines are along the wall. In a cupboard beside the door, are slickers and rubber boots, mittens, hats, and worn but serviceable towels. A blue speckled-enamelware coffee pot stands on a camp stove, and a black kettle, set upside down, stands as an absurd hat topping a broom.

Jan sets down the backpack next to the cupboard, and I follow suit. I'm waiting to hear about the birdhouse.

"Let's go for a hike." Jan stands, stretching his shoulders and pushing up against the beams in the cabin with his fingertips.

In the dimming light, we walk through the copse of trees, and I pause to listen. Other than the funicular's clang, I hear no voices and see no one.

Stars and constellations, including Thor's Hammer, dot the northern sky. The lights below block the Aurora Borealis, but if we hike farther in on the plateau and spend the night, we might see the lime and emerald-green lights dancing across the sky.

Floien's restaurant stands as a black hulk in a navy sky. Two gas lanterns with elaborate scrollwork stand lit beside the doorway.

As I walk closer to where the two funicular cars discharge passengers, I feel the lights are toying with me. As my body moves within the lantern's reach, my shadow explodes onto the pavement—a distended version of myself. A second later, the light flickers in another direction, and my body loses any distinction it might have.

The snow lining the trail tempts me to make tracks, announcing that I, Kory Mowat, am here, that I outsmarted the Germans and will continue to smuggle and outwit our enemies at every turn.

Like children set loose in a closed amusement park, Jan and I continue to shadowbox the barricade, our shadows growing sharper as the stars appear in the night sky.

Faint voices come from beyond the restaurant.

Jan heads back to the cabin, and though I have been to his place a million times, I'd be more comfortable being within line sight of his retreating lope.

As I walk inside the cabin, Jan is reaching for the flashlight in the cupboard nearest the door, as he must have done a thousand times before. He walks to the lantern and lights it with a match. His curly hair, against the light, is exaggerated against the shiplap boards separating the sleeping area from the living room.

The packs are gone.

Jan reaches into the cupboard, pulling out tins of stew and a cast-iron pot. He lights the fireplace.

Settling in, we quietly eat the warm stew, drinking the beer Jan retrieved from the cabinet with the irreparably broken lock. Hands squared, foreheads and knees centimeters from touching in our hunched-over-decision-making position, we are ready to soldier on.

I raise my eyes to Jan's. "We can do this. There is nothing for us here. I'm mechanical. You're good with languages, and you're learning to fly...or at least wanting to. It's the only way we can do this." I poke his knee. "Are we men or mice?"

Jan sighs. "I've talked to Stein, and he says since his

brother Bill went to England, we have an in with the people doing this. We need to go and talk to the guys. We can pass for eighteen—"

"But our passes say we're sixteen," I interrupt halfheartedly. We can lie…we can lie.

In years past, we have concluded other soldiering-on decisions with a stare down. Whoever blinks first loses. Jan's not blinking, and neither am I. We stand up.

We can lie.

Chapter Twenty

Paul's eyes widen, and I gasp at how many printer's ink tubes Jan has brought from his father's office this time.

With the subtlest shake of my head, I hope Paul remembers not to ask about what is becoming painfully apparent to our group.

"Surplus office supplies," Jan says.

Paul and I take the metal cylinders from him, being careful to stack the tubes and our friend's pain into safe places.

Not long after Jan turned twelve, his mother cleaned out Herr Anderson's closet and found a woman's name that she didn't know in his pants pocket, along with a hotel receipt.

"There was," Jan spat out to me one afternoon, days after the discovery, "a discussion and a departure."

Though I never confided in him, Gramps began suggesting that I bring Jan over to our house after school.

Over three-handed games of Solsvik Bridge, while Gramps invented techniques for teaching us how to play, he and Jan talked of history, especially Napoleon. Peering over his spectacles, Gramps instructed us on exacting a finesse or a squeeze play, and Jan gave voice to the pain he was witnessing at home.

Gramps told us of Lapskaus Boulevard in Brooklyn-America and Napoleon's complicated life. After letting

Jan's pain spool out like the waves crashing against Smuggler's Rock, Gramps led Jan to a type of accordance under history's guise, giving Jan another story to read, and us, new bridge and life techniques to practice.

At the time, I didn't recognize the substitution.

A wall of pilfered ink tubes now grows between Jan and his father. Between Jan's go-along-to-get-along attitude, which passes as the new normal, and Herr Anderson's behavior, which verges on that of a collaborator, Jan's seethes with defiance of his father in silence and anger.

Rolf, through his modeling for the Germans—still a subject he rages over—heard of the Atlantic Wall, which we report in *The Whole Truth.*

With a smile, Paul quietly comments on the terrific source stories Rolf gets. He asks if he would continue to act in that capacity, but cautions that he could never forgive himself if Rolf came to harm because of our thoughtlessness.

Put that way, how could we not agree?

Our stories, never attributed to a single person, tell of the increasing harassment of ordinary citizens doing ordinary activities, like playing bridge or going to the movies at the Forum Kino. Our latest edition featured an anonymous source reporting being spotlit while fishing by a passing German cruiser and circled by swastika-bearing planes canvassing the coast for escapees.

Quietly, imperceptibly, the walls of our resistance arise.

Chapter Twenty-One

On a late spring evening, with the sun still warming those standing by the shore, Jan and I watch a white-trimmed mahogany boat slice through the water.

The birch trees near the shore droop with caterpillar-like pods, while pussy willows sprout near the little stream running past the Anderson and Carhart houses.

Alighting from the boat, Ingrid runs up the dock, carrying a rope. Tying the boat to the pier, she cups her hand over her eyes and squints at the boat's captain.

It isn't the way she holds her hand to her face to keep the breeze from blowing her chestnut hair or the way she looks back at us questioningly as if we have been up to no good, but it is…and more.

Paul steps onto the pier and walks to her. Silhouetted by the sun, he takes her hand, dipping from his waist in a bow.

She smiles and curtsies.

The sight is among the most romantic images I have ever seen. I'm in awe. My friend already knows what pleases a girl like Ingrid. I don't know him, after all.

Jan starts to speak, but for whatever reason, he stops.

Ingrid's laugh flows like a far-away stream. Her face shadowed by Paul's, Ingrid grabs hold of his arm, bouncing her head against his shoulder. When Paul reaches to pull her closer, she pulls away, slightly tap dancing down the pier toward the shore, her light blue dress swaying around her legs, inches from his reach.

Ingrid's arm extends, fingertips waggling, mocking. Her eyes locked on his, she shimmies and slinks away from his grasp in a comic dance move. She bends slightly, rocking her shoulders, and runs toward two transfixed boys.

Paul stands for a second, a look of bemusement on his face.

But the message is clear. Both know where they stand with one another. No words. Just a surety that he is hers and she is his.

Paul excuses himself to walk Ingrid home.

They walk side by side, almost as colleagues might, until they reach a trellis.

Paul pauses to open the gate. He gently takes Ingrid's chin, tilting her face upwards.

I blink, willing myself to turn away from the intimacy. I do.

When I open my eyes, they walk side by side, as colleagues do.

Chapter Twenty-Two

Paul, Jan, and I have been smuggling gunstocks and munitions over the past six weeks and have been successful. Until now.

Lighting a cigarette, I lean against a stone wall near the Goat Trail. I'm probably five meters behind Paul. I can't decide if I should tamp out the smoke or run my thumbnail against my teeth. I'm having trouble breathing.

The smuggling started the Friday after Paul's boat party. Now, when I open my work locker on Friday afternoons, a playing-card deck with the Ace of Spades sticking out lies on my hiking clothes. I don't recognize the deck's cover. My knapsack contains gunstocks and ammunition when I leave Techworks. I pass through the checkpoint, hike up the Goat Trail, then leave the pack in the Andersons' cabin.

Each successive Monday afternoon, my knapsack sits empty in my locker. Clearly, our actions have the approval of parties unknown. But just as clearly, I have no candidates as to their identity.

But now, I have three problems. Firstly, Herr Henricksen's mother has been ill, and he has not been in the office, so Fru Martin has been the person in charge. Secondly, in the past two weeks, we've had two random visits from Germans taking inventory of the cylinders behind the curtain. The list checked out both times, and the Germans even commented on how untouched the catalog seemed to be.

Third, I ache to write about my smuggling, but that would be too much. Too many questions, too few places for a cabin, such as what I'd like to describe. I can't risk exposing who we are.

This Friday afternoon, after climbing the small hill past the Leper hospital, I spied a familiar curly head in trouble. And I can't help him. Make that four problems.

Paul, waiting on others—always waiting in that deferential way he has—has announced to the German guards that he *does* have black-market items inside and opens the sack.

The two office workers behind him in line immediately step back.

The guards pull Paul aside. Judging from their scuffling feet, the bags slapping against their thighs, and their crossed arms, the factory and office workers trying to get home appear frustrated by the nonsensical delay.

Paul pulls out a succession of kipper tins, setting them on the ground next to the guard's checkpoint.

The guard, his eyes widening, asks, "Why so many kipper tins? Are you sick?"

"My Gran likes them a lot," Paul says. "She always asks for them, and she gets into a storytelling mood. The kippers keep her happy, you know?"

The guard stares at Paul, the bag, and the shiny tins. He waves Paul through as if Paul has escaped from an asylum.

A middle-aged man, hands in pockets, wearing a red knit cap, juts his chin and shoulders at the soldier. "And *you* are protecting us? Against what? Kippers for an old gran? What a load!"

The soldier turns red.

The woman behind the man holds open her bag. "Hey, Kippers!" She says this in the way a farmer would call a pig. "Have you seen enough?"

Down the line, people snicker, and as each one goes by the guard, they pull out their coat linings, fingers spread wide, catcalling, "Seen enough, Kippers? Here you go, Kippers!"

It's time for me to get into line.

Kippers doesn't check my rucksack, and I don't call him *Kippers.*

The tips of his ears flush, and the guard waves me through as he tears a long strip of a cuticle from his nail.

Twenty minutes later, after taking the Goat Trail's easy route to the Andersons' cabin, I arrive to find Paul unloading the kippers from the sack and putting them in the kitchen cabinets.

I pull out the phonograph records from my pack and put them behind the Andersons' radio cabinet. Against the wall lies Paul's steel-grey rucksack, chock-full of gun components. As I lay my knapsack down, which is nearly identical to his, my fingers trace the narrow, contrasting ribbing of his rucksack. As with mine, there are at least twenty bullets encased in the ribbing. Inside, ten gunstocks lie beneath my clothes.

Paul steps outside.

I crane my head and see him walk past the birdhouse and turn toward the funicular.

Stepping outside, I turn to lock the cabin door. Behind me, through a copse of trees, a poorly executed bird whistle carries on the breeze. All clear. But to whom?

Chapter Twenty-Three

The man who has always reminded me of a starving bird struggles with his foot placement as he passes outside my open bedroom window. I'm translating an English text into Norwegian for Herr Tveit's class.

"*Jeg er Beten og Gandheben og Livet; ingen fommer til Tabern uben veb mig,*" my father says. His footfalls on the stone walk above my window sound like someone learning to walk with crutches.

" 'I am the Way, the Truth, and the Light. He who believes in me will have eternal life.' " I stop translating, having just heard and translated a phrase my father, given his religious views, would never say. But I *heard* him.

"Klara?" My father's voice, usually a pleasant rich baritone, rasps as he climbs the stairs to our kitchen.

I run up the two flights of stairs to see my father reach for my mother's hand.

Her smiling face folds in upon itself like punched down bread dough. "No!" she cries, running to my parent's bedroom and shutting the door behind her.

With a cacophony of chairs pushed back from the dining and kitchen tables, the Mowat family has an impromptu roll call, huddled outside my parent's bedroom door. All, except for Jules, are present.

"Mother! Mother!" I exclaim. "What happened?"

Taking a deep breath, Papa hesitates, then squares

his shoulders. The door opens wide enough to reveal my mother clasping a hand-stitched wedding pillowcase to her chest. Slipping his wing-like legs and arms inside the room, my father shuts the door.

"No!" My mother's voice is a muffled sob. "Oh, God, this is awful!"

Gran—all one hundred forty-five centimeters of her—elbows past me and muscles the door open, leaving it—I think—purposefully ajar. Her maternal instincts to fend off the evil that has entered our house are instantly razor-sharp.

Mother, her back resting against the high-back bureau, is hugging herself tightly. Her nose is red, and tears stream down her coarse, doughy cheeks. She holds a white paper in her hand.

Gran walks to and removes the pillow from my mother, handing it to my father, who places it on the bed. As she takes the paper from her daughter's dazed grasp, my grandmother, with her ramrod carriage and steely gaze, assumes the shield protecting her beloved family from more harm.

Papa has joined Mother and Gran. He whispers into Gran's ear.

Gran listens carefully, her child-sized hands smoothing her cotton apron pockets. "What? Killed? Oh, no! He was so young."

She turns to Gramps, Ray, and me, who are hovering in the doorway. Although she's a tiny woman, her clear and steady voice fills the room.

"Harold"—Gran pauses to choke back a sob—"Harold's dead. He was sailing, taking people—including a teacher from Bergen—to the Shetlands. The Germans found and executed everyone. Then, the

Germans blew up the boat, dragging the remnants and remains to Solsvik's harbor and leaving them to drift."

In my mind, I see bodies swirling in the eddy near Smuggler's Rock. And then I picture who should be here, and who I'm convinced is probably behind Harold's death. Bile rises in my throat, and beads of sweat form on my brow. "I'm going to tell Jules. The bastard needs to know. He and his friends are behind this. I know it," I say. I'm expecting a barrage of protests, but no one steps in to contradict me. "He needs to be told," I state, grabbing my coat from the hook in the hall. Running down the stairs, I open the door, calling over my shoulder. "As if we need another reason why he's not welcome in Solsvik. He needs to hear what he has done."

Stepping outside into the beginnings of twilight, I realize it has probably been only fifteen minutes since Papa brought us the dreadful news about Harold's death.

Herr Eklund, our neighbor, nods at me as he walks on the sidewalk toward his house. Barely glancing at him, I run down the street toward the bus stop.

I climb on the bus heading in the general direction of the West Indian bordello. Because this bus is heading toward the city center, there are only three other people on board.

A couple sits two seats in front of me. The young man keeps sliding his hand around his date's shoulders, and she keeps pushing his hand back. He blows in her ear. When she turns to him, a tear is running down her cheek.

I wonder if the girl on Harold's boat wiped her eyes. I wonder if Harold did, as well. Harold. Wiping tears from my eyes, I rise, but the passenger on the seat opposite me beats me to it.

Leaning into the boy's head, the man speaks, and the young man quickly moves to another bench. As the man turns, he places his hand on the girl's shoulder, and she nods, wiping her eyes with the back of her hand.

****

Staring out the bus window, I think about the saying of yes, initially, but then changing your mind. What of the girl in front of me, the girl on the boat, and Harold? All consented, and all paid for it.

Over the Easter holiday, Jules and his friends, Petter among them, went to Solsvik.

On Easter Monday, Gramps was yelling at my mother and Jules in the kitchen.

I tiptoed to the basement door and crept up the stairs, straining my ears to hear better. Not quite. I forgot the third step from the bottom squeaked.

"Get back in your room, Kory! Stop eavesdropping!" Gramps shouted.

I moved back to the second step but considered stretching to stand on the fourth step.

"Now!"

I tiptoed around, returning, then crouching on the second step, listening, and holding my breath.

My mother admitted to Gramps that Uncle Bertin had sent a telegram to her about Jules. That she'd had to telephone her brother from Fru Eklund's, who she was sure had listened in on the conversation. Mother thought Bertin would consider the matter closed, but she was wrong.

To reinforce his displeasure, Bertin had told Gramps—*in great detail*—about Jules at the weekly bridge game.

"Jules, do you know how embarrassing your actions

are?" Gramps thundered. "You aren't welcome any longer!"

Then, Gramps' voice dropped. His next words dripped with horror. With revulsion. With unmasked fury. "You *wanted* to watch? Who *does* that?"

Jules didn't talk back in his usual cocky way.

My mother's voice raises in denial. Big mistake.

Gramps levels his aim at her, letting loose a barrage of words, using one I hadn't heard before. "Coddling. You know I'm right. No one from our house treats girls that way. Or tries to take advantage of Harold. I just won't stand for it! It's sick!"

My right calf cramped, but I couldn't move. I couldn't breathe. I heard the squeak of a shoe on the floor and the rustling of fabric.

"Let me go!" Jules cried out. Two jars rattled on the wall behind me as something—or someone—moved something heavy—*the couch?*—which must be directly above my head.

"You sit there and listen to me!" Gramps' heavier footfalls moved, and again the jars in the basement rattled. "You knew Harold would trust you. He did, but now, you, Jules, aren't welcome in Solsvik."

A lighter footstep retreated from the living room, but Gramps wasn't finished with his lecture.

"And you! Don't you dare defend him! Coddled. Always." Gramps' voice takes on a jeering sing-song tone. "Playing favorites. That's over."

The boy got off a few stops after being confronted for his actions. I don't know if he felt shame or remorse, but he didn't look back. In fact, he didn't look back to apologize while on the bus. Nothing.

My chest tightens as I consider what I want from

Jules. An apology? Surely, he would be sorry to hear about Harold. Surely, he would accept some blame for his actions. But he watched. He must have liked watching. He had no problem with watching.

Alighting from the bus, I present my papers to a soldier. He's curious as to why I'm in the town's center so close to curfew.

"Our family had a death in the family," I explain. "I'm on my way to notify my brother."

The guard pats my arm and offers his condolences.

I don't mention that Jules is my mother's favorite.

A year has passed since the invasion, and the last time I walked Nostegaten. That day, I glimpsed an olive-skinned arm and ruby cufflinks going past a doorway. At the time, I couldn't believe that Jules would be a part of this world. But I have changed my mind. The Bibop is four blocks from here, on the fringe of the respectable area. Two blocks south is Gold Dust Pawn. Jules' living here makes perfect sense.

Long ago, when I was eight or nine, my mother and I accidentally walked this street, past the Four Lions and its larger competitor, the West Indian. We were to take a ferry, north, to visit Papa's family, but a large van unloading supplies had blocked our intended route, so we turned down a street I had never been on before.

My mother clutched my arm, hustling me along the narrow, cobblestoned street, but I heard clicking, like typewriter keys, on the gabled windows above me, and I looked up. A black girl was waving and blowing kisses at me. In the next window was someone who looked older than my mother. She had no teeth. Girls were in every window—young, old, thin, fat, and all of them incessantly tapping their window panes.

"We shouldn't be on this street!" my mother said, clutching her purse and her dignity. She sped up, but as we galloped along, I continued to gape upward, thrilled and curious at the pinging on the glass and how the girls eyed me.

A woman leaned over, and a breast spilled out of her shirt.

Open-mouthed, I pointed.

My mother glanced up and then slapped me hard across my face.

The following Monday, while playing marbles in the yard at Granvin, Stein explained what the West Indian was to a dumbfounded Jan and me.

"Sheesh! Where have you been?" asked Stein. "The West Indian is the oldest and largest bordello in Bergen, and Bella is the madam. The story is, in the olden days, one in five of the people who lived in Bergen was a whore."

From that moment on, Jan and I looked at our classmates with a whole new view. I'd count out loud while Jan pointed. Then, he'd point at me, and I'd raise my eyebrows practically to my hairline, making sure I counted Jan as a fifth person.

Stein always glared at us as if we were idiots. "Do I have to explain *that* to you, too?" he asked the first time we tried to estimate how many whores would have been present in olden days. "Many whores descend from Caribbean or African slaves. That's how the West Indian got its name. Anything you want, any type you want, that's what you can find at the West Indian."

Rolf helped us further our knowledge of the natural world by showing us magazines he'd found near his family's cabin. While Stein and Jan made wisecracks about farm animals, I studied the women in the magazines Rolf held and then—curious and mortified—thought of the girls in our classes. Jan pointed at a picture, snickering about an old spinster teacher, and we rolled around on the ground laughing. Stein made curving motions with his hands and nodded toward Fruken Simone, a young French teacher exiting the building.

Then, Rolf said, "Our mothers."

Within seconds, I tore the magazines from his hands, pummeling him, feeling sick to my stomach. My mother wasn't like that.

Stein and Jan howled in protest, so they must have thought the same thing.

Now, on my journey to let Jules know of Harold's death, I must admit that my curiosity is getting the better of me. How is it, *exactly,* that Jules came to live here? Does he—and I picture him as a baboon—is sex part of what he does for Bella? His ease and sophistication with girls, his sales skills…are they things he learned here? How can he compartmentalize his life? I want to catch him in the act. Make him stop his lies. I want him to admit that he is a whore, too.

I'm nursing that thought when I hear tapping on the windows. My heart pounds. My breath comes rapidly. Maybe my plan is stupid. I told my parents that I wanted to leave a message for Jules about Harold's death. But I've never seen a madam. And I want some truth about what Jules really does.

A man, nearly hidden in an empty storefront's doorway, calls out, "Hey, buddy, you got cigs for a guy? I can help you find the right pearl for you."

Walking closer, I see a plaster with graying edges

taped to his neck. The dressing has a rust-colored splotch.

The man looks up uneasily at the inns across the street.

Stein told me all those inns were bordellos.

A mist blows in from the wharf. I hadn't thought to bring my raincoat.

A catcall comes to me from a window. "Get you out of those wet things? I can keep you warm!" The woman's loose breasts sway under her shirt. She crooks her finger at me. "C'mon, honey. Let me warm you up. Keep me company?"

"I'm looking for Bella. Know where I can find her?"

The woman smirks. "Aren't we picky now! I bet no one has popped your cherry. Let me do it for you. I got a special place, and you will just love it." A white breast, looking like a pig's udder, swollen and chapped, falls out of her shirt.

Shrinking back, I flash onto the memory of a little boy walking along this street with his mother. Then, I had been curious and pleased by the fawning attention. But this woman, with her knowing leer, turns my stomach. "Know where I can find her?" I ask. "I need to talk to her or a friend of hers. Is she at the West Indian?"

"You just come in, and I'll get you fixed right up."

I turn away.

"Oh, go screw yourself," she says. "Just trying to be friendly. It's the third door on your right when you come down this street. You need to knock four times. That way, she knows you aren't a cop. You aren't one, are you? We were just having a friendly conversation— trying to be neighborly." She drags on her cigarette and then coughs, wiping the drool from her gums onto her arm.

Drawing closer, I'm surprised at how satisfied I am that the flowerboxes, the white siding, and the green gables of the West Indian are splintering and could use a fresh coat of paint. I push on the doorway's frame, which is spongy. Testing my theory that I could dent the door with my fist, I rap four times, concluding that the door must be a recent replacement. I call out in my deepest voice, "Bella, let me in! You can't just keep me standing here."

A radio clicks off, and I hear a shuffle inside. The door opens, and a woman more diminutive than Gran peers out at me.

The woman, despite the cold, is wearing a sumptuous royal-blue brocade kimono with bright-yellow frog closures. She bows slightly, but as she comes up, bearing a warm smile, I step back with shock and pity.

The cake makeup—like the kind used in theater productions—can't cover the damage. One half of the woman's face is an ugly shade of purplish green. A sideways V runs along her upper and lower eyelids. Her freckled nose has large, crudely sewn $X's$ running across it like a poorly made fence. Her swollen upper lip nearly touches the tip of her nose. If I had to guess, I'd say she is in her early twenties.

Standing next to her is a teen-aged girl, and I smile at her She is wearing a powder-blue and brown kimono and her hair coils at all angles. I've never been near a black girl before. One eye is blue—a bright, light blue—and one is a dark, chocolate brown. She holds out her hand to me. Her shyness is appealing. My core rights itself as I realize she's offering herself to me.

"Bella?" I ask.

The woman shakes her head. "What do you want? I can help you, but I don't feel well. Maybe Rachael can?"

Upon hearing her name, the young girl smiles with a toothy grin.

"I need to talk to Bella," I say. "Or Jules. I'm his brother." Above me, I hear whispering and I look up.

Two young girls giggle. They crook their fingers, waggling their tongues at me.

"Are you Bella?" I ask, again, glancing around at the seascape art on the walls, the brass décor, and then back to the woman. "I need to talk to her. It's important."

"What do you want? Come on in, and we can talk. "

I follow her as she hobbles through a doorway. A light down a narrow hallway reveals several doors. A repetitive "Oh, oh, yeah, big man" comes from behind a door.

She motions down the hallway to a place I imagined very differently. The artwork is similar to what Mother and Papa have on their walls. The couch resembles what is in our living room. Other than the peeling paint on the walls outside and the ecstatic voices coming from behind a door, the brothel is…well…*homey*.

The young woman is asking me a question. "Ya cop? I didn't say anything you can get me on."

A tall, bronzed woman steps into the hallway. She wears a black suit with a large red cloth rose pinned to the lapel. Her hair is blond and swept up in a chignon.

I can't determine her age, but she looks like she stepped out of a fashion magazine. Or an advertisement for a secretarial course.

"Kristen, I will take care of this," she says and turns to me. "I'm Bella. Who are you?" Her voice is soft and expectant. The way she asks me who I am makes me feel like she has all the time in the world to hear whatever I have to say.

As I come closer, I see that she, like the young girl in the entryway, has one light blue eye and one brown eye.

I blurt out, "Yes, so you are Bella, I hear. I need to talk to Jules. I'm his brother. Is he here?"

"You are a friend of Rudy's?" she asks. Her voice continues to be one of curiosity. I have the overpowering sense that I am, quite willingly, being drawn into her sphere.

"Rudy?" I frown.

Someone behind me is tracing an *S* from my shoulders down my spine and, skipping my belt, proceeds down my——. I jump.

Bella peers over my shoulder.

Kristen moves beside me, her fingers still curled. "Ya know…Rudy," she says. "Rudy- toot. Always blowing his horn. That and he's over quick. It's like Rudy and *tooooot!* All over. You're his brother?"

"Kristen?" Bella says with a warning tone. She smiles, baring the whitest, straightest teeth I have ever seen.

Kristen swipes her finger from my butt to my neck and then leaves.

"What's your name?" Bella asks. Again, softly. Warmly. She appears to be ready to take dictation—or any other directions I could give her—if I had the nerve.

"Kor—Ray. My name is Ray."

"So, you're Rudy's brother. Well, well. Come. Let's get to know each other." Bella motions to a door, and as I look over her shoulder, a settee and a carved headboard and all that entails could wait for me.

I have fare for the bus. "I don't have any money. I wanted to talk to Jules…er…Rudy. Can I leave a message with you? Tell him Harold died. That's all."

At that, Bella straightens up. She doesn't blink. Placing her hand on my wrist, she leans toward me. When she bares her teeth again, she looks like she could eat me. Her voice, once coaxing, comes out in a hiss. "Come back, little boy, when you have money. And as for Rudy, message received. Get out!"

For someone in a tight-fitting suit, she moves fast. I'm yanked down the hallway and shoved into the street. The door slams behind me. Above me, giggles and tapping on the windows come from the young girls I had seen earlier standing in the window. They wag their fingers at me, making the motion for money. Then, the little whores disappear, but I'm sure I hear laughter coming from the building.

I go home, unsure if I have accomplished anything.

****

I walk into my house to the heavenly aroma of caramelizing onions.

Gramps is in full-blown Brooklyn-America mode, wearing an apron and whisking eggs in a bowl with a fork. He takes two eggs from a container, and cracking them with one hand, tosses the shells into a soup bowl.

Papa stands beside him, tending to a cast iron skillet with butter, sugar, and creamy, shiny onions.

I stand in the doorway, loving that I'm in my familiar, which is not as familiar as I thought. I have never seen Gramps or Papa cook before.

Gramps is in the middle of a story filled with what sounds like gibberish. "Take those rafts, add axel grease, and I"—he points at the skillet—"I'm going to make this cry. Are you sure we don't have anything that squeals?"

Papa looks at him blankly, and I'm bewildered. "Back on Lapskaus Boulevard." Gramps paws through the icebox's contents for a treasure he might have missed, "we prepared the recipe, poured the bowl into the onions, added what we could scrounge"—he holds up a tin of smoked salmon in triumph—"and created…" Gramps hovers over the skillet, taking a spatula and folding one half of his masterpiece over. "Then…" he continues as he takes the handle, looks up as if offering a prayer, and lifts the skillet. The concoction flips and lands perfectly into the sizzling skillet.

Behind us, hands clap. Mother sidles by me and kisses Gramps' and Papa's cheeks.

The Denver Omelet is delicious. Mother coos over every bite, grateful to be the one tended to today.

Gramps speaks up. "Sonny, we need you to watch Ray while we go to the funeral. What did Jules say?"

"I want to go!" I protest, but the four adults shake their heads. "I passed the message along to his friend." Eyeing Gramps, I shake my head in a silent *Don't ask!* motion while flicking a glance at Gran and Mother.

****

The next morning, Granvin's principal, Herr Sjursen, is teaching Herr Tveit's English class.

Petra Johnson raises her hand. "Where is Herr Tveit?"

Herr Sjursen clears his throat as he gathers the papers on the desk. "I don't…err…there was a family emergency that he had to attend to."

The next day, we have a substitute. And the next.

Thursday morning, walking past the teacher's

lounge, I hear Herr Sjursen talking to an English teacher.

"Herr Larsen, we checked his apartment, and all is in working order. We're trying to reach his family to find out more."

At Granvin, I become a minor celebrity. As I walk from class to class, my classmates rehearse their condolences about Harold, the bolder ones asking, "Did your cousin's body drift into the harbor? How could the police identify him?"

My family boards the bus to Solsvik on Friday morning, full of repeated instructions.

I had asked and received time off from Techworks.

Stein and Rolf, no less subtly than anyone else, ask about Harold's death every day. I go easier on them. Harold's attempt to go to the Shetlands has put a crimp in our plans.

Sunday afternoon, Gramps and Papa sit in the kitchen in their usual spots, drinking beer and peeling potatoes over some newspapers spread out on the table.

"Sonny, get yourself a beer, a potato peeler, and sit down," Gramps commands.

I pop off a bottle cap, chugging the frothy, yeasty beer while noisily rummaging through the kitchen tool drawer.

"Sonny," Gramps says, "Harold was trying to be a foolish hero. He and that teacher. Blown up. For what? You and your friends, you put that crap out of your head."

"I—"

Gramps cuts me with a stern look.

Papa taps Gramps's sleeve, using the tip of his peeler like a surgeon to extricate an eye in the potato. "Andreas," he says softly, drawing out and placing the eye on the newspaper, "his teacher. I don't think Kory knows."

At this, I straighten too fast as I grasp the peeler and the truth.

My father and grandfather rise to steady me as I find my chair.

Papa's next words come to me through what seems to be a thick pane of glass. "Your English teacher— Herr Tveit?—he was on the boat with Harold." My father's teeth come down on his lower lip, and he breathes out slowly. "I'm sorry. The police weren't sure until yesterday morning who, besides Harold, was in the boat. Bertin could identify Harold from the boat, but the others…" He drifts off, his voice lowering further, debating, releasing another drawn-out breath. "The others—we'll probably never identify them. Tveit…" He pats my arm. "I'm sorry."

Gramps breaks in as he mounds the brown strips of skin onto the newspaper. "Sonny…no. Just no. We can resist in other ways. Maybe Jules will let us know what's happening since he seems friendlier with the Germans. But Sonny, none of this foolishness. The bodies…dumped like fish guts into the ocean, and the Nazis blew up the boat. We would have believed his death was an accident and a storm was the cause. But no, they sent a message to whoever was watching, demonstrating what happens to those who try to leave. Their bodies…dragged for miles in fishing nets…"

Gramps stares down at his beer. "Like chum." He sits, flipping the potato peeler between his fingers. "A point was made."

Gramps' eyes turn dark blue when he's angry—or scared like he is now.

"Bertin...he's aged a hundred years. The whole family. The town was gossiping, eyeing us as if we knew about the escape, but get this, the Germans come by and tell us we must break up the *party*. A guest started shouting. He told that damn German punk it was a goddamn funeral. I haven't seen anger like that. Sonny?" Gramps looks me straight in the eye. "No."

Papa looks at Gramps and me. "Kory?" His tone is kind and gentle, but I know as sure as the sun rises in the east what the next question will be. "Kory, where is your head? What are you thinking?"

I have no plausible excuse. "Um...I don't. Sorry. I was thinking about Harold. He was a nice guy."

Papa stops peeling potatoes and taps his finger on my forearm. "You. Your friends. Gramps is right, and Jules hears things. He might share his information with us, but reprimanding him is uncomfortable for me. Not my kin, but I raised him. He's like my own son, though."

Gramps nods toward the growing mound of potato peels. "We need to talk to you about this."

My face flushes. Folded in the middle is a small insert with a script I know well.

"What do we have here?" With a harsh stroke, Gramps shaves off a sliver of potato skin, which hits the edge of *The Whole Truth* like a slap. "Says here"— Gramps' finger points to the script I had helped to typeset only a few days before. "Says here, people had a boat with a radio picking up the BBC and Radio Andorra. The Nazis will kill anyone who houses a traitor or someone from England." He picks up another potato. "In fact"— his finger points to my article— "says here, *practically word for word*, what I told you two weeks ago. The exact phrasing. Whaddya know about that?" He looks me up and down.

Unmoving, as if frozen, I stare at the insert lying on the table in front of Papa.

"Sonny," Papa says, "you have to be careful. You are going to be questioned if the war drags on much longer, and you'd better have a satisfactory answer."

I pull a potato from the pile and lean forward to avoid eye contact with Gramps and Papa. Then, digging in with the peeler, I create what looks to be a long, satisfactory strip from the top. But their hands are not moving. Instead, their fingers curl over the tabletop like soldiers in formation.

Don't look up, Kory. They will know, Kory. Hell, they already know.

The tip of my potato peeler catches on an eye and nicks the web between my thumb and index finger. I put my mouth on the cut, not daring to raise my eyes.

But didn't they describe Harold and Herr Tveit as *chum?* What a great headline.

****

The sight of the Ace of Clubs in my parents' ice-covered mailbox makes me happy. I have the perfect headline and story. But contrary to what Gramps and Papa think, *The Whole Truth* is causing problems for the Germans. Our news is being torn down around town by the guards, only to reappear again. The Shetland Gang—the people transporting is increasing.

Three hours later, Paul asks about including Harold and Herr Tveit by name in our newsletter but decides to call Harold *an island boy* and Herr Tveit, *a celebrated teacher*. He writes of both as heroes and uses the English word *chum* to explain that Harold and Herr Tveit were not fish bait, but friends. Friends and colleagues. One of his articles reads, "As true heroes, they will not be forgotten. Brothers to the cause."

Cranking out the edition, Stein stops for a moment, snapping his fingers for me to pass my cigarette to him.

Jan and Rolf lean in, reading the text. Jan rubs his nose with his thumb, and Rolf's eyes are downcast.

I crank the printer's wheel, waiting for a protest from the others. Like a locomotive pulling out of a station, the wheel spins faster and faster.

And, as a late spring squall covers the ground with snow, sheltered among my chums, I cry.

****

Several days later, the Ace of Clubs is in my parents' mailbox. That, in and of itself, is not newsworthy. However, a small envelope addressed to me in a woman's hand lies beside the playing card.

Juggling the book bag I hold, I clench the perfumed envelope in my teeth as I open the door to our home. The invitation, written in Ingrid's neat hand, is for a party at Paul's house. Of course, I must buy a gift, which means another trip to see Jules.

An hour later, I swing open the Bibop's door to get an album for the birthday boy. Easy as pie if they have Alfredo Brito.

Jules is playing the piano for an appreciative audience as I come inside. His fingers curl over the treble keys while his left hand is splayed out, coaxing a boogie-woogie from the bass keys. Next, he switches to Bach's "Minuet in G," his shoulders squaring, his posture straightening, his mouth forming a pious, holier-than-thou line. He smiles at a young boy, calling over his shoulder to the boy's mother that the Bibop offers piano lessons. Jules finishes his showcase by playing the beginning of Gershwin's "Rhapsody in Blue."

Swinging his legs around to face his customers, he smiles. "Never a lesson! Except through the Bibop, of course." He holds his smile, his bright enthusiasm not waning for even a second. That's until they turn toward me. Then all emotion, like a wet rock drying in the sun, evaporates.

The mother and son depart.

Jules closes the piano's fallboard and pushes in the bench.

"Do you have any rumba music? 'Siboney' or 'Green Eyes,' maybe?' " I ask in an even tone while scanning his shirt for a tell.

Although today's shirt has button cuffs rather than the French cuffs he prefers, his fingers seek a cuff, stroking the buttons. Meanwhile, Jules eyes me like a seasoned Solsvik Bridge player. He doesn't appear to be breathing.

My guess is that neither do I.

I launch into the conversation that has gotten us through the last three encounters. How are you? Fine. You? The parents? They're fine. Pause. We're like first-time actors that have forgotten our lines.

I remember what comes next. "Techworks and school are fine. How is the Gold Dust? And the Bibop?" That's his cue to talk about the pawn shop. I don't mention Bella. My internal stage manager prompts me on my next lines. I ask—brightly—about the ration-card committee.

Jules is snide. "That's what this visit is all about? Not a concern for your dear older brother. Why are you interrogating me? You can't rat me out. Get that through your thick skull! It's going fine. I'm respected, and that's all you need to know. I wish you'd stop gossiping with those people and grow up!"

Jules' voice has risen, and his cheeks are flushed. "I know what you are doing. Every single time"—Jules draws out these words as if he's pulverizing them— "you have a party with your fair-weather friends, you come in and ask me questions. I don't think you're as innocent as you want us to believe. People are starting to watch you and your friends." He turns to leave.

I grab one of his suspenders. "You take it back!"

He pushes me back. "That's all you have? Your big talk? Your pretty words from your pretty friends? Such a big tough guy. Wow!" Jules's fingers spread across his face in a picture of fake surprise. "Wow! You terrify me!"

My elbow draws back, and as I ball my fist to hit him, the door opens, the bell clangs, and my life changes forever.

Chapter Twenty-Four

"Wowza!" I have seen cartoons where the character's eyes bug out, and their jaw hits the floor. I now understand that.

Smiling at my outburst, a copper-haired girl says, "Hello to you too!" in halting Norwegian with a strange accent.

Jules, adjusting his suspenders and knocking me on the shoulder in a we-were-just-fooling-around way, scurries to where the girl stands.

She surveys the record store, her eyes running over the pianos, trumpets, and guitars. Wavey, coppery hair tied with a black satin ribbon lies over one shoulder. She wears a royal-blue jacket and gray tweed trousers, and as she walks to where I'm standing, something on top of her loafers glints in the light.

Bringing my eyes from her feet to her face, I gaze into the blackest eyes I have ever seen. "Coins? In your shoes?"

"Pennies. Did I interrupt anything? I thought you two were going to go at it for a second. Reminds me of a story about a bar fight my dad saw back when he was working near Spindletop. That's in Texas."

Deepening her voice, she continues, "My father said, 'The juke joint was going to get messed up, Anne. Hell of a thing! Best barbecue in four states, too.' One of his favorite places. I'm Anne, by the way, in case you two are being…oh…what is the word?" She mutters in another language.

Jules' face lights up. He speaks back to her in a language that makes him seem to gargle.

She nods, talking back to him in the same gargling way.

I cough.

Anne turns her charm back on me. Her eyes, I now notice, are jet black with green flecks in them. She has narrow eye sockets. The effect is mysterious. She peers up at me with a bemused smile. "You don't speak Dutch? Too bad. How's your English?"

Jules and I chime in at the same time. "I speak English!"

"We'll see about that." She peels off a glove, revealing pale, freckled skin and lacquered blood-red fingernails. Reaching for us both, she commands, "Now, you boys shake hands! Be done with it! And who do I talk to about getting decent bayou music?"

Jules never says, "I don't know." Instead, the master of sleight of hand guides her to American music, studying her as she flicks through the albums. He's a good salesman.

As we draw her out, her shaky Norwegian steadies, and we learn that her fluency in Dutch and English stems from having spent time as a child in both Amsterdam and Texas, America.

"Is Texas close to Brooklyn, America?" I ask. I'm planning. She and Gramps can talk, and I can spend time with her.

Anne's tawny eyebrows knit together. She snorts with laughter, and Jules chimes in at my stupidity. "Oh, not hardly. I've been to New York, of course." She tosses that off as if it were an ordinary occurrence. Curiosity gets the better of her. "How do you know of Brooklyn, America?" She steps closer to me, her coal-black eyes searching mine.

Jules' hand brushes Anne's. "We have Fats Waller. I tell you what"—he walks to the piano he had used only minutes before to awe an audience—"when I play the music you like, you can tell me." Lifting the fallboard and pulling out the bench, he once again plays "Minuet in *G*," assuming the same posture and poses as before.

Giggling, Anne shakes her head. He plays a few bars of a boogie-woogie tune.

Again, she shakes her head.

Jules plays a riff on the piano, his fingers dancing down the keys.

Anne raises her voice. "I'd like to hear the music played in some backwater juke joint near Shreveport that serves dry rub barbecue, cold beer, and even colder watermelon."

"W. C. Handy," I say. "Robert Johnson."

She rifles through the bins, flicking her blood-red fingernails, even though nail polish is supposed to be unattainable. Finally, her fingers stop, and she puts her index finger on my chest.

I think my heart is going to stop.

"So, how do you two know each other?" She taps her nail against her teeth before turning to give us both the once over, as if sizing us up. "And where do you go to school?"

Jules wades right in. "Kory and I are half-brothers. Two halves of the same coin. I'm two years older, work two jobs, speak two languages, and try twice as hard as my dear, younger brother here. I'm enrolled in the school of the world."

Anne seems flustered by his anger toward me, and I see my opening. I practically coo— after all, she did put her finger on *my* chest. "We're brothers. We both like music and want to better ourselves. I want to become an engineer and am learning work's practical side."

With a satisfied air, I make my play. "If you won't think me forward, I'd like to take you to my favorite bakery and introduce you to Bergen's famous roll. Then, we can talk about W. C. Handy and Robert Johnson. Would you like that? I'm sure Jules has work to do." Another Brooklyn-America expression creeps into my head—*shit-eating grin.*

Giving said grin to Jules, I offer my arm to Anne.

She looks up at me and dazzles me with a smile, promising me the world.

My heart is going to stop.

Jules glowers at me but smiles pleasantly at Anne, encouraging her to come by and visit the shop any time. He gently kisses her hand. "Until then."

I catch a glimpse of Anne and myself in a store window. Arm in arm, we are sauntering like movie stars.

"Mercy! Your brother! Well!" Anne, clearly flattered, laughs, and then waves her hand over her face as if to conjure away the rivalry between Jules and me. "Where is this bakery?" she asks, clutching my arm and giving it a good-natured squeeze. "And how do you know about Robert Johnson?"

Neptun Konditori is just ahead, and I put my nose in the air, drawing in the delicious aroma of baking bread. Taking her hand, I lead her into my favorite bakery as if I own the place. We sit in the same chairs where I met my source for Robert Johnson and W. C. Handy. Over several coffees and a shared Bergen's Skillingsboller, Anne laughs boisterously as she regales me with tales of Houston and Amsterdam, the boarding school she attended in England, and being brought to Bergen, as her father's company likes keeping families together.

Later, as we walk to her bus stop, she entwines her arm with mine. "Mercy! This was wonderful!"

I lean in to kiss her cheek.

She reaches up to stroke my face. "You are the cat's meow. Toodles!"

My heart stops.

I walk into Paul's shed empty handed.

Jan is bent over the printing press, inserting another ink cartridge for *The Whole Truth*s' latest edition.

Elbowing Stein, Rolf groans.

Paul looks up. "No! He's mooning. Look at him!"

Jan's neck snaps up. He shakes his head in mock terror. "What's her name?"

"Her name is Anne Thompson," I begin. "She's from America. And Amsterdam. And England."

Stein and Rolf make kissing noises.

I wave away the teasing. "She says "Mercy!" and "juke joint" a lot, and I don't understand half of what she says, but who cares? She's gorgeous!" Placing my hand over my heart, I pat my chest.

They stop talking.

"I met Anne at Jules' shop," I continue.

Paul and Jan eye each other.

"Jules met her, too? How did that go?" Stein asks warily.

I give them the highlights—the near fight, Anne coming in at the right time, Jules fawning over her, and her having coffee with me.

"So, Jules met her too. Hmmm." Paul nods slowly. "He won't give up. Especially since you like her."

As we leave the shed, and Paul turns off the lights, the ink's metallic smell and our activities catch in the door before being closed off from the world.

I walk across the manicured lawn, past the petunias closing shop for the evening, into an early morning news drop. I'm touching my face and remembering.

Chapter Twenty-Five

"How does drilling for oil work, exactly?" I ask, spending the last of my week's pay on the espresso and skillingsboller before me.

A vibrant red index fingernail grazes my arm, arranging the reddish-blonde hair on my wrist into a heart. The finger reaches onto the plate, dipping into the cinnamon-laced powdered sugar. Anne, using her finger as a paintbrush, begins dabbing the sugar onto the heart.

"I wish I could see you more often." She sighs, signaling the waiter for another coffee.

That's two more bus fares I will have to forego.

"Daddy... er... Papa doesn't talk about his work. He works for the same company as your friend Jan's father, but in a different department. My dad is a drilling engineer, so he works with geologists and determines where the best places are to drill oil. He was in New Orleans and Houston. He went to Amsterdam. This is boring to talk about, don't you think?"

"Why did you come to Norway?"

Anne's hooded eyes flash at my question, their green flecks darkening. She lifts the demitasse to her crimson lips and empties the contents, the string of pearls at her throat rising and falling as the liquid slides down inside of her.

Reaching for her raincoat with the black-rust-and-beige checked scarf, she waves her hand, weighing the question. "Dad has a government contract. One moment, I'm in London at a boarding school, preparing to go to school in Switzerland, and the next thing I know, I'm on a ship from Amsterdam to here for who knows how long. Bergen is *not* Amsterdam or London. Not by a long shot." Anne looks at her wristwatch and leans over to kiss my cheek. "This was fun, but I have a piano tutor coming by the house in an hour. Good to see you. Maybe you can change your schedule so we can spend more time together. That's what my tutor did. He rearranged his schedule. For me."

Watching her depart, I count the cash I have left. I will be walking everywhere until payday.

Ten days later, my heart quickens as the reflection of a copper-headed beauty strolls toward Caspian's Cafe. Caspian's isn't a café, with its table linens and fancy menu. As Gramps and Anne have told me with their American phrases, it's a place to get *dolled up.*

I breathe a sigh of relief, and my friends gasp when Anne strolls into the cafe as if she owns the place. Anne's coppery hair hangs in loose ringlets around her shoulders. Two tortoiseshell and pearl clasps pull her hair up and away from her face, which is flushed with excitement, I hope, to see me. The hem of her ruby and black polka dot dress grazes her knees. As she turns to take off her black wrap, the faint sheen of silk stockings flickers in the light. Red toes peek out of her black patent-leather open-toed shoes.

She sashays to the table. As I rise to greet her, Anne captivates me by stroking my cheek. "Never mind my *y'alls* and my Scarlett-meets-Amsterdam drawl. I'm happy to meet you," she says eagerly, introducing herself to Ingrid, Stein, and Rolf and nodding to Paul and Jan.

Tossing her head, she turns to me with a fox-like grin. "Mercy! So, these are your friends? I never!"

Ingrid looks back and forth between Anne and me, shaking her finger at me in a mock scold. "Kory! Why didn't you pick up Anne at her house?"

Anne pats my arm. "I had a million errands to run, and I had to squeeze in a piano lesson, so I told Kory I would meet him and all of you here. It was no bother." She squeezes my arm, leaning into me. "Kory understands my busy schedule." She nudges me and gives everyone else a captivating smile.

A rumba comes on, and Paul and Ingrid quickly excuse themselves to dance.

Anne looks at me expectantly.

Taking her hand, I lead her to the dance floor. Fortunately for me, Anne has been taught the style Paul, Ingrid, and I have been practicing, so I rumba my way across the floor. All the while, I am retreating, counting a million reasons why I can never be the extravagant boarding-school and casual-shopping-trips-to-London-and-Paris golden child that she is.

As we start, the second song is a foxtrot. Thank God! A dance I know.

Anne whispers in my ear. "I'm so lucky to have met you. I think you are wonderful."

I smile down at her, kissing her cheek, twirling her, and making her laugh. The world once again becomes my oyster.

Except that the Spartan and Rolf, who have nursed their drinks and bruised dating egos all evening, are scowling. At me.

As Anne and I walk back to the table, she excuses herself to "powder her nose" while Paul and Ingrid step outside.

I slide onto a chair next to Jan and Rolf when a loud belch rumbles across the room.

Uniformed Germans have commandeered a piano that stands in the café's far corner.

They remind me of cartoon characters as they try to remain upright by clutching the top of the piano. Two of them, whom I nickname *Drunk* and *Stupid*, point toward our table and then lean over to the pianist with an apparent request.

He looks over his shoulder at us and nods, earning the moniker—*Boot-Licking Collaborator*. With no hesitation, the pianist launches into the strains of "Erika," a German war song.

There isn't any doubt as to whom this song is dedicated.

A pimply-faced boy who I dub *Ugly* spreads his doughy fingers across his face, stretching his mouth into an unnatural, hideous smile. "The *Face!*" he calls out.

Jan and I clamp down hard on Rolf's arms.

"Sit. Down. Now!" Jan hisses into Rolf's ear. "Don't even think about it!"

A soldier, whom I christen *Smart*, grips the pianist's shoulder. He draws his finger across his neck in a kill-it motion. As he leans over the pianist, Smart says, "We shouldn't sing this. Not here!"

Ugly is far from finished. "Let's dedicate this to The Face. He's right over there."

How much longer do I have to smile like an idiot to everyone while keeping my friend from tackling everyone in sight? My hand is getting tired of holding Rolf's arm, but this evening will be over if I let go. Rolf's arm is trembling and hard. Remembering his anger at the lake and at other times over the past year, I clamp down harder.

Undeterred, the pianist begins singing a song about what the German soldiers will do to the English soldiers.

Hoots of laughter come from a nearby table.

Still smiling like a goddamn idiot, I look across Rolf's tie and chest to where Jan is taking cues from *me*. I lean over to Rolf, smiling like I'm ordering coffee. "Knock it off," I say. "Do you want to be arrested? Think of the publicity about that."

There are bows by all, but Ugly, and the soldiers leave.

Anne slides a compact into her purse and smiles at the departing soldiers. "That taught them, didn't it! I mean, they're supposed to be here and all, but that ruffles people's feathers. We see the good the Germans do and how the English can't be trusted. That song. It's about the English, not the Norwegians. They aren't rubbing the Norwegians' faces in it, do you think?"

Rolf rises, excusing himself from the table.

I don't catch all he whispers as he rises, but I do hear, "I'm not the one with the problems here."

The Spartan stands up. Then, putting one hand behind his back like a butler serving drinks, he takes Anne's hand, shakes it, and wishes us a good evening. He turns to me, saluting sharply. It could be a joke, but his eyes say otherwise.

"Probably time to get back home," Anne says. She opens her evening bag, dabbing at her lips with her finger. Resting her arm on my forearm, she rises.

"Can I walk you home?" I ask.

She nods, curling herself into the crook of my arm.

Half-listening to Anne's talk about a bicycle she

rode in Amsterdam, I reflect on how Paul and Ingrid interact. So, I decide I will be the perfect gentleman, like Paul. But Anne isn't like Ingrid. She's skittish, direct, naive, and worldly all at the same time. Trying to be courtly is not working.

Anne squeezes my hand and nestles harder into the crook of my arm.

Paul's way is the right way. What was I thinking?

I'm beginning to think things are going well, when Anne starts talking about a boy in England and an invitation to a coming-out at a debutante ball in Houston. My brain and stomach somersault. Those are things that don't matter to me.

She takes my hand and tugs on my arm. Pulling my collar down, she kisses my cheek and murmurs about a lovely evening. She walks backward, blowing me a kiss. I step toward her, but she shakes her head.

I'm ten meters down the road when I hear her voice. Her surprise. His tone, even from this distance, is clear. Ever the salesman, he's overcoming an objection, performing a sleight of hand that might conjure love.

I stop walking. Wishing for another conclusion, I step closer. Their laughter is killing me.

****

All during church, Sunday supper, school, and now at Marine Techworks, I have replayed the evening at the café a thousand times in my head.

Her drawing a heart on my wrist. Her smiling at me. The way she said my name. The piano tutor. The boyfriends in Houston and who knows where else. Her expensive tastes. Her bluntness. The way she laughed in the dark after I left. With Jules.

Herr Henricksen calls my name as I'm putting

together a design for a canning machine.

Putting down my work, I walk with him to the swinging doors. As Herr Henricksen passes through the doorway in front of me, I see the pennies in her shoes. I wish I could say I'm excited to see her.

Anne's invitation is for an evening of music. As she burbles on about how excited she's to see me, she peers at the door, widening at the hive of noise beyond it.

I want to believe. I do.

She's reaching out to me. I'm an idiot if I don't go. I need to know.

****

With its rose garden, the Thompson's house lies in clear sight of BST. The artwork in the living room is not European but displays horses and cowboys. A bouquet of yellow roses sits in a cut-glass vase in the shape of a boot. Anne's mother wears the most massive earrings I have ever seen and bright florals. She, like her daughter, says "Mercy!" a lot. And "Bless your heart!" which Anne does not say. Maps and pictures of tall towers with black clouds funneling out of them line Herr Thompson's study. In the bay window overlooking BST's turrets is a grand piano. As I sit down, I read the name of the manufacturer and give out a low whistle—a Steinway.

I pick out the first strains of "J'aime Suzy," replacing Suzy's name with Anne's.

Anne coos with delight. "I know this one! Jules visited me earlier today to say hi and to give me additional piano assignments. He played this song. He said you bought a present for Paul at the Bibop. Jules wants to be a music teacher. He's encouraging me, too. Isn't that sweet?"

Her mother bustles in the kitchen, making a big clatter, pretending not to eavesdrop on us.

Like a cat rubbing against a sofa leg, Anne arches her back as she settles on the piano bench next to me. Her shoulder and arm seek and find shelter in my body, and her hair, now flecked with golden strands, brushes against me. As I span an octave with my right hand, her index finger, its nail, now a lacquered burgundy, circles my pinky.

My upper chest tightens. She squeezes my hand and giggles; however, I have seen her with Jules, and I heard her laugh. I'm not wrong about her laugh, am I? Swallowing hard, not wanting the answer that lies in her deep-set eyes, I concentrate on the piano keys.

Fru Thompson comes in with a tray of cookies and milk. "You must have worked up an appetite. Here. Do you know 'Fur Elise'? That's a favorite." She plops into the brocade chair beside the piano.

Anne shimmies away from my hip and toward her mother. "Mama, Jules is so good at that song. Kory wants to be an engineer like Daddy. Jules is industrious and is working three jobs. He never stops!"

Is she an idiot? What's she doing? I stare at both of them. Her mother dusts the cookie's icing from her fingers onto a cloth napkin and sniffs. "This is such an old, small town."

Anne stares into the distance, a faint smile playing about the corners of her mouth. Then, she lowers her head toward the piano keys, closing her eyes and pressing a finger to her lips.

Ah…a good thought.

But not about me.

****

"Edvard Grieg was as tiny as your grandmother? Did you see him once?" Anne asks.

I flatten out the blanket so Anne can press her perfectly pink toes on my legs. Massaging her big toe, I feel the ribbing and webbing on the sole and the shiny-as-glass toenail. I smile and give her toe a gentle shake, plucking a tulip from the garden behind us, waving the flower toward the Music Pavilion and back at the girl I love.

Two weeks after going to Caspian's Café, Anne and I are enjoying a warm summer afternoon picnic on the flower-edged lawn of Bergen's Festival Park. Ducks and seagulls swim lazily in the park's lake. There has been no more talk of Jules or her piano lessons. From the way her face lights up when she sees me, I'm convinced that she has made up her mind about me.

I point to the aquamarine statue near the Grieg Music Pavilion, where the Norwegian composer's statue stands in perpetuity, ready to stroll around his beloved Bergen. "He died in 1907. Gramps saw him once when Grieg was walking near here. Gramps brought Gran here to walk around the lake, tell her he was going to America, and propose marriage. She turned him down. He didn't listen to Grieg's music for many years because it made him sad."

I hand the pink tulip—nearly the shade of her toes—to my beloved. "Later, after my great-grandfather died, Gramps returned to Norway. He again asked Gran to take a walk here and asked her the same twenty-year-old question. She said yes."

Anne sits up and kisses me. "Yes," she says, her eyes wet with tears.

Drowsy with lunch and what I hope is mutual love,

we stroll beside the lupine and tulip-lined path around the park's lake.

Anne rests her head against my shoulder, swinging the picnic basket. "I can add another item to what I like about living here." As the basket bounces against my thigh, she continues. "The summer here is like early February in Houston. July in Houston is a swampy soupy mess. And Bergen doesn't have cockroaches the size of garbage trucks!" She smiles and glances at my face. "I liked hearing that lovely story." Following my gaze, she looks across the street.

Our eyes meet. We join hands and dash toward the bus station's brick arched entrance.

Moments later, as we stand by the open door of the bus, she raises her chin, her eyes searching mine. "Well…"

I bend down to kiss her.

She turns her head, murmuring, "I will see you soon."

****

I wouldn't describe Bergen as swampy, but the breeze coming through my basement window feels good that evening.

Outside, six booted feet are pushing aside my mother's prized bayberry hedge.

"I'll call out," says Jan. "He'll know it's us. Hoot!"

I tap the window in return and run up the flight of stairs, flinging open the front door. Paul, Rolf, and Jan stand waist-high in the shrubbery. I'm about to salute when I see tears running down Rolf and Jan's faces.

"Mathias— Christ! What are we going to do? We have to tell Stein," Rolf gasps.

I don't understand. "What are you talking about?"

Paul looks down. "Mathias was executed last night, Kory. Late last night, the neighbors heard shouting and shots, and all became quiet. A neighbor claims he saw three young men running from Mathias' house. Mathias, his sister Katrina, and their parents—all executed. The murderer wrote *traitor* on their living room wall. In their blood."

I take a step back. Tears sting my eyes. "For what? What did he do?"

"We heard Mathias' neighbor keeps a list of the people who come to see Mathias and who's from the neighborhood and who's not. The neighbor also attends the movie theater and knows about what you and Stein have been doing. To make the Forum janitor talk, the killers pulled out his fingernails. He's dead too. They cut off his finger, too, and wrote *traitor* on a wall inside his house. We will get found out. We have to stop what we're doing."

"We need to avenge their deaths!" I bluster.

Paul purses his lips. "We can't. They will find us and kill us. We must keep our mouths shut and be more discreet about what we do…or…we stop now. If Mathias can be outed, we can, too. We need to be more careful."

"Or stop," Jan and Rolf say together.

"We need to use the King of Spades," I say. "We agreed on that. That's our stop card. We stop now."

I hear Gramps inside, talking to Gran about dinner and how much he loves her. As my three friends depart, I remember that we never voted the King of Hearts as the *stop-love* card.

Over lamb and potatoes, Ray is bursting with a secret. "I heard that a whole family was wiped out last night for fighting the Nazis. A kid told us Mathias tried to fight, and he screamed when they broke his fingers one by one." Ray takes his hands and pretends to break them. His body twists, and he crosses his eyes in mock injury. "His tongue was cut out and used to write on the wall."

A sharp slap cracks through the room.

I'm not the only one that has heard enough.

"Mamaaa…!" Ray races out of the room, knocking over his glass of milk as his plate of food hits the floor.

"Disgusting talk if you ask me," says Gran. "We don't need that at the dinner table. Kory, did you know Mathias especially well?" Gran's voice is as soft and fluid as the cotton yarn she knits.

I slice my lamb chop, chewing for several seconds before answering. "No, not really. He's a kid I know. He plays…er…played at the Forum Kino."

I think back to the evenings when Mathias played piano and Stein ingested information found under the piano bench. Who is going to do that now?

"Since that's a good job, and Jules is talented, I think he should apply for the job," Gran says. "He's a genius when it comes to playing popular pieces. I'll tell him about it." She picks up her china plate. Scraping her knife across it, she brushes the leftover food onto an empty platter, signaling that the subject is now closed.

****

I'm not a traitor. My friends and I are not traitors.

Later that evening, I hear a tap on the window and a low hoot. Scissor legs are shadows on the ceiling. I tiptoe up the stairs, avoiding the dreaded second step, and open the door.

"Come inside and come downstairs," I whisper.

I walk to the third step down and hold up my hand.

"Step over this one." After closing the bedroom window, I pull up the desk chair, knocking aside my canning- and knitting-machine designs.

Jan sits on my bed.

As we have done when making over a million important decisions, the Spartan and I sit across from each other, bodies squared, heads nearly touching.

"How'd Stein take the news?" I ask.

"Scared shitless. How'd you think?" Jan's blue eyes are wide with fright. "I'm glad I'm from here. I took every back alley and crept through every yard I could to get here. Stein—he's a wreck—but he told me the strangest story."

My fingers flick his hand. "What?"

"Stein says he's not in trouble. We aren't in trouble. And you're not going to believe this next shit. Stein thinks his brother Bill played a part in the killings."

I pull back, my mouth gaping. "Bill"—I snap my fingers—"he kills people and leaves for England? That's not possible."

"Stein swears he heard footsteps in his kitchen three nights ago, and when he went to Bill's bedroom to get a book, the closet door was open, and Bill's favorite boots were gone."

I raise my hand, and Jan stops talking. Fru Eklund's front door opens with a loud squeak.

Jan and I watch the shadows of the long leash, the thin silhouette clutching its chest, and the figure scooping up and nuzzling the wriggling puppy. The door closes.

"Fru Eklund got a new puppy," I say.

"So, Anne? Is she the one?" The Spartan knows how to cut to the chase.

With a wave of my hand, I knock down a cobweb I've meant to clean for months. I nod, looking for a tell in my best friend's face. "I think I'm in love with her."

Jan's smile is rueful. "Yes, you think you do."

"Anne says her father works with your father."

Jan shrugs his shoulders. "Government project." His tone has changed back to one more take-charge. "I mentioned Herr Thompson to Papa, and his reaction suggested that he doesn't know him. Herr Thompson is on a government assignment. That's all he knows."

The Spartan clicks his tongue and changes the subject. "She must keep you on your toes."

I shake my head. "Jules is not giving up. But I'm in love with her."

Jan stands up, slapping my leg as he moves off my bed. "Yes, you think you are."

****

The lunchtime crowd has thinned out. "I'm looking for sheet music for 'J'aime Suzy.' Do you have it? My brother Jules says he has ordered it."

The Bibop's new clerk smiles. "Oh, your brother Jules bought it for a girl he likes. He has a girl he talks to, and he thinks the music will seal the deal. Those were his exact words."

I stammer out a thank you or think that I do, my face flushing with embarrassment.

The clerk's smile fades. His eyes lower to a sheaf of paper near the cash register, then look up as if hoping that I'm dropping the matter.

I'm not going to give her up and certainly not to Jules. Hurrying back to Techworks and ignoring the sign forbidding personal calls, I telephone Anne from Fru Martin's desk at Techworks and ask her to meet me at the Bibop.

The afternoon drags on, but at last, I'm able to leave work and go to the Bibop.

Anne glides into the record shop wearing a red-striped shirt, pearls, and white linen pants. Her finger- and toenails, now a sherbet red-orange, compliment her outfit.

"I wanted to give you a surprise," I say in greeting. "Pick out the music you want. I'm paying for it."

Anne hugs my neck and picks up a songbook costing half my week's pay. I swallow hard and plunk down the money, mentally calculating what I will have to give up. I have roughly enough left for bus fare and maybe a coffee, and that's it.

Crooking my finger, I lean in toward her and whisper, "I have a secret I want to tell you, but you have to come with me." Then I reach out to stroke her cheek, but she turns, and my hand catches on her clavicle.

She jumps back, slapping my hand away.

The clerk's eyes widen, and he starts toward us, but Anne waves him away.

"I can't wait any longer to tell you!" she says. "I got a new job at the Forum Kino. Finally, I get to play the music I miss doing. It's going to be great!"

She leans over the keyboard and studiously begins playing a piece from the songbook, craning her head out stiffly. The piece isn't difficult, but she keeps hitting all the wrong notes.

She's nervous. I think Jules has already won, but not without a fight. I know how I can win her over. I need to be alone with her. She will be proud of what I'm doing.

"Come with me." I reach out, and she takes my hand.

We leave the store and walk to Bergen's main street. The streetlights glow in the falling dusk.

"Look up." I point to the funicular's twinkling lights. "I have a secret to tell you, and I can't wait to show you. But it must be a secret. Do you promise?"

She nods, her eyes more curious than proud.

"Are you going to be in the army, joining with the troops and helping us become better neighbors and allies?" Anne clutches the songbook to her chest against an incessant breeze.

"What? No," I say, exasperated by her interruption. "Do you see that third twinkling light from the top? We take a trail to a cabin near the summit, and we use that trail to take things through checkpoints. We're good at it."

Anne steps back. "Where?" Her tone is accusatory. "You? No! I don't believe you. They will kill you. How long have you been smuggling? With whom?"

Questions tumble out of her mouth faster than I have answers. Her tone is not full of the pride I hoped for, but much worse than I could have imagined. She doesn't believe me. She thinks I'm lying.

"We smuggle gun parts and ammunition and take them to the cabin, and we can go through the line," I say with pride, knowing that my words will surely convince her. With a smirk, I recall *Kippers* and the catcalls that he got. "The Germans are so stupid. They don't know who they have. One time, we brought through guns—"

"Guns? You took *guns?*" she shrieks, as the syllables reverberate off the store windows and passersby slow to stare at us. "To kill the Nazis?" she continues, her voice now ricocheting down the street. "They're going to be good for our economy and will help us. How can you go against them?" Her rebuttal concluded in triumph, Anne takes two steps away from me.

What is the matter with her? I look at her hard. Have I mentioned anyone's names? "You can't tell anyone," I say, lowering my voice, horrified by the pleading that has now replaced my prideful tone. "We'll go to the cabin, and I'll tell you about the good we're doing." I reach to take her fingers in mine. My eyes search hers for a capitulation. Anything. Anything at all. "The guns are in a little cabin by the stream in those woods, near the lake. It's a short walk," gesturing with my free hand. Are the lights on the funicular fading? Or is that my hope? "It would be good to show you. You'll see that what we're doing is good for our people."

She had to believe me. We're doing good. Why doesn't she believe me?

She narrows her eyes and then pokes me with her finger. "No! My Papa says we must cooperate and collaborate. It's good for our business. My Papa has more contracts now than he ever did. They're so happy to have met him, and we even get extra ration cards! Jules has been so nice about that, and we can go to different places without a pass. The Germans treat us so well. Those lies you told…they're lies! The Germans want to help us get back on our feet. The people who are against that…I don't know how anyone cannot be supportive. It's good for our country."

I shake my head. "I will show you, and you will be proud. I'll bet I know where I can get a German uniform." I know I'm babbling, and I should stop, but my mouth keeps moving. Anything to keep her in front of me. Anything to let her know who I am and how she will be proud of me and ashamed of what Jules is doing.

"You think smuggling is good? By lying? You're trying to overthrow the government! The one that stepped in to help save Norway. My papa says—"

"My papa, my papa, my papa! What do *you* say, Anne? Am I a hero? Do you want to see me again? Trust me, it's heroic, and you should change your mind."

"For the last time, Kory, no! Please leave me alone, and don't you ever come to see me again. I'm going straight to Jules and Papa. You're going to get what's coming to you."

Anne flings the songbook into my face, then stalks away as the pages meant to captivate her fall to the ground. Her crimson hair streams down her back, forming a capital 'L.' For Liar. Or Loser. Or Left. As she fades into the evening crowd, my last image of her is of her pushing her arm back, palm up. Leave.

Picking up the smudged book, I gaze at the funicular lights twinkling brightly in the night sky. But not for me. As one tear, then another, and soon a torrent streams down my face, the realization of what I have done settles upon me. Lost.

Chapter Twenty-Six

I'm most definitely breaking a family rule. And probably the rule about being a good co-worker here in Techworks' kitchen. Tamping out the third nervous cigarette in an hour, I tap the ashes into a half-full coffee cup that belongs to one of the machinists. Like passengers clinging to a life raft, the ashes line the cup's sides. I drop the cigarette butt into the cup. As I run my fingers along the rim, sloshing the coffee back and forth, I watch the butt rise against the cresting liquid and then fall back to bobbing complacently.

Gramps found the Craven *A* tobacco can floating near Smuggler's Rock on his latest fishing and bridge trip to Solsvik and gave the tin to me.

My leaving a butt in the cup at home would have Gramps sputtering with what he calls *a walleyed fit*.

Brooklyn-Americanisms be damned.

Anne won't tell. She's upset, but she would never do that.

I walk through the doors leading to the boneyard, rubbing at my neck. For the fourth time today, the bile rising in my throat burns.

The parts—categorized and memorized—have conspired against me. All I want is an unbattered tin sheet that I can rivet as a prototype for the canning machine Techworks is designing. I step up on the pile of metal. Righting myself, I survey the battered, dented, rusted possibilities.

I bring a half-assed candidate inside. Not much wiggle room, but workable.

Anne won't tell.

I'm planing the burrs off the tin, my nose centimeters from the flying confetti, much like Herr Henricksen's so many months ago. I smell the caramel fragrance of the cologne Jules wore at Solsvik.

A finger adorned with a ruby-encrusted gold ring turns off the machine. Jules claws my uniform, his hot breath pushing against my face, nauseatingly sweet with the odor of rum. "*You* think you can get by with your dealings? *You* aren't man enough. We're on to you."

Small, shiny metal curls fly onto my cheek and imbed into my hand as I grip the worktable. I look down at my hand, cowering.

Herr Henricksen appears like a vengeful specter. Glaring at me, he points an oiled bony finger at Jules. He doesn't honk. He shouts, "Jules! What are you doing here? Kory, you know the rules about bringing people back here!"

Ever the consummate salesman, Jules' smile is nothing short of dazzling as he pushes at imaginary creases in his suit jacket. "Excuse me, Herr Hendricksen. I needed to talk to Kory." His hand waves upward and toward the office. "The front was empty, so I…"

Herr Hendricksen towers over Jules, continuing to glare at me for breaking the rules.

I shrug my shoulders.

Herr Henricksen turns toward the office.

Jules leers at Herr Henricksen's back, his nose an inch away from mine. His eyes are bloodshot. The combination of cologne and rum is cloying. "Anne told me. Everything. *You?*"

I retch, swallowing the foul bile of coffee and cigarettes back down.

Henricksen whirls back, grasping Jules' wrist. "Jules, you can't be here. Get out!"

Jules' eyes are steady pools of brackish water. His voice is low and placating as he wipes the grease from his sleeve. "Kory, I will be waiting at home. But your lies. Anne told me all about your activities. We're on to you."

My boss whispers gruffly in my ear, his voice no longer a honk or a reedy whine. "Kory, he is…activities must stop…no more chances. Understood?"

I shake my head in agreement. With his words, he's damned me.

Numbly, I go to the boneyard. Trembling, I separate the parts having a use from the ones that are too far gone. Anne told Jules. Why? My warning from Henricksen…I must warn the others. Henricksen doesn't understand. He, Anne, and Jules must understand.

Chapter Twenty-Seven

Coming to the spot where Anne blew me a kiss a few weeks ago, I'm horrified.

Jules stands outside Anne's house, tapping his cigarette ashes into the rose garden, his hand resting ever so lightly on her shoulder. Anne giggles but is doing nothing to push him away. I slow down to eavesdrop and watch as she brushes his hand off, smoothing her skirt with her hands.

"Anne! Jules!" I call out.

Both let out a cry of surprise as I stride into the yard.

"I thought he should talk to you." Her tone is contrary. She juts her chin out as though she has every right to her opinion. "Big spy!" she taunts, "I can't believe you think you can stop these people. Nazis bring jobs and opportunities."

"Jules," she coos rapturously, stroking his sleeve, "he tells me about the people coming into the shop. Jules, you are just so sweet to offer to bring new music over." Her hand touches his jaw, and Jules takes her hand, kissing her fingers individually. She giggles and draws her hand back, cupping his face.

Jules has a smirk on his face. I've seen the look before with the other girls he's won over with his stories and gifts.

Not this time. Lowering my head, I barrel into them. I reach for Jules, but he pushes me back with surprising strength and then runs away. I turn to face Anne. Her hands shield her face, protecting her mouth and nose.

"Bitch! You are a bitch! And I hate you," I scream as the façade drops. For the first time, I realized what an idiot I've been and how my friends, in their way, tried to warn me. She was stroking Jules' face just like how she stroked mine. I see her differently. She never loved me. She never even cared. It was all an act. Well, I'm going to set that record straight right now. "My family is going to die because of you," I say, as the walls of our future, my future, come crashing down around me.

"And what about the kid whose job you got? Ever think about that?" I raise my voice, needling this bitch. She deserves all of what I'm going to say. "The Nazis cut out Mathias' tongue. They wrote on the wall with his tongue. My cousin died because you are goddamn collaborators. They're heroes. Mathias' family is dead because of people like you."

I curl my fingers into fists. When I find Jules, I'm going to enjoy pummeling that snake-oil salesman into the ground and watch him beg for mercy. Hot tears threaten to undermine me, and I wipe them on my sleeve.

Anne draws back, and then, she *smiles*.

Does she think I'm acting? "You—How do you think you got the job? You have no talent. "

With a flourish, I bring my raised fist in front of my face and pretend to study my fingernails. I speak in falsetto as I mimic Anne. 'Oh, look at me, I can sing only one song and play the same stupid song repeatedly.' You... you traitor! You bitch! Jules set the job up. Jules got passed over, and Mathias got the job. Now Mathias is dead. People will *die* because of you, you stupid, dumb piece of shit...because of you and Jules. Every time you hit a wrong note, *that's* how many people you will be killing. Me. My family. My friends. You will have all of us on your conscience."

Globs of my spit dot Anne's face. She wipes her eyes, a fingernail drawing a large scratch across her cheekbone. A long blue vein courses up her pale forehead. She brings her other hand up and shrinks back, her hands now covering her face as if I'm going to pummel her.

I no longer care. "Jules is lying to you. He lives in a whorehouse. Did he tell you that? And he steals from little kids."

Anne's face goes white.

The front door to Anne's house slams against an interior wall. A tall, red-headed man with deep-set black eyes, wearing the most oversized belt buckle I have ever seen, strides toward me.

Anne runs to him and clutches his arm. "Daddy! He called me a traitor and said that you are a bad man—"

Herr Thompson pushes Anne in the ribs, sending her reeling into a hedge by the front steps.

His first blow to my head makes my teeth rattle. I fall, and as I fall, he kicks my ribs, my knees, and my balls with pointed, heavy boots. I double over in pain, convulsing, seeing red- leather with white stitching before another kick to my head sends me into gravel next to the flowerbed.

He kicks again, and as he does, my legs separate. Another kick to the balls. A kick to my head.

Gripping his thigh, I bite his pants, hoping for flesh, hoping he'll stop.

He laughs at my feeble attempt to ward him off, trying to kick with his other leg, and falls on top of me.

The heavy metal buckle lands on my nose.

I smell the starch and urine. I don't care.

"So, you pissed on yourself hitting a kid?" I taunt. Then I scream in his ear, "Asshole! You are a piece of shit and a traitor. You're a collaborating asshole." I bite again, this time through his shirt, finding soft flab covering a rib. My nose feels his heartbeat.

Another kick by him.

A warm stream of urine runs down my leg.

Shaking me off, he jumps away. "Look at you, a piss-soaked baby, trying to be a man. You're a traitor, not me." He takes a good look at me, clears his throat, and spits right in my face. "Come here again, and I will kill you."

Another kick by the cowboy boots wedges my ribs apart.

"As for your family, they will pay. All of them. We're trying to do good for you and your traitorous friends."

I don't doubt his intentions.

Rolling over onto my side, I see him hobble to the door. A cowboy hat hangs in the foyer.

Herr Thompson is finished with me, but not with his family's reputation. Tilting his head back like a wounded Old West gunslinger, he bellows for all to hear, "You can shut your goddamn doors and windows! Some asshole made a pass at my daughter, and I set him straight. Shut your goddamned doors!"

Up and down the street, windows slam, and doors bang shut.

A loafer with a penny is all I see. I try to roll over onto my front. "No more." I'm crying. "No more."

"You are nothing," Anne sneers. "You will die, and

I'm so happy my daddy kicked your ass. Die, why don't you? Just die."

The Thompson's door slams shut.

Once, while on a bus, I saw a car hit a dog. The blow crushed the dog's hind leg. The beast howled and snapped and mostly tried to save itself. As the dog tried to run, its crushed leg dragged behind it. All the while, every howl, every tortured movement, was a wish to go somewhere quiet, somewhere away, somewhere to die.

The dog stood for a moment in the road, its howl a high-pitched scream, its frothing mouth open, spitting blood, repeatedly snapping at the leg, shuddering, and twitching. The dog dragged itself across the road, and a car door slammed.

Our bus lurches into motion. I craned my neck, relieved that someone wearing an oversized coat grabbed the dog and enveloped the tortured creature in his arms. The dog wrestled and pulled, but the man was stronger. Another man ran forward and instinctively held the other half of the writhing dog. All the while, the second man leaned over, apparently talking to comfort the animal.

I don't know what happened to the men or the dog, but I saw kindness triumphing over apathy and indifference that day.

Nobody will rescue me from this situation now. I know that. I have put my family in the line of fire all because I needed to prove that what we do matters. I might as well be dead.

A centimeter from my nose, a yellow rose petal lies next to the butt of a hand-rolled cigarette.

Pushing myself to my feet and receiving a last swipe from the rose's thorns, I assess the damage. Blood trickles from my eyes, nose, and lips. I taste blood in my mouth. Swallowing, I wipe my eyes and cheek on my sleeve. The overwhelming stench of urine makes me gag.

As I stagger out of the Thompson's garden, an old, wooden garage offers a refuge twenty meters away. Sliding down its splintered exterior, I settle against a dented garbage can. I know one thing. I can't go home.

So, this is what my life is. I don't understand why I can't get one thing right. Wrong girlfriend. Wrong brother. Jules ran off and, judging by the fact that no one being here to help me, *not* to get help. At least not for his brother. And Anne and her father will not keep quiet. Herr Thompson has figured out what we're doing, and I'm in real trouble.

My head rests on a scratchy, cold chunk of cement. Lifting my head, I see a blurred movement—four legs followed by two legs. The ground's dampness seeps into the crotch of my pants. The situation I'm in seeps into my soul, and with that, a solution makes me slide a little.

It's hopeless. Maybe I should take myself out of the equation. Maybe if I'm gone, my family will be safe. Maybe that's the solution, after all. All I need is a piece of glass, and my life will be over. A quick cut, some writhing, and I will be done—such a simple and easy solution. I will wait, find a sharp object to slit my wrists, and burrow where no one will find me.

I cough again, and blood spurts onto my sleeve. All slips into darkness.

****

"Kory? You all right?"

I nearly don't catch that I'm being called by name. A sharp beam shines in my eyes. As I roll toward the light, I double up, coughing and crying.

"Oh, sweet Lord, what in the hell happened to you?

Oh, my God." Herr Carhart squats, his shirt hanging over his khaki pants, his knees bumping mine as he shines a light in my face. "Can you stand?" Showing surprising strength—his days as an Olympic biathlon competitor still with him—he pulls me up. His legs are like cords of wood.

I lean against him, feeling his biceps flex.

"C'mon, young man. I'm right here."

"Herr—" I sob, but he sharply cuts me off.

"No names for right now, all right? We'll talk in the car." Wrapping his arm around my shoulders, he half-carries me toward his automobile, a Rover 10 that Paul calls the *mini-tank*. "Another few steps."

As I get into the car, I put my fist into my mouth and scream. Like the wounded dog, I understand the terror and relief he must have felt when he was rescued.

"How—?" I bite my fist again.

"A friend of yours living near your girlfriend called me."

Unballing my fist, I mutter, "She's…bitch…

"Right, my apologies, Kory. Her father's business and political-cowboy ways have come to our attention. Your friend is his neighbor. When your friend saw the scuffle and your brother running off, they called me. I'm sorry it took me so long to get here. I had to wait until I was sure the neighbors would be asleep."

Herr Carhart's car smells of leather and, not surprisingly, wood.

"I know your boss, Herr Henricksen." Paul's father shifts the mini-tank into gear and starts the car after rolling down the hill for a few seconds. "In the morning, I will call him and let him know you fell while helping at the cabin after work and are resting up for a few days.

Nothing too serious, just a bad fall. I can come by and talk to your parents if you like. They will worry, yes?"

I squirm, trying to find a position in which taking a breath doesn't feel like getting stabbed. One of BST's turrets peeks out above a streetlamp.

"Kory, if you can, tell me what happened."

"If I can?"

His question tells me he knows what we're doing. *Of course,* he does! Who just so happens to have a printing press? Out with it, Kory.

I can lie, but I no longer want to. Paul's father is here, but can I trust him? But he's here. He came to rescue me. No one else did. No one else *showed up.* I close my eyes, and as I roll mental dice, betting on my life and that of my friends, I pray my next words are the right ones.

"Herr Carhart, I'm going to get us all killed."

Herr Carhart turns right past Rosenkrantz Tower. "Why do you say that?" His voice is placid, as if reporting the weather.

"I told Anne what we store at Jan's cabin."

"And Anne did what? Your brother—he was there, too? He didn't try to help you?" Herr Carhart's tone is casual, but his questions are not.

"Anne told Jules and Anne's papa about the guns, I think. Now we are…we are in danger, and the Nazis will find out."

He slows the car as we come to a checkpoint near his offices and lumberyard.

On other days, I smiled as I passed the Carhart lumberyard with the intertwined C, a tree, and a saw painted on the office building's facade. But today, I'm not smiling, especially when a light shines in my eyes.

Herr Carhart rolls down the window of the Rover 10 he brought over from England a dozen years ago—right-hand steering be damned!—and reaches across my chest to hand over his papers.

The lantern glances over me and my face.

"What happened to you?" The guard's question contains no trace of sympathy, only suspicion.

"Paul's my son, and he was working on our family cabin." Herr Carhart's hands and eyes are as steady as he's setting up a target to shoot.

The guard holds up a staying hand. "I'm asking him!"

"We found a small leak in a corner on the roof. I needed to get tar, and as I climbed down the ladder, one leg gave way. I fell, hitting my head and ribs. And I peed on myself." I'm shocked at how easily the lie rolled out.

Herr Carhart gently tousles my hair and pulls my chin up.

"I'm taking him to my doctor. Can't be too careful. Your papers, Paul? Did you bring them with you?"

I bite my hand, and a tear rolls down my cheek.

Herr Carhart leans back to look at some clothes in the backseat. "Paul, I have told you a thousand times!" He turns to the guard. "If there is a problem, I can bring the papers over tomorrow. Paul is bruised and banged up. I want him to get into a hot bath and have him checked by our doctor."

The guard lets out a long sigh, running the flashlight up and down me again.

Herr Carhart sits quietly, as if this happens every day.

"Um, yes, bring the papers by." The guard shakes his head, pointing to his jaw and cheek. "Okay, take care of that. We don't want him getting sick."

"Thank you. We will do that. I apologize for my son leaving his papers, but he will get a stern lecture."

Herr Carhart puts the mini-tank in gear, driving a few blocks before speaking. "Why don't you tell me what is up at the cabin."

My voice hovers above a whisper. "We hide the parts for guns, and we get regular guns and ammunition at Jan's cabin." I take a deep breath, spasming, and coughing. A blood clot splatters onto my arm.

Herr Carhart points to the curb and raises his eyebrows.

I shake my head. "I'm okay. Really. Jules is friendly with people sympathetic to the Germans. He thinks the Nazis are good for business and that we need to cooperate."

Herr Carhart's jawline, so like Paul's, clenches.

He's angry with me. "Please don't throw me out. I don't know what to do!" I cry out, overwhelmed by the horror of what I have admitted and by the knowledge that I've put people in danger, people I care about. "Look, let me out, and I will go away."

Herr Carhart tilts his head down, taking a bead on the information I gave him. "Your brother, you think he will talk to his collaborator friends about your plans and what you have done?"

I'm reminded of when Jan told me about Herr Carhart's winning a medal in Chamonix. "You take a bead on the target and control your breaths, so they're at one with your heart. Doing that will steady your eyes and your aim." I'm reminded of that biathlon competitor now and not sure if I or someone else is the target.

"Yes." My voice is ragged, and I'm crying again.

"I'm going to get all of you killed and my family, too."

"Hmm…"

"Herr Carhart, you believe me, don't you?" Herr Carhart's calm is scaring the shit out of me. "It's true! It's all true!"

"What of your parents? Do they know anything?" he asks, shifting the gears of conversation and the mini-tank at the same time. "You are out so late. Won't they worry? We'll have to let them know, but the gun smuggling…how long have you been doing this? And who, besides Anne, knows?"

I snuffle into my sleeve. "Jules, probably Anne's Papa, and I don't know who else." I feel so guilty. "Herr Carhart, my parents, they will think I'm staying with a friend. They ignore me and don't seem to worry much. Should Herr Henricksen call a neighbor—my family doesn't have a telephone—they would worry."

"Ah, they're raising you to be independent. I like that. You're a good friend to both Jan and Paul. And what you have done for Paul?"

I'm incredulous. "Herr Carhart, the guns…Your family and Jan and my family, they're going to die because of *me*. Our friend Mathias is dead. The Germans wrote *traitor* on the wall with his tongue."

Herr Carhart gasps. "You knew him? Such a horrible situation to get caught up in, and all for trying to get extra rations—"

"What?" I exclaim, my voice rising in pitch. I'm utterly confused. "No, no! Mathias passed notes at the theater. He's on *our* side. He and the janitor, they're on our side—they pass notes—"

"To the Germans. Yes. That, they did." His voice drops, and he shifts the car into a lower gear. "Mathias slipped up. He gave notes to the wrong people. His mother and sister—*Ugh!* Horrible women. They kept lists and would check with Mathias about who he saw at the theater. Your friend, Stein's brother, left so people would think he had an alibi when Mathias and his family were murdered."

My eyes widen, remembering what Stein told me about the noises in his kitchen and Bill's missing boots. So, Bill killed Mathias. I shiver.

A sharper staccato creeps into his voice. "The killing had to look like the Germans killed an informant family. Mathias' mother and sister were trying to get extra ration cards for themselves and would lie." His jaw muscles clench as he clicks his teeth.

Herr Carhart has his bead on a target. ****

It's not rare for people to own a car. I've heard of people, usually those who live on a farm, having a work truck and a go-to-town car. Rarer is a two-stall garage. But a carriage house with two garage stalls replicating the main house, right down to the flower boxes and Dutch doors, a miniature tank, and a car looking like a racehorse? That's *rare*.

Herr Carhart eases his mini-tank into a stall. As he has teasingly explained, sitting regally in its bay beside the mini tank is the fourth most important thing he loves after his wife, family, and Norway—a cherry-red Jaguar sedan with a Swallow sidecar. The sidecar is partially covered with a cloth to prevent the buckskin interior from fading.

For reasons defying any logic I might possess, the Jaguar's sleek lines remind me of the racehorse Man o' War.

A familiar figure eases through the Dutch door as

Herr Carhart closes the garage door. Paul's smile fades, and he steps back, his hand clutching a pillar. "Kory! Holy shit! Uh, sorry, Papa, but, oh, holy shit."

Pulling the mini-tank's ratchet-like door handle down feels like I have shredded my bicep. The door defies opening.

As if the very act of opening would bring about world destruction, the door finally sighs its release.

I shriek as my groin muscles relive the pummeling received from Anne's father's cowboy boots. Focusing on the floor, I test my legs' endurance as I traverse the three meters that separate us.

As Herr Carhart opens the door to his house, I catch the scent of cake. "Let's go downstairs." His arms encircle me as Paul's arm slides away from my back. "Paul, can you sort through your closet and find clothes for Kory?"

Paul nods at his father's request and disappears in the direction of his room. "Hot bath," he says, his voice fading.

A clod blocks my right nostril. Nevertheless, I smell coffee and cake as I hobble through the kitchen. I want to find the cake, but my right eyeball can't move, and my left eye is swollen shut. I gasp as my toes curl over the top of the stairway. The entrance to the basement looks cavernous and is longer than I remember.

I weigh eighty kilograms, and I'm convinced that my legs will buckle at any second.

Herr Carhart has a solution for that. Easing me down the stairs like I weigh no more than several bags of groceries, he lifts me, so my toes barely touch the stair's treads.

A young hand smelling of soap squeezes my

shoulder in gentle reassurance. Paul. I'm guided onto the couch and gently released. My weight shifts back onto pillows of starched clothes. Lights flicker on, revealing shelves filled with old planers and files, a tribute to the family business. The sofa is the softest thing I've touched all day.

Lolling my head back, I reassess myself. Herr Carhart's soothing voice and his checking of my limbs remind me of a joke. "I have one eye that works, one leg that works, and one ear that functions. Call me *Lucky*," I say.

Father and son snort.

"Come here, Paul," instructs Herr Carhart. "Right. Hold his head with both hands."

Paul strokes my forehead with his thumbs. "We're going to fix this. You shouldn't fret. We value loyalty."

"A an ne…" I stammer, "Paul, I messed up. I told Anne about the cabin. She told Jules. I thought if she knew, she would be proud. She's going to tell the Nazis."

Paul pulls back. "Jesus! Are you serious? Oh, God! How could you?"

Herr Carhart's knuckles are nearly white as they pinch Paul's arm.

"Ow!" Paul bats at his father's arm. "What—oh, good God!—what have you done, Kory?"

"Paul, Kory," Herr Carhart says, "listen carefully." This time, his eyes draw a bead on two targets—Paul and me. "The situation with the guns is handled. Do you understand?"

I whimper.

Paul's face, now crimson, is wet with tears. He's nowhere near through with me. "You idiot! What could have possessed you? Did you tell her anything else—the newspaper, the people you see, where you get things?"

"Paul...*Paul!*" Herr Carhart's sharp tone is like a finger on the trigger of a gun, forcing us to listen. "There will be nothing for them to see. Do you understand? Nothing."

I shake my head as I think about the conversation. "My brother...He came to me. He said, 'We're on to you.' He knows about the smuggling. Anne told Jules. He was at the house. I think he's her new boyfriend."

Herr Carhart's voice rises in anger, blowing us to bits. "The guns are being dealt with. That is all I can say. Do you understand? Not—" he raises his finger as if signaling the end of the discussion—"another word!"

I lie on the couch, drifting in and out of the low chatter around me.

When I come to, a man stands behind Herr Carhart, his black satchel glowing in the lamplight. With his hint of an unshaven beard and twice-used clothes, the man appears pressed into sudden service.

I have seen him before.

He adjusts his tortoiseshell spectacles and kneels beside me, murmuring, "Do you mind if I unbutton your shirt?"

My eyes widen. Such an odd question. How else is he supposed to examine me? "Do people ever say no?"

He unbuttons my shirt and directs Paul to point a table lamp toward me. "I'm going to press down, and you let me know where the injuries hurt the most."

As the doctor examines me, I know where I've seen him. Chamonix. He's in Herr Carhart's Olympic-team photograph. Furiously, I kick as he seems to pick out and press on my sorest rib.

"I'm sorry, but I must do this." He continues to

examine me. "Were you kicked anywhere else?"

My hand covers my groin.

"I'll have to look. I promise to be gentle and fast."

As he turns me on my side, my suspicions of the doctor being a former Olympian are confirmed. His legs are like cords of wood, and his biceps are powerful.

He asks Paul for water. "Bruises are appearing, and there's swelling, but that's normal. Kory, I need you to follow my finger with your eyes. Can you do that?"

The doctor slides his hand under me, gently tugging me upward. "You have badly bruised ribs, but I don't see anything broken. A hot bath and sleep are what you need. I'll give you a shot to help you sleep, but I recommend that you not go to work for the next three days. Andrew explained the situation, and I will state that you were at Andrew's cabin and fell while doing work for him and hit a rock. The medication will be delivered here. You should rest for a few days. See you tomorrow." He squeezes my shoulder, then rises to leave. "Andrew? You'll keep me apprised?" he calls over his shoulder as he opens the sliding doors.

Paul goes into the bathroom. Soon, the sound of running water slows to a trickle.

When Paul returns, he and Herr Carhart help me get up, and the three of us walk to the bathroom. With the greatest of care—almost discretion—they strip me of my clothes. Then they leave the room, giving me my privacy.

The water feels like a bad sunburn when I first step into the cast-iron tub, but as I slide in, my whole body and troubles melt. I close my eyes, and my mouth falls open.

Paul opens the door and, seeing me like this,

squeals.

I open my eyes. "The bath feels great. I'm fine."

Herr Carhart pushes the door wider. "Everything all right?"

Paul sits on the toilet, and Herr Carhart leans against the marble-topped vanity.

Sinking deeper into the tub, I close my eyes again as if going into a trance.

Neither one says a word the whole time I'm in the tub.

"I may need help getting out."

They swiftly lift me out of the tub, the water swooshing from me with a loud *smock!*

Herr Carhart envelopes me in a body-length Egyptian cotton towel, and not for the first time do I marvel at how well they live.

Paul dabs at the water on my face, but I wince, my body tensing up.

"Sorry, but Jesus!" Paul says in a strangled voice. "God, I have never seen anything like this. I'm going to kill the person who did this. But you're still an idiot, you know."

Wiping steam from the mirror, I take stock. I look like that whore at the West Indian. A dark, boot-width bruise lines my jaw. The worst bruises are on my torso. Starting just below my nipple and encircling me are fourteen bruises, each one the width of a red-stitched cowboy boot, with deeper purple blasting out from my ribs.

Paul continues to lean against the sink, as if looking a second, third, or thirty-third time will make the injuries go away.

I'm not sure he can forgive me. I wouldn't blame

him if he never did. I don't forgive myself. That leaves one choice. I'll leave Bergen as soon as possible.

Chapter Twenty-Eight

"Kory? You awake?" Paul stands, his sleeping bag puddling on the floor. "They want me to watch you. I need to make sure you don't have a concussion or a punctured lung. If you hurt, you are to tell me. No bravery and pretending to be tough."

His tone has an ordinary pitch, but the way he's stretching his arms and shoulders—his preciseness—shows a cold calculation, as if he can't let himself off his inner leash. He'll kill me in my sleep if he can.

I'm teetering between defiance and despair. Out with it, Kory. "I have to go to work in a few hours. I'm grateful, but I can't pay you back. There's no way, and this sense of obligation is gnawing on me. I've imposed myself on too many people. Paul, let me rest, and I'll leave."

I want to say, "Take a look around. You have everything. I have nothing. You have parents and family who love you and support you. You snap your fingers, and people come running. My parents, my family, can't be bothered to even think about where I am." The truth is, I'm angry. At Paul, Herr Carhart, and my parents. At Jules, Anne, and that asshole father of hers.

"You should sleep." Paul sits on the sofa's arm, his voice tethering me to the reality I see for myself and an alternate reality where everything wrong is fixable. "You have an ability none of us can ever buy. I would have thought about the press and printing copies for our family and those we trust, but it takes someone heroic to walk out the door with that news. You are the first one out the door. And I believe I can do it, too. You stick to the plan, and if plans change, you change. You live with no regrets, and you inspire us to do the same."

I'm less fearful that he's going to kill me.

****

From the chatter above me in the kitchen, I gather I've had a busy morning with the doctor checking on me, giving me another shot, and talking to me about my recovery. I remember little.

Wincing as I put one foot down from the sofa, then another, I limp gingerly toward the bathroom. *Steady.* Last night, the doctor told me to notify him quickly if I had blood in my urine. Investigating the toilet bowl, I see nothing frightening.

The man with the tortoiseshell glasses and strong biceps said my remaining injuries are the time-will-heal variety.

Maybe.

A razor is in a mug by the sink. Soaping my hands, I slide one fingernail under the others, removing tiny, rusty-brown remnants of bad decisions. Clean clothes are piled on the coffee table.

Wash me of my iniquity and cleanse away my sins. My parents think I got nothing from Luther's Short Catechism.

Squaring my shoulders, I climb the stairs to the kitchen.

"Coffee? How are you feeling?" Gretchen Carhart, a tiny woman with rouge applied a bit too thick on her apple cheeks, reminds me of a Russian nesting doll.

When she explains her talking points, her hands fly up in the air and trickle down to her conclusion. She's a singer and has told us that she uses her hands to get people to pay attention to her. "Raise your hands," she says. "People watch that."

"I need to see Jan," I say. My tone has the dulled sound of inevitability.

Bustling by me, Fru Carhart slaps Paul's hand as he reaches for a slice of cake by the stove.

Ration cards are more plentiful in this kitchen, I notice wryly.

"Jan?" Paul asks, his hip resting against the counter. He wolfs down a small piece of the cake, then smiles at his mother, who shakes her head.

"Yes, we contacted him." Herr Carhart takes a long sip of his coffee and turns back to his newspaper.

"Your ribs?" Fru Carhart touches my face. "Oh, and a nasty bruise on your chin. I think you should stay here for another day."

The ease in which the three of them speak of my injuries and decide what's best for me is a new experience.

"Andrew? You spoke to Karl about Kory?" Fru Carhart asks.

Herr Carhart nods.

"All right, the plan is settled. Do you want me to call your mother? I'm sure she will be wondering where you are." Fru Carhart's hands fly up to the telephone on the counter.

"We don't have a telephone, and they won't worry," I say as simply as if asked their kitchen countertop's color.

Paul's parents' eyes widen. Their blinking shows a

lack of comprehension as they check my face for anger or denial.

They won't find either. I'm beyond that. My mother isn't likely to wait and worry about me. She cooks, cleans, and tries to pay attention, but we demand too much of her energy—the three of us and my grandparents. So, she expends only what's necessary to deal with whatever crisis is heating up. I should be that crisis now, but that would mean someone else wouldn't get the attention they need.

I persist. "I need to see Jan, and I don't want to overstay my welcome. I'll find a way to pay you for the food and the doctor. Please let me know what the bill is, and I'll work the debt off."

Paul and Gretchen raise their heads to the same angle and regard me.

Herr Carhart sets down his newspaper, clearing his throat. "Kory—?"

I open my mouth to speak, but Herr Carhart holds his hand up, giving me the kind of thin smile reserved for a petulant toddler.

"Kory, no questions. Of course, you can see Jan, but you cannot leave here. That's certainly impossible today, and most certainly impossible just after breakfast, which you have hardly touched and most assuredly need. I understand the desire to run away, but we need to think of a plan to keep everyone out of danger. Can you give me a day? Just a day? I promise you I will get a plan for you."

Mr. Carhart stands up, kissing his wife's head. "Good breakfast. I need to go." He turns to me. "We will talk more tonight, yes?" Walking to me, he examines my face from this side and that. "Gretchen, if Kory complains of dizziness or anything else, get Bertinson over here again. Tonight, then!"

Paul opens the patio door and turns to me. "I thought we could sit outside on the deck if you like. Jan will be here shortly."

Gretchen follows us onto the patio with a coffee pot and then reaches out to touch the bruises on my jaw and my eye. "Your mother *will* be worried. I will go to her house and let her know you are helping Paul with a project at our cabin. Do you have everything you need?" When I nod, she hurries toward the front of the house.

Fru Carhart greets someone.

Jan's familiar chatter would usually be music to my ears. Not now. I'm terrified. Maybe I can explain before Paul does.

Forgetting the agony in my groin and ribs, I galumph my way off the deck and back into the kitchen.

Jan stops in the kitchen doorway, his hand covering his mouth and part of his eye. "Jesus! I'm going to kill him. Bare hands. The bastard and the cowgirl."

"Jan, I…uh…I…screwed up. Big time," I venture, hoping Jan won't hit me when he finds out the truth.

"Yeah, I heard that. Paul told me." Jan nods to Paul, who comes up behind me and rests his hand on my shoulder.

The Spartan shakes his head. "I never thought you were that stupid. But you were in what you thought was love."

"Mathias was working for the Nazis." I blurt out. "Jules, Anne's father—they're Nazi collaborators. I screwed up, and I don't know how I'm going to fix the problem." As I gaze at my two friends, what comes out next doesn't seem real. "I need to leave today, and you are going to help me. I will row for England—go somewhere they can't find me—and I'll let you know when I arrive."

Paul and Jan practically howl their displeasure.

Clapping my hands mere inches from their noses, I shout, "No! Just me! *You* will put me on the boat. *I* will cross the sea by myself or go on the boats as part of the Shetland Gang. The leader, the captain, leaves from Sotra, and patriots serve our country from England. I'm going to do that."

Through the Carhart's expansive kitchen windows, the outlying islands I know are Sotra and the islands won by my great-grandfather appear in the summer haze. I point at the outcroppings. "I need to go around that bend. You will take me to that place. Just to that point, and I will hike or swim or something, but only me. I'll find someone who knows someone who can help me, and I'll go. Me. Only me. "

Jan's voice is firm. "*We* go. There is no *you*. Us."

Jan and I turn to Paul, who hasn't chimed in.

Paul's eyes cloud, and he shakes his head. "I can't go. I can't. Papa has a plan for me, and I was going to tell you. I'm escaping to the mountains and going far away from here. Disappearing will make people suspect, but now I have to." He turns to Jan, pulling his arm. "Say nothing to Ingrid. Nothing. Promise me. Promise!"

Jan pulls his arm back, glaring at Paul. With a defiant shake in Paul's direction, he juts his chin to me. "I'm already involved. Kory, I'll go with you. The guns are…er…were at my family cabin. Stein's brother is in England, and maybe we can get word to him that we're coming, somehow. If that guard had checked my knapsack further, he would have found the guns. Kory, you're not so different. And Stein will go and Rolf, too, since he has the boat. The four of us. We'll leave today or tomorrow at the latest."

All the pieces have tumbled into place.

"Let me go pack," says Jan, "and I will be back in an hour." He starts toward the hallway. Then he stops and turns. "We do need to leave letters to our parents. Paul, you'll meet us tomorrow, and we'll give the letters to you to mail. When our parents get them, we'll be far from here. It's the only way."

Chapter Twenty-Nine

Paul's fingers run along the bookshelves lined with wooden planers. "His name is Klaus Stinson. He's nineteen and from Lubeck, Germany." He winds the skin on his forearm like a clock. "Kory, there are secrets I haven't told anyone. Don't say anything to Jan. A week ago, I—God, this is so hard. I'm not perfect, either. I'm scared they'll get my family because of me."

"You? What have you done?" I'm incredulous.

"I took care of a German who was bothering Ingrid. That's why I must flee to the farm. I took care of him."

The sound goes out of my ears as I look at my friend. The one I told everything to and the one I thought would do the same. The one to whom, moments before, I'd made a big speech about obligations and loyalties. My first reaction is to justify whatever he did and, more importantly, to protect him at all costs.

His mouth is moving again. I hold up my hand.

"You need to start over. Jesus, Paul, what have you done?"

"Two weeks ago, Ingrid came to me. She was terrified. She'd been walking to see a friend. A German soldier saw her and catcalled about how pretty she was." Paul's fingers twist his skin, creating deep ridges that resemble the hands of a watch. The angry lines appear to be at nine-fifteen. "She kept walking, and the guy called out, 'I'm going to get you. You will like it!' " Paul stopped. "He made a circle with one hand, thrusting his index finger toward it."

Paul's knuckles turn white. "Ingrid tried finding a different route, but she saw the man again a few days later. He brushed past her and whispered, 'Get you when your friends aren't around.' She was petrified, but when her papa asked Jan to start walking with her, Ingrid insisted she was entirely capable."

Paul releases his fingers from his forearm. "She told me she was pissed. You know Ingrid. She will not back down."

Paul pulls at the tufts of hair on his arm, ready to wind them up, too. "Ingrid was hurrying from the store with groceries. A different soldier decided to harass her about whether she had the right ration cards or not. He kept saying, 'I'm going to get you.' So now there's two of them doing it...I think."

Paul continues to pinch the tufts of hair on his arm.

I reach over and swat his fingers.

"I asked her what the guy looked like. She didn't want to tell me. Finally, she said he had a long, thin nose and dark eyes. His hair was brown. I yelled at her—big mistake, by the way—and she told me she didn't remember anything more than that. "Thin? Fat? Anything weird like a laugh, a high- or low-pitched voice? Anything?"

Paul's voice rises in exasperation. "She told me it didn't matter. She was going to face him down the next time it happened. I was mad at her. She wasn't telling me anything. But Jan walked with her the next few days. And no one harassed her. She figured she might be in the clear." Paul shakes his head.

"A few days later, she went to the post office, and

one of the soldiers followed her. He seized her wrist and pressed himself against her. He tried to kiss her, but she pushed and kicked him. When he jumped back, she noticed he had a long scar on his hand from an accident. It was like a burn. She came to me and told me she remembered the burn on the man's hand."

Paul's cheeks flush. He looks upward and then around the room, as if deciding whether we're truly alone. "I decided to go to the store to get groceries for my mother. As I was leaving, a soldier opened the door for me. His hand had this big scar. I looked up at him, and other than the scar on his hand, he was average looking. I was pretty sure this was the guy Ingrid described. When I asked Ingrid, she said, "Yes, yes, that's the one." She begged me again and told me not to do anything. I told her she was not to worry."

Paul begins to twist his skin again. "I went to the store the next day. He wasn't around, but I figured he had a certain route he would take." Paul gazes through the panes of the sliding glass doors. "Sure enough, I saw him walking to the store. I had a bag with me so I'd look like just another shopper. I'd brought some wire that I got from the tool shed. I went up behind him just before he got to the store. You know the small alleyway there? I put a wire around his neck. He started fighting, struggling to get at me, but I dragged him into the alley. It didn't take long."

I gasp. "Did you kill him?"

Paul is plucking hairs from his wrist. He doesn't wince. "There was a lot of blood. It drenched his collar and the shoulders of his jacket. I didn't care. I needed to have proof Ingrid would be safe from now on. I rolled him around and took off his uniform, shoving it into the bag I was carrying. The bag had apples and other things in it, so I'd look like I had gone shopping."

He swallows and glances over at the hallway behind us. His shoulders slump, and he appears to be deciding if confession really is good for the soul.

"Go on," I say, half fearing that I haven't heard the worst of it but, nevertheless, wanting to hear it all anyway. I hope my voice is neutral enough for him to continue.

Paul's words come out in a torrent. "I came into our basement and put the uniform into a back closet. There was so much blood and dirt on it." Paul begins twisting his skin the other way.

I slap his hand.

Rubbing the reddened knuckles, he looks past my head, his pupils widening as if staring into an abyss. "The blood. Good God Almighty, I had no idea! And on me! It was everywhere!"

He inhales as if discovering the last drops of redemption he might have available to him.

"I grabbed towels, bundled the uniform up inside of them, and went for a swim. I know…stupid, right? I dunked everything. There was a wallet inside with the guy's name. Klaus Stinson. Age 19. From Lubeck, Germany. That came floating out, and I had to get rid of that. I pitched it into the ocean. And the blood came floating off the uniform and stained the towels. I wrung them out as best I could. I brought them up to the house to dry."

I lean over and pat his hand.

Paul shrugs, glancing at a small anteroom. "Do you want to see it?"

I nod, following him past the bathroom to a small,

cluttered storage room. In the corner is a bureau with an ornately carved mirror.

"The towels, I laid on the floor, here"—his foot swipes the floor. Then he grinds the spot with the ball of his foot— "and the uniform"—he points, as if detailing his confession— "I hung from this mirror to dry. After everything was dry, I turned the bureau against the wall so people have to pull it around to get it open."

Paul pulls the bureau around, squatting and tugging at a drawer, fishing his hand inside. Gray tweed cloth appears.

I don't need any more proof. "No! Put it away! I believe you. People are going to ask questions. Are you sure no one saw you?"

Paul grimaces. "If I go to the mountains within the next couple of days, they'll have nothing, and they'll have to spend a lot of time searching. I'll probably get rid of the coat. But not a word to Jan. He can't know about the uniform. I need to protect Ingrid any way I can."

****

Jan slides the glass door open, revealing Paul and I leaving the anteroom, our hands raised defensively like prisoners caught in a prison break. "I left the playing cards for Stein and Rolf. I think I have everything I need, but what do you think we should take with us?"

Paul and I walk to the door. I look over my shoulder to where the evidence lies not ten meters away and exhale in relief. I don't think Jan saw where we were because of the water's glare on the glass.

Jan clasps Paul's shoulder. "And it will be the five of us? I've been working out how we can take turns rowing and sailing. You have reconsidered?"

Paul shakes his head. "I can't. It's all arranged. Papa stuck his neck out. I leave in three days. Papa's friend is a highly placed general who has a farm in the mountains. His farmhand's wife is pregnant, so I'm to help on the farm while he's with her. I can't make any changes because what if someone talks?"

I limp and wheeze as we walk up the terraced steps outside.

Jan and Paul slow their pace to allow me to catch up.

Paul's tone is casual. "You can wait a day or two. Do you think the Nazis are going to come that fast? I don't. Come on. A day more."

"I'm fine," I say through gritted teeth. "I alternate a deep breath with a shallow one, and that seems to be working."

Paul excuses himself to wash his hands.

Jan helps me as I ease into an Adirondack chair the Carharts brought back with them from a trip to America.

A tall figure taps me on the shoulder. Dr. Bertinson is standing beside me.

Paul blanches at the angry look I send him and ducks back into the kitchen.

The doctor kneels beside me.

I follow his finger and smile in a fake happy way as he presses on my bruised face.

Jan rats me out. "He says he's breathing deep and then shallow, but he struggled to climb the steps up here."

My other rat-friend in the kitchen sends out a confirming grunt.

"Tell him about how you can't roll over or raise your arms, Kory. Or how you needed help getting into that chair."

I try to slouch into the deep chair but groan.

The last thing I remember is being hauled down the steps to the basement couch by my rat-friends and a voice saying, "This may sting."

I awake with a start. Swinging my legs off the couch, I see one rat and two other friends hunkered down, intently playing Solsvik Bridge. An ice bucket is being filled loudly by the other rat. On a tray are more sandwiches and slices of cake.

Paul puts on a blues record his parents brought back from Greenwich Village. Motioning me over, he has everyone bring me up to speed about what has been decided while I was comatose.

Paul is still going to the farm in the mountains. We're not to breathe a word to Ingrid. Jan and Rolf are going with me to the Shetlands. Stein thought he was coming over to make a newsletter delivery, but Jan asked him point-blank if he wanted to go to the Shetlands with us and he said yes on the spot. Mathias' death at the hands of the Nazis has freaked Stein out. And for reasons unknown, my injuries have been explained to Rolf and Stein as my falling off the roof of Paul's cabin. Jules has been presented as the culprit for turning me into the Nazis. There has been no mention of Anne.

I'm not sure why, but I decide not to tell Stein that his brother might have killed Mathias. I also swallow sharing the idea that Paul's father knows a lot about Mathias and his family's death.

We're to write letters to our parents explaining what we're doing, and Paul will mail them in three days when he goes to the mountains.

"You've been busy!" It's all I can think of to say. I'm incredulous that they've worked out our escape plans. And how they all—though they don't say anything directly—believe I'm the holdup. Based on the you're-out-of-your-mind looks I'm getting from the four of them, my idea of cowboying my way to the Shetlands is viewed as ludicrous, insane, and selfish. The fact that I'm spending a lot of time doped up on the couch—the rats reported that to Rolf and Stein with no hesitation—ensures that I'm to be watched like a hawk in case I get another harebrained idea.

Rolf pulls a lock of his perfectly cut hair. "I have another photo shoot in a few days as *The Face*. Now I'm being presented as the perfect specimen, and those who have deficiencies— that's what they call people who don't look Nordic—are not to have babies or even marry. They say I'm the face of the *master race*. I'm supposed to be proud, but I—it makes me sick."

Angry red splotches mottle Rolf's face. "And my parents. I'm getting paid for this. The money is coming to my mother, and she loves to tell the neighbors and others about how I'm Norway's Face. Brags about it. I asked her not to accept the money, and she was appalled. 'That's your future,' she says. My future. Right. My future, all right. She bought a car on the black market. My papa is so disgusted that he now stays out at our cabin. I think they're going to get a divorce."

Rolf looks at us, his dimpled face smiling its recruitment-poster smile. "So, I'm in. The Face of Norway. I hate everything the Nazis and the collaborators here stand for. I hate my mother for going along with this, and I can't stand what they have in mind. I want to fight, and I want to go with you. We can use my boat. The plan is perfect."

Jan elbows Stein. "Do you know who got Bill to

England?"

Stein shakes his head. "I've asked people I think I can trust, and no one knows for sure. Maybe the Shetland Gang. Ivar, Bill's best friend, might possibly know. I think he got a present from the Gang, the signal letting us know Bill was safely in England, and left it on the door for us to find, but he denies it."

Stein eyes me, reaching out to touch my jaw. "Are you sure you can leave in two days?"

Cowboying or not, I'm going.

****

Two curly headed boys, one blond and one brunette, have their elbows propped on a table holding a Norwegian Sea shipping-routes map.

It seems the Carharts lack for nothing.

"We're at 60.3913 degrees north latitude and 5.3221 degrees east longitude, and we need to go"—Jan's long finger traces an old shipping route between Bergen and Lerwick in the Shetland Islands—"here. Two-hundred-eighteen nautical miles."

Paul gently nudges Jan.

The Spartan moves over so I can look at the map, too. "You have to be careful of mines," he says. "I wish we could put out one more edition of *The Whole Truth*. Papa heard that Germans are leaving tin cans around that look like they have food in them, but they contain bombs."

I met Paul while carrying a canning-machine part. My latest project involves streamlining a new canning-machine part. I shudder.

Two curly heads snap their necks around to look at me.

"I'm fine," I say. "I realize how much I need to

leave. That's all." I hear footfall on the deck.

Stein taps on the window, crooking his finger at us.

"Why's Ivar with Stein?" I whisper to Paul and Jan.

Ivar Kristiansen, Bill's best friend, pulls on the sliding doors and steps inside with Stein.

Stein skips introductions and launches in. "Rolf's out. He went upstairs to his attic and started pulling out camping gear for the trip."

I hold up my hand. "Ivar, this is Paul Carhart."

Stein waves his hand irritably at me. "Rolf's mother overheard Rolf talking about wanting to go and spoke to his father. Not only is Rolf forbidden to talk to us, but he's also to go on a photo shoot in the fjords in the morning. I'm afraid we'll be ratted out, and I think we need to go sooner rather than later."

Ivar's lanky frame is stooped over the table. His calloused finger, unlike our softer fingers before, traces a route on the map. "Here." He points to a shipping route between Bergen and Lerwick. "In a sailboat, the journey will take three days. Bill said there are sea stacks to look for after we cross the fjord so we can avoid detection."

He's in. That was easy.

Paul places a finger across his lips and puts on blues music just loud enough to cover our talk.

'Sweet Home Chicago,' by Robert Johnson. A favorite and how I won over—

Ivar pushes back a white-blond shock of hair from his eyes. He's deeply tanned. "I will show up wherever you want. I should get my gear, and I'll meet you when you want to go."

I press on my ribs, now a puke green where the pointed cowboy boots dug in, intent on separating them further. They don't hurt. "With Rolf out, how are we going to go to the Shetlands? We were going to use his boat. It's not like we can borrow it. Right?"

Jan raises his eyebrows and smiles.

Stein replies, "Tomorrow. Kory's house. Kory, I think you should go back to see your family and get your gear."

Short months ago, in the dead of winter, I stepped from Paul's shed, unsure how distributing a newspaper would change my life. I don't regret doing that for a second.

I slide the glass door open, and we file outside onto the deck. A German cruiser passes by the house, a swastika painted on its hull. I raise my hands and clasp the shoulders of Jan and Stein.

They, in turn, hold the shoulders of Paul and Ivar.

Standing side by side like a bulwark, we watch the ship pass.

Jules stroked Anne's face, and she smiled. I shake the image away, knowing I stand with my true brothers.

Chapter Thirty

My climbing the stairs was only slightly easier than yesterday... so, effectively, it remains torture.

My mother, her head down, stands alone at the kitchen sink in our blue and white kitchen, washing a bowl bearing the remnants of mashed potatoes. Tortuous climb or not, my mother remains deep in thought and does not look up and has not heard me. The amber light above the sink turns her deep reddish-gold hair to the color of the sunset. Like doughy pillows, her cheeks will smell of soap and lavender. The sleeves of her red dress are pushed up, showing her muscular forearms. Her hands are not delicate like Anne's but blunt like those of a fisherwoman. She wipes her eyes and cheeks with a blue towel she wraps over her forearm, plunging her hands into the water. Her mouth is moving, and I know she is in her church, offering penance that might be of my making.

I peer in at her for a moment longer before reaching for the back door's handle.

Opening the door, I step into my familiar with the smell of potatoes, lamb, and cardamom.

Dropping a plate into the soapy water, my mother wipes her hands on her towel. Her face is at my neck level, and warm water runs down my neck as she squeezes me with the fervor of an answered prayer. "You should have let me know you were at the Carhart's cabin.

Jules searched everywhere for you. He wanted to make sure you were safe. I spoke to Fru Carhart. She said you were resting up at their cabin after your accident. She said the injury wasn't too serious, and you were safe. And you are. I'm so glad."

Out with it, Kory.

"Mother, my friends think we should get away from work for a while, so we're going on a hike. I leave tomorrow morning. Jan and others will be going. I need to pack."

With her index finger, my mother traces the bruises on my cheek and under my eye. Her brow furrows, and with a deep inhalation, she locks my hands in hers.

Bowing her head in the amber light, she decides, her hands pushing mine away. She wipes her hands and turns to the sink, watching me in the window's reflection. I stand, my hands in the same position, trying to absorb and remember the feeling of her hands on mine in what I think was tacit acceptance. I believe she will try to stop me, but as I gaze at her reflection in the glass, my eyes sting with unshed tears. Her face is one of admiration, fear, resignation, and maybe respect.

Chapter Thirty-One

My parent's bedroom door closes. I reach for a cup from the cupboard and wince as my back spasms.

Don't gasp or cry out!

I'm sure my mother has not gone to sleep. I imagine she's listening at the bedroom door, waiting for me to move about the kitchen. She can—or the other adults in the house can—then catch me in the lie I'm telling myself. I am badly injured, and what I will be doing in less than —the teapot clock on the wall shows it's almost eleven—eight hours is complete madness.

My hand trembles as I grasp the cup's handle, willing myself to hold on.

I peer at my reflection in the window above the kitchen sink. As always, my hair is a mess, and I have stubble on my chin and upper lip. Breathing deeply, I raise my arms, testing for more spasms. Bearable. I exhale and utter a prayer of gratitude.

Filling the cup with water, I raise my hand to my lips, again testing my resolve.

Some rest and no one will be the wiser.

My mother's faint snore is absolution.

Creeping downstairs, I take a long look at the hand-me-downs that are my surroundings. Everything in my room has been used up and cast aside. It's time for me to create something new.

I sit on the floor and write.

Dear Mother and Papa,

When you get this letter, I will be nearing the Shetland Islands, fighting for your freedom and mine. I know you recognize that it is important I contribute. I am strong and capable, and you will be proud of what I do. As soon as I can, I will return to you, but I want you to be proud of me and what my friends and I are trying to do. *We* believe the Nazis do not belong here, and we want you to be safe and to feel safe in talking with your friends. I have had to keep secrets, and I never meant to hurt anyone, but now is the time to act. I will send a message to you talking about the daisies of September, and you will know I'm safe and sound.

I'm going to make you so proud of me.

I love you,

Your son,

Kory

I close the envelope and lick the gum to seal my future.

Chapter Thirty-Two

"Ivar? Don't you play Solsvik Bridge?" asks Gramps. "Shall we give him a tutorial, Jan? Stein, you sit here. When I was a busboy on Lapskaus Boulevard, we would eat rafts with axle grease on them. Do you want some?"

Through the kitchen floorboards, I hear Ivar sound polite and noncommittal and utterly confused. As I roll out of bed, the camp stove I had been so careful to set out last night tips with a loud clang.

Dammit!

"I'll be upstairs in a second!" I yell.

The Spartan hoots back, and I hear cards being shuffled.

Ray's freckled arm reaches inside and turns on the light, putting my lack of planning in plain view. Stepping over my shirts, shoes, and shorts, he climbs onto Jules' bed and begins jumping. "When can I come along on your hikes? I bet you meet up with girls, and I bet you kiss them and everything."

Ray's bouncing is causing the bedframe to squeak. I can't concentrate.

"Ray, it's a hike in the mountains. That's all. I'm going with my friends for a week. Now, I need to think, so can you leave me alone?"

"I bet you are thinking about Anneee. I bet you kiss her, and I bet she tries to run away, and I bet—"

"Ray, leave me alone!" I bellow.

Ray's face crumples into tears.

I hear his rumbling and tumbling footsteps as he runs to his room, slamming the door.

I'd tried to convince myself that the Nazis wouldn't find and question my family and friends. That could never happen to me. I'm too smart, too clever for the likes of them. And yet, here I am, slinking away, hoping the Nazis don't put my family into work camps or kill them. I'm the one who has put us all in danger. What if I don't see them again? What then?

I can't leave Ray with that memory.

Climbing the stairs, I hold my hand up to the seated card players and knock on Ray's door.

"Go away! I hate you!" Ray cries.

I hear an inhalation of snot.

Shit.

I open the door.

Ray sits on his bed, rolling a truck up and down his blue chenille bedspread. Sullenly, he turns away.

"I'm sorry," I murmur, picking up a car and driving up and down the chenille rows. "I'm thinking about where we should go on our trip to the mountains. Maybe next summer you'll be old enough to go with my friends and me. We stay at a hut above a lake, and the fish... oh, you won't believe the size of the fish you can catch!"

Ray's chin trembles as the truck slowly traverses the mountains that are his bent knees.

"The camp is near the place where the big monsters are in the mountains," I continue. "Trolls eat little brothers. That's a well-known fact."

Ray rolls his eyes and continues to pout, his brown, freckled hand releasing the truck down the steep slope of his shins.

I gingerly take a dented, scraped tin car and run it up a chenille ridge. "One time, Jules took me up, and he tried to feed me to a big troll looking like, well, like you!" I tickle his ribs, and the cloud passes. "I want my brother to be with me. No trolls for you!"

Ray giggles. "Tell me another story about your camping trips," he pleads.

I needed to pack, but I didn't know when I would see him again. "Listen, I have to finish packing. Ask Gramps about the time he almost bought a bridge in Brooklyn-America." I take his chin and peer down at him, memorizing his freckles, the way his lashes cross one another at the corners of his eyes, and his hand's softness as he holds on to my index finger. "I want you to know you're a good kid. I'll see you soon, you little knothead!"

Standing in the doorway, I give Ray a wave. Then I walk down the stairs past my familiar to the kitchen.

Ivar is smiling at the teapot clock. He pats Gramps' hand and then taps on his wrist as he finishes his coffee. "We have to get going, or we're going to miss our train."

He and Stein stand and head to the back porch.

I hang back for a second. "I'll meet you out front."

Boy, that didn't turn out as nonchalant as I'd hoped. I go downstairs, walking past the family photos and the paintings, then past the canned goods and the rakes into my bedroom.

Looking at the rumpled bed, the unused suit, the work boots, and the album of Django Reinhart meant for an upcoming birthday, I pick up my backpack—spasm be damned!—and climb the stairs to the front door. Taking a long look up and down the staircases, I open the front door and step outside.

On with it, Kory.

The Spartan stands on the sidewalk near the rhododendrons and salutes. "Spart—" he begins. Then he dabs his eyes.

"Spart," I return, raising my hand to salute, my back muscles grumbling but, luckily, not spasming. I hear a tap on the window above us and see Gramps saluting.

We salute back.

A small stream comes from Jan's eye. He, then, snaps a heartier salute to Gramps and plasters a full smile in his direction.

"C'mon, we're going to be heroes, and we'll be fine," I say to Jan, whose smile seems to be glued to his face. But I don't feel right. Our departure from my house was so abrupt. A wave of fear hits me.

The reality of the situation is nothing like I had thought it would be. Damn Jan—him and his being all emotional. Why couldn't he pretend to be casual? He never tears up. Now, I'll bet our families will see we're not on a hike. Gramps's salute...They know! Shit, shit, shit!

Jan sniffs. "Kory, your family cares about you, and I'm part of your family. My parents—I didn't tell them anything. I don't know if they would care. It's all about missing shipments."

People's shapes shift with green edges to their forms as I move past them. My heart races. I want to rest, gather myself, maybe put my head between my legs. I pause.

Jan stops, waiting for me, his hands tucked in his pockets. He jerks his head toward Ivar and Stein, who are traipsing ahead.

I hold up my hand.

He strides to me. "Spart? Your rib? I can—" He points toward Stein and Ivar's disappearing forms.

If I say the word, the journey will end. I shake my head, smiling the most radiant smile I can muster, and continue walking.

As I bounce and jostle among the people near the train station, I tune out the easy banter between Ivar and Stein and don't pick up the conversation threads Jan occasionally throws out to me.

Jan's pace slows to match my flagging steps. "Spart?" he asks, his next words coming to me through a stationary jaw, like a low growl. "Herr Carhart could, I bet, find work for us. We could ask…"

I fix my eyes on the blond curly-headed boy standing outside the train station and raise my arms in a hallelujah. Beads of sweat form on my forehead, matched bead for bead with internal pangs of panic, guilt, and anger. I don't know who I'm trying to convince more that this is a great idea. My best friend? My friend who saw the cowboy-boot-shaped kicks on my ribs? Or the idiot that put this whole thing in motion?

"Let me hold the door." I hold it high enough, exaggerated enough, and long enough to pass muster with Stein and Ivar. Paul passes under my arm next and is in conversation with Stein.

The Spartan mutters, "Nice," as he walks by me.

I drop my arms in relief, as much for the performance as in convincing three-quarters of my party that I'm fine. We buy chocolates and a newspaper, jabbering to Paul as if he's a shirttail cousin we haven't seen in a long time, commandeering a small table near the train platform. I take the newspaper from Paul.

Bending over and remembering that my instructions

are to create a diversion, I fan open the paper. Pointing to a headline, I raise my voice. "Married? She's getting married?" The boys cluster around me to see what's going on. Deposited into the folds of Paul's newspaper are three letters.

Paul gathers the newspaper under his arm. He claps us on our arms. Then he turns and strides away, becoming one with the crowd.

Our journey has begun.

****

The train ride to Vika reveals secrets. Jan gets sick on boats but swears he'll be fine if he looks at the horizon. Ivar doesn't like riding backward in trains. Stein likes little kids and can talk their parents into allowing us to use them as props to get through inspections.

My secret, which is worse than the one my best friend is choosing to keep, isn't so good. My back spasms while walking. My ribs are sore, and I have no idea how I'm going to row two hundred nautical miles. I'm praying for sunny days and winds. I'm praying. I'm flat-out praying.

So it is that I depart from the train in Vika with a spring in my step for Stein and Ivar and a told-you-so smile for my best friend.

Walking past the apple orchard, buzzing with bees, and the German's tent city, I spy good news and hear some bad news.

The bad news is that my German lessons are paying off. I understand the word *gun* and that they intend to drill within the hour. I point my finger toward the Wiks' cabin and speed up my pace.

The good news is that Herr Wik is making an effort. Birch saplings no longer block the entrance to "the hillside manger." A new handle and a sturdy lock secure the door. Two sawhorses have lumber stacked on them, and the wheelbarrow isn't a tripping hazard. As we get closer, I see newly cut boards nailed on the balcony.

Rolf's instructions were clear. Herr Gunderson's gifts of food and any other supplies we need in the manger are ours for the taking.

Stein, spying the lock, wipes his hand on his sweaty forehead and then fumbles as he removes, not the usual chocolate from his pocket, but the lockpick set, dropping the tools on the ground next to the wheelbarrow.

Ivar sets down his pack and motions for a cigarette. He takes a drag and expels the smoke, tilting his head back as if in salutation to a beautiful day.

Jan and I turn, facing east toward the camp. Along with Ivar, we create a half-circle in front of our friend.

Stein steps around the sawhorses, and—*click!*—the lock disengages.

I make a mental note to stop harassing my friend for this habit. Maybe I should take back all the teasing I ever did—every word.

Slipping inside the manger, we stand in the hollowed-out cavern.

We're not alone. Less than a meter above our heads, and in the loudest, most horrible way, a fart rumbles, and the fumes seep down through a knothole.

I light a match, as much for illumination as to cut the horrendous odor. Recently cut lumber is stacked haphazardly in the corner. Hammers and a saw lie on a table. I become painfully aware that the match is burning my fingers. Lighting another, I see Stein pull a candle from an earthen cubbyhole. Grateful, I light the candle, and Jan and I slide tins of peas, oatmeal, and kippers into our packs from two shelves.

Ivar examines the tools.

Stein shoves a small barrel into a sack.

Another eruption sounds, longer and worse than the last. I would laugh, but the smell is so atrocious that curiosity takes over. I must look. Three sets of hands move quickly in a quelling motion, but I must know.

Diagonal daylight floods the cellar opening as I lift the trapdoor a few centimeters. Covering my mouth and shaking my head in disgust, I rear back on the ladder. Exactly how much alcohol does it take to pass out? Rolf's father, sprawled on the couch, has his pants undone, a girlie magazine and a big bottle of clear liquid on the floor beneath him. From where I'm standing, I have a direct line of sight up his nostrils. Herr Wik's bellow-like grunts are straight out of a jungle movie.

When I come back from England, I won't ever be able to look Herr Wik in the face. Herr Wik is my family's banker. I've never seen him without his felt fedora or Panama hat stylishly slanted on his head. I used to think Rolf got his looks from his father. And now this.

"Wha—?" he grunts. Herr Wik swings his feet down, his hairy toe barely missing my nose. The girly magazine falls, sliding on the top of the trap door, giving me more information about couplings and contortions than I've ever imagined and an opportunity to close the door.

The secrets that man has!

We flatten ourselves against the back wall.

Another footfall and gaseous eruption—the worst of the bunch. The floorboards squeak, and the door slams.

Ivar's head cracks open the manger's door. He motions with his hand for us to be silent. Circling his finger in a *wrap-it-up!* motion, he walks his fingers to let us know that Herr Wik is walking across the lawn to the outhouse. The outhouse door slams. Ivar holds up two fingers.

Two minutes? We're sure to be caught. Two minutes isn't enough.

Ivar evaporates like smoke.

Stein follows him, clutching his pack in front of him, tamping down the noise.

Jan's long legs seem to take the thirty meters to the small copse of aspen trees in seconds.

My turn. I ease out, my back clenching, and I lean back, inadvertently closing the door to the manger.

Rat-a-tat-a-tat-a-schrown! *Rat-a-tat-a-tat-a-schrown!* A high-pitched whistle passes by my head, and I want to scream. A rock next to the terrace moves. I've been seen, and I'm dead. *Schrown!* I hear splitting wood, and I want to puke. Nearing the shrubs, I look—finally—to where the shots are coming from. *Schrown!* Apples—the target practice—fly over the Gunderson's wall. A vision of my being the knife-throwing target at a carnival pops in my head. No sign of Ivar, but a few meters from the overturned boat, I see a movement to my left that must be Stein.

Hurdling a downed tree, the Spartan crouches behind a rock that barely conceals him.

Go! I'll bet everyone can hear the kippers clanging like a peddler's wagon in my pack. I'm breaking a sweat. My back hurts. I can't see the outhouse. What if Herr Wik opens the door? Diving behind the trees, I tackle Stein and Ivar. Sitting up, I apologize, when Ivar firmly claps his hand over my mouth.

Herr Wik lumbers out of the outhouse as voices,

laughing at a German joke, waft across the road and cove. Cocking his head toward the road and flipping off the soldiers, he pulls a flask from his robe and takes a sip.

I will have nightmares about the sight under that robe.

He dashes past the manger door, up the stone steps, shoulders the squeaking door, and disappears.

Thank God we didn't try that!

Five meters away, a rowboat lies on the beach like a beached-whale carcass. A tree branch, the thickness of my pinky finger, sticks out of the hull.

If that's the boat that will take us to the Shetlands, then we are in trouble.

****

Ivar reminds me of an otter as he not so much crawls but slips through the twigs and branches, making only the slightest splash as he dives into the ocean.

Stein, always a quick study, follows suit, as does Jan, who deftly negotiates the branches and rocks without a single problem. Their feet pop up with the briefest move, but Jan yelps as he hits the water.

My turn. As I crawl the five meters to the water's edge, I scrape my hands and knees on every rock shard and broken branch while my back muscles find new ways to cramp and seize. At the water's edge, I not so much dive as careen into the breathtakingly cold water, taking stones and dirt clods with me.

With silent consent—to hell with the sound!—we flip the whale carcass.

If we expect the tree branch to pop away from the cozy home it has made for itself in the hull, think again.

Ivar twists the limb, trying to break it in half but with

no luck. Reaching into his pack, he pulls out a knife from a sheath, and with what looks like a we'll-see-who's-tougher smile playing on his lips, raises the blade, bringing it down with the force of a guillotine.

Problem solved. Ivar wipes the edge of the blade with his hand, sheathes the knife, and moves on to the next task.

Jan spins his arms. "Where are the oars?" he whispers.

"They have to be in the cellar. Who doesn't have oars?" I whisper back.

Ivar's voice is slightly louder than the crashing waves. "I didn't see anything." Craning his head, he offers a solution. "Oars are usually in boathouses. The Gundersons, or rather, the Nazis, have a boathouse. Let's borrow the Nazi's oars."

And I thought I was the crazy one.

Ivar and Stein drop their packs on a speckled granite boulder, leaving Jan and me behind as scouts.

Jan swims out far enough to see the edge of the Wik property.

I hold the frayed, gray tow rope in my hand, welcoming the rest.

Ivar and Stein move like otters, their heads barely visible, cutting the water with sure, long sidestrokes until the boathouse and the Nazi Camp are in clear view. In tandem, they rest for the briefest moment before disappearing under the waves.

Like everything else Herr Wik's owns, the rowboat isn't much and is long overdue for care. I run my fingers along the boat's flanks, looking for softness and rot on the peeling, brown surface. I'm surprised to see that the exterior is sound. Uncle Bertin has a craft like this. Hell, everyone who lives within a meter of the coast has a boat like this.

A lifetime ago—was it only a year ago, after a night of Solsvik Bridge?—we took Bertin's identical boat to Smuggler's Rock. Roughly five meters long and a meter-and-a-half wide, this boat also has two benches and a storage caddy.

When a series of *rat-a-tat-a-tat-a-shrowns!* erupt, my head jerks up, and my eyes dart around. Then I smile. About ten meters out, three otter friends appear above the water's surface, carrying what looks like tree limbs.

With froglike motions, Ivar, Stein, and Jan swim toward shore, hauling the oars.

Climbing aboard the craft, we push away. The boat eases into the current. Unlike the rivulets of people on that day last April, as the Germans tramped into our city and country, we are no longer coasting or consenting. On a fjord of dissent, we're rowing toward our freedom.

Chapter Thirty-Three

Ivar is checking the boat's contents for usefulness. Sitting cross-legged in the hull, he has helped himself to our packs, picking at their contents like a scavenger.

The fjord's currents lap up the distance like a gentle river. I want to sleep—and I should since, according to Ivar, I will be rowing with him in less than an hour—but his intrusive method is unsettling to watch.

Ivar doesn't use his whole hand when pulling articles out of a backpack. He uses his thumb and index finger to extract an item. Then, mercilessly eyeing it against the cloudless sky, he brushes the shock of white-blond hair from his eyes and puts it in one of several piles according to its suitability. Food tins, stacked by type and shape, prop open the storage caddy.

Stein carried a small wooden barrel as he raced across the Wiks' lawn, but while I was staring at Herr Wik's nostrils and crotch, Ivar apparently handed several barrels to the others. These barrels appear to have a specific purpose.

As Ivar encounters our clothes, his face takes on the same look of apology Dr. Bertinson had last week when he asked to check my groin for damage. Ivar folds the clothes into thirds, smoothing the fabric with his hands, and places them along the bench like toy soldiers. Ivar returns the clothes, using his fingers like pincers to take the clothing and stack it back into our bags.

I remember Ivar standing by the stack of wood and tools near the manger and the way he seemingly evaporated into thin air. To my astonishment, his pack contains small wood pieces in neat piles, two hammers, boxes of nails, three screwdrivers, and a roll of stiff material. Ivar has also thought to bring the Norwegian flag with him.

The sail. I didn't think to include that or any tools. I was more concerned with Herr Wik's farts. Well, I'm not going to stack up. I can see that right now.

I feel a gentle kick against my foot. Opening my eyes, I see that the caddy door is closed. My pack rests at my feet with a tin cup tied to it. I have an assigned latrine bucket.

Clearing my throat, I decide to hatch the plan's next part. "I think two of us should row for two hours, and then we should switch."

I point at Stein and Jan, who toss their heads in Ivar's direction. Ivar must have covered the subject. I thought he was making suggestions, not taking over the trip's logistics.

"It's important to look like we're on an outing. We should point and talk to one another." I continue. "No rushing. We're four boys on an outing before going back to school."

Again, Jan and Stein nod, but they aren't looking at me.

Ivar has covered the subject.

A wave of anger comes over me, and I open my mouth to speak, but Ivar slides an oar into the holder, and mechanically, I do the same.

"I didn't ask, Kory," Ivar says. "Are you left- or right-handed? I don't want you wrenching your ribs."

His smile is open and genuine. His teeth are a shade less white than his hair, and I feel like an idiot for being angry.

Stein's knees are jackknifed in the space by the caddy. His hand rests against the lid as if protecting the contents. The Spartan, also jackknifed, is using his pack as a pillow.

Ivar pulls up his oars, and I do the same. He reaches down and extracts two packets and two oranges, handing one of each to me. "Lunchtime. I've been thinking about my sandwich all morning. And I love oranges, don't you?"

As I tear into the sandwich's creamy cheese, spicy cured meat, crusty homemade oatmeal bread, and the orange, one of Gramps Brooklyn-America phrases pops into my head. I'm not too fond of it.

Bit off more than you can chew?

****

After lunch, the sun's early afternoon glare on the water looks like a spear. While gentle and allowing Ivar and I to guide the boat out of trouble, the current has picked up and seems intent on hurling our boat against the rocks at the base of a lighthouse two kilometers ahead.

Jan stretches from his nap, motioning for the water barrel resting at Ivar's feet. Putting his dented tin cup to his lips, he wrinkles his nose in disgust as water spews from his mouth. After running his hand in the seawater, he tries again with the same result. "Here, taste it."

I take a sip. "Fish." I spit out the salty brine. "It's bad and does taste fishy. Who brought the barrel labeled *kippers?* I would have thought someone would have cleaned it out before filling it with water."

Jan's cold stare practically says, "Jerk!"

I raise my hand, accepting the admonishment. "We can stop and ask for water. Surely we have another barrel." I look at Jan, "Are you okay?"

Ivar holds up a sandwich and an orange, passing it to Jan. "Sandwich?" He picks up his oars again. "You need to wake up and eat these in the next twenty minutes. We'll switch to you two rowing, but I have to instruct you."

Stein wakes up and takes the last orange and sandwich.

I look around, thinking of a plan. "Ivar, can we stop at a boat station and get water? The kipper barrel's water is awful."

Ivar shades his eyes with one hand. "We'll be okay. It's a little salty, but we need salt. We don't want to get sick. We'll be in the Shetlands in less than seventy-two hours, and with us eating the food we brought and drinking the water, we'll be fine."

Ivar never says *could* or *should*. He states facts with certainty, just as he was certain we'd need two sets of oars and fabric to create a sail. He knows about sailing and voyages. He's right. We'll be fine.

Ivar points to me and pats the bench beside him. "Jan and Stein, we'll all row to the dinghy in the middle of the channel so we can assess how many ships are going each way. We all might need to row, or we can switch off until we get to the other side."

A fishing trawler chugs past us, and the captain waves.

We wave in reply.

The lighthouse is less than a kilometer away. A stiff breeze comes over the point, and the temperature drops several degrees.

"Stein," Ivar says. "Sit next to Jan. We're going to need to row together, especially—" Ivar points to a swirl of water where the fjords meet. "Let's avoid that eddy. We need our strength."

Our mission, clothed in the anonymity of the ordinary, is now subject to the scrutiny of the main fjord.

Chapter Thirty-Four

A low-riding gray boat with a spotlight perched on the wheelhouse, passing a kilometer away, causes the oars in my hand to vibrate, making my hands tingle.

In unison, the four of us straighten up, gripping the oars, and on an unspoken signal, launch ourselves into our next hurdle—rowing across the fjord undetected.

The alarm on my friends' faces mirrors my own, and I hear their thoughts as clearly as if they're speaking aloud. It's though we're thinking one thought. *Is that boat slowing down to look at us?*

Ivar reads my mind. "We have fifteen minutes from the time we see the ship entering the fjord to the time it passes by us. We need to be well outside their channel, or they'll blare their horn in warning. And that"— Ivar munches on an apple and points at the long channel, marked by the sheen of oil and the occasional buoy— "invites scrutiny. I've noticed that no two big ships ever go directly past each other. We must time our crossing so we're rowing hard for fifteen minutes, and we reach the dinghy."

Against the sun's spear-like glare, the red buoy bobs like a child's toy in a bathtub.

Ivar continues, "We can go slower for five minutes as we wait for the ship. We'll need to have our buckets ready in case we take on water from the wake."

I point north at a troubling sight. In the distance, a

German patrol boat is heading south.

Ivar nods. "We must look like four boys out for a day on the water. That's our plan. That's our story. We know nothing about the food and supplies in the caddy." His mouth is a grim line, and he's frowning, but his voice might as well be reporting the weather. "Are we in agreement?"

Our benches start vibrating.

Stein points, and we collectively gasp. A cargo ship is barreling northward through the entrance to the fjord.

As we inch across the water, straining against the current, my ribs ache. The vibration of the bench is at a hum.

Suddenly, the ship is within a half kilometer. The cargo ship's crates are stacked ten high. The sound of the vessel is deafening. As the waves course toward us, I'm positive we'll be thrown overboard. The first wave crashes over the side, lifting us, our boat skittering across the calmer sea behind us. We throw our weight against the wave to counterbalance the boat.

For what seems minutes, we're pelted by sea spray and thrown back from the ship's wake. The vibrations slow, and the waves flatten.

I breathe a sigh of relief. "That went okay."

The dinghy's gentle bobbing—maybe two hundred meters away—coaxes us, and we row again.

Stein points to the north. Lying in the water is a German cruiser, and the searchlight is swiveling unmistakably in our direction.

"Bullshit." Jan stands up, undoing his shorts. "Get us to the dinghy."

The current and our determination move together, and soon, the red dinghy jars our arms as we put our oars in to rest.

"Jan! You can't be serious!" I chide, but we're all starting to laugh. "Taking a leak, here?"

"Bullshit!" Ivar stands up and proceeds to take a leak in the middle of the channel, facing the Nazi cruiser.

Jan snorts. "I had to anyway. They can't arrest us for peeing in the ocean, right? What are the Germans going to do?"

They can chase us. That's what they can do. We're in trouble. The German cruiser we saw earlier is heading toward the other side of the channel, and a second cruiser meets them. I see two men in its wheelhouse. One is talking on a radio and pointing toward us. Even though the sun is beating down on us, I'm shivering. The captain's head turns. Jan turns pale, and Stein's jaw clenches. The man continues to stare at us. He reaches for controls, and my mouth goes dry. I don't know if our story is going to hold. There's a momentary glint from his sunglasses, and the boat's engine idles. The cruiser slices through the water for a few seconds.

To my mind, decisions are being sliced in the wheelhouse, as well. I watch as the captain cranes his head around the other man, to take another look at us. His head disappears behind the other man. *Would we be worth pursuing*?

The engine speeds up. The captain is facing away from us. I can make out his sunglasses as he appears to look north and west.

"Row, dammit, row!" Ivar bellows. "The cruisers are nearly upon us, and we're up shit creek. Let's go for that small channel ahead, and we can figure out if a boat is waiting for us on the other side."

The aspen trees and rocky shore of the channel's

western edge are about four hundred meters away.

With two—or is it eighty?—more strokes of our oars, our boat slides between the sun-dappled trees. Sheer cliffs rise thirty meters above us. My temperature and anxiety drop in the narrow channel as the cruisers' spotlights dance on the water behind us.

"They've turned away. We beat the Nazis!" Jan howls as we shoehorn into the crevice.

Well, not quite.

The cruiser blares a reverberating warning.

Stilling a low-hanging aspen's branch, I see a faint yellow circle trained on my hand. *Don't turn around. They don't know who you are! Don't give them an excuse to track you down.*

"Listen to me," I say, "and don't turn around. Don't. Turn. Around." I repeat this in case my friends can't hear the terror in my voice. "If the cruisers could come in here, they would. But they can't. That doesn't mean—"

Clearing his throat, Ivar pulls out a cigarette holder. "Kory's right," he says. "They probably have already sent a radio transmission to a cruiser near here, and it will be waiting for us." Ivar hands his cigarette to Stein, who takes a long drag before passing it back to Jan.

"But," Ivar goes on, "they can't wait forever for four kids in a boat."

I know two facts about Ivar. He's the calmest person I've ever met, and he holds everything as if he has pincers, even his cigarette.

"I need to make repairs," he says. "My feet are soaked, and I must find the leak. We're probably no more than two kilometers from the open ocean." Ivar pulls out an oar and pushes away from a rock. "Stein, I will need you to be my eyes as we go through the crevice." As he says this, we're jarred by a rock scraping against the hull. Unfazed, Ivar continues. "Jan and Kory? When we round that corner up there, I'll need you to sit here and use the oars to keep the boat away from the rocks."

Rippling waves—the cruiser's final retort—propel us toward a downed tree. With this, for the first time today, comes silence.

Ivar makes an impressive gondolier. Pushing against submerged trees and rocks, we come to a small waterfall. We dip our cups again and again, washing away the kipper taste and fright from our mouths.

Opening the wooden kipper barrel, I dump out the fishy water. Impetuously, I remove my shirt and dig in with my shirtsleeve to give the barrel a good rinse, rinsing the slats and crevices a second and third time.

"Jesus!" Ivar—he who is calm and relaxed under pressure— is alarmed. He points at my chest and then, in a modest gesture, points back to himself, diagramming my injuries. "Are you going to be okay? When did that happen?"

"I—"

Jan interrupts. "He got kicked by—"

Dammit! The Spartan cannot help himself.

"I fell off a ladder at Paul's cabin. I was kicking away a hornet with my foot. The doctor checked me out, and there are no serious injuries." I want to strangle Jan. "The reason they're circular is there was a barrel of flowers below the roof, and I fell into that."

Ivar takes this in, remaining quiet for what seems like a minute.

Through telepathy, I send a message to my best friend. *Don't blow this for us. I'm fine.*

Ivar cranes his head as if leaning to hear a faint

question. In answer, he poles the boat until we all hear the same question.

"Ready?" the water asks.

The Atlantic at last.

****

We nearly didn't see the advantages of stopping at the rock resembling a warty tadpole.

Green with a rounded head facing west, the monolith's north side is littered with small, smooth, flat recesses, the longest being a meter above the water and seven or eight meters long. Catapulting onto the ledge, Jan grasps my forearm and pulls me up.

Ivar and Stein are swiftly becoming an intuitive team. Stein's questioning of Ivar in a measure-twice-cut-once manner reminds me, again, that Stein's curiosity marks him as having the makings of a great engineer. Together, they seamlessly hand supplies to Jan, who continues his high-wire act.

Holding the rope in one hand and balancing like an acrobat, Jan suspends himself between the rock, the boat, and the water. For his final act in this circus, he pulls Stein and Ivar from the boat.

Ivar surveys the tadpole rock. "The ledge isn't wide enough for me to do my work. Pull the boat up onto the top. I need to see where the leaks are coming in."

Like a minke whale speared by a harpoon's lily iron, the boat twists and strains against the rope, skittering and dropping toward the cove once or twice, but like the mariners of old, we wrestle the craft up. Again, Ivar seems to have all the time in the world. His hand runs along the hull, fingers pressing and prodding at aging points, finally coming to rest upon a barely discernible dent. Reaching for a centimeter-long shank of wood, he breaks the piece, manipulating it as if working out a jigsaw puzzle. Nails appear in a nifty sleight of hand, and a ball-peen hammer materializes from his pocket. The old wood, forced to close the breach, squeaks in vain protest.

Standing up, Ivar wipes his hands on his shorts and pushes the ice-blond shock of hair back from his face in the manner of a man content with his labors.

The voice behind us doesn't come from Bergen. It's male, older, and possibly dangerous. "Do you think you will make it?"

When I turn around, I see that I guessed two things correctly. A man is in a boat, and he's older than me. But I didn't count on there being two men in a boat strewn with lobster traps and rope, and I still don't know if we are in danger.

Jan speaks up. "We're going fishing for a few days—going to see friends south of here."

The Spartan's voice has an assured cadence. I'm shocked and pleased at the same time. I glance at Stein, whose beet-red face and balled-up fists show him as anything but assured. Is he starting to cry? Oh, Christ on a stick, we're dead, finished, doomed!

In my mind's eye, the Spartan is in full battle dress as he strides to the edge of the rock, his carriage suggesting that our being here on a godforsaken rock in the ocean, miles from anywhere, is an ordinary occurrence. An incredible performance.

Maybe not.

The two men in the boat merely smile, coughing gently into their hands.

"Boys," the older man begins, "you are making repairs before going out fishing. Always a smart plan.

Can't be too careful."

Jan, his posture still in battle-ready Spartan mode, has his hands in his pockets.

Ivar is flicking his fingernail in what must be the biggest act of nonchalance I've ever seen.

The younger man smiles. "Having gotten out as you have, away from the coast in good weather, you will, of course, already know about the planes and ships going by—you, with your experience."

Ivar's head tips back slightly. "Right. The planes come two or three times per day now, don't they? We don't want to be shot at, so we're going to stick close to land. If we were to venture out to a better fishing hole, how could we avoid being spotted by the planes?"

My mouth drops open at this ballsy statement.

"I'm Torgeir, and this is my cousin Ole," the older man says. "We live up the way from here and heard the hammer's pounding. We came by to see if you need help." Torgeir hesitates as if plunging into an unknown pool. "Yes, the planes come by here around noon every day, so if you are fishing, you will be spotted and used as target practice. I would be out about eight miles over the horizon before eleven tomorrow morning to be on the safe side."

No hint of we're up shit's creek breaks Ivar's calm façade. "We encountered three German boats earlier. One looked like they were going to check us out, flashing their lights and turning their bow toward us. But, since we're fishermen, going to visit our friends in a few days, we didn't need to worry."

Ole slides his arm up, revealing a bigger gun than I ever smuggled through Nazi checkpoints. Then, he draws his oar through the water, bringing him and

Torgeir closer.

Call it instinct, or the fact that we're in this venture together, but we line up, our shoulders squarely touching one another, facing down the men below us.

Ivar stops his nail flicking. Coolly, he looks from Torgeir to Ole. "We can't be too careful. Nazis are all over the place. All we're doing is going to visit friends, going fishing. The boat is leaking, but, as you said, you really can't be too careful, so I brought extra supplies."

Ole taps his gun, which has a particularly sinister gleam.

I do not doubt it is loaded.

"Listen, boys," Ole says, "we might get ourselves shot over this, but you are going to Shetland. I mean, where are your fishing poles? This is not a sailing boat. You are not out to visit your friends unless your friends are over there." Ole jerked his thumb due west. My lower lip is bobbing worse than the buoy in the channel, and I've forgotten how to breathe. "We support what you're doing. We won't say anything. We have family that has tried to cross, but we don't know if they were successful. A cousin is in London. You are going to need help along the way."

Torgeir clears his throat. "Luck is on your side. The weather is supposed to be good. The wind should help you along. Just be over the horizon by no later than eleven tomorrow morning. It's eight now, so get some rest and get up in a few hours. You should be okay."

With that, I exhale, but my lower lip continues to bob up and down.

Torgeir pulls hard on the oar and steers the boat around the corner, heading north.

The sun lies low on the western horizon, cutting a

red swath above the blue ocean. A cloud blocks the sun for a moment.

I nudge Jan. "Look! The red sunset, the blue ocean, and the cloud…like our Norwegian flag."

"Such a poet!" Jan guffaws. "A flag on the ocean. Man, I can't believe what you say."

Jan is teasing, though I think he's surprised since he's always the one with his nose in the books, not me. I wave my hand at the water, sun, and sky, suddenly overcome with exhaustion. "We need to rest. How are we going to sleep?"

Stein and Ivar walk a few meters north, pointing to a rapidly drying boulder about the size of a car.

"Here's a spot where the German patrol ships can't see us, nor the planes, for that matter," Ivar says. "We'll sleep under the boat. The tide is going out. We're over two meters tall, so we'll have to squish down under the boat, keeping our feet from sticking out, and making sure not to tip the boat over by moving too much."

Jan tucks his rucksack under his head and looks at me. His furrowed brow tells me that he's scared, but he smiles. "Soldiering on."

My bed for the next few hours smells of seaweed and seagulls. The tiny gnat in my ear has a low guttural whine. Joining the gnat is another noise going thunk-cutta-thunk-cutta-thunk. I draw in a long breath and close my eyes. I want to look. If I were on my belly, facing the sea, maybe I could see what's happening. We didn't think to do that. We're lying on our backs, staring at a bench, with no idea of what's out there. In a minute… or less…I'll find out if I get to live another day.

Ivar hisses, "Nobody moves a muscle!" Instantly, we lay with our hands by our sides, our legs scrunched up to our chests, unmoving. The gnats are growing louder, coming closer but are not yet directly overhead.

The suspense is killing me. "I want to look out," I say impatiently.

Ivar, who up to this point has not said an angry word, snaps, "Kory, do it, and I will bash your skull in. Do you understand me?"

My gut wrenches at this, but I know he's right. We need to get up, but we need to wait.

The gnats brought company. Just as its motor fades in the distance, another loud motor drones above the lapping waves.

"Another plane, or maybe they see us?" Ivar asks.

I close my eyes and listen.

Stein says, "If they get close, and we don't move, they'll wonder why there's an abandoned boat out here and will come to investigate, so we're up a creek without a paddle. I say we jump in the water and swim for a rock or go underwater if we can. Maybe we'll be okay."

The din grows louder. The vibrations cause the metal oar rings to hum. The boat inches over to the drop-off. The plane is probably no more than a kilometer away, the sound is different. The engine…the engine…it isn't going *thunk-cutta-thunk*.

I whisper, "It's a different plane. There are two of them, one going north, one going south."

The boat shifts. All arms reach out to keep the rowboat from toppling over. I hear a collective intake of breath.

Ivar exhales with apparent relief. "I think the plane has moved north. Let's wait until we don't hear it anymore and get out of here."

The gnats fade away. Within a few minutes, the only

sound I hear is the gentle lapping of the water against the rock.

The sun casts a faint glow in the west, giving us enough light to see.

We flip the boat, spending a few minutes hoisting supplies onboard, tucking them into a small space at the stern, and placing the extra set of oars under our benches. There is a moment of silence as we glance around, looking for any stray tool we might have missed.

My shoulders straighten. I glance at Ivar, who is looking at me as the leader. "All clear?" I ask.

There are murmurs of yes.

There are no speeches. So, with a small knot in my stomach, I say, "Okay." I study the black core twisting around the Milky Way, which offers no answers to my unasked questions.

Pushing past tadpole rock, we follow the golden trail of the setting sun into the open ocean.

Chapter Thirty-Five

Ivar and Stein take the first shift. Their hands and arms move together, making a steady *slap-whoosh-slap-whoosh* as we course through the powerful currents, the fjords rushing and spilling their contents as we venture into deepening waters. Ivar is a patient teacher, and Stein, an apt student.

Stein points. "When we see a calm spot, we know we're heading south and west, right?"

Ivar nods. "We'll feel a little shudder and a shimmy as the two currents collide. I view that collision as a good way to sense our surroundings."

Above us are a purplish-gray myriad of stars, a barely perceptible moon, and the Milky Way's twisting cord. Sitting upright in the stern, staring at Ivar and Stein's placid faces, I'm soothed, as when my mother tended me in a rocking chair, long ago, and I drift into a dreamless sleep.

Jan and I are nudged awake. Stein and Ivar take our identical sleeping positions.

A breeze flutters against my collar and thighs as I sit down. I signal to Jan to let the oars rest, and we let the boat drift for a few minutes as I take stock. The water appears to flatten in the darkening light. The shudder or shimmy of the fjords meeting the ocean must have passed while I slept.

Jan and I create a steady rhythm, the creak of our

oars chiming in unison.

My shoulders sway as I row, the rhythm of the oars in my head as they swoop up and catch, pull and pull free and pull again, creating what resembles the beat of a tango. I begin a chant in my head, silently counting out a beat.

T—the oar's at two o'clock; A—the oar's at eleven; N—dip at nine and pull; G—to six; and O—at four. Tango!

I hear tango music in my head, and I picture my clumsy, halting steps in the Carhart's basement. Panning the violet-tinged horizon, I hear a Paris accordion and piano and see myself swaying from the sidelines. I imagine Paul and Ingrid. They look so good together.

Jan is muttering about people being lost at sea.

I snap around to look at him. "Sorry. Lost in my thoughts. Rowing feels like a tango."

His hand cups down into the water, and he splashes me.

I grin.

A shooting star streaks across the coal-dust-gray sky, and I make the only wish that makes sense right now.

We row for another hour. By agreement, we nudge our friends awake.

They stand wearily and, without objection, exchange places with us.

Tucking my head against the prickly canvas Ivar chose to rest on earlier, and despite the fabric being unyielding and scratchy, I nod off.

There's a tug on my shirt once again. I start raggedly, but soon, I lose myself in the rhythm of the tango music playing in my head.

I glance back to see that the mountain tops deep in the fjord are disappearing with only a line of thinnest charcoal showing above the faintest pale-blue sky. How can the sky appear so serene while my stomach and water have started to churn? Have we hit the convergence of the currents? Will we be out far enough by eleven to escape detection by the Germans? How far is far enough? To help control my fear, I count how many oar strokes we do in what I think is a minute. Fifteen? In my head, I multiply that by ten minutes, a half-hour, and an hour.

With the next switch, Ivar devours two cans of peas, liquid and all, heaving the cans into the sea like the baseball player Lou Gehrig.

Stein curses in a barely audible tone about how this had better be a short trip.

The two-on and two-off situations may not have been a wise choice.

I think my calculations will give us a goal. "I've been counting," I say. "We need to cover fifteen thousand meters to be out of harm's way. With our rowing, I think we gain probably fifteen hundred meters in an hour. Probably more. To be out of danger, I think we need to be doing two thousand meters per hour."

Stein mutters under his breath and, like Ivar, hauls off a can of carrots into the waves.

Jan groans, and as I turn to fill the Spartan in on my grand plan, my nose and ears are assaulted by a foul retch and the even fouler smell of bile. As Stein reaches for the water, Jan doubles over, furiously covers his mouth, and waves the barrel away. "That awful water! Is that all we brought?"

I recall Harold and Jan's insistence on keeping a

dead aim on the horizon when we were at Smuggler's Rock. I hadn't put it together that he might be seasick. At least not until now.

I touch Jan's shoulder blade. "Can you pick a spot on the horizon and continue to look at that? Don't look up or down, just ahead. Do you think you can do that for me?"

Jan pushes me away.

Ivar heaves a long sigh, the sound—I think— continues longer than necessary. "We need to get moving," he says. "We're not that far out, and trawlers and other ships might see us."

His words, said as if he was discussing the obvious to a toddler, cut me to the quick. Half rising off the bench, I shout, "That's enough! We are risking everything to be here! People have died! I know what we're not doing, but we're not getting any clear instructions on what we should be doing. How much longer do you think this should take? Do you think all four of us should row until we're over the horizon?"

The boat rocks, and I lose my balance, sitting down hard on the bench. Flushing in embarrassment, I purse my lips, looking for a smirk from Ivar. "We need answers. Clear answers," I say.

Ivar opens his mouth, but I cut him off. Ivar doesn't know my friends as I do.

Touching Jan's shoulder, I glare at Ivar. "Here's what you need to know about us. We hit specific targets. We don't like uncertainty but give us a mission, and we'll complete the task. Back home, well, you don't know what we have done, but we complete things. Dangerous things. Answers," I say, my rant ending like a deflated balloon, "we need answers."

Ivar gazes at me and out to sea. Rather than accept my challenge, he shrugs. "Let's let out the chip log and see what it tells us."

Ivar reaches into his rucksack, taking out a wooden board in the shape of a quarter circle, its lead weight dulled by years of use. Three lines dangle from the instrument. He hands a twenty-eight-second hourglass to Stein and raises his hand. "On my mark, let out the line and stop when I say stop."

Our bodies tense as Ivar waits until the last grains of sand fall into the bottom of the hourglass.

"And now!" Ivar commands. The white cords pull away from the boat's stern. Jan and I watch as the knots slip between Stein's fingers, and we count aloud.

"And stop!" Ivar holds up his hand and pulls up another painted board. "We need the number to be at least eight nautical miles out." He reaches into his rucksack again. "I'm going to use the traverse board. Then I'll be able to get a dead reckoning."

Ivar looks at the oil compass, drumming his fingers mechanically up and down in an ancient ritualistic rhythm. His eyes evaluate the distance. "I think we're about seven miles out. We need at least another mile. More would be better. As long as we're beyond the horizon, we should be safe."

He glances skyward, pulling out a sextant from his pack. Taking a sighting off the horizon, he leans forward and twiddles his fingers. His head nods. "I'm double-checking—I do that—confirming roughly seven miles, I reckon, and a generally western direction. Let's eat and take stock. All who aren't too tired can row."

Ivar continues to row, his muscles arching in a constant rhythm.

I offer a can to him, and he waves me off.

"I'm fine," he says. "I'm used to this."

"Look," I say, "I need for us to be far enough out that we cannot, under any circumstances, be spotted. You know that, but I'm scared we will be, and then this will have been for nothing." I think we both know how weak my apology is. A vague headache throbs, and I rub my eyes.

"Are you doing all right?" Ivar's face is impassive. He glances over and smiles. "I've spent a lot of time out here, and I've grown used to the little pitfalls that come my way."

Ivar is taking stock of me.

He grimaces at my sorry sight. The next time he speaks, his tone is neutral. "Are you getting headaches? I squint a lot and try not to look into the sun. The water's glare can bother you. I tend to listen rather than look at the water. Not much can get us that we won't see ahead of time."

And with that, the gnats return.

****

The sun is overhead when I hear a plane's faint hum coming from the south with the unmistakable *thunka-thunka-thunka* I listened to the previous day.

At the sound, Jan scrambles up onto the boat's edge.

I take the opposite perch to keep the boat from tipping. The sun warms my back, and everything would be wonderful if I weren't worried about being shot.

The others shift their weight on the boat's railing, trying not to lean too much in one direction or the other.

The gnats are swarming. My voice sounds calm, but I'm ready to bail. "Can you see it? If we can see the plane, they can see us, so we'll jump in. They can't shoot all of us, so dive and swim away from the boat."

The hum grows louder still, and my stomach gets tighter, willing the shooting star I wished on, or anything at all, to grant my wish.

Jan retches, and we all turn angrily toward him.

"God, not now! Please, not now! Please!" I shout in fear.

The *thunka-thunka-thunka* grows louder. Now, I retch, and my friends tell *me* to shut up.

The boat rocks, our gangly legs hanging in the water, our white knuckles grip the boat's edge. Then, as if a scissor has sliced the ribbon of sound tethering us to the plane, the sound grows fainter, finally unspooling, until all is silent again.

The wind picks up. My shirt flutters in the breeze, and I throw my shoulders back to capture more warmth on my back.

The others swing their legs into the boat with a resounding stamp.

We're now far enough out that we can't be seen or heard, and three of us are celebrating outwardly.

Ivar pulls a long canvas tarp from the caddy. "No sail." He pulls at the material, letting out a sigh. Pulling out his backpack, he finds a nail. He taps the nail into the canvas, creating a small pucker in the fabric. Ivar hammers again and again. Finally, a small tear appears.

Ivar tears more holes, and he and I thread the rope through the holes, pulling on the fabric to create a sail.

Jan and Stein set themselves to the task of tying knots on each side of the holes. Soon, we have a sail made.

Ivar puts an oar into the mast hole.

The boat lurches forward, and Ivar and I quickly

reach for the rope to hold it steady.

"Easy, Man o' War!" I call. The blue-gray water slaps the bow as the boat speeds across its glassy surface, skimming the waves. "Look how far we've come and how fast we're going! Sparta!" I pump my fist in the air.

Jan, Stein, and Ivar's hands all rise, the sea spray catching them.

Jan jockeys the boat's stern as if it's a horse. "On Man o' War! Dammit, on! You know you have it in you!" he shouts. His eyes, though, are fixed on the horizon. He doesn't glance at anyone, just the horizon.

Our laughter continues as the sun rises higher in the sky.

I can almost taste our success. It will be easy now. Another day, maybe two, and we will be victorious. We'll be heroes!

The little boat makes good headway. Although we don't have a rudder, we follow the sun, knowing the Shetlands are, at most, two days ahead. Even the kippers and peas taste good. We break out the chocolate, too.

"I don't eat chocolate," Ivar says, "as my parents consider it to be a luxury." Ivar nibbles on the chocolate, breaking off small pieces, savoring the morsels as if swallowing fine wine.

I arch my eyebrows, stunned by this peek into a side of life I've never considered.

"Bill is the one who brings some for us when we go on hikes," Ivar says.

Stein leans in at the mention of his brother.

"I wonder how he's doing. When we fish and hike, Bill uses the chocolate as a treat for me if I get the most fish or ski up a hill faster than him." Ivar's eyes crinkle at the memory. "Bill and I began training for the

Shetland Gang the morning of the invasion,"—he passes a sliver of chocolate over every taste bud in his mouth— "and we found ways to climb up Ulriken Mountain at least four or five days per week when I was in town. When I'm on the ship, I run up and down the stairs. The Gang wants strong men, yes, but with discipline and experience, too."

Swallowing the chocolate as if it were from the finest chocolatier in France, he looks westward, his face wistful. "I'm glad you thought to ask me. I have wanted this opportunity for so long."

Chattering about the Shetlands, Jan, Stein, and I talk of Paul's newspaper sources, who state that the Norwegians and English are making headway in the war and that Lerwick is full of opportunities to make an increasing difference.

Ivar whistles, shaking his head in disbelief at our newspaper and gun exploits.

I speak up. "Jules."

A large cloud passed over Ivar's face. "Yes, your brother. I know of him. He's why you are here?" He inhales, his eyes darting back and forth. "Does he know you're here? How we got here?" Ivar's eyes, now the shade of ice before it breaks, look into mine.

I shake my head. "No, I left Paul's cabin and got my things from my house quickly. Jan and Stein never saw Jules." I look pointedly at my friends. "Right?"

The Spartan and Stein vigorously shake their heads, and Ivar's shoulders relax. "You will pass for eighteen," Ivar says as if it were a foregone conclusion. "Armed with our bravery and willingness to do what's necessary, we will put our pasts behind us. Those traits are our calling cards."

I push Anne out of my mind, thinking of Shetland's green hills, how the food will be better, the girls, prettier, and how people will read of our work with pride.

And we'll do it.

The wind shifts. Once again, we take our heading off the sun and tend to the sail in shifts as the miles click by.

I become sleepy, my thoughts jumbling together as I close my eyes. Small sprays hit me from time to time, but I don't care. I go to sleep with one word in my brain.

Heroes.

Chapter Thirty-Six

I hate seagulls. Their beady eyes, their greediness, their insolence, and their complete unwillingness to take no for an answer make me nervous. And with Bergen being a seaport, seagulls are around all the time. So, when I hear their awful screeching, practically feeling their wings brushing my head as they sail right over me, my mood upon waking up is not good. Seagulls have discovered us and are swooping down for a snack and an investigation.

"Stop feeding them! They're getting too close to us." Jan's voice oozes irritation.

This is one of the reasons why the Spartan and I are best friends. We hate seagulls.

Sitting up and rubbing the sleep from my eyes, I'm startled by two discoveries. Firstly, Ivar *enjoys* feeding those damn birds, laughing as he tears off salt-encrusted bread while the birds cartwheel and dive for the morsels. Secondly, Ivar, who is not the most demonstrative person on earth, preferring to keep his emotions *deeply* in check, is hugging Stein's shoulder and pointing excitedly. Is he giddy? *What's* going on?

"We're getting close to land," he says, beaming. "You know you can tell where we are just by looking at the currents."

Ivar is...jubilant?

Closeness to the Shetlands smells of salt air and

sweat. Another gull swoops over us and decides my back is the perfect place to unload.

Ivar takes in a long breath, announcing he's tired and needs a rest soon.

Another tin of kippers, sardines, and peas provide a tasty snack. I slurp the oil and, feeling lucky, take another swig from the water barrel before passing it to Ivar.

Ivar pinches his nose, guzzling the water.

I don't know which is worse, retching on awful water or hearing the gnats return.

In unison, we look south in terror as the unmistakable sound of a plane comes straight for us.

We aren't going to escape, no matter how hard we try. Jules was right. I'm not man enough to be here. I think of a fly I once saw land on a mirror in our living room. The fly seemed to be preening, admiring its wings in the afternoon sunlight. Gramps' newspaper made short work of any notions of survival. We'll look the same way after the plane comes by. I sob and retch.

The Spartan reaches out, resting his hand on my shoulder.

Stein wears the same expression as me, his eyes scanning the air, darting every which way.

Farther back, Ivar is ready to spring.

We are all coiled and still.

We are going to die.

You? A smuggler?

We are trapped. Pulling our oars in, we scramble onto the boat's edge.

The gnat's guttural buzz grows louder.

A black dot, the size of a pin, pulses ten degrees above the horizon. As the pin draws closer, a red flashing light appears.

Jules' voice purrs in my head. *Your lies are what brought your friends here. All your doing.*

"Do you hear that?" asks Jan, his black curls hanging lopsided across his face. "It's different!"

The gnat's din is getting louder, and the pin is twenty degrees above the horizon.

Jan continues, "It's not German, or it's a different German plane!"

Forty-five degrees above the horizon. With two blinking lights.

We hold our heads up in the air, like setters hearing a capercaillie ruffling its feathers.

Seventy-five degrees above the horizon. The plane is round, green, and displays unmistakable letters as it whizzes above us.

RAF.

Royal Air Force. England. Are we in English waters?

I whirl around while Ivar and Stein scramble through the caddy's contents. My eyes never leaving the plane, I absently take a corner of our Norwegian flag. Realizing what I'm helping to hold up, I snap to attention. We wave our colors, our symbols, and our pride for the world to see.

The plane circles around and descends. Little spitting circles jump up in the water. The noise is deafening. Our boat nearly capsizes as we wave the flag back and forth, but I don't care. Tipping the plane's wings, the pilot salutes us. I drop a corner of the flag and salute back. Hot, snotty tears roll down my cheeks and chin. Loud snuffles coming from either side of me tell me that I'm not alone.

The green tail and flashing red light disappear in the northern haze, the red light blinking in time with my breath. Within a few minutes, the din is gone.

For an instant, my being splits wholly into two. Externally, I scream and howl like a wolf. My friends and I burst into joyful tears, singing and whooping and howling like deranged wolves. Internally though, I'm on mute.

We've done it. We're close enough to be in English waters. The Resistance will send a boat or plane to pick us up. We've made it!

A breeze returns. Ivar frowns, balling his fist, kneading the base of his skull. He breathes in quietly and repeats the process. "The wind has changed direction. We're a little off course, but we can correct that. We need to shift the sail.

We take the sail down, and after shifting the pole and ropes, our little boat skims through the water.

Jan begins to sing that horrible German song we heard at Neptun Konditori with Anne. That day seems a lifetime ago. Jan, Paul, Rolf, Anne, and I met at the bakery. She smiled at the song. Now I understand the looks that passed between my friends. Paul and Jan had stared at me. They were obviously deciding whether or not to voice their opinion on what an idiot I was.

Now, Jan is bellowing the song with apparent disdain. His eyes affixed on the horizon, his middle fingers pointing to where the enemy lies, he cackles and grunts. I join him, middle fingers extended. Soon, Stein joins us. The three of us oink, bray, and make every disgusting noise we can think of.

Ivar is deftly changing tack, and the boat slows as water sprays over the sides.

I lay my head on top of the bow, my enthusiasm and vocal cords exhausted. I let out a large sigh, ready to sink into a nap when I see something serrating the waves a few meters from me. What's bobbing on that wave? What appears to be an oar, splintered with teeth-like edges and plumped with water, has been nearly split in two. "Look at that!" I exclaim, pointing.

The others peer over the side.

I grab a spare oar and kneel on the port side. Leaning over the water, I reach out with the oar as far as I can and sweep the water toward me, trying to coax the floating derelict to come like a reluctant stray kitten. "An oar? Jesus, what happened to that?"

Another bit of wood, unidentifiable, drifts past us.

Ivar reaches into the water, snagging a large, polished piece of wood, scorched on its sheer, jagged edges. He pulls it up for us to examine. His voice is awestruck. "It's a piece of a hull, I think. See the curves?"

"Mines?" I ask of no one in particular.

Jan breaks the silence, his eyes never leaving the horizon. "Herr Mitchell called my father four days ago, and Papa spoke to a group of people, so I heard much of the conversation."

I break in. "He continues to be in contact with your father?" The Spartan's and my shorthand are leaving Ivar and Stein in the dark, so I quickly bring them up to speed.

Ivar pulls in the oars, his hand lightly holding the rigging.

Jan picks up where I left off, his eyes fixed on the horizon. "Papa said, 'The English are putting mines in the water, but English boats would know to avoid them and how to have them attached to German submarines.'

The English attach the bombs in the fishing lines, or in what looks like fishing lines. Norway is to contact other countries, such as Sweden or the United States, if possible, to let them know the areas to avoid when they sail to England."

It might be a trick of the light, but I could swear that both Stein and Ivar shiver. Ivar's long fingers curl under his nose, and Stein looks like he has been slapped. Neither friend blinks.

Jan flicks salt from his arm as he continues. "It has become a brisk trade. Herr Mitchell talked about how the client thought we were so stupid that we wouldn't catch on to the fact that we were producing mines that would kill us."

The Spartan's head swivels to look at me directly. "Hilda was at our house the next day. She talked to Papa about a Techworks cannery-parts project order. I overheard her saying how Herr Henricksen created three projects. You carried those parts, Kory. You mailed them out."

"Why do you call her—" I cut myself off, sitting back to think of the broader implications of what I unknowingly carried to the post office, what Paul and I brought. Tools to kill people.

Flicking the last of the salt from his arm, Jan looks westward. "Herr Mitchell asked Papa, again, if he knew of any Resistance groups."

The boat tilts as we lean into where Jan is seated.

"The conversation was four days ago?" Stein is doing math. "Does your father know about us? Does Herr Mitchell?"

The Spartan shakes his head. "The English may want us dead. Herr Mitchell might be right. Why shouldn't the English defend themselves? I know they support us, but why not try to keep us from coming over?"

Jan looks warily into the water, quickly resuming his steady gaze outward. "I don't think we're out of the woods yet. I don't think that boat was any larger than the one we're in right now. If that—" Jan points to where the debris was. "If a mine caused that, we need to be vigilant. Our mission might not be as easy as we thought."

Stein's fingers point skyward, and his tone is defiant. "We're going to be picked up. We made it this far, and they know about us. We'll be in Shetland by tomorrow, I'll bet."

"I wonder how many people were on board the boat. I wonder what happened?" Ivar asks. He's as curious as I am.

The Spartan is rowing with rags wrapped around his hands. He's not exactly green around the gills, but he's turning pale. He continually brushes salt off his forearms, sloughing the skin underneath.

Absently, I pick at the tiny scabs on my skin, as well.

The wind shifts, and again, we pull the sail down, adjusting the ropes to line up with the air currents.

Ivar looks north and west at a few thin wisps of clouds beginning to form along the horizon. Then, pulling out his compass, he smiles. "We should be in Lerwick tomorrow."

****

I smell warm, rotted fish.

Breathing in, I wave away the horrible smell and open my eyes. Stein is pushing my shoulder and pointing. Ivar sits a meter from me, his head oscillating like a farm sprinkler. My thoughts are a jumble, and a voice within barks orders at me. *Straight ahead. Snap ten degrees. Snap ten degrees. Snap ten degrees to the shoulder. Straight ahead.*

Stein climbs over the bench, facing Ivar. They become twin sentries as his head movements mimic Ivar's.

The sea, or creatures in the sea, are playing percussion. Even I recognize this as an idiotic thought, but I don't know how else to explain the way the bow is shimmying as if reverberating from gigantic bass drums far below us. The muffled *clank-clank-clank* are like gigantic cymbals or a xylophone. The sound, coupled with a rhythmic whooshing, must come from a whistle.

As I lift my head off the bow, I catch another whiff of the rotten kippers, and I retch. The sentries pause before continuing their oscillations while the percussion around us and below us amplifies its presence. There is a cloud—white, pillowy, and tinged with the faintest yellow—above me. I look down and see a perfect mirror image of the cloud and a red-haired boy, a blond boy with a hand cupped over his eyes, and a rail-thin young man whose hair nearly matches the cloud's color. Craning my head to look around, I hold my hand over my nose to block any more whiffs of a putrid carcass. We are the sole occupants in all directions. I retch again because we're most assuredly prey.

I begin to oscillate. When I press my fingers on the boat's edge, they tingle. As the clanking grows louder, the oar rests inch back and forth. Although fastened tightly into the boat's frame, the screws loosen. I watch in horror as the boards darken and water leaks through the boat's wooden frame.

The gigantic cymbals crescendo.

It's a ship. We can't see it, that's all. Right?

The sea has a sheen of smooth navy damask. Our heads snapping at ten-degree intervals, we watch the damask pucker as if thin fingers are under the fabric. The splashing waters move quickly like a drummer giving a bravura performance to thunderous applause. I suck in my breath and point.

Stein opens his mouth to speak but stops himself as the fingers withdraw from the puckered fabric, and the ocean is, once again, a bolt of satiny damask.

The clanking fades like kettle drums quieted by a firm hand. Soon, all is silent except for waves lapping against the boat. The sea mirrors an image of the cloud above me. The red-haired boy in the mirror is pale but appears to be as calm as the surrounding sea.

I think back to the day of the invasion. Jan and I stood in the harbor, holding our noses. From a distance, the creature in the sea appeared to be a whale, right down to its gray color and blowhole. As we drew closer, the smell of the churned kelp, seabed, and fish was nauseating. Then, from the beast's protruding blowhole, which, in reality, was the hatch, soldiers emerged. The behemoth heaved a long, hissing sigh, and the timpani-like engines quieted.

Stein points downward. "I wonder if they know we're here and if they're friend or foe."

Chapter Thirty-Seven

I don't have an overactive imagination when I say the kipper barrel is drooling slimy, gray strings of ooze, which is the only available drink…other than kipper juice. The kipper barrel also rumbles. My ribs are reliving being kicked by Herr Thompson and straining a muscle while rowing, and my breath seems to come from the upper part of my ribcage. I want to rub my butt on the bench, but I know that will gross everybody out. Rubbing my hands on my back isn't working. I slither my back up the ship's hull, looking for relief. When I feel a *pop!* and liquid trickling down my back, I'm glad to have a shirt on.

The Spartan and I now share the same shift and row with our backs jammed against the hull in the same pose. Keeping our other-purpose buckets at the ready, only inches from our noses, we stare at the horizon, counting our strokes and willing the voyage to be over.

Stein and Ivar are developing a kind of speech shorthand.

"Remember," says Ivar, "I said the depths off the Shetlands were not as deep as those by Norway, and we could expect higher waves?" Ivar's finger draws a long line from north to south. "There's a trench," he says, "and we have lots of water spilling into the sea. The Gulf Stream feeds in up there." Ivar points north. "The closer you get to the Shetlands, well, the water has no place to go, so it gets choppy. We may start seeing that, and that's okay. The choppier the water is, the better it is, as that means we're getting close to the Shetlands."

The Spartan stops rowing, and his face disappears into his bucket. He kneels, holding the caddy and displaying his backside. "Yeah, I know, great news, but look at this." The bottom of his shorts underneath his butt has worn through.

"I can give you a pair." Stein quickly rummages through his pack, handing over the shorts to Jan.

Jan's face disappears into the bucket again. Licking his lips, he wipes them with his hand. "I just want to keep my lips from getting so chapped."

Stein picks up an opened tin of kippers, dabbing the oil on his fingertips. "See if this will work, Jan. You'll smell like a fish, but you won't hurt so bad."

The breeze, which I welcome, as it helps me stay awake, has changed and is colder. Stein repositions the mast as Ivar scans the horizon.

"Mackerel clouds." Ivar points at the high, thin clouds. I remembered they're a harbinger of a cold front on land, but out here, I don't know if that's all they mean. He turns toward me and isn't paying attention to the wind. His eyes were on the northern and western horizon.

I follow his gaze, and so does Stein.

Ivar dips his hand in the water, and as I follow his arm, he appears to be making a figure eight.

Stein gasps.

When I look over at the Spartan, I see that he, too, saw what Ivar did.

Solsvik. I gulp, remembering the look on Harold's face, how he passed the clouds off as a casual occurrence. I think he didn't want us to panic. But he looked at the lighthouse, which turned on its warning lights, and said we had to hurry back to the village to avoid the danger.

We're nowhere near Solsvik. And Lerwick is only an idea.

The sun disappears behind a cloud I didn't see forming a few minutes ago.

Ivar pulls out the logline, having Stein count off the knots as he holds up the twenty-eight-second hourglass. He hasn't asked us to do that for a couple of days. Finally, Ivar grows still, calling out, "Stop!"

Stein pulls the log in. Once again, Ivar calculates, his fingers moving this way and that in the air. "I think we're about thirty-five miles from the Shetlands." Ivar declares, unsmiling.

The waves are splashing higher on the port side. "Look! The water…the trenches…we must be so close," Stein says with a grin. "We can find Bill! Then, we can help with the Resistance. Just a few hours more."

Ivar studies the northern and western horizons, which have grown even cloudier during the past few minutes.

A fog descends on the horizon as if curtains are closing to reveal the narrowest of vistas, obliterating half the sun within seconds.

Ivar declares, "We're all going to need to row as hard as we can and take advantage of whatever breeze we have available." He pointedly looks at Jan, who is picking at scabs on his arm. "We'll need to row."

Jan and I nod.

Ivar points to the fog that has now nearly enveloped the sun. The clouds, now a dark gray, rumble and tumble across one another. He points again, and we all turn to look as the fog engulfs more of the sunlight.

"Well, boys," he says, "you are about to find out what you signed up for."

Chapter Thirty-Eight

July 30, 1941

The sun is gone, and the fog, or what we think is fog, has coiled around us like an insidious specter. The coil smells of Gran's cinnamon Christmas cookies, lemon, and Uncle Bertin's lambing pen. I hear the faint cries of a newborn lamb, and I'm hopeful.

Lerwick. Lerwick has sheep.

The wind intensifies, creating an unrelenting screech of anguished, tortured animals in my ears. The overpowering smell of cinnamon smacks me in the face again. I'm brought back to the scent of Herr Tveit's tea and his instructions about the Bean Nighe.

My favorite teacher wears a vest of the Sinclair clan, laying on a Highlands burr worthy of Robert Burns himself.

"Laird Mowat and the rest of you Milesians," Herr Tveit says, snickering. "Your homework is to read the story of the *Bean Nighe,* the fairy washerwoman. She's small, almost insignificant, but her songs and her voice, like the Mongols, carry across the meters, promising success. Sailors rationalize that they're smarter than her, but she is clever. All the while, she meekly tends to her washing. As she begins twisting the cloth, inspecting, slapping the clothes on the rocks, her voice rises in anger."

Herr Tveit sets down his cup of tea on the desk. He brings his hand up in the air. Then, as he strikes the edge of the desk, he raises his other hand, encouraging us to slap our desks as if taking out our frustrations.

Our hands slap our desks, our thighs, our books. We laugh, but Herr Tveit's extra-thick burred speech silences us.

"She raises her head, and for the first time, you see her features. Toothless, crimson-haired, warted. Green-tinged skin and the blackest, coldest eyes. Her fingers grow longer, her nails turn into claws that tear your flesh, begging you to hear her.

"Or, she can resemble the person you love the most, and you will trust what she says. Make no mistake. Her cooing voice pulses in your head until you go mad, pleading for mercy, promising her your life, your soul. All the while, she washes the bloodstained clothes of those about to die." Herr Tveit raises his arms, dropping his hands in a ghostly, I'm-coming-for-you fashion over Frida's head as my classmates and I giggle at the mock horror of what we know… or believe… to be a fairy tale.

As I hunker down in our small craft, at the mercy of the elements, the Bean Nighe is no fairy tale. Death's specter is here, with her unearthly keening threatening to rupture my eardrums. Her wind savages us from all directions, and the water she commands begins to swamp our boat.

Jan seeks refuge, squirming and shoving his head and shoulders into the narrow recesses of the bow, his head bent, his curls pressed flatly against his pale head. He waves his bandaged hands in protest or resignation. We have angered the washerwoman, and our penalty is clear. We or a family member, even if they're far away or don't know yet, are going to die.

Dropping my oar, I hoist my vomit bucket and begin baling water. I can't row and bail simultaneously, but I decide to keep our feet and bodies dry.

Ivar's screams circle with the wind. "Row! Jesus Christ, Kory! Row!"

In the winter before the war, Jan invited me to Voss to see a family friend, who I now know is Herr Carhart, participate in a biathlon event. The skiing center of Western Norway, Voss, had cross country and slalom skiing, a lake for ice skating, and a bobsled course, for which the family got participation tickets.

Participation meant that we could watch—which we did—as Herr Carhart received a medal for winning in his age bracket. Participation also meant that we could try a new sport. In this case, it was going on a bobsled course with my best friend at the helm.

The sled wasn't much. With pitiful rusted scratches running its entire length, dings nearly a hands-width deep peppering the top, and scrapes obliterating the name of a disgraced racing team, the sled gave every indication of not surviving Jan's and my maneuvers. I had a million logical reasons for not putting myself in harm's way, and I objected, but having heard the chicken clucks of my friends behind me, any argument I might have prepared was fruitless. Sliding into the sled, I became temporarily Catholic, praying to any saint protecting idiots in bobsleds.

Like a Roman candle, we shot down the course. Exhilarated, I thought we might be masters of this. On the first curve, the sled pitched to the right, and we rolled. My knee slammed into the wall, and we skidded sideways.

I had the sensation that everything within me was trying to calibrate to my surroundings. My head turned sideways so that my lungs and heart were at a perfect ninety degrees to my head. My legs became untethered from the sled, and I was defying gravity. I was, for a moment, airborne. I knew beyond certainty that I'd be ejected from the sled and slammed into a tree and that I'd have zero control over anything that happened to me in the next second and a half.

Miraculously, Jan steered us back onto the course, and we finished.

Until now, I have suppressed that memory of possible ejection.

Digging in with my oars, the boat stubbornly resists my movements, continuing to nose its way east. I pace myself, which does not necessarily mean keeping time with Ivar and Stein. I have no idea if we're making headway.

I look down at the Spartan, who is still a huddled wretch in the bow. Red splotches have appeared on his cocooned knuckles. A long, wet, pink stream courses down his inner arm.

Ivar mutters to Stein, who stops rowing. Then Ivar bellows, "Stop rowing! Stein and I will try to row diagonally and head northwest across the waves. Maybe that will work better. You can start soon."

Jan's head lifts. With his enveloped hands, he takes his head and gently places it back in its original position as if correcting an incredibly bad idea.

I shift into neutral, watching Ivar and Stein's shoulder blades threaten to tear through their shirts, their backs straining with every stroke. All the while, I'm anticipating our next calamity.

The waves pitch us heavily to our right, giving me the sensation of being back on the bobsled.

"Row, damn you! Row!" Ivar roars. Gone is the giving of orders in a crisp tone. "We're in a storm, and we're trying to make it to shore if we can."

Jan looks at me with raised brows and mouths, "If?"

Jan and I take the second set of oars and dig into the churning water, which cuts like a tough piece of meat.

Jan's head is down, his eyes closed. He's rowing by feel.

I dig in with my left side and feel a tear beneath my ribs. I try to level the pain against the churning ocean. The vomit bucket sloshes at my feet, and I cannot hold back any longer as remnants of food and hope disappear into the bucket.

The rain pours down on us. At last, I can drink. Opening my mouth, I take in deep gusts of the sweet, cool rainwater. Jan has his head up, as well. Our jaws snap and snatch at the drops.

Stein's shoulders are wracking. He's in pain. Like me, he's overcome.

Ivar rows for a few strokes and then stops.

A more massive wave sends us scrambling to the port side to keep us upright. The Bean Nighe apparently doesn't think we've paid enough homage, as she's spinning and throwing us relentlessly. Wave upon waves pour into the boat, and I'm back in the bobsled with one question. "How far will I be thrown?"

Ivar points and shouts, "We'll head northwest. It's the only way out!"

Our reprieve, drinking good water, is over, and we inch northward into the dimming light.

Jan's movements mimic mine, which means digging

into the water with full strength is out of the question. The pain of stretching my arm out and of putting pressure on my bruised hand implies that the torn muscle will tear further. Cold water courses down my spine. I clench my shoulders, shaking them to dislodge the unrelenting wetness. Squinting, I sob out of frustration with my plight.

The flickering, amber glow from a lighthouse appears out of the corner of my left eye. I shout to Jan and point. "A lighthouse! There! Ivar, look! There!"

Ivar glances back, shaking his head in response. "There is nothing there, Kory. Keep rowing."

Another wave of revulsion hits the vomit bucket. The contents now bear food, hope, and seasickness. The beacon light revolves and shines intermittently.

"There! There! How can you not see the light?" I cry in wonder.

Ivar's head remains down, but Stein gazes into the distance, trying to see what I see.

To me, it's obvious. The lighthouse is there. I catch a whiff of the lambing pen, which smells of curing mutton. We're closer than we think. Then, as if to prove my point, something buzzes in my ears. Gnats! I break into a grin, welcoming the pests like long-lost friends.

Faintly, through the storm, light shines upon the roiling sea, and I hear the unmistakable drone of a plane circling north of us.

Ivar yells at Stein, "The flares! Get the flares!"

Stein scrambles to the caddy, retrieving two rust-orange fusees stamped with the Norwegian railroad's name.

I nod, remembering that Ivar's father and Stein's father work with my father on the railroad.

The plane circles slowly. Red lights and the spotlight cast a beacon of hope in the darkness. I smell diesel, and my heart leaps.

Ivar breaks the flare, and the flame explodes, a burst of orange against the sky. He sets off the second one, the orangish-white light flaring off into the dark. The flames fizzle ten meters above our heads, raining down on us a faint smell of oily smoke and snuffed out sparks of hope.

The plane circles around again. Its lights blink in the distance before it turns west and disappears into the rain.

A few minutes later, we spy another plane, this one farther away heading west. Then, in the rain and fog, we watch as a red lights moves across the sky and fades from view.

In the quietest portions of my mind, my heart, and my soul, I know that we are done for. And I can't tell anyone. Thinking about the twenty-eight-second hourglass that Ivar uses to determine miles accomplished, I wonder if there is a twenty-eight-second hourglass to show how much time we have left. But I can't let on. I can't. If I shout, "What's the use? We are done for anyway!" then all that the Bean Nighe means, all that we have worked for, slaved for, believed in—

My moroseness is interrupted as another wave hits us, and it is time to row again. This wave, higher than the others, catapults me sideways. I sense we're heading into the worst of the storm.

The lighthouse dims until, all at once, it's gone. I crane my neck in both directions to locate it and either plane, but it's as if they never existed.

"I'm sure at least one of the planes saw us," says Jan. "They must have. It's just us here. I bet they saw something out of the corner of their vision, and now they know where we are and will send help. I'm sure."

Taking Jan's forearm, I smile. "Yes, help will be coming. I'm sure, too."

I sit for a moment, contemplating, before being jerked back to reality as another wave swamps the boat, pushing us east, away from the Shetlands.

Stein speaks up. "Look, Jan's right. The planes must have seen us. They know our position. They're waiting for this storm to pass, and then they'll pick us up. As simple as that."

I will myself to believe, but why didn't either plane fly over to investigate us?

Once again, my body seems to split in half. Externally, I nod, cringing as a wall of water crashes upon us. Spluttering, I grab my bucket and bail water as the boat tips upwards, a torrent coursing above my waist. I pitch forward as the boat slaps down and shakes. Internally, my view is tunneling, and the terror I feel has turned into a calm, even into acceptance. I don't know how many more minutes or seconds I have, but I don't think I have much time left. Strangely enough, I hear faint music, as if I'm standing outside of a church. The pipe organ is soft, and the music is a hymn from my childhood. I cannot remember if it's from a Midnight Mass or an Easter service, but it's beguiling.

My mind is drifting with the music when a wave rises before me like a snow-capped mountain. The torrent of water extends its claws, drenching me. The Bean Nighe is here. As I shake the water out of my eyes, the bow tilts upward and keeps rising. I fall backward.

Ivar slams his head into my back, and I do the same to Jan, who is sitting in front of me. It's the only way we won't capsize.

"We're going to pitchpole!" Ivar screams. "Lean forward when we go up!"

I haven't heard the term before, but our boat is nearly vertical as we ascend the wave and will flip over if we don't take drastic measures. My back aches. My ribs seize up, but I don't care. I lean forward, and so do the others.

We come over the top. Then we're slammed down and turned hard.

After the next onslaught, the water filling the boat swirls around our calves. Stein, Jan, and I cup our hands and bail furiously, but our efforts are futile. We're basically treading water—taking in more water and sailing backward.

Ivar does the most curious thing. He yanks open his rucksack and starts shoving things into the storage caddy.

Stein shimmies into the bottom of the boat and starts pushing the contents of Ivar's backpack into his own.

Jan and I continue rowing through the furrow of waves.

Even though he's sitting less than two feet from me, Ivar's voice fades in and out. "Kory, get two short pieces of wood that I have stored under your seat."

I reach under my bench as another wave rushes over us.

Ivar stretches his sack open. He fishes around in the caddy, extracting a hank of cord. Forming an X with the two boards, he lashes them together within seconds and shoves the device inside the pack. He ties a sturdy knot to each of the straps. Taking long pieces of rope, he rapidly counts off several arm lengths and then cuts them.

Our boat tips to one side, and we all lean in. The side isn't quite vertical, but it's rising higher, causing water to pour into the boat and cascade over us like a shower. The water in the boat is now up to my knees.

The next wave is the steepest yet. Roaring, the water spits and slaps us. I have my head resting on Jan's thigh. Stein has followed suit, and I feel his breath warming the back of my knee. A half-full can of peas splatters, ricocheting off the hull below me. I tuck my chin down, which allows me to see what Ivar is doing.

Ivar's voice is firm. "Stein, you and I need to attach strong knots onto the back of the boat."

Stein shakes his head. "I'm confused."

Ivar's voice shows his exasperation. "We have to tie them as tight as we can," he shouts, pointing. "Here, and here!" Taking a length of the rope, he ties one end to the rucksack. He ties the other to the bench.

Stein looks puzzled.

Ivar opens the rucksack, and he tosses the device into the water. The bag snaps back as the ropes unfurl behind the boat. Stein's fingers fly open as the line whizzes past him. The brown sack gulps the seawater and sinks.

"Jan, Kory, row as hard as you can now, and stop when I say!"

Pulling on the oars, Jan and I turn the rowboat southward, and we head into the waves.

Ivar calmly says, "We're going to ride up the wave and row as hard as we can, and that will spin the boat. Just you, Kory, and Jan. Okay, up we go! Now row, row, row!"

The boat inches slowly to the left.

A gigantic, bluish-black monster, steeper than the

last, hurls over us with a roar. We rise, sheets of water coursing off and past us. We're cresting.

And then…and then…and then?

In the dim light, I feel the cool mist of the wave, the crest of the wave, the light sprinkling of the wave as it courses past us, and then…a miracle.

Air.

We're on top of the wave, coasting downwards, yet we're being held or dragged back. Again, cool mist and a sprinkle of sea spray fall onto our heads, and, once again, we have crested the wave. Then, once again, we dip behind the wave.

"We'll be better now, at least for a little while, but we need to keep rowing," Ivar says. "If we push off a little when we get to the top, we'll go farther and get that much closer to land."

The tunnel is gone, and I can feel everything. I burst into tears. "How…what did you do? How did you think of that?" I shake Ivar's arm, snot billowing out of my nose. "How did you know to do that?"

Ivar points at another monstrous wave coming toward us.

Instinctively, I brace myself by leaning forward.

For the first time that day, Ivar laughs. "We don't all need to do that now. A few months ago, I was on a ship going north. We ran into awful waves. One crewman talked about how he and a friend were caught in a similar situation when they were kids. The friend created a sea anchor that acted as a counterbalance."

Ivar continues, his hands mimicking the motion of the waves. "As the boat goes up, the anchor's weight pulls against the wave, acting as a counterbalance to keep the boat from pitchpoling or capsizing. I should have thought of the idea earlier, but I didn't know the storm would be this bad or even if the sea anchor would work."

He sighs in satisfaction. "Stein and I will need to sleep soon, but for now, how about you, Jan, and Kory, take a nap if you can, and we'll wake you."

I scramble into the hull of the boat. Grabbing a bucket, I paw at the trash lying there. Flinging cans with an exuberance that overlooks my wrenched ribs, I toss everything dented and disgusting overboard. I know Ivar will soon need help navigating the shallows as we get closer to land, but I'm exhausted. I close my eyes to contemplate the end of our journey and soon drift off to sleep.

In a dream, I see a bright light. A lighthouse.

I call out to Ivar, "How long do you think it takes for the lighthouse beam to go around? A minute maybe? Maybe less? If we time it, we can figure out how far away we are. A good idea, yes?"

A wave takes us up again, but now, the motion reminds me of when Jan and I neared the bobsled finish line. I count the beacon light's cycles. First, they're brighter, with a lapse of about twenty seconds. Then, they're darker. Though I can't make out the colors, I sense we'll almost be there when the storm has passed. Reaching to wake Jan, I reconsider. He looks so peaceful. I'll let him sleep.

Stein glances at the distant shoreline. "So, that's the Shetlands. I see the shoreline. There are low hills and, in the distance, stone fences just like Solsvik's. There will be plenty to do with my friends and in a place that looks like home."

My eyes follow the flicker of the beacon light. The light grows brighter. The sound of the waves changes.

They're calmer; I'm rocking and rocking as I do at home.

Familiar figures appear, waving and calling to us.

Startling at the sight, I touch Ivar on the shoulder. I see who they are. There is my beloved favorite teacher, Herr Tveit, with an oversized bowler hat yanked down around his ears, his Harris Tweed coat, the edges singed. And there's Harold, who has a gaping, red gash where his face has been, but he's wearing the same clothes he wore on our boat trip from Solsvik. And there's one more person. Looking up, I see the pale skin and the pennies in her shoes.

I scream in shock.

Chapter Thirty-Nine

"Kory, wake up, man!" Stein says.

Claws rake my face like fish hooks, jerking my head up as I inhale seawater. Spatting the oily, fishy brine from my mouth and pushing angrily at my assailant, I compound my injuries by twisting my ankle under the rowboat's seat.

"God almighty, what was that? Buildings and a lighthouse? You damn near threw us overboard!" Stein grips his wrist as he gasps in pain. "We pulled Jan's and your head above the waterline. Otherwise, you would have drowned."

"Kory." Ivar's hands move as if balancing a scale, then stop, palms down, marking a decision. "Kory, we're off course. I think we've missed the Shetlands." Twisting his head around, Ivar wedges his fist against his skull. "I think we're south of the Shetlands, but we might be able to make England. It's probably a couple hundred miles minimum, but with fair weather, we'll arrive in another three or four days. If we're careful, we can make the Orkneys or drift straight south and be on the outskirts of Scotland."

"Off course?" I ask. Ivar's words don't register. Are we lost? Impossible! My words tumble out. "Ivar, I don't understand. What about the Nazis? Our food? Our friends? Why not go back north?"

Ivar leans forward to Stein, giving him the briefest

smile. "Kory," Ivar says, his voice raspy, "we're out here. If we row when we can, there's a chance we can make it to England or the Orkneys. A ship will see us, maybe another plane."

Stein shakes his head. "I think a day passed. We drifted for a long time. We couldn't go on, so we slept."

"Impossible!" I exclaim. "You're wrong. There's no way a day passed from the time we started to when the plane flew by us. We would have woken up. We can't be that far off course. That's the stupidest thing I have ever heard!" I slap the bench. "Stupid! Stu-"—my hand points at my head—"-pid. Off course? Utter bullshit!"

Cautiously, Stein starts again. "You did seem to be awake. You talked about a lighthouse and kept pointing. I have weird dreams, too. Jan has gotten weaker. He says he hurts all over. And look at the kipper barrel."

Our water source burps, oozing a sticky, orange fluid from its seams. Stein gingerly turns it. "The resin from the wood is leaching into the water. We can't drink from the barrel." He nods toward the faint, gray, diagonal sheets of rain along the horizon. "If another storm or rain shower comes, we can get more water." His voice cracks.

Jan's long frame fitfully edges to the boat's hull and pulls back from performing any more contortions.

"Look at Jan. He's not doing well. None of us are," I say.

Ivar looks askance at the suggestion that he's slipping into sickness, too.

"Are you sure we can't make Shetland?" I ask.

This is my fault.

A coiled metal ring that looks like an apple peeling floats next to my elbow. Unbidden, Jules creeps into my thoughts.

The hand with the gold ring turned off the lathe. Jules gripped my shirt. His breath, rummy and sticky sweet, pushed into my face. *How long were you going to keep up these lies? A smuggler? You? You aren't man enough. We're on to you, and we'll turn you in.*

My bloated fingers wipe away a tear.

Impossible.

The towels protecting Jan's hands lie upon his chest, resembling giant puffed-up mittens. Jan's mouth hangs slack-jawed, his skin beginning to draw in over his cheekbones. He's already in a deep sleep.

Gently, I pat him on the ribs.

"Ow! Oh, God! Jesus, that hurts!" Jan's voice crackles. Coughing, he blinks, his glassy eyes taking several tries to register me.

"Do you think you can manage chocolate or kippers? You have to keep up your strength." My hand smooths back my best friend's hair, taking a good, hard look at his chapped and sunburned face.

Scrunching down, Jan recoils as if being forced to lie on a bed of nails. He twitches as I push away an empty can bobbing near his ear.

"Do you want to rest against my bag? I think there are soft things here."

Jan's cough sounds like a dry heave. "I want water. I keep seeing my family, and it's like they are here. I miss them, Kory." His voice drops to a whisper as he turns his head to where I sit. "Kory?"

"I'm right here." I look at the bloodied bandages on his hands. His fingers are like sausages. His neck has plumped over his shirt collar. Reaching to unfasten his shirt's top button, I look at my distended fingers. If I can't undo it, he's going to choke—my fault.

"Kory?"

"Jan, I'm right here."

I see Jules' face sneering at me. *You aren't man enough.*

Jan's voice breaks as he reaches up and tugs at my finger, pulling me toward him.

You? A smuggler?

"Kory, if it weren't for thoughts of my family and friends, I would want this hell to be over."

We're on to you, and we'll turn you in.

Chapter Forty

I don't have an honorable way to tell my best friend I think he's dying, and we're lost. And I may die, too.

Jan's first seizure comes as Ivar asks, without blame or malice, a simple question that's now impossible for the Spartan to answer.

"Jan, are you able to row?"

Jan nods but brings his swathed hands up to his collar and digs, trying to pull himself free. His cough is less an exhale than a rearrangement of the dried blood clots he wipes on his oil-splattered shirt.

I lean over, raising my hand to stop whatever Ivar is about to say. "Jan, is your collar too tight? Let me unbutton it for you." I can do that. The oil has saturated his shirt and the shorts he borrowed from Stein. "You want to borrow my shirt?" I ask.

Jan shakes his head and slips backward with a sharp clatter on the boat's bottom.

We stare as the Spartan's limp body contorts.

He shudders, his arms and back stiffening, his feet pressing against the bench. His tongue protrudes, and I push down on his spasming face, keeping my hands away from his feral, snapping jaw.

As quickly as the seizure happens, the grayish glassiness of his eyes dissipates, and with that, the Spartan is back.

For now, I decide to lie.

"Look, it's not the best thing, but if you rest and drink kipper juice, you'll keep your strength up. It's what we have now, and you can live on that. We'll get into a shipping lane, and a ship will pick us up. They must. Or they'll be sending a boat from the Shetlands. We'll wave, and we'll be on that boat, and we'll go. Maybe to England."

No matter how I fidget, residue from the kippers and sardines continues to harden and create pockets of dried oil in odd areas—behind my ears, under my nails, on my kneecaps. Peeling and picking at my knees is providing me with a fresh start.

Stein is now peeling the sediment off himself, too.

He must think I'm having success at giving myself clean knee caps, but my picking has only caused uneven, scabby, crusty patches of skin to form. When I rub the tinned oil over my skin, it resembles putty. My feet look like plumped up prunes from a twisted Dickensian Christmas dinner. I reach down and poke at my ankles, fascinated with my new toys. When I poke where my ankle should be, the rubber-like skin sinks. My stomach clenches at the sponginess, but my curiosity about this atrocity has taken over.

When Jan and I were kids, we found a huggorm snake eating a mouse. We cornered the viper, fat with prey, against a cement block, taking turns poking at the snake's belly with a stick. Finally, when we poked the twig down about a centimeter, the snake hissed, baring tiny, deadly fangs, and we ran Now, I watch as my three fingers sink into my ankle. The fingers' imprints are visible as I pull away, the bluish-purple swelling connecting in a zigzag pattern like the huggorm's scales.

Ivar moves like a marionette.

Stein has absently opened his shirt's top button. Now his fingers are too swollen to close it. He turns back to look at me. His neck looks like a bull's.

None of us are rowing. Did I say that we should row? Or was that someone else speaking? I'm unable to remember. The boat creaks, and tins bobbing in the water at the bottom of the hull ping as they hit the sides.

I have begun to think about death. While I'm not rational enough to determine if I'm talking out loud, the consideration I'm giving the ending of my life is leisurely, almost contemplative, and *rational*. These thoughts aren't impulsive or angry like the ones I had in the alley. My thoughts present a perfect solution to the predicament in which we find ourselves.

Stein and Ivar hoist the sail. Ivar makes a yanking motion as he hands me a fraying, gray rope, and I understand that I'm to grasp it.

My hands, now bloody and chapped, make small splotches on the cord. My body obeys the command, but my mind thinks about my death.

The sail catches, and we sail on a southern course ahead of the squall line. "I'd welcome the rain," I say. "Now, we won't get any water. How is this going to help?" Did I say that out loud? I'm not sure.

I think about how Jan's thoughts of family and friends kept him going. Though I'm not quite sure, I think I'm slipping into a place where the logical step, the most rational thing to do, is find a way to end my life. I am memorizing my friends' faces in case I can keep those memories where I'm going. The clouds in the west look like a girl's hair—Anne's hair as I saw her running across the street to the bus station on the day of our picnic in Festival Park. To *Jules*. I picture the way she looked at him and her laugh, and I vomit.

I think back to the day of the invasion. Of the submarine that Jan thought looked like a sardine. Of the German drum corps; their cadence, loud and crisp as they passed; the sound, muffled as they turned the corner, growing stiller until all you heard—if you strained—was a faint rhythm. My heartbeat is slowing as if my life's cadence is disappearing.

"If I slip into the sea once the storm comes, this horror will be over. I can fall into the ocean. They wouldn't be able to catch me and pull me in, and I would sink."

Jan's eyelids flutter.

I whisper, "Storm coming but not like before. We might even outrun it."

He drifts off, indifferent to the news.

Maybe that is it. Maybe that is how I will be remembered. A choice but really no choice because you don't fear either consequence.

Chapter Forty-One

I hear a voice behind me. I turn. Up close, the tweed is not singed and doesn't smell of kerosene. A mittenless white knuckle appears below a sleeve.

"You could have come closer to me," the voice coaxes softly. "You were nearly over the edge. I would have guided you."

"But—" I clamp my hand over my mouth.

"Yes, I know, but you are here, aren't you? You are here with me." The voice is musical, low, and inviting.

I had plans. Harold and Herr Tveit understood that, I think. But where is the Robert Burns Highland burr?

"What you want isn't that painful, you know, just a pinprick, a bee sting. It's not bad. You come with me," the voice coaxes.

Where is the bowler hat? Or the facial scar? Why is the skin so white?

My stomach clenches as I pull away. "No! My friends—I dragged them out here, and I can't leave them!"

I am shouting now. "No! I'm not…! I can't. I have my friends with me, and I can't do that. They will have died because of me. Me! I will be remembered for my stupidity. That. Only that." I am pleading with the figure to understand.

A tendril of crimson hair falls forward, and I stare into coal-black eyes, familiar and terrifying. The smile is benign. The accent is indistinct. *Why not the voice of the Sinclair clan or of Solsvik?*

"It'd be over in a second," the voice says, in a beguiling manner. "You wouldn't need to worry. Your friends won't blame you. They all have their reasons to be out here with you. You didn't force them. They wanted to go. To be heroes. Just like you."

"You died a hero," I say. "I don't think you counted on that. I don't think you set out to have that happen, but it did."

A cascade of crimson hair falls forward from the figure sitting, utterly complacent, beside me. "Do what you want."

Balling my fists, I want to punch the specter. I scream with agony, frustration, and now—to my horror—with complete realization of who the Bean Nighe is.

Herr Tveit's Scottish burr, that day in the classroom just before his own death, his hands held teasingly—like a ghost's—over Frida's head. "The Bean Nighe comes for those about to die," he said. "She takes many forms, some horrible, some cruel, and some forms that we trust and love the most."

The figure caresses my arm, its hands nearing mine. The black lacquered fingernails circle my wrist, squeezing tighter and tighter.

I stare into the narrowest, deepest set black eyes I have ever seen, and the drawling bray from her mouth tells me the Bean Nighe now has me in her grasp.

I know who the Bean Nighe is.

She's not worth dying for.

I look at my surroundings, seeing landscapes that are my familiar and not. I see land.

Land is home. Land is life. Land means hope.

I remember Ivar in Paul's basement, looking at the map, regarding the shipping routes like old, trusted friends. And that's where I am. I'm among my friends.

Tunneling, surfacing, pushing the evil away, I awaken as I inhale grease and seawater. Lifting my head from the hull of the rowboat, I dislodge the oil seeping into my ear. Bits of food stuck to my eyelashes partially block my view of a tin bobbing in the water at eye level. Grease trickles down my neck. I shake off whatever liquid is in my hair.

I'm still alive.

The gnats are back. After days of hearing the oars slapping the waves, I don't know if I should be happy or frightened. I freeze in place.

"A plane!" I shout. "It's a goddamned plane! We are going to be rescued!" I sit up.

Stein and Ivar sit up as well, and Jan raises himself on his elbows.

"It's not like the ones before, though." Jan points a wobbly finger. "The plane is German."

Ivar and Stein perch on the boat's edge. They face in this time, their legs purplish and swollen, faces chapped, eyes dull.

"Oh shit, it *is* German. It's close, and what now?" I look at Ivar and Stein and down at Jan.

The swastika is unmistakable as the plane heading south passes by us. It is not as close as the English plane, and this time, there is no recognition, no tipping of the wings.

Jan's mouth looks like a dying cod's. I kneel to get closer to him. "I don't care," he whispers. "They can do what they want. I just don't care."

Chapter Forty-Two

Haze masks defining forms like an Impressionist painting, and I'm drawn back to the memory of a summer day at Bergen's fish market just after a rainstorm. An artist used a painter's knife to throw large globs of green and blue paint on a canvas. He took a brush and painted random forms—savage, yellow, diagonal lines, red and green squares set at odd angles, and a long smear of muddied brown along the bottom. He then took a bucket of white paint and splattered the entire painting. Along with the skeptical crowd, I gasped at the artist's anger and audacity, more than ready to turn away from his madness.

The audience began clapping, and the artist bowed. His canvas revealed an abstract perfectly capturing Bergen's harbor.

The live canvas before me bears the same handiwork.

The current carrying the boat has become more assured, and I'm startled by a honk and a vehicle shift from a low gear to a higher one.

Ivar and Stein are kneeling, their heads just barely above the boat's rim.

Stein points at a red splotch in the haze. "I see a house."

Ivar glares at Stein. He puts a finger to his lips. "We're back in Norway, not far from Stavanger. I was here earlier this summer. I heard there might be a Nazi camp, so you need to be quiet."

"What kind of camp did you say?" I ask. My throat is dry, and I don't want to talk, but I need to find out where we are. I have not seen this landscape before and want to know where the camp is. I have other worries, too. My hands are on the bench, vibrating, and I hear a quiet purr coming from across the water.

Ivar, Stein, and I scramble into the hull, dislodging tins and oars with an annoying clatter. I know I should tamp myself down into the bottom, but I want to see what is coming toward us.

A navy-blue triangle, a red circle, and a yellow rectangle are frightened and arguing as they bob in the water.

"Back up! The Nazis will blow us to bits if we touch it!" the triangle says. His voice is male, older, and panicked.

The boat's motor idles and then shifts into another gear. The red circle and the triangle disappear.

The argument takes another turn with the sound of a gun being cocked. "Hello? Is anyone on this boat?" says a strong voice with a Western Norwegian accent.

Ivar glares at me.

Stein shakes his head.

"They might be Germans. Not a word!" Ivar whispers.

"Hello? Is anyone on this boat?" the strong voice repeats.

The argument has escalated between the triangle and the circles. They're close. Close enough that I hear another click of a gun. One of the three shapes says they should get the hell out of here. *Now.*

A bellowing grunt—cracked and guttural—explodes behind me. *"Help me!"*

The boat's motor cuts off. Then, above the lapping of the waves against our boat, I hear voices and the cocking of a third gun.

"Help me!" Jan's voice is not a plea, not plaintive, and is beyond hope. It is primal. It is miraculous.

"We're armed," the voice says, "so if you have weapons, know we can—and will—shoot you. Know that!"

The voice means business.

"Gawd! Help me!" The sound of Jan's voice is a gasp, a bawl, and a scream.

We turn our heads and gape at where Jan is lying.

"We're pulling up beside you," the voice says. "We will shoot you if you even think of trying to mine us. Everybody will die."

A large trawler pulls up alongside of us, bringing with it the hated seagulls screeching and diving at us, indiscriminate as to whether the food it seeks in the boat is canned or merely barely alive.

The voices above us are Norwegian.

"Are you German?" asks the strong voice.

"Look, they're just kids," says the panicked voice. "Jesus, how long have you been here? Jesus!"

"Jesus!" exclaims the man who said it was a lousy idea to come any closer. "Will you look at this boat? God, how long have you guys been out here? What the hell happened to you? The one in the back —is he dead? Oh, God, what are we going to do? A body. What the hell are we going to do?"

The question has stopped Ivar from his incessant picking at the hardened oil on his skin. He looks up. "We went sailing to visit friends," says Ivar, with a raspy voice. He coughs and then glances at Jan. "Him? He's seasick. That's all."

A yellow blob with black tentacles and a web dances in front of my face. Confused, I utter a cry as I swat at the tentacles. Unfortunately, I completely miss my target as it appears that my hands track three seconds behind my brain.

Ivar's eyes bore into mine. "Grab this! Hold this!"

Numbly, I follow Ivar's directions. The hemp braids cut into my hands.

Jan, his skin stretched back thinly over his skull, is slumped next to the caddy.

"The redhead. Can he stand?" says the older man with the strong voice. "What about the one over there? Is he dead?"

Jan answers this with a roar—a painful primal scream. The Spartan is not going down without a fight.

The man who isn't panicked anymore laughs as he says, "Okay. Some fight. That's good. We must get you up here and inside before it rains again. Can I come down into the boat? Is that all right?"

I feel the boat sinking as a heavy weight tips it back.

"Red? Can you hold my hand? Here. Up," says the man wearing a blue slicker.

Another voice. This one is younger—the one who thought coming aboard was a lousy idea says, "Jesus, look at this kid's ankles. My hands are trying to grip him, but they keep sinking in. Gross!"

With a whoosh from the bow, I'm tossed into the air like today's catch. A second later, and with a sharp pain against my rib, I roll onto a metal floor that smells of fish and gasoline. I slam into more metal. Squares.

Something bright and silver is waving in front of me. I raise my hand, moving my fingers to wave back. "Hellooo…"

"…more dead than alive."

I think the panicked man could be describing me, or he might be referring to Jan, who hasn't come up on the deck of the trawler.

Stein slides beside me like a large fish.

"…fine… fine…"

Someone is flipped over the rail without a word. Jan?

Ivar grunts. He's last.

One footstep follows another. The yellow rectangle comes closer. Overalls—the rectangle is wearing yellow overalls. I see blurry printing on the side of a boot and the inside of a pants leg above me.

"Red. Give me your hand," says the man with the strong voice.

As if working a child's puzzle, I'm putting the voices and shapes together. The man with the strong voice is the yellow rectangle.

The rain is spitting on my face. Like a dam bursting, a torrent of oil gushes from my hair.

Another set of hands appears and grabs my arm.

"Hey, are you German?" I blurt out, trying to shake the man wearing the red rain slicker off.

Hey…hey! We're not your enemy. You need to get inside the trawler, and we need to get your friend help."

I put the second piece of the puzzle together as I recognize the voice of the man who thought this was a lousy idea.

As he drags me across the door jamb, my ankles have the same sensation as when I poked the huggorm.

A map and pencil rest near a steering wheel. I'm near the door in the trawler's wheelhouse.

The voice coming from the radio speaks English. I'm happy that I recognize the announcer's voice from our source for real news—Radio Andorra. The volume is too loud, creating pain in my ears. I pull on them, shutting my eyes against the noise.

"Thass Thadio Andotha. Stop! Stop!" I say, shaking my head back and forth. "No!"

"Red recognized Radio Andorra," says the man who thought this was a lousy idea.

Ivar comes into the wheelhouse last, but another man stands behind him, giving directions. "We need to get the boat hooked up for towing and will need people to help."

Ivar and Stein grunt agreement, disappearing with the men.

A loud screech clatters behind the trawler as a chain secures our rowboat.

"At first, I thought the gulls were snatching your food, but it was your knapsacks," says the man who thought this was a lousy idea. "I have never seen so many pea cans. And no water. Or lifejackets. And kipper tins everywhere."

Outside, a yellow slicker lies over Jan, covering his torso and all but the top of his head. Perched on his chest, two seagulls prepare to peck at either Jan's eyes or a fish in his hair. I grab the door's frame. "No, no, *no!*" I scream, pounding the door. Bile rises in my throat, burning my mouth, and I dry heave.

The seagulls, chastised by my outburst, fly away. The man who thought this was a lousy idea motions for me to keep the door open. He lifts Jan, his arms encircling the Spartan's chest. His distorted feet and ankles splay as the man steps inside and gingerly places Jan's body on the floor. Pulling the yellow slicker back, he asks, "You have been through enough rain, yes?"

"We need to get all of you help," says the older man, "especially you two." He points his finger at Jan and me. "All of you, stop this nonsense about a fishing trip to see friends. How long have you been at sea?"

I glance at Stein and Ivar, as much because I'm unwilling to break our code of silence as because I don't know.

"Dunno. A few days at most," says Ivar. "We were fishing and going to see friends," he adds, sticking to the lie no matter what.

The man with the strong voice speaks. "I'm Lars." He points to a younger man, who has to be the man who thinks this is a lousy idea. "This is Michel, and downstairs is Bertrand. We're from near Stavanger."

Lars starts the trawler. As the trawler lurches forward, a kipper tin flies off the deck, hitting the wheelhouse window squarely, leaving a bit of fin stuck to the glass.

"We have to be careful," says the voice I now recognize as being the panicked one. "But I am going to bring medical help to you." Now, his voice filled with confidence, Bertrand has brought up coffee for us.

Jan stirs and moans.

Michel kneels near him and hoists him up so his back rests against Michel's knee. He takes a small cup from Bertrand and opens a corner of Jan's mouth, pouring a small stream into it. The liquid flows back out and onto the floor.

"Hey! You need to swallow. Can you do that for

me?" Michel shifts position. "We live just north of here. I want to find out how long you have been at sea. The truth, please."

Stein asks, "What day is it?"

"It's August fourth," Lars answers.

I think back to when we left. I croak, "You can't be right. We couldn't have been out for more than one week. Please don't lie to us."

Opening a cupboard, Lars pulls out a log and holds it to my face. "Look!"

I lean in very close to the man's hands and stare. The figures are jumbles.

The rain pelts against the trawler's windows. Again, the landscape is reduced to a steamy haze. Lars uses his shirtsleeve to wipe away the fog, making a loud squeaking noise.

"Rain. Storm. Not again. We're not in it," says Jan in a low, strained voice.

"Wait…" Lars turns, his eyes widening. "How long were you out there? Were you in that storm a couple of days ago? No ships went out for three days. Not even the German patrols or planes. The ports closed. The weather was too severe."

There is a sharp intake of breath from Bertrand and Michel.

Lars gasps. "You were out in that?" His mouth falls open. "Were you heading to Shetland? How close were you?"

Ivar is silent.

I no longer care. "Lighthouse. I saw."

Ivar shakes his head. "No! No lighthouse. He's crazy."

"Yes! Lighthouse! I saw." I cough again.

The trawler slows down. My consciousness fades. I catch only the snatches of conversation Lars has with Ivar or maybe to Stein about staying here, hiding the boat in the boathouse, and the need for a doctor.

Jan is slowly rocking on the trawler's floor. He rolls his shoulders and tries to cover his ears.

Lars turns the radio off.

Jan's head comes up, and so does mine. A small smile is on his face. "Thank you," Jan whispers.

****

The Spartan is nude, sprawled in the middle of the trawler's wheelhouse floor. Like points on a compass, four tubes radiate from his salved body. Eye droppers, the size used to feed newborn kittens, lie near his outstretched hands.

We're to listen and listen hard to Jan's sounds.

I pray we don't have to blink the trawler's wheelhouse light tonight as an SOS signal, as that would mean Jan is nearing death.

Stein and Ivar have positioned themselves along the wheelhouse's walls to watch *me*. Like Jan, I'm slathered in salve. The liniment's odor stings my eyes, but I'm unable to cry. Using my hands to wipe my face is out of the question. But I don't need my friends' attention.

The sky is an angry gray. People are walking rapidly on the wooden pier. As they come closer, I catch only phrases

"Two of them…not much longer… I think…morgue…what to do."

The door opens, bringing wind gusts and nearly horizontal rain inside. Lars and a bearded man squat, then look at me inquisitively as if choosing questions to ask after long, careful deliberation.

Instinctively, Stein and I flatten ourselves, our arms stretched out, bracing for the rowboat's uplift. Then, as the door closes, we are restored to warmth, no longer tossed about, feeling nothing but the vibration from the trawler's engines.

Lars takes my chin in his hand. "Red, here, is the least sick of the two." He points to the Spartan's sprawled figure. "Him, I don't know."

"I will do quick work," says the bearded man.

A bright light shines into my eyes while a wet hand probes my neck.

"How long?" the bearded man asks Lars. "And these bruises on his ribs? And his swollen back? From the storm?"

Lars shrugs. "Eight days, maybe more. Don't believe the fishing story if you hear it. They were heading to Shetland. Caught in the storm." Lars' voice betrays a mixture of derision and awe.

"Cut the shirt off the dark-haired one. His collar is strangling him."

Bertrand takes the scissors the doctor hands him and, after struggling with Jan's collar, resorts to cutting upwards from his chest.

Jan draws a long breath as Bertrand cuts the salt, grease, and blood-spattered fabric's final threads.

"He has severe dehydration, burns, and chafing," the doctor says. "Probably will be dead within a day, at the most. The others are dehydrated too, but this one is bad." He prods Jan, asking if anyone has pants that might fit him. "He can't wear these. He has sores on his bottom, and blisters are forming. In addition, he has an infection that can kill him."

Lars rummages behind the wheelhouse door, pulling

out a pair of pants.

The doctor shakes his head, promising, "I will bring clean clothes for the two of them. For now, the skin needs nothing on it but salve. The problem is how to get them off the boat," he says, pointing. "I know of a cabin where they'll be safe. I can get nurses who live nearby. But we're too close to the Nazi camp. We can't attract attention. They will sleep here tonight, and I'll get them—at least these two—stabilized. But they need help. They all do."

With cups in their hands, Ivar and Stein kneel next to the Spartan and me.

Ivar looks up at the doctor. "Is it okay for me to give them food?" he asks. "Me, I'm fine."

The doctor shakes his head. "Give them small sips of broth or tea. Or water, of course. You all should be drinking that. But small drops of water."

Lars nods. "I will be here tonight with you," he says. "If he takes a turn for the worse, I will flash a light inside, and the doctor will come at once. I don't have much, just crackers, water, coffee, and broth, and I have now been given a crash course on what to watch for."

None of us are talking. And the three of us—Stein and Ivar along the wall, me on the floor—are breathing along with the Jan. Hoping. Praying. Listening, listening hard.

****

Over the past four days, we've learned things. The cabin where we're staying lies in a cove blanketed by fog from six until around ten in the morning. The trawler that picked us up was one of two with a blue flag and red buoys hanging from its sides, and I will never see our rescuers again or even know their full names.

I sit at the kitchen table, being retaught how to move a spoon from my bowl of fish soup to my mouth. Kristi, my teacher, is unwilling to smile at me, though Stein makes her laugh regularly. The soup, made by my other nurse, Marta, is delicious.

Sitting beside me, Marta tosses her brown braid over her shoulder as she searches my face for approval.

"Mmm …you're the best, Marta," I say. "Will you marry me?"

Unlike Kristi, Marta laughs, dismissing my proposal with a push of her hand.

Kristi observes our exchange without cracking a smile.

Ivar lounges in the corner chair, the cabin's prime piece of real estate. If he moves the chair a half meter from the corner, he has a view of the village across the cove. He scrutinizes me, his blue eyes and white-blond hair standing out against his tanned skin. "Your great-grandfather created Solsvik Bridge?" he asks.

"Yes," I say, "my great-grandfather created a barter system using playing cards."

I open my mouth. In Kristi's hands, my spoon gets ninety percent of its contents in my mouth. If nursing doesn't work out for her, she'll make a great schoolmarm.

"And," I continue, "he won the town of Solsvik and two islands in the process."

Kristi feeds me another mouthful of soup. This time, one hundred percent of the broth and fish dumplings make it into my mouth. The expression on her face says, "Great. Can you do that again?"

Ivar shifts in his chair, eyeing the pack of playing cards our nurses brought from the village.

Through the haze, I hear a trawler's engine go into gear and its anchor chain wrested and wrangled onto the boat. The trawler emerges from the mist. Yellow buoys bob alongside its hull.

The fishermen who rescued us handed my friends and me off the trawler and onto their boat as if we were small whales or sharks. I remember a faint light, the smell of wood, and being grasped and pushed. I was patted dry, and the mattress I slept on was soft.

I have no way to thank them. "I don't even know who they were."

Ivar shuffles the playing cards like Gramps taught the rest of us.

Stein walks out of the bedroom we share, setting the book he's been reading down on the kitchen table. "We need four."

The Spartan appears in the kitchen doorway and salutes me. "Spart."

"Spart," I reply. Ready to soldier on. Again.

As the days pass, Jan and I move from the back bedroom into the front room, curling up by the windows, reacquainting ourselves with old childhood friends. Jan finds several Crimshaw Brothers novels in the cabin's bookshelves, reminding me of those books' possibilities. The Brothers never wavered. They were always there for one another, and they resorted to teamwork when faced with a challenge.

We spend our afternoons playing Solsvik Bridge and returning to a familiar routine.

One day, Ivar goes into town under the guise of being a fisherman, in case anyone asks. He goes to the doctor and calls his parents. He did not tell anyone he was leaving, not even his parents.

The next day, Doctor Sussman comes by with his medical bag to check on Jan and me and give us an envelope. "These are your tickets back to Bergen. Ivar called his parents, and they sent money for your journey home." Doctor Sussman squares his shoulders and smiles, clearly delighted that he's made us well. "It is time to get your lives in front of you."

As the door closes behind the doctor, I speak up. "So, what happens now?" It's an obvious question, but we have not thought to talk about it.

Jan is quick in his response. "We went hiking. That's all. We went hiking, and we'll never speak of this. Not a word. We all have to swear to it."

Jan's eyes are clear and steady. "Spart, it's the right thing to do."

I snap a salute, and The Spartan snaps one back. "Tomorrow. On a boat and back to Bergen," I say. "When we land, we say nothing to anyone."

Ivar and Stein look at us, saluting to chime in. Of course, that isn't their signal, but it is a way to bind us together.

The next morning, tickets in our hands, sun on our faces, we walk through the door of our familiar into the unknown.

Chapter Forty-Three

Genoa October 1947

"*Cian-cianno*," I say haltingly as my fingers trace the collar of her blouse.

Mia's laugh is playfully mocking as she waves her finger in my face. "You Norwegians...you think Italians are the answer. You drink our wine. You eat our food." She waggles a piece of the anchovy pizza I have come to love during previous visits. "Here, you Viking!"

I snatch a bite, the cheese dribbling down my chin.

"You think love must be the answer. And you tuck my necklace around my neck. My hands—they're not so good. You must have more wine, yes?"

Turning away, she calls out, "Christof, another bottle!" She shakes her fist at him in mock anger. "That brother of mine!"

Standing up, I maneuver to where Christof stands, his bow tie slightly askew with tufts of gray chest hairs spilling over it. "No, Christof, no! I have had my fill. I have to get back, but...oh...what food! And you...you... Mia! There will be no cian-ciano with you next time!" I kiss Mia's hand and cheek.

Christof waggles his finger. "In parts of Genoa, you would be married now. Many bambinos to follow!"

Mia puffs out her belly. "Oh yes, a miracle!"

"You must tell us more stories next time, Kory!"

enthuses Christof. "You tell Paul, Ingrid, Stein about us. They should come here. We'll feed them well. We'll look for your beautiful friend Rolf, too. Mia, Kory has a boyfriend for you!"

Mia claps her hands in mock joy.

"Until next time, my friends." I blow a kiss to Mia, who pretends to catch it. Then, I wave to Christof, step out into the night air, and head for my ship on foot.

Carlo's Ristorante, located up a narrow alleyway from my employer's ship, has become one of my favorite spots to eat in Genoa. Mia and Christof, the owners, have introduced me, in their warm, boisterous way, to ravioli, anchovy pizza, and delicious octopus.

Genoa, with its dark alleyways, laundry hanging overhead, beggars, whores, and sailors, can be described as a scary maze attracting society's worst sorts. After looking at the labyrinth of streets, many fellow crewmates shake their heads and stick to the harbor.

Genoa's industry is the reason I'm here. My employer's company is building a new ship, and my assignment is to work on the electrical schematics. I revel in my increasing responsibility, the respect I'm earning as I work alongside seasoned engineers in designing the ship's electrical system.

Soon after I arrived in Genoa, I wandered down an alley, still in sight of the ship, looking for company. The smell of ravioli cooking led me to Carlo's Ristorante and Mia and Christof.

In the six months I have been in Genoa, I have come to love the city, and when my schedule permits, I always seek out Carlo's for Mia and Christof, their food, and their love of life. I find myself talking easily to Mia and Christof about my friends. Mia asks me to tell stories of my boyhood and about what my friends are doing now.

I tell of how, during the war, Stein and Ivar joined an elite mountaineering corps called Bjorn West and how they hid in the mountains just to the north and west of Bergen, bravely working with the Norwegian Resistance to bring an end to the war. "Both Ivar and Stein saved my life and Jan's. I owe them so much. Their heroism saved Jan and me. They're true heroes."

During the last three years of the war, Jan became interested in flying and was given tasks near the airport. He became a pilot and now lives in Oslo as a member of the Air Force.

Paul and I joined Jan in the mountains as we worked with the Resistance. As planes dropped supplies, Jan turned wistful and repeatedly told us that he'd like to fly once the war was over. He now gets to do what he loves.

Herr Carhart offered both Paul and I jobs at his company. I was tempted, but Herr Henricksen had previously suggested I talk to a friend who is a shipbuilder. The engineer liked my suggestions and hired me.

Jules and I had little contact after the trip to the Shetlands. He and Gramps fought about Jules' "collaborator friends," and Gramps kicked him out of the house. For once, my Mom agreed.

Our lives went separate ways, with Jan going to Oslo, Paul working for his father, and me taking a job on a ship, first, as an electrician and, later, as an officer. Stein and Ivar moved from the neighborhood. Both continued to serve with distinction after the war. My parents sent me notices about them. Rolf began to travel to France, London, and even to New York for photographs.

I often talk of Jan's flying career and of his becoming a flying instructor and participating in an elite group of the Norwegian Air Force.

Christof makes swooping motions with his hand and pronounces Jan's name as Giovanni, and of course, Mia chimes in with "like Don Giovanni, the good loooover."

I relay the invitation to Jan, who seems delighted and talks about coming to Italy.

Mia asks about my family. "A big family, yes? Brothers as handsome as you?"

I sigh.

"Ah," Christof says. "I have people in my family that can't be from my tree. They're dropped like cookoos into our family. Do you understand?"

I smile at that and talk of Ray, of his musical ability and his being in a band.

"My older brother is Jules." I begin. "He's complicated. He said he was neutral during the war, but he had his hands in everything. He's clever. He always says, 'It's business.' He puts business above everything, his family included."

I'm thinking back to immediately after the war as I continue. "Collaborators were rounded up to be questioned and imprisoned. Stein came to see me. He said Jules was going to be questioned and would probably be sent to prison. They needed someone to corroborate his activities. Would I do it?"

I take a drink, remembering that day. "The office was large, with many legal books lining the shelves. The desk had leather on top. In the distance, I heard the church bells strike two. I swallowed and reached for the cut-glass water pitcher. A door opened, and a young man with heavy tortoiseshell glasses and jug ears strode over to me. He said, 'Kory? I'm Captain Johnson. Please have a seat.'

"The questions over the next hour related to Jules and his dealings with German officers. Did I know about this? From the questions, I gathered Jules sold ration cards on the black market, even going so far as to arrange so-called *visits* between dignitaries and the women from the West Indian."

Mia looks at me questioningly.

Christof's translation causes her to clap her hand over her mouth.

"I don't know if Jules was associated with them. We haven't had much contact. I saw him after my grandmother died, but that was nearly a year ago. I know he worked at a pawn shop and a record store and made deliveries. He visits my parents, but he and I do not get along very well. He comes over when I'm not home."

Mia breaks in. "Is your brother guilty?"

I nod. "Jules is guilty of many things—probably more than they knew. Telling the truth, though—the real truth? It would destroy my parents, my relationship with my family. I couldn't go through with it. I told the truth but not all of what I knew. There is much I did not—do not— know about Jules. If they wanted to imprison him, they should have found someone else. I could not do it."

The three of us sit silently for a moment, sipping our drinks.

Leaning forward in his chair, Christof asks about happier subjects—Paul, Ivar, Stein, and Jan.

I brighten. "Paul, now busy with his papa's business, is making a name for himself. Ivar and Stein have become best friends. Ivar never ate chocolate until he met Stein. And Stein, he has given up lock picking. He prefers to hike and sail with Ivar." I frown as I think of the Spartan. "With Jan, I'm happy and sad," I say ruefully. "Our letters often cross in the mail. I'm sad because I'm out to sea and have to wait to see what news has come for me and because he is stationed in Oslo. I'd have to either take the train or figure out another way to see him when he comes to Bergen."

I look at my watch and then stand. "Another lovely evening. I have to go back to the ship."

I kiss Mia's cheek before shutting the door behind me. A stiff breeze comes up. Laundry strung from multi-storied apartment buildings flaps like sails. I find myself staring at the *sails,* thinking back to our boat adventure.

Rain pelts my back as I scurry up the gangway. Walking past the mailroom, I hope for a letter. I'm excited to see two letters, and as I turn them over, I'm even more delighted to see they're both from Jan.

Opening the first letter, I walk along absently, automatically lifting my feet as I pass through the bulkheads leading to my room. He sends birthday greetings to me, mentions how the Michaelmas daisies are blooming, and wants to know if I want flowers since I'm born on Michaelmas. The Spartan's happy stories involve tales of the latest recruits. These young men are a promising bunch of pilots with good instincts. The Spartan is sure he can teach them to fly. Coming into my room, I settle on my berth, where I can see the statue of Christopher Columbus, Genoa's native son. A pigeon is sitting on top.

The wine and great food have made me sleepy. Rolling over, I indulge myself with a cigarette, savoring the wonderful evening.

A call comes from the hallway. It's a young voice,

clearly looking for me. "Kory! Kory! Where is Kory?"

I open my door and peer out.

"Kory, you are to go see the radio officer. It's important!" I thought I knew everyone onboard this ship, but this kid I don't recognize. I put on my shirt and head to the radio transmission room.

As I enter the room, the chatter slows.

"Sir, a transmission for you," says the radio operator, who turns back to the keyboard on the console.

The paper is ripped along one edge and smells of the same ink used to print *The Whole Truth* so many years before.

Jan in plane crash near Gardermoen airport STOP Expected to recover STOP

Fru Anderson STOP

I run my fingertips along the edge of the paper, turn the transmission over, and flip it back again.

I read the day's date. It happened just a few hours ago. *And they contacted me.*

"The telegram," I say, pointing out a protocol that the teletype operator clearly slept through, "there's no black band. Bad news telegrams always have a black band around them. So why isn't there one? Is someone trying to cut corners?" I cock my head at the operator, my mouth open in a sneer. I hold up the telegram and stride over, shoving the telegram under the boy's nose. "Are you trying to go cheap on me? Huh?"

The control room dials aren't moving, and neither is that stupid kid, whose hands remain coiled over the keyboard.

I slam my arm on the console, aching, no lusting to flip every toggle, every switch that surrounds the boy.

From the corner of my eye, I see a considerate hand rising like a benediction to quiet my outburst.

Meanwhile, the kid's fingers remain poised over the keyboard.

"Sir," a voice says, a hand pointing to a machine with a hand crank, "do you need to make a phone call? We can connect you." Slowly, fingers take my forearm, steer me to the apparatus, and gently push my arm down, causing me to sit. The man who has taken my arm is my age, and I recognize him as a pipefitter, though I don't know his name. Not my department.

I can't think of who to contact as I turn over the telegram. "The black band. Why doesn't this have one? I don't understand why Fru Anderson cut corners?" I look up as the pipefitter and the kid nod in agreement. As I ask my next question, I realize—too late—that my voice is reverberating, and they don't know the answers. "Where is Jan, and what happened?" I ask.

As the young men ask me questions, I'm reminded of playing Solsvik Bridge. A lever, like a hand, is raised, words are spoken and responded to, and the next transaction lies before us, like Knuckles and my cousin, Hansen, developing a game plan to thwart Jan and me. Even the dim lights of the control room remind me of the smoky haze inside the bridge club at Solsvik. Then that problem, like a bridge hand, is assessed. There is strategy in placing an overseas telephone call.

I have an urge to pass the telegram over my shoulder to Jan's expectant hand as if waiting for another problem for the Spartan and me to solve.

At last, I am connected to Jan's parents' house. Unfortunately, the sobbing girl who works for Fru Anderson can't tell me anything and stumbles over her words.

"N-no, she doesn't know w-what happened...or when," the maid stammers between sniffles. "Oh ...b-but Ingrid is at Paul's house, and Fru Anderson doesn't want them to go—s-so sad—but they're flying to ...to Oslo."

I return the telephone receiver to its cradle.

"First, there are no black bands, and now that dumb maid doesn't know anything," I say, drumming my fingers across the cradle.

Giving me grace and benediction, or maybe absolution, the pipefitter says, "Paul? Is he a relative or a friend?"

I nod, and another logistical exercise, another hand of Solsvik Bridge is performed.

Paul picks up on the first ring. His voice is measured, as if his current purpose is to keep himself and those around him calm. He relays that a student died and that Jan's leg is broken, but he is expected to recover. However, Paul's voice, usually calm, has a break in it. "He is badly bruised."

I hear Gretchen and Ingrid in the background.

"Tell him how serious it is!"

I can't avoid hearing the panic in Gretchen's voice and make my decision.

During my conversation with Paul, my captain has been summoned to the control room with his lieutenant.

"Permission to fly to Oslo, Sir. This evening if possible, Sir."

Sitting next to the captain, the lieutenant makes small talk about the wind and the rain and the next port, a clue that he doesn't see the rush in getting me to the airport. I would be flying to Milan, London, and Oslo.

He keeps repeating, "Oooh, boy. Long flight. Oooh boy. Long flight."

I sit in the control room for a few minutes to gather myself. Then, as I leave, another squeal comes from the transmission phone.

I whirl around. "No, no, no! Not a black-banded telegram!"

The next few hours are a blur. Finally, I find myself at the airport and board the plane. As the propellers drone, and the mountains surrounding the city and the blue sea fade below me, I stare numbly out the window. I need answers, and all I got were sobs from a housemaid and evasive, measured words from one of my best friends.

My seatmate tries to make conversation in Italian. Then in English.

I shake my head and gesture, placing my hands under my face, a universal symbol of sleep.

During my layover in London, I call the Anderson house. This time, the maid is openly sobbing, and I can't get any idea of what's going on. I call my home. My mother knows nothing and starts to cry at the news. There is no answer at the Carhart house.

Now, I am petrified.

*

The MacIntosh clan valise sits on a metal chair. The man, his salt-and-pepper-spit-shine haircut now a steel gray, is seated by the hospital bed, holding my best friend's forearm.

A solitary tear trickles down the Spartan's stitched cheek and disappears under a white bandage.

"A priest, a rabbi, and a minister are out fishing, and the priest says…"

I have heard this joke a million times; I'm sure the Spartan has, too. As Gramps delivers the punchline, I mouth, "Do you think we should tell him about the rocks?"

Jan's joyful laugh is a sharp contrast to his appearance.

Gramps stands to hug me, and I see my shock in the room's mirror. The image takes me back to that day at the bus station when Gramps embraced Jules and commanded him to say nothing. My eyes widen as his hug holds more firmly and a second longer than usual. I'm to be brave.

I look for a positive aspect and come up empty. Half of the Spartan is bandaged or oozing, and the remainder seems like he's been rolled in coal dust. His jaw, tinged black and smelling burnt, is slathered with orange goo. A long patch of gauze and tape extends diagonally up his blistered cheek. His eye sockets are puffy, burgundy-colored *V's*. Two black ringlets have managed to escape the skullcap bandage encircling his head. His eyebrows and the area in front of the skullcap has been singed or shaved off. The toes of his right leg peek out of a cast suspended by a cable. The long fingers of his left hand are encased in tape.

"Spart." I salute, holding up my hand to stop him from returning my greeting.

He smiles weakly, his deep blue eyes seeking truth in my face.

"All in all?" I say, assessing the damage, "I've seen worse."

Jan's smile fades.

My bravery has failed the test.

"I...tried...I..." he says, wincing.

I touch his fingertips. "Shhh. I know you did. I hear you've canceled tango lessons for the next few weeks, but you're going to be stomping over Baby's feet shortly."

Gramps quietly picks up his valise and tiptoes out of the room.

"Spart," says Jan, "it's just bruising and a busted leg. I'll be fine." He coughs, and I hand him water. His lips move. "I will rest awhile. Maybe we can walk together later. I want to get out of this bed." His hand reaches out to me as if he wants to swing around and face me.

"Well, Spart, you're in that contraption. Let's see what the doctor says. Or maybe you can chew your leg off?" I make noises like a rabid dog attacking something as I pull a chair closer to his bed.

Jan laughs at my silliness. He presses his arm down and tries to wriggle back on the mattress. The leg doesn't budge, and there's a sharp yank in his body as the metal proves stronger than the man.

Jan's singed eyebrow rises, and he grits his teeth.

I try, again, to lighten the mood, noting Gramps is smiling at me from the doorway. "I'm going to stick around for a few days, I think."

Jan's face brightens as Baby pushes back the curtain.

She kisses him.

"My girl," he says. "Baby, when did you get here? I wasn't sure you would come."

Baby's nurse's training apparently hasn't prepared her for Jan's appearance, as she wails her surprise.

"Baby, it's just a broken leg," says Jan. "I'm fine. We'll be fine. You, Herr Molder, and Kory…you came. Will you all be here when I wake up?"

Instinct or good manners wins the day as Baby goes to the bottom of the bed and studies the chart. She glances at Jan, nodding as if he meets all the tests shown on the form. This information seems to bolster her confidence. She has medical knowledge, and she now knows what the situation is.

"Jan," she says, "the leg will be in traction for a few days, but other than the break and your burns, all of your vital signs are stable."

Jan gazes at her with pride, tenderness, and love. "My girl." The Spartan scrutinizes me and finds me lacking. "See, this is what you need. A girl who is smart and pretty and who can put up with your weirdness. When do you need to be back? I would like all of you to stay."

"I can stay as long as you need me here. I'll explain the situation to my boss," I say, working out how exactly I'm going to pull this off.

"Nah," says Jan, "I can rest, and when you get your next leave, you can come here, or we can go back to Bergen. We'll go drinking."

I look up. Fru Anderson stands next to Gramps, watching the three of us. She must have come in quietly so as to not distract Jan and me.

"Kory and Herr Molder, you can stay with us," says Fru Anderson. "I'm glad you came. Baby, if you like, we can take your luggage to where we're staying. Would you like to come with me or stay here?"

"Mother, I'm fine. You didn't need to ask Kory to come from Genoa. He's a big shot on that boat, don't you know? Spartan!"

Fru Anderson's hand lightly squeezes my shoulder. "You can stay. I will be down the hall should you need any help. Baby, let's let Kory and Jan visit. We can come back after you have settled in, all right?" She nods to me and takes Baby by the hand. They both wave to Jan, who waggles his fingers at them as they leave. Seconds later, and out of Jan's sight, they pull out their handkerchiefs.

Turning back to Jan, I smile as if I saw nothing. The chair is situated close enough to get him water when he needs it, and I can wander down the hall to get him a blanket if he begins to shiver.

The nurses come by to change the bandages. Gently, they cut the gauze and put compresses and salve on Jan's face. His face is an oily mess. Just as gently, they manipulate his head and put on fresh compresses.

Baby comes back. Her eyes never leave the monitor, and she peers over a nurse's shoulder at the information recorded in the chart. All the while, his heart and breath are being monitored.

Gramps comes into Jan's room and takes my arm. "Sonny, let's take a taxi and see if that relative of my boss on Lapskaus Boulevard still owns that Italian restaurant I heard so much about. It's supposed to be on Karl Johan Street. Maybe we'll get a free meal out of it. We should, considering how many dishes I washed for his cousin."

****

Lodgepole pines and birch trees thin out as the taxi we're in descends into the bowl that is the city of Oslo.

"Too many people visiting Jan," says Gramps. "He needs his rest."

I nod, ashamed of the admonishment. I open my mouth to apologize, but Gramps sighs and continues.

"Where is Herr Big Shot? He brags about his pilot son, 'the second youngest instructor in Norwegian

348

history,' and he doesn't show up when the chips are down. At bridge last week, a cousin told me that Edvard has a woman he brings with him as his assistant. Assistant, my ass!"

My face reddens, absorbing the honesty and anger seething below Gramps' humor.

We chatter about Brooklyn-America family and friends for a few minutes. Then, over wine and ravioli rivaling Mia's, I summon my nerve to ask a question. "Is Jan going to be okay?"

Gramps adjusts his spectacles, motioning for another glass of chianti, which the owner happily supplies. He studies the wine, swirling it around, and draws in a long breath before eyeing me. "He's young, and he's survived far worse," he says, as if he is stating a well-known fact. He looks out the window at the passing cars. A bus rumbles by and honks at a pedestrian who narrowly avoids a collision. "Look at that guy, playing cards against death. One minute, fine..." He searches my face. "Jan comes by to see me, especially after Mali...Gramps's lip trembles. The loss has been less than a year now.

He brings his glass up to the light, swirling the red liquid. "We play bridge at Solsvik when he's in town. Did he tell you?"

I shake my head.

"Jan needs to set a date for the wedding. No one is engaged for four years unless he's waiting for a better girl." Bringing the wine to his mouth, his head tilting back. Gramps' gaze is neutral. "Jan is in good hands."

After feasting on the hotel's breakfast smorgasbord, Gramps and I go to the hospital.

As we enter Jan's room, Gramps whistles. "Now

that's spit and polish."

Another Brooklyn-America.

The two men in the Norwegian Air Force uniforms, gathered around Jan's bed, resemble Rolf's Face of Norway recruiting ads. One of the men holds a clipboard.

Jan motions for me to stay.

"We're just here to get what you recall," says the man with the clipboard.

His thin smile and unblinking eyes make the hackles on my neck rise.

Jan is deferential. He clarifies that he was in the back of the plane when it stalled, dropping rapidly in under a minute. Everything leading up to the accident seemed routine. Stefan, the student, panicked and repeatedly tried to restart the engine, but the smell of gasoline told Jan the engine had flooded.

"I couldn't get it to start," Jan says, "but I told him we'd turn around and head back to the airport. I alerted the tower, which alerted the fire brigade. We glided for no more than a minute, losing altitude rapidly, and the plane hit the ground nose first."

Jan's fingertips curl back, imitating his actions in the cockpit. "I pulled back on the stick to bring it up, but Stefan panicked—I think—pushing the stick back the other way, so we ended up tipping forward. The plane landed on its nose, and Stefan hurtled against the side windshield. His head butted up to the windows and..." Jan stops, remembering, waving the memory away.

He sobs. "The engine started to smoke. All I could hear is one of the propellers trying to turn against the ground, dirt hitting my window." With glazed eyes, he tosses imaginary clods in my direction, not *at* me but at something only he sees. "There was dirt, and I thought—

I don't know…maybe—I thought the dirt might stop the flames. I started coughing and then…Stefan's head. He was unresponsive. I got out of my harness and tried opening the door. Tapping on the glass, I finally pulled it open. I unlatched it, reached down, and snapped him out of the harness. I pulled him up and out. His head…his eyes were staring."

Jan's eyes continue to stare through me. "He fell on top of me, and I rolled him off. I could hear, or thought I heard, breathing. I yanked off his helmet, and his neck rolled around like this." Jan's head rocks from shoulder to shoulder. "Stefan lay there, and I called his name. There is a pulse, I thought. I needed to keep his head still."

Jan's voice rises. "I pulled him and dragged him. The plane caught fire." Jan's hands clench into fists and then fly open with spread fingers—one, two, three times—mimicking explosions. "Flames shot from the engine, the nose, and they seemed to follow a line inside. I saw a glow inside the metal, like a lighted trail."

Jan's eyes dart back and forth. "I heard the fire trucks. Birds flew out of the trees as the brigade came closer, and I heard my name. The firemen ran through the trees to where we were. I tried so hard to get to the runway." Jan begins to cough and sob.

From his expression, I can see he's going over each detail to make sure he didn't miss a clue.

"The fire brigade arrived a minute or two later, I think. I tried to get him going again." Jan gasps. "I'm so sorry. I don't know what I could have done. I tried, I tried. I want to talk to Stefan's parents. I need to explain how we tried, how we went over this situation in class and how he had experienced this scenario before and restarted the plane fine. This wasn't his first time. He had done it before and, well, he panicked. And the smell of the gas…We had flooded the engine. We could not quite see the runway. We nearly had it in sight and…" Jan winces as he touches an area under his rib.

"My leg…" says Jan, "I don't remember breaking it, but I needed to get him out." Jan's voice betrays his frustration. He coughs, producing red spittle, and rubs his rib. Then he wipes off his mouth.

Alarmed, I look at Fru Anderson, who has just entered the room carrying broth and water. Both clatter across the linoleum as I lunge out the door, colliding with a doctor.

"He's coughing up blood!" I exclaim. "Is he supposed to do that?"

"It can happen," the doctor replies as he enters Jan's room.

I follow the doctor inside.

Jan is speaking to the airman with the clipboard. "Yes, Sir, I am sorry, but I don't think I could have prevented this. I want to speak to his parents when they get here and explain what happened. I need to do that."

I sit down next to the Spartan, my legs slightly spread, my hands clasped on my knees. "Sparta, you're going to be better. I can stay for a few days, or I can leave tomorrow morning and go back to Genoa."

Jan laughs as he points to how I'm sitting. "You're plotting something again," he says. "You go back to Genoa. I'll be fine. Everyone says so."

Baby nods as she studies the chart. She smiles at me, agreeing with Jan's assessment.

I'm startled by a sharp rap on the door. Gramps jerks his head toward me and waggles his eyebrows at Baby and Jan. "Let's let the *lovebirds* court, Sonny," says my wily grandfather.

Baby blushes, and Jan gives a dismal rendition of a wolf-whistle, but both laugh as Gramps and I wave.

"We'll go to the airport and be back in a jiffy," Gramps calls over his shoulder. "So, no hanky-panky, you two!"

Baby and Jan call back in unison, "Another Brooklyn America!"

The ride to the airport is brief and reveals that there are no flights for the next day, but I have two options. I could leave in two days or later tonight.

Gramps looks at the schedule. "First time on a plane for me, and I loved it. Look at all the places you can go. If I were a younger man, I would come to the airport and say, "Let's go"— he rotates his finger in the air as if spinning a globe and then taps an imaginary spot— "here. And we would go."

A few hours later, I stand in the hospital room again, talking to Jan.

Fru, and now, Herr Anderson stands in the corridor with Gramps. I don't catch what Herr Anderson says, but my grandfather appears to be having none of it. Squaring his shoulders, he turns to face Jan's father. "Yes, I am happy to come," raising his hand, but then stops as to Fru Anderson, whose eyes have welled up, utters a cry. He lowers his hand, reaching over to pat Jan's mother's arm. "Yes, I'm sure it's nothing. He's young, strong."

Jan is sleeping, and I lean over his head to whisper in his ear. I smell his singed hair and wonder how he stands that.

"Spart," I whisper, "I'll talk to you in a few weeks. I have leave in November, and we'll plan a party. In the meantime, clean yourself up. We have girls to impress."

He stirs, squeezing my arm. "Spart, you can't impress anyone without me. See you in November."

I gently rub his head, and he groans, trying to laugh.

"November." I turn and leave.****

Coming back to Genoa, I look forward to doing the one exercise that will take me away from what has happened to Jan—settling into my ship's berth to read electrical wiring diagrams and make notes with my pencil.

The analysis and structure lets my mind wander away, away from hospital rooms and grim faces and worry. Diagrams are a sure thing. Structured diagrams allow me to plan and gain control over at least one aspect of my life.

I've grown fond of the sound of diesel engines and like the rhythm they provide. I count to them; I think to them, and I fall asleep to them. Their *throck-throck-throck* hypnotizes me, soothes me.

My pencil lingers over a schematic. Lost in thought, I draw in a long breath, then cough. Smoke—musty, acrid, and definitely not my brand—rolls up my nostrils and drops into my throat, providing no comfort. In fact, the smell reminds me of when I licked a metal pole on a dare back at Granvin. Searching my room for a likely culprit, I center my gaze on my ashtray. It's empty, having been cleaned while I was in Oslo. With fuel tanks everywhere, smoking areas are strictly limited to our rooms and offices. Am I being poisoned? My shoulders droop, and shooting pains, far worse than what I felt in the alley, slam the base of my skull. I am suddenly exhausted. It's taking everything in my power to stay awake, and I'm fighting a losing battle.

The fire alarm by the door should be clanging—another item to add to my list of diagnostic problems. Pressing my hand against the door, I can tell there's no heat outside, so I carefully pull the door open. All is silent. All I smell is diesel fuel. That's normal.

I gasp as pain, far worse than seconds before, floods my head, causing me to double over. My shoulders spasm, then clench tight, as if the heaviest weights I've ever lifted threaten to crush my skull.

Reeling, I close the door behind me and sit on my bed. The smoke smell has vanished.

Pushing the wiring diagrams aside, I lie back. I've been through enough. What I need is a good night's sleep. Then the headache will go away. I close my eyes and welcome sleep.

The blurry edges of my mind gradually come into focus. Something bounces at the foot of my bed, jostling me, pulling the covers with its weight.

It's Jan, sitting there, inspecting his nails. He turns to face me and salutes. "Spart."

I automatically salute back, ready to be soldiering on. "Spart." As I have done a hundred times before, I turn to him, my knees touching the rough edge of his pant legs. I know the Spartan is plotting something.

Jan studies his thumb. "Spart, I have to be going. It was good of you to come." He picks at a hangnail until he peels it off.

"Yeah, I'll see you in November. Like we talked about."

Jan flicks the nail away, pushes curls from his forehead, and looks up at me. "It was fun. It meant a lot to me. All of it. I just wish we had more time, that's all."

My head jerks, and I sit up in bed. Other than the

throck-throck-throck of the engines, all is silent. My headache is gone, and so is the smell of smoke. Smiling at the comforting dream I had just had, I lie back down. The cotton sheets, cool against my cheek, pulled me into a wonderful, weightless darkness.

The clock shows three o'clock when I'm startled awake by a pounding on the door. My heart jumps as the pounding continues.

I open the door and shield my eyes against the glare of the overhead light.

"Kory," exclaims the control officer standing before me, "you need to go to the radio room now!" His breath smells of coffee and maybe something with liquor in it. I can't be sure.

Shimmying into my pants, I run barefoot over the barricades, stubbing my toe on a small ladder, swearing at whatever crisis I need to deal with now.

I fling open the control room door. The console's flashing green lights are the only things visible in the room. An odor of stale coffee and sweat comes from the operator sitting at the console.

The operator passes a message to me. It's from Paul.

"Jan is dead," the letter reads. "I will send more in a letter to you." The light is too dim. That's the problem. I misread the message. So, I read it again, and my tears fall on the purple teletype ink, causing the words to smear and be absorbed into the thin paper.

"Sir?" says the teletype operator. "Sir?"

I turn to him, noting his long legs, blue eyes, and black hair. Too bad for him, he is leaning forward, his legs apart, plotting. Plotting just like the Spartan.

"The problem with this outfit that you operate is that messages, messages like *these,* I say, pointing at the thin message in my hand, "*important* messages are left to some cheap paper, horrible ink, and an idiot who has the gall to interrupt a superior."

I stalk over to where the boy sits, and instinctively, he shields his face and torso with his hands.

Taking the coffee cup from his desk, I throw it like Jackie Robinson at a wall full of dials. Then, lifting the roll of teletype paper straight up, I use it as a discus to shut off as many of the switches as I can. My forearm swings along the radio room console as I turn off the toggles.

"The problem," I say, pointing to the teletype, "the problem is that your radio is too slow. I should have gotten messages. I should have been told. I could have seen…I could have saved…this is your fault. He's dead because of you." I take the crumpled paper and shove it under the boy's nose. "Do you see? Do you?"

The boy cries out, pushing his chair back farther from me. "Sir! No! I don't understand. What has happened? Who died?"

My brow furrows at his ineptitude. "Who died? What happened?" I shout. "My friend, my *best* friend is dead. He was fine yesterday when I saw him, but now he's dead. How does that happen?" I glare at him. "Why wasn't I informed that he was getting weaker? If I had the right information…current information…correct information, I could have turned back. I could have turned around. I could have…"

The boy pushes back the curls from his forehead and reaches out to take the message from me. He inhales snot and wipes his eyes. He then reaches over to flip on a toggle and waits.

The only sound is the *throck-throck-throck* coming

from the engine room, my breath, and a snuffle coming from the boy. I hear a *click* as the boy flips another toggle.

"Sir? Please sit." The boy's voice is low. His hand reaches for mine, and he pulls me down to the chair beside him.

With the flick of a finger, he flips another toggle up and waits. He looks at me out of the corner of his eye and wipes at his cheek. "Sir, can I call the captain for you? I'm sure you have some plans you will need to make." He leans toward the intercom.

I stiffen.

"Your best friend." The boy's voice is quiet, and his eyes look at the intercom. He leans forward, his fingers inching toward the button.

"The dial over there has a crack in it. You'll need to get that fixed," I say.

"Yes, sir." The operator leans over to the intercom and speaks into it.

What will he think now? Jan will shake his head and admonish me in that way he has. "Spart—" he will begin.

Not now. Not possible. Jan can't be gone. He's here. I just heard from him, saw him, joked with him. He came to me. That dream. Was it a dream, or is this a dream?

Chapter Forty-Four

Had the Solsvik Bridge protocol failed Jan and me?

Pondering this question, I climb the etched flagstone stairs leading out of Cathrinekirken's graveyard. At the iron gate above the church, I stop and lean down. My fingers flick at the sphagnum moss, looking—no— hoping to find the rest of the doll's hand.

Earlier this afternoon, while in the basement of my parents' house, digging through a drawer of my battered desk, I found an identification card with the name of *Stefan Nelson* and the porcelain finger of the doll.

As the bells strike the hour, pigeons flutter from the twin-towered belfry. Taking the smooth, pink remnant from my pocket, I'm startled as snatches of German lift on the breeze.

"You!" calls another voice below me.

Turning to answer, I'm disappointed that it's not the Spartan but a gravedigger calling to his fellow worker to finish the work, as a body will be in the hole in an hour. I descend the stairs to where duty awaits.

My brothers have all gotten older. Their eyes have dulled, and lines have developed seemingly overnight along their jaws and around their mouths. As they come through the church door, there is a nod, a brief handshake, and a hug.

It's all of that, of course, but it's more. To a man, they step toward one another with leaden feet, downcast eyes, and all is coupled with the briefest of grim smiles. Then, they square their shoulders as if willed by some inner force to be resolute. To be brothers.

Inside the gray stone church, the music has started, and I want to believe that the ceremony is a sick joke. But the flag-draped coffin; the crumpled faces of the Andersons, Ingrid, and Baby; and the fact that I'm led to the front to sit with them, pulls me out of my tunnel of grief. They consider me family.

"Here you are." Herr Anderson pulls me down beside him. "My son." He points to the coffin and the picture of Jan in his uniform. "My son." He claps my shoulder, turns his head, and sobs into my coat. His body rocks against mine. "My boy...my boy."

Paul slides into the pew beside me, and a powerful hand touches my shoulder. Herr Carhart.

I hold on to Herr Carhart's extended hand, continuing to stare at the flag-draped coffin. Releasing his hand, I look down at my gray overcoat, twisting a button with my fingers. Absently, I pull on the thread. The button clatters to the floor, spinning to the far recesses of a neighboring pew.

Jan's mother reaches down, stopping its trajectory in an instant.

The casket is covered in roses and sprays of white carnations. The organist's rendition of the Second Movement of Beethoven's Seventh Symphony is rushed, not legato, played softly and then slammed through to the finish. Jan liked Michaelmas daisies and begrudgingly came to like Robert Johnson and Django Reinhardt. The casket is closed.

I was not consulted. Jan's aunt stepped in and made the funeral arrangements.

Fru Anderson clutches a telegram from the King, alternately shoving it into her purse and then removing it, as if in acceptance and denial.

I half-listen to the benedictions and platitudes picked and spoken by people who have no idea about loss. My anger, my horror, and the futility of never being able to see Jan again should have been wiped away. More than anything, I want a sense of redemption, but this service and the plans for this afternoon will have no part in that happening.

Gramps' invitation for this afternoon was cryptic. "After the service, we will gather in Solsvik. It's what Jan would have wanted. You'll see."

****

Man o' War creeps carefully around the final corner, followed by its bodyguard, the mini-tank. Both cars stop, and the occupants eye the low-slung dilapidated building that I'm standing in front of.

A man leans against a telephone pole. He looks at the cars and then at me. Lighting a cigarette, he jerks his head, I nod, and Knuckles saunters into the bridge club.

Four car doors open. Herr Carhart and Fru Carhart come out of Man o' War. Paul opens the driver's side door of the mini-tank, and waiting—always waiting—extends his hand to Ingrid. She stands, straightens her suit, and drops Paul's hand. A young man exits the back seat of the mini-tank, and reaches for her. Arm in arm, she and her beau walk behind Paul into the club.

Idly, I flip the Ace of Clubs. Gramps groused about needing "to go to every tobacconist in town to get enough decks of playing cards," but he did it because "that's what Jan would want." My grandmother's death, unexpected and quick, quieted a portion of Gramps' wily ways, but right now, Gramps is back to being the mischievous maestro, organizing an event for someone he came to love deeply. I suspect that once this event is over—Gramps has been uncharacteristically tight-lipped about what will transpire—another door within him will slam shut.

Paul sidles up to me, holding the lighter I stole from Jules. "*Always, Bella*, you still have it, I see. I found it after—" Neither one of us can say the word *funeral*. "So, is Jules going to get into the U.S. or Canada, you think?"

"Canada. The U.S. turned him down, even though I testified for him. I mentioned his work with us, and so did Gramps."

As if on cue, Gramps comes out of the bridge club, his arms moving like windmills. "Gather round, gather round," he calls with a note of exasperation. "Well, so much for going to Smuggler's Rock today. The tide is too high. We'll have to do it here." Walking to the entrance, he opens the door, motioning for us to go inside. Coming inside the dark entryway, I note that no attempt has been made to eradicate the smell of smoke, sardines, and mustard that permeates the building. "Go through the club to the *smoke-hole* patio in the rear," Gramps repeats to everyone who walks past him.

Knuckles and the man I recognize as Hansen—from when we first played cards at the club—have set out sandwiches and coffee. I open the back door to a patio offering a clear view of the town and Smuggler's Rock. At last, the back door slams, and a loud "Ahem!" interrupts my thoughts.

Paul and I hold up our identical Aces of Diamonds to Gramps. We then surround him, as much to brace against the afternoon breeze as to hear the reason we're here. Deciding this was the signal, the Carharts, my family, and the Andersons hold up their cards.

Never one to *pussy-foot around*, my grandfather begins. "Jules did not do our family a whole lot of good being friendly with the Germans," says Gramps. "Still, he went to bat for you, Kory, after that thing with that girl—What's her name?— Anne. I wish you had mentioned that when you talked about him to the immigration officers. He might have gotten into the U.S., after all. Your girlfriend and her mother barely made it back to America. And they used your help, didn't they, Edvard?"

To my left, Edvard Anderson nods.

I hadn't expected him to get a playing card.

"Herr Mitchell pulled many strings," Edvard says. "He knew people in the War Department who got them out. Herr Mitchell was annoyed by Anne's father's cowboy ways."

Gramps' eyes cloud as he rests his hands on Paul's forearm and mine. "Jules came home that night. He admitted to flirting with Anne and wanting more, but her father, well, you know all about that. Her father ended up dead shortly thereafter. Very strange circumstances. Some say he got too close to a bomb. Others think he was executed."

Herr Carhart is standing behind Gramps, facing me. A look I either can't or don't want to read crosses Herr Carhart's face.

As Paul and Herr Carhart open their mouths to speak, I grasp Gramps' arm hard. "He ran away. He told me he knew about the guns," I say, dumbfounded. "Herr Carhart came…" I break off, realizing that I can now ask a question that has been puzzling me for many years.

"Herr Carhart, who told you that I was in the alley?"

"Hilda Martin. Hilda called me," Herr Carhart answers.

I interrupt. "Why was Jan allowed to call her Hilda? Who is she? I've wanted to know…"

"Edvard? Can you fill us in on her?" says Herr Carhart.

He's using the same tone as when he told Paul and me not to worry about the guns. I think he has a bead on Herr Anderson.

Edvard coughed as if bringing up a painful subject. "Hilda Martin was my mother's best friend, and Jan was her special favorite. Almost like a grandchild." He then sniffs. "But she and I had a falling out some time ago as she disapproved of my lifestyle. I didn't talk to her after that. Jan was always allowed to call her Hilda, but she insisted on being called Fru Martin while at work. She lived down the street from the Americans before the father's accident."

The silence that follows allows me to hear the cries of gulls far from shore. No one speaks. I don't dare breathe.

Gramps clears his throat. "Listen, I'm freezing my tail off out here." He opens the door of the smoke-hole, and our families go inside.

Paul and I mutter in unison. "Another Brooklyn America."

Going inside warms my hands and cheeks, but not my mood. I still have so many unanswered questions.

Clapping his hands together, Gramps gathers us in. "Jules had no intention of telling the Nazis about you," he says. "But he did tell that madam, Bella. She owns the West Indian, the Bibop, and Gold Dust Pawn. The businesses are all under different names, but she is the owner, just the same. Did you know that? Jules and Bella concocted a scheme to get the Nazi's guns back, of course, but at a good price. You know your brother—everything for a price. And, now, we know where he learned that."

Gramps glances around at us. "I contacted your boss at the machine shop on my weekly visits to the fish market and told him there would be a delay in shipments that week. Some of my friends from Solsvik moved into town not long after I did. They aren't part of my bridge group, but they're friends of mine, nonetheless—I see them. I would get the guns and supplies and go to the back of your shop. Your boss put the equipment into your bedroll."

Unburdened at last, he points toward Smuggler's Rock. "I made contact with a doctor. I can tell you now. That doctor's father is one of my friends from Solsvik. The Germans came looking," he says, "but they didn't find anything, did they, Andrew?" He looks over his glasses at Paul and Herr Carhart, whose faces vacillate between respectability and freedom. "Of course, Paul, I didn't know Andrew and the doctor were neighbors, and the guns were moved to a safe location while the doctor was treating you, Kory, for your wounds." He says this as if he has found the corner piece of a jigsaw puzzle.

His voice drops to a whisper. "So, you boys disappeared for weeks. All of us thought you had died." He sighs. "So, we thought the Nazis had gotten you. We got your letters, but we thought the Nazis made you write them."

"No, not true!" Paul sputters. "I mailed them."

Gramps tugs on my sleeve, smiling at me, turning

around to look at all of us. "I have had good friends in my time. Friends who have lasted a lifetime. They know my history, and I know theirs. Background, education, social standing…none of that matters." Reaching up, he tousles my hair. "It's a rare thing that you and your friends have. A rare thing indeed."

I want to smile and feel better, but my friends know the truth. Jan is not here. He's in a box. And I, despite everything said today, helped put him there.

Chapter Forty-Five

The aspen's golden leaves flutter as I walk up the Goat Trail. I stop, looking down at Festival Park, rubbing my thumbnail along the mysterious Ace of Spades I received in my parents' mailbox this morning. I pause and turn, remembering the day the Spartan and I stopped here after the Germans nearly caught us with smuggled guns in our backpacks.

We were boys. It was so long ago. We're men now.

Gravel crunches behind me, and a young boy with a skinned knee and curly hair tramps up the hill.

I rock back, startled to see him. Jan? No. The boy nods at me, and I watch as his form disappears over the rock and up the trail.

I'm wearing the wrong shoes for a hike. I had not thought I would come up here, but I had gotten the card. I needed time to myself.

Jan's face floats in my head. He nods and salutes. I press on up the hill.

Internal injuries. A slow leak. He bled out, and by the time they discovered the damage, they couldn't perform surgery to save him.

"He was twenty-three," I say, shaking my fist in the air. "You bastard! Twenty-three."

The war has brought improvements to the trail. A graded path now leads to Jan's cabin. Ducking underneath a low-hanging branch, I listen to the wind and try to recall where the bird feeder once was. Then, spying the tree, I walk to it. The only remnant of the feeder is a neat dark hole in the pine branch, nearly obscured by new green needles.

Through the clouds, a sunbeam shines on the ground around where I stand. A solitary Michaelmas daisy stands sentry in the copse.

Gasping, I lean over to pluck the flower but stop myself.

"Jan," I whisper. "My friend…my best friend."

The daisy's petals stand still.

"I will miss you more than you realize. You had no right to leave. We had our lives ahead of us—you, Baby, me…with someone." I chuckle.

It seems the flower is lifting its head to either catch the sun or hear what I have to say.

"We were something, you and me. How could you leave me? You are a hero. We're Spartans; you were right. You had that within you. You had honor and strength. You gave me your strength. You. How is it you never questioned? Even in the end, you rose, and you fought to save others. 'It's our duty,' you said. You rose again and again."

In my mind, I see Jan shaking his head at me.

I speak to the flower, the cabin, and the trees. "And you lifted me, as well. Always including me, always knowing that my circumstances didn't bind me. You knew better than that, and you encouraged me. We were like brothers—like the Crimshaw Brothers. Where would Tom and Ned be now if the brother they were honored to know, privileged to be with…if that candle were snuffed out? How would they handle that?"

I gulp back my tears and my voice grows stronger.

"I have you in my heart, and I will hope to be like you—courageous, strong, empathetic, funny, and valorous. Honorable."

Nearby, a twig snaps.

"A daisy. This late in the season, too." Paul, nonplussed, stands beside me, reaching out to pick the daisy.

I slap his hand.

Paul pulls back and waiting—always waiting—looks at me questioningly.

"Jan...we used the code *the daisies of September*," I begin. "I think he's here now. But I can't forgive myself for not realizing how sick he was. I left too soon."

As Paul speaks, it isn't his face I see. I see his father's face as he pulled me up in the alley.

"I know." Paul brings his hands together under his nose as if readying himself for prayer. "Friends forgive. We all do. We all have. We always will." Paul dabs at his eyes.

"But the way he rubbed his rib, I should have known, I should have said..." I rub my rib as if I could grant Jan some of my strength now—will my power away to Jan. Give back what belongs to him. His life.

"I left him—" I say, raising my hand to stop Paul from soothing me. "Friends don't leave. Friends with any sense of decency or moral code go back to get their fallen comrades. And I, of all people, the one who knew him best, should have stayed. He had fallen. And I left him there."

In all the years I have known Paul, I've never seen him cry. When he finally speaks, his voice barely matches the rustling leaves.

"He had a voice. And he didn't know. Given how

much he did complain about his leg and his burns, he would have said something about the leak inside of him. But he didn't know. You didn't leave a fallen comrade. You honored his wishes, and you honored your instincts."

"Jan taught me about myself," I say, studying the flower in front of me. "About things I wasn't sure of. He allowed us to be our best. He had that ability." I look at flower's green stem. A thin scar marred its base where the stem had been trampled. "Look at this daisy. It is bent, and yet, here it is, stronger than ever." A lightness begins to fill my chest.

Paul leans forward, looking at the stem. "He would not want us to cry. He would have made a joke. I was envious of you and Jan. Did you know that, Kory? Not envious in a bad way but of the way the two of you always had this inside language. You fought together, nearly died together, and your friendship—your brotherhood—was absolute."

I stand up, holding out my hand to Paul. As he rises, I tell him what I should have said to Jan. "I have brothers by blood, and I have brothers by honor. If I had to choose, I would choose honor every time."

Paul was right. Jan gave us, or rather, he identified our honor and made both of us better for having known him.

We remain silent as we make our way down the mountain to where Jan's legacy waits for us.

A word about the author...

Janet Yeager is the author of Brothers by Honor. She is the recipient of numerous awards through the Tulsa NightWriters and Oklahoma Writer's Federation. A Montana native, she lives in Tulsa Oklahoma. janetryeager.com

Thank you for purchasing
this publication of The Wild Rose Press, Inc.

For questions or more information
contact us at
info@thewildrosepress.com.

The Wild Rose Press, Inc.
www.thewildrosepress.com